LOST IN TRANSLATION

Edward Willett

DAW BOOKS, INC.

DONALD A. WOLLHEIM, FOUNDER

375 Hudson Street, New York, NY 10014

ELIZABETH R. WOLLHEIM
SHEILA E. GILBERT
PUBLISHERS

http://www.dawbooks.com

First Paperback Printing, October 2006
1 2 3 4 5 6 7 8 9 10

DAW TRADEMARK REGISTERED
U.S. PAT. OFF. AND FOREIGN COUNTRIES
—MARCA REGISTRADA
HECHO EN U.S.A.

PRINTED IN THE U.S.A.

Then, with no signal at all, the Hunters dropped from the trees.

Black as night against the bright green, blue, and yellow of the tents, they swept in a hundred-strong flock across the camp and back, firelances lacing the ground below with blood-red beams. Tents blossomed into orange flame that brought aliens naked and screaming into the light, hair ablaze, skin blackened, only to be cut in two by the next wave of Hunters. A half-dozen aliens close to the ship made it inside, but others had time for only one startled look, time to open their mouths wide, before the beams found them and sliced them apart.

In two passes, the Hunters utterly destroyed the camp and every alien in it; but with an ear-hurting whine, the sliver ship came to life, rising into the air, its lifters sending the smoke of the burning camp twisting and dancing across the carnage. One Hunter, more brave than wise, dove toward the ship, beam reaching out to caress the silvery skin, but the lance didn't even mark it. Other Hunters followed the first, but suddenly the ship's whine turned to fang-rattling thunder, white flame exploded underneath it and it rocketed into the sky, vanishing in a matter of seconds. In its fiery wake, the Hunter who had first attacked it fluttered to the ground like a burning leaf.

We won, Jarrikk thought fiercely. *It's over!*

Two days later, when the first S'sinn warships arrived and the fortification of Kikks'sarr began, he knew he'd been wrong.

It wasn't over at all.

It was just beginning.

LOST IN TRANSLATION

Prologue

Jarrikk watched the humans crossing the polished black basalt floor of the Great Hall of the Flock as closely as if they were prey, hearing their strange footsteps echoing back from the distant walls. Spidery red columns, studded with perches and platforms, soared to the haze-hidden roof, S'sinn clinging to them in dozens and hundreds. Jarrikk could feel his people's hatred of the humans beating down like desert sun, hot enough to turn the bitterness in his own hearts into bloodfury were he to allow it.

His crippled left wing ached, ached as it had not since the day of his injury, the pain throbbing in the withered flight muscles in his shoulder and chest and into his left arm. Humans! The plague of his childhood, the cancer that had eaten away the best parts of his life, the poison that now threatened the Commonwealth itself. He had first seen the ugly, flightless, four-limbed creatures twenty years past. War had followed. He would gladly have gone another twenty without seeing them again, but the Translators' Guild had called him to this duty.

These negotiations had almost not happened at all. Without Full Translation, they would be impossible. S'sinn Translators were few and far-flung among the Seven Races; at this time and this place, he was the only one available, though he had never Translated with humans before.

He wished that could have remained true, but his Oath bound him. He would do his duty.

If war came this time, it would not be *his* doing.

The giant hall whispered with the rustlings of the S'sinn, here stretching batlike wings, there yawning to display gleaming white fangs or grooming themselves with their ventral arms, but mostly just staring, staring with the blood-red eyes of a thousand nightmares.

The damp chill and near-choking scent of musk pervading the Hall of the Flock might have come from those same dark dreams, Kathryn Bircher thought, shivering in her sleeveless Translator's uniform. As might the sense of foreboding that gripped her. For a moment, she envied Ambassador Matthews and his aides, cut off from the seething sea of alien emotion she'd begun to feel the moment she stepped out of the shuttle. She knew the other five races of the Commonwealth considered humans and S'sinn primitive, almost barbaric, barely free of their animal pasts. Maybe that was why she could read the aliens so clearly, with very little effort, as clearly as she could read Matthews himself, his cold, passionless soul a spire of ice among the smoldering red fires of the aliens' hatred.

Or maybe it was because the last time she had been exposed to the raw emotions of the S'sinn, her world had shattered.

She stared ahead at the waiting S'sinn leaders on the small, circular dais, still impossibly far away. The fires of rage in this room could shatter a great deal more than just her world; they could shatter a thousand.

She wondered if anyone could stop them.

Jarrikk focused on the human Translator, sharpening his gaze to hunting mode. He could see every strand of her blond hair, every tiny imperfection in her pale skin, could even count the stitches that held the triangle-within-a-circle-within-a-square symbol of the Translators' Guild in place above the curve of her left breast. He raked his eyes over her figure from a distance of fifty spans, memorizing every claw's-breadth of her within the space of five of her steps. Within that time he knew how she walked, how she breathed, which hand she favored, and where her uniform chafed her. Within minutes, he would know her interior landscape just as perfectly.

He didn't even notice his claws gouging splinters from the golden wood of the dais.

Feeling that she carried not only her small metal Translator's case but also the weight of a thousand S'sinn, and the lead ball and chain of her own night-mares, Kathryn stumbled as she mounted the platform. Ambassador Matthews steadied her with a strong hand. It was all she could do to keep from flinching; she could shut out much of the hatred beating down on her from the S'sinn, but touch strengthened empathy a hundredfold, and for that moment of contact, his little candle of hatred burned brighter than all the red eyes of the S'sinn—and he held the fate of negotia-tions in his hands as much as she did.

She pulled free, took a deep breath, straightened, and looked around. The dais bore a black, glass-topped table and metal chairs for the humans and, for the S'sinn, the padded resting racks called *shikks,* which to Kathryn looked more like torture devices than comfortable body supports, even for creatures with two wings in addition to the normal complement of arms and legs, and bizarre musculature to match. Matthews and his aides sat at the table; a female S'sinn, already reclining on one of the shikks, watched them in silence. Three others stood just behind her.

Each S'sinn wore only a broad metal collar, marked with a sign. The female on the shikk, on whose red-gold collar a sapphire-studded lightning bolt slashed across a spiral of rubies, would be Akkanndikk, the Supreme Flight Leader. The other two, male and fe-male, would be her Left Wing and Right Wing, her aides and bodyguards. On their copper collars, dull red stones picked out the spiral, minus the lightning bolt. As Matthews sat down, they spread their arms and their wings, revealing the insignia repeated in metallic red on the black, leathery membrane.

The fourth S'sinn also unfolded his arms and wings in greeting, but though his arms moved normally, only his right wing extended fully; the left opened only halfway, and Kathryn glimpsed lurid purple scars zigzagging across it. On his silver collar and on his one good wing gleamed a triangle inside a circle inside a square. Translator.

Kathryn felt him trying to read her empathically, and blocked frantically, instinctively, though the effort made her head throb. By Guild etiquette that was unforgivably rude, but she couldn't help it. Facing the S'sinn Translator, all she could think of was the first time she'd seen a S'sinn this close, and the memory threatened to send her screaming from the room.

Yet now she had to get even closer. Now, she had to Link.

As the human blocked his polite probe, Jarrikk growled deep in his throat. *How dare she!* What it had cost him to make the effort, she could never know . . .

Except she would know, in a moment. His anger dimmed slightly, damped by curiosity. Why block the initial contact when the deeper contact was heartbeats away? Did she fear it as much as he? Was fear the sharp smell that mingled with the humans' strange salty stench?

Fear or not, the Link could not be avoided. They were sworn to Translate, and that meant they must Link.

It seemed the human recognized that fact as well as he; she stepped to the center of the dais, set her case on the floor, opened it, and took out the injector, a small glass cylinder with an absurdly tiny needle. *Is human skin really so thin?* Jarrikk wondered. He stepped forward with his own case, removed the much larger metal injector, and without giving himself time to think, drove it into his left arm.

As the warm tingling of the Programming spread through his blood, he looked at the human. She still held her tiny syringe in trembling hands, staring at it as though it might explode, and the sharp scent was strong in the thin film of moisture that had suddenly covered her skin; but then her strange blue eyes came up to meet his gaze, and with a jerky, ungraceful motion, she stabbed the little needle into her arm. The syringe still shook in her hand as she returned it to her case.

Jarrikk reached into his own case, took out the warm silvery cord of the Link, and touched it to the contact patch behind his right ear. He proffered the other end to the human, but she didn't take it, staring instead at his polished black claws. Behind her the dominant male, the Ambassador, stirred and muttered something, but the human Translator didn't respond. Jarrikk wondered if even now she would refuse the Link, and felt shame at his half-born hope that she would; or, more accurately, shame at his lack of shame at the thought.

Confusion, he thought. *Humans bring nothing but confusion. Confusion and pain.*

But he had sworn an Oath, and so he kept the Link extended: and, at last, the human took it, careful not to touch his clawed hand, careful to the last, though it seemed she, too, would uphold her Oath, and all her care would mean nothing momentarily.

For the last time, the human hesitated, staring at her end of the Link. Then the Ambassador cleared his throat and said something, his voice deep and painfully harsh to Jarrikk's ears.

The human Translator snapped something even harsher and louder in return, and firmly touched the cord to the patch under her own ear.

As human and S'sinn memories, terrors, and anger melded and fused, a great many things became clear.

Chapter 1

The wind caressed the leathery membrane of Jarrikk's wings and tickled the soft hair of his belly like his brood mother used to, to soothe away a nightmare. For a thousand heartbeats he'd been holding his wings imperceptibly angled, spoiling the airflow ever so slightly. His chest and shoulder muscles ached with the effort, but he would have shrieked with excitement if it wouldn't have ruined everything, because Kakkchiss and the others now flew thirty lengths ahead of him and had yet to realize that he lagged behind.

With relief, he drove toward the clouds with powerful strokes. This time he had Kakkchiss. The young-flight leader would never know what hit him!

High enough. Jarrikk focused prey-sight on the sleek black hairs rippling over the powerful muscles in Kakkchiss' back, folded his wings, and dove.

Kakkchiss flapped on, his attention apparently entirely on the forest below. "You wait," he said to Llindarr, on his right. "Flight Leader Kitillikk will threaten to rip our wings off when we get back, but she'll be glad to hear a clear-eyed report of what these aliens are doing, just the same. She'll probably make us full-fanged Hunters on the spot, *isn't that right, Jarrikk?*" And at the last possible instant, Kakkchiss side-slipped smoothly out of Jarrikk's way. As Jarrikk hurtled through empty air, Kakkchiss' laughter followed him down.

Claw-rot! Jarrikk snapped his wings open, grabbing

air so suddenly he almost tumbled out of control. He righted himself but stayed put a good fifty lengths below Kakkchiss and the other four members of the youngflight, their good-natured abuse raining down on him. "Give it up, Jarrikk! Kakkchiss is Leader to stay!" "Noisiest dive I ever heard!" "Hey, even those aliens could fly better than that!"

That stung, because the strange aliens who had just landed on their planet of Kikks'sarr—*their* planet, Jarrikk thought, with a familiar sense of outrage that the aliens had *dared*—flew only with noisy motors and stiff artificial wings. "There's one now!" Jarrikk shouted suddenly, pointing down, and had the satisfaction of seeing all but Kakkchiss spill air, proving pretty conclusively, Jarrikk thought, that they weren't nearly as unconcerned as they claimed to be about this flouting of Flight Leader Kitillikk's command to roost until she decided how and when to contact the aliens.

Not that they planned to contact them, Jarrikk hastily reminded himself; just spy on them.

Kakkchiss hadn't put a wingtip out of place. *He really is good,* Jarrikk admitted to himself. *An excellent leader. But I could be better.*

Still, Kakkchiss caught his eye and clawed the air with his arms in a gesture of respect, and Jarrikk felt a little better. One thing about Kakkchiss, he never begrudged Jarrikk's attempts to dethrone him, and Jarrikk thought if—no, *when*—he finally succeeded in catching Kakkchiss off-guard, Kakkchiss would accept it—and then, of course, immediately set about getting the leadership back.

Well, it was no good sulking down here all day. They must still be at least two thousand beats from the aliens' landing place. Jarrikk strengthened his wing-strokes and started to climb.

Something flashed, blindingly white. Jarrikk blinked. Lightning? Out of a clear sky? "Kakkchiss, did you—" he started, then stopped, gaping.

Kakkchiss' wings, those smoothly powerful tools

that never stumbled in even the roughest air, fluttered uselessly, spasming like they had suddenly developed minds of their own; and then they stopped altogether, and Kakkchiss dropped from the sky.

He plummeted down toward Jarrikk, and for a moment Jarrikk thought he'd been wrong and Kakkchiss intended to take revenge; but as Jarrikk spilled air and swung out of the way, he glimpsed the gaping, blackened hole in Kakkchiss's chest. Trailing a thin stream of smoke and blood and the smell of burned meat, the youngflight leader hurtled a thousand lengths into the forest below, striking the treetops with a terrible breaking sound that carried clearly to Jarrikk's horrified ears.

Jarrikk's own wings suddenly didn't want to work anymore. He circled down toward the scar in the forest canopy, while above him the other younglings whirled, shouting in confusion. "Jarrikk, what—" Yvenndrill called, then the strange bright flash came again and the call became a choking shriek that dopplered toward Jarrikk.

Jarrikk tore his eyes from the place where Kakkchiss had fallen just in time to see Yvenndrill spinning helplessly down, blood streaming behind him, his agonized shrilling ending abruptly as the sharp splintering branches of the trees broke his fall and his back. His severed wing, still twitching, fluttered down seconds later.

Stunned, almost numb, Jarrikk spiraled down to the trees and clung to a high branch, staring back up at the sky, where Llindarr and little Illissikk, the youngest, still circled in terror and confusion. The light flashed again, and this time Jarrikk saw an energy beam split the air between the two bewildered younglings and realized at last someone was shooting at them. "Dive!" Jarrikk screamed at them, just as they reached the same conclusion and headed for the trees.

Llindarr had only descended a few lengths when the beam flashed again. For a moment Jarrikk thought it had missed, because Llindarr's dive still seemed in control—but he never pulled up, and the upthrust tip of a forest giant impaled him.

Illissikk almost made it: might have made it, if he hadn't tried, at the last minute, to pull up low over the forest and join Jarrikk. The beam flashed one last time, and Illissikk's headless body slammed into the clearing below Jarrikk's perch so hard it shook the tree he clung to. A thin pattern of deep scarlet drops spattered the dark brown fur of his chest.

Jarrikk wanted to shriek himself, then, wanted to throw himself in blind panic into the sky, but fought down the instinctive urge to flee with reason—and rage. If he left cover, he would die, too, cut in two by the beam, and the Flight Leader might never know what had happened. But if he stayed, he would see the hunters who had used this horrible weapon come collect their "trophies." And then he could tell the Flight Leader with absolute conviction what he already knew in his hearts: that the strange aliens who had landed on their planet were bloody-handed murderers. *And then it will be the S'sinn's turn to Hunt!*

And so he waited, and watched, a hundred heartbeats, and a hundred more, and a thousand after that, absolutely still, absolutely silent, until at last, as he had known they must, the murderers emerged.

There were three of them, hideous, near-hairless four-limbed monsters, like wingless, bald S'sinn. Two were much larger than the other, whose face had the unformed look of a youngling. They wore brightly colored coverings like the S'sinn sometimes wore on holy days, and both carried black, evil-looking tubes with knobby handles: the murder weapons, Jarrikk thought. It was all he could do to keep from diving on them then and there and tearing out their ugly throats.

The youngling seemed agitated about something, pulling on the upper limb of one of the adults, his voice shrill and painfully loud, but the adult pushed him away and said something in a deeper, harsher voice.

As the youngling alien watched with wide eyes, the adults knelt beside Illissikk's corpse. Then—Jarrikk's claws dug deep into the branch—one of them drew out a glittering knife and began cutting at the dead youngling, skinning him as though he were a jarrbukk!

Worse followed. One of the large aliens went into the forest and emerged moments later carrying something wrapped in giant leaves. With a flourish, he swept them aside, revealing Illissikk's head. A branch or rock had ripped out his left eye, but his right remained, wide with his final terror.

The aliens seemed to take forever going about their grisly business, but Jarrikk held down his impatience with the same cold calculation he had already applied to his revenge. There *would* be revenge, and soon enough, but first he must bear the tale back to the colony. First, Flight Leader Kitillikk must know. And then—

—then it would be the aliens' turn to feel the cut of knives and beams in their hairless, pale skins.

At last the monsters finished, and disappeared into the forest again, leaving behind a pile of bloody meat indistinguishable from any dead beast. Illissikk had vanished as if he'd never existed, reduced to less than nothing by the aliens' cold knives. They had moved on, no doubt to do the same to Kakkchiss and the others; and now at last Jarrikk moved, too, unfurling stiff wings and sweeping silently away into the gathering twilight, low to the treetops, where he knew he would be all but invisible.

He would not allow himself grief; he clung to his need to report to the Flight Leader as he might have clung to a slim green branch in a thunderstorm, refusing room to the other black thoughts that tried to shoulder in to share it. Thirst and hunger soon joined the throng, but he refused them a place to land as well. Cold rage and the hope of hot revenge were all he needed to sustain himself this day.

They'd been a half-day's flight from the colony when the aliens attacked; deep night's bitterly cold black wings covered the world when Jarrikk, with ever-slower wingbeats, finally began flapping wearily up toward the high mountain caves into which the S'sinn had withdrawn with the coming of the aliens. They had abandoned their airy tree-top structures with a prudence Jarrikk had thought foolish at the time. No longer. A dark shape slashed down to meet him, briefly silhouetted against the star-lit glimmer of snow-capped peaks before swinging into position wingtip-to-wingtip on his right. "Jarrikk?"

"Ukkarr," Jarrikk rasped, with barely enough breath to talk. "Must see—Flight Leader."

"So you shall, since the Flight Leader left standing orders to bring you younglings before her the instant you returned. Where are the others?"

"Dead."

Ukkarr's steady wingbeats stuttered. "Dead? How—"

Jarrikk concentrated on keeping his own wings beating. His story was for the Flight Leader first, not for her lieutenant. Just a few more beats . . .

Ukkarr didn't ask again. Silent, he climbed with Jarrikk, guiding him away from the cave complex's main entrance to a smaller, isolated cavern higher up the slope. "Wait here," Ukkarr commanded, and plunged back into the night.

Wings still at last, Jarrikk slumped in the cold dark, chest and back ablaze with pain. He pressed the backs of his hands hard against his eyes, then slowly massaged his wings' muscles. Thank the Hunter of Worlds that Ukkarr had thought to bring him here first. He couldn't face their brood mother—not yet. What if she had seen him and asked about the others? He couldn't lie to her. And the bloodparents . . .

Alone, no longer able to concentrate solely on the act of flying, the magnitude of what had happened threatened to overwhelm him. He folded his wings flat against his back and crouched on the cold stone floor. Wind whispered across the opening to the cavern, a soft, keening sound like a youngling just taken from its bloodmother, before the brood mother came to nurse and comfort it: but this night, Jarrikk knew, no comfort would come at all.

Flight Leader Kitillikk rested on a shikk outside her dwelling caves, overlooking the large central chamber that had served as their Flock Hall since the arrival of the aliens on Kikks'sarr drove them underground. Blood-red and smoky from a thousand torches and fires, it seemed a primeval place, like the legendary hot, hollow center of the home world of S'sinndikk, where the Hunter of Worlds was said to dwell when not soaring through the universe on space-black, star-studded wings.

Or so the priest who had just left her had described it, but Kitillikk was of a more prosaic turn of mind. To her, it looked like a prison—a prison they had been forced into by the alien invaders. Her lips drew back in an involuntary snarl. The priest had all but ordered her to attack and drive the aliens back into space—had almost accused her of cowardice. But the priest didn't have to answer to Supreme Flight Leader Akkanndikk back on S'sinndikk, who had given unequivocal orders: no attack unless attacked. To strike first would contradict the First Principles of the Commonwealth.

Kitillikk had her own opinions about the Commonwealth, opinions she intended to one day make S'sinn policy, when she became Supreme Flight Leader. But achieving that goal meant first succeeding at her current task of leading the colonization of Kikks'sarr, and that meant following orders. No attack unless attacked.

Just give her an excuse, though . . .

Ukkarr soared across the cavern and settled beside her. "Excuse my intrusion, Flight Leader, but you asked to be informed immediately upon the return of the youngflight that sneaked away to spy on the aliens."

The youngflight that *thought* it had sneaked away. Kitillikk had known all about the younglings' "secret

mission"—she'd have had Ukkarr's head if she hadn't—
but had chosen to let them go. She could use whatever
information they brought back, however garbled the
report. "They're back, then."

"Only one of them, Flight Leader. Jarrikk. He says
the others are dead."

Kitillikk turned and stared at him, then grinned savagely, showing all her teeth. "At last!"

Ukkarr led her to the cave where he had wisely
stashed the youngling out of sight. Jarrikk slumped
motionless inside, so that for a moment she thought
him dead, too; but he jerked up when they entered,
and unfurled his wings in salute. Kitillikk motioned
him to relax. He folded his wings, but every other
muscle in his sleek young body remained tense.

Ukkarr drew a lightstick out of the Hunter's pouch
he always carried and cracked it against the floor. A
cold blue light filled the cave and illuminated the
snowflakes beginning to fall outside its mouth. "Tell
me what happened, Jarrikk," Kitillikk said.

The youngling told her, his voice high and strained,
but admirably under control, considering what had
happened. She remembered her own youngflight; they
had lived for each other, would have died for each
other. Had she lost her sisters as he had lost his
brothers . . . *he has strength,* she thought. *Great
strength.*

When he finished his story, she turned to Ukkarr.
The aliens had given her her opportunity; even the
Supreme Flight Leader could not fault her now, and
her name would echo in every Flight of the S'sinn
after this. "Summon and arm the Hunters."

"Yes, Flight Leader!" Ukkarr spread and snapped
his wings in salute, then leaped into the snowy night.

Kitillikk looked back at the youngling. "Can you
tell your story again, Jarrikk? Can you tell it to the
Hunters?"

"I can. I will."

"Then come with me."

A thousand beats later, she stood overlooking the Flock Hall once more, Jarrikk beside her. More than a hundred Hunters now filled the red-lit space, clinging to every possible roost, and this night the arms they bore weren't the knives and spears and bows they used on game, but slim black S'sinn-high rods: firelances. The weapons of war, not the hunt. "Tell them," Kitillikk ordered Jarrikk.

He repeated his story, his voice going hoarse by the end of it, and her hearts beat faster at the shrieking roar that answered his tale. Her claws gouged the stone beneath her feet. An alien flung from her roost into the cavern at that moment would not have reached the floor before being torn to bloody shreds. She wished she had one to try it with. "We waited, and hid, to see what kind of creatures these are," she cried to the Hunters. "Now we know—they are murderers, savages, child-killers! Kikks'sarr is *ours!* Let us take it back!"

The second, greater roar of the Hunters filled her with the wild, fiery elation she felt only when fighting or mating. She spread her wings and arms again for silence. "We know where they camp! We can be there by dawn. By the time the sun sets, let there be no aliens left alive on our planet!"

This time the roar went on and on as the Hunters rose and swirled around and around the Flock Hall, then swooped out through the short tunnel leading to the surface and burst into the snow-filled sky. Kitillikk spread her wings to follow; but the youngling Jarrikk touched her wing and said, "Let me go with you!"

Annoyed, anxious to join the flight, Kitillikk snapped, "You are not a Hunter," and spread her wings again.

But the youngling didn't withdraw. "They were my brothers. They were my flightmates." His voice grew hard and desperate. "I want—I have to see the creatures who killed them die. I *have* to."

Admirable. Kitillikk considered. "I cannot arm you."

"I know."

"It is a long flight. One you have already made twice."

"I *know.*"

"We cannot wait for you."

"You won't have to."

He's tough, Kitillikk thought. *Or thinks he is. Good.* "Very well. But you are not to take part in the attack. You will only watch. Understood?"

"Understood!" With his own shrill shriek of defiance and bloodjoy, the youngling spread his wings and flapped away.

Kitillikk flew after him thoughtfully. It would be good to cultivate a young male with such loyalty and fire. A personal bodyguard and aide of unquestioned loyalty—all Flight Leaders needed such. The Supreme Flight Leader had two, black as night, the Left Wing and the Right Wing. Kitillikk had Ukkarr, of course, but a second would not go amiss. A fine-looking, strong young male.

She grinned as she flew after Jarrikk. Oh, yes, he had to be male.

Jarrikk hurled himself into the night on wings made strong by his thirst for revenge: but that thirst could only take him so far. Within a thousand beats his wings felt like lead and his lungs as full of fire as his blood had been, except this fire slowed him as much as the other had filled him with energy. He began to lag behind the Hunters. No one waited; he didn't expect them to. The strong owed it to themselves and to the Flock to fly as hard and fast as they could. The weak must keep up the best they could, or silently turn back. Fly or die, the Hunters said. Fly or die.

Jarrikk kept flying.

When dawn broke, Jarrikk saw the alien camp ahead of him, marked by the glittering silver egg-shape of their ship, surprisingly small compared to the huge black sphere that had brought the S'sinn to Kik-ks'sarr. A half-dozen tendrils of smoke twisted lazily skyward in the still morning air, proof that at least some of the aliens were watchful. Jarrikk dropped to treetop level, then below, swooping through green-pillared corridors with his wingtips brushing leaves. He looked for Hunters with every beat, but saw and heard nothing—right up to the moment when something swatted him from behind and sent him tumbling ungracefully to the ground. "Find a roost and stay there!" Ukkarr growled, then somehow disappeared into the forest again.

More cautiously, Jarrikk worked his way from tree to tree until he had a clear view of the camp, which consisted of two prefabricated plastic shelters, a dozen brightly-colored tents—and a drying rack on which were stretched at least twenty pelts of various animals.

Three of those pelts Jarrikk recognized very well indeed. He gripped the branch so tightly he felt it split in his claws.

And then, with no audible signal at all, the Hunters dropped from the trees.

Black as night against the bright green, blue, and yellow of the tents, they swept in a hundred-strong flock across the camp and back, firelances lacing the ground below with blood-red beams. Tents blossomed into orange flame that brought aliens naked and screaming into the light, hair ablaze, skin blackened, only to be cut in two by the next wave of Hunters. A half-dozen aliens close to the ship made it inside, including, Jarrikk saw with fury, the small one he had seen with the adults who killed his brothers, but others had time for only one startled look, time to open their mouths wide, before the beams found them and sliced them apart.

Jarrikk saw one of the two aliens who had killed his brothers running for the illusory safety of the pre-fabricated buildings, before beams set the buildings alight even more spectacularly than the tents. He half-unfurled his wings, prey-sight focused on the base of the male's stubby neck, ready to fly after him himself, promise or no promise, when a beam slashed at the alien's legs and he went down, blood spurting from half-cauterized stumps that ended where his knees had been. The alien tried to crawl away, but the next beam touched his head, which exploded into red steam and bits of charred flesh and bone. His torso bizarrely crawled another half-length on its own before falling forward, limbs twitching once or twice and finally lying still. Jarrikk's lip curled in an involuntarily snarl. He only wished he'd fired the lance himself.

In two passes, the Hunters utterly destroyed the camp and every alien in it; but with an ear-hurting whine, the silver ship came to life, rising into the air, its lifters sending the smoke of the burning camp twisting and dancing across the carnage. One Hunter, more brave than wise, dove toward the ship, beam reaching out to caress the silvery skin, but that alloy was far tougher than the plastic of the prefabs or the fabric of the tents, and the lance didn't even mark it. Other Hunters followed the first, but suddenly the ship's whine turned to fang-rattling thunder, white flame exploded underneath it and it rocketed into the sky, vanishing in a matter of seconds. In its fiery wake, the Hunter who had first attacked it fluttered to the ground like a burning leaf.

We won, Jarrikk thought fiercely. *It's over!*

Two days later, when the first S'sinn warships arrived and the fortification of Kikks'sarr began, he knew he'd been wrong.

It wasn't over at all.

It was just beginning.

Chapter 2

Katy pushed the mashed potatoes on her plate up and up into a shape like Mount O'Bagnon, framed in the dining room window just across the table from her. Then she began picking up her peas one at a time and sticking them into the potato-mountain, pretending they were the dekla trees that covered Mount O'Bagnon, although they were entirely the wrong shape and not even close to the right color. She pretended really hard that they *were* the right shape and color, because pretending really hard helped her not to feel how worried and scared her parents were. When they were scared, she got scared, and she didn't like being scared.

Pretending really hard sometimes helped her not to hear them when they argued, either, but they were right there at the table with her and she couldn't help it, even though she pretended Mount O'Bagnon suddenly turned into a volcano and all the dekla trees got covered in the thick brown lava she poured from the gravy pitcher.

"I can't believe you're letting them go ahead with this carnival," Mama said, her voice all tight and strange. "After the news from New Atlanta? My God, Mike, just before we left Earth the Sootangs said they were planning to move to New Atlanta. They could be dead!"

"They could have been dead since the day we left Earth," Daddy said. His voice stayed really calm and low, but it didn't fool Katy; she could feel his worry just as strong as Mama's. She decided the peas didn't look anything like dekla trees and had to be punished. One by one, she started squashing them.

"You know what I mean. Mike, we're at war!"

"Earth is at war. We're a thousand light years from Earth. We've got nothing anyone would want."

"We don't know what these monsters want. We don't even know why they attacked the colony on Petra to begin with!"

"They're still intelligent creatures. They won't attack a place just to be attacking. Luckystrike has no strategic value. We're just a farming planet."

"What strategic value did New Atlanta have? They killed a quarter of the people in the colony, Mike! Over three thousand dead!"

Daddy took a deep breath, and Katy could feel a little bit of anger inside all his worry. She squashed another pea, lining it up carefully under the middle two tines of her fork, then pressing down little by little until the green skin burst and the inside gushed out. It made her think of squashing the little green worms that kept trying to eat their garden, and she giggled, thinking how shocked Mama would be if she said that out loud. Daddy glanced at her. "That's still no reason to cancel the carnival. You know how Katy's been looking forward to it. Not having the carnival won't make us any safer."

"It just doesn't feel right. Having fun when all those people—"

Daddy reached over and squeezed Mama's hand, his anger receding and the undercurrent of love Katy could always feel welling up. "How's this, then: we'll have the carnival, and we'll all go, just like we planned, but we'll try really hard not to enjoy ourselves."

Just for a minute Mama got a little angry, and Katy stopped squishing her peas and looked up. Sometimes when they both got angry together, they argued and she wanted to be ready to run up to her room where she couldn't feel them quite so much. But then Mama's anger faded away and amusement replaced it, and Katy relaxed. No fight this time!

"It's a deal," Mama said. "But Mike, what if they *do* come here?"

"We've got shelters set up, just like Earth told us. If we get enough warning, they won't be able to do anything but burn some buildings."

"And crops, and livestock, and . . . how would we survive the winter?"

"Earth would send relief." Daddy slid his hand under Mama's and squeezed it. "It's not going to happen."

"I hope not," Mama said.

Daddy smiled. "You have the Governor's word on it."

Mama smiled back, and Katy smiled, too, turned her fork over, and ate her squashed peas.

Landing Day, four days later, dawned bright and clear, and Katy bounced out of bed the minute the sunshine touched her face, put on her best play-dress and sun-hat, and was downstairs for breakfast almost before Mama started making it. Mama wore blue shorts and a sleeveless white top and Katy thought how pretty she looked with her sun-freckled skin and long red hair. She turned and smiled at Katy and said, "Happy Landing Day, Katy!"

Katy bounced up onto the green-topped stool behind the breakfast counter. "Happy Landing Day, Mama!"

Mama frowned. "You know, seeing you makes me think I'm forgetting something important. But I can't think what . . ."

Katy giggled.

"I know!"

Katy waited expectantly.

"I forgot to salt the eggs!" Mama turned around and sprinkled a little salt onto the scrambled eggs in her skillet, and Katy laughed out loud. "But you know," Mama said, putting the salt away in the cupboard, "I'm sure there's something else . . ."

Daddy came in from the dining room and scooped Katy out of the chair and swung her around. "Happy Birthday, kittenkid!"

Katy squealed with pure joy, and then laughed again when Mama said, "Birthday? No, I don't think that was it . . ." But then she turned around, too, as Daddy set Katy down, and gave her a big hug. "Happy Birthday, Katy."

Katy jumped back up on the stool and bounced up and down, barely able to contain her excitement. Six years old, and Landing Day, too, and that meant they were going to the carnival, and somewhere there had to be a present for her, she couldn't know exactly what, of course, but the only thing she really, really wanted was a synthibear. Misty Pendergrass had a synthidog, but a synthibear was better because it could walk on two legs and use its front paws to hold things. You could have a tea party with a synthibear and all you could do with a dumb old synthidog was play fetch, but every time Katy played with Misty she could feel how Misty thought she was so special because she had a synthidog and Katy didn't. Katy thought she'd really enjoy the new feeling she'd get from Misty the next time they played together if she had a synthibear.

But that made her feel a little bad, because she didn't really like unhappy feelings from anyone, even Misty. And maybe it wasn't really fair, because Misty never said anything out loud about her being special because she had a synthidog, and Katy had recently realized that because most people couldn't feel what other people were feeling, they figured she couldn't, either, so if Misty hadn't actually said anything out loud, then maybe . . . maybe . . .

Mama set a plate of steaming eggs in front of her, and a slice of toast smothered in big, sticky, gooey, blue gobs of muffleberry jam, and Katy quit trying to figure out Misty and started eating.

"Weather should be clear all day, SatCom says," Daddy said, coming back to the table from the comm unit. "And the carnival people arrived in orbit right on schedule yesterday and landed before nightfall. Everything's set." He winked at Mama, and Katy knew he was keeping a secret of some kind, not from Mama but from her, but that was all right. Birthday secrets were almost always good secrets.

Half an hour later they set off down the grass-covered street toward the Landing Field, turned into a carnival ground "For One Day Only!" as the posters that had appeared everywhere in Luckystrike weeks before proclaimed. Katy loved those posters; she ran ahead of her parents to look at the one on the side of the two-story red-brick building where Daddy worked. A big smiling clown juggled Ferris wheels and danglepods and grav-ups and other exciting rides in the center of the poster, while down at the bottom young couples laughed while they threw balls at bottles or ate zipmud or rode into the Tunnel of Love, but the one thing Katy always looked for was the synthibear that sat on the shelf in one of the game booths in the background. She touched her finger to her lips, then reached out and touched the synthibear. "Mine," she whispered. "I wish, I wish, I wish . . ."

"Really, Mike, letting them put a poster on the capitol!" Just for a minute Katy thought Mama was really mad, but then she felt the laughter underneath the words and knew Mama was joking, and she could tell Daddy knew it too, so she touched the bear one more time for luck and scampered back to her parents.

Daddy ruffled her hair. "Shocking, isn't it, defacing such a classic structure?" He laughed. "Some day we'll have a real capitol—and a real governor, too."

Mama put her arm around his waist and snuggled up to him. "I like the one we've got."

Katy copied her. "So do I, Daddy!"

"Well, we'll see what the colony thinks at election time. But that's nothing I'm going to worry about now." He scooped Katy up and put her on his shoulders. "Now, it's carnival time!"

"Wheeeeee!" Katy squealed, and clapped her hands as they headed down the street, and then they turned the corner and there was the Landing Field, all the rides the poster had promised and more rising out of the middle of it like a little brightly-colored city all its own. Early as it was, laughter and music and the smell of popcorn spilled out of the carnival, and Katy felt Mama and Daddy's worry slip even further under the surface and that made her feel even happier. "Fun!" she yelled, and patted Daddy's head. "Let's go have fun!"

"Your wish is my command!" said Daddy, and into the magical city they went.

The day passed in a blur of rides and zipmud and hot dogs and cotton candy and smoking iceys and acrobats and clowns, and only once did the worries come back to Mama and Daddy, when a tall, skinny man with a crooked nose and scraggly black beard came up to them while they waited for their turn in the bumper cars. "Governor Bircher. A word with you, if I may."

Katy instantly felt Daddy go all tight inside, and she pouted. This was her day, her day and her parents'. Why was this stick-man trying to spoil it? She could feel him, all prickles and indignations and puffery, and she folded her arms and pointedly turned her back on him, staring into the dim interior of the bumper-car arena, where the red and green and silver cars floated and bobbed and bounced into and off of each other and the walls and the floor and the ceiling like a box full of balloons. Was that Misty Pendergrass over there in the silver car . . . ?

"We'd like to ask you yet again to—"

"We?" Daddy interrupted.

"The Luckystrike Concerned Citizens' Coalition, Governor Bircher." The man radiated disapproval.

Katy inched away from him, but it didn't help. "As you well know."

"Ah, yes, the L-Triple-C. And which of your many requests are you reiterating this time, Al?"

"The most urgent, Governor Bircher. Surely—"

"They're all urgent, or so you would have me believe when you bring them up at great length in the Assembly."

"In view of the news from New Atlanta, Governor, the LCCC has put aside its more parochial concerns for the good of the greater all. We have collected more than two hundred names on a petition insisting that Luckystrike formally declare its neutrality in the Earth conflict with—"

Katy felt her father's rising disgust, but it was her mother who broke in suddenly, with, "Does this mean you want to secede from the human race, Mr. Bastion?"

Bastion's confusion momentarily overwhelmed everything else. "I don't see—"

"What my wife is suggesting, Al," said Katy's father, "is that the only way you could remain neutral in this conflict would be to change species, because that seems to be the only thing these aliens have against us—the fact that we're not them."

"They are rational creatures whom we must have offended in some way," Bastion spluttered. "They will not attack us if we clearly disassociate ourselves from the rapine policies of Earth Planetary Survey and Development, who—"

"Who built this colony and recruited you and your fellow concerned citizens," Katy's father said, his anger becoming hot enough that she was glad it wasn't aimed at her. "If you consider their policies so misguided, perhaps you should ease your conscience completely and return to Earth. I would be glad to sign the necessary transportation orders . . ."

Bastion blinked. "Return to Earth? In the middle of a war? I'll do no such thing."

"Good. I'm glad that's settled. Now if you'll excuse

us, I believe it's our turn at the bumper cars." Katy's father turned his back on Bastion, took his wife's and Katy's hands, and marched them into the arena, where the previous crowd of drivers was just disembarking on shaky legs from the cars, which had now all settled to the shiny black floor.

"Doesn't he care about New Atlanta?" Katy's mother whispered furiously to her father as they crossed that floor. Katy tugged impatiently at her father's hand, hoping if she got the two of them into cars and having fun again, the black cloud the stick-man had wrapped them in would lift. "Or the rest of the people who have died? Declare neutrality? It's us or them! What kind of neutrality can there be in that?"

"The only people Al Bastion cares about are himself and his like-minded friends," Katy's father growled. "I imagine he'd much prefer that those of us outside the L-Triple-C simply vacate the premises and leave Luckystrike to them. Then they'd build a nice little insular ant colony and live—if you could call it that—happily ever after." He took a deep breath, and his mood lightened a little bit. "But come on, forget about him. This is Katy's day. We're here to have fun, remember?"

Her mother patted Katy's head in an absent-minded fashion. Katy stared up at her and frowned. Mama never done *that* before! She hoped she didn't do it again, either.

The bumper cars were suitably bumpy, and as they all staggered out of the arena again after their ten minutes were over, Katy's parents seemed to have forgotten most of their worries. A couple of more rides and a zipmud cone apiece took care of the rest of them.

They stopped at one of the game booths that lined the temporary streets of the magic carnival city, and Katy's father smiled at her and at her mother, said, "Wait here!" and went to talk to the man running the booth. Katy busied herself with her cone, and just as she finished up the last sweet, crunchy bite, her father came back. "We're up!" he said to Katy. He boosted her onto a stool behind the counter of the booth, and put a little laser pistol in her hands, then pointed at the holograms of bats and dragons and goblins and dinosaurs flying or walking or marching through the fog-filled darkened space beyond, and said, "Go on, kittenkid! See how many you can hit!"

Katy nodded happily and started firing the laser pistol through the fog, and though it seemed to her she wasn't hitting very many holograms—maybe none at all—a light kept flashing and bells and sirens kept going off, and when her time ran out the man in the booth shouted, "What shooting! What an eye! We have a winner, ladies and gentlemen! A big, big winner!"

Katy turned around to see that a crowd had gathered outside the booth, and they all laughed and applauded as the booth man ducked behind the hologram chamber, and came out with—

Katy squealed. "Is it really mine?"

"It really is! You won it fair and square, kid! Fair and square!" He set it down in front of her.

Katy stared at it. "A synthibear," she breathed. "A really, really, truly synthibear. For me!" She hugged the bear hard, and suddenly it wriggled to life in her grasp.

"Hello, what's your name?" it said cheerfully. "What's your name?"

"Katy!" Katy said. "My name's Katy! What's yours?"

"What would you like it to be, Katy?"

Katy had figured that out a long time ago. "Your first name's just Bear," she said, "and your last name is Bircher, just like mine. You're Bear Bircher!"

"Bear Bircher," the bear repeated. "Okay, Katy! Do you want to play now, Katy?"

"Time to go home, Katy," her father said. "Then you can play with Bear until bedtime."

"All right." Katy studied Bear doubtfully. "I don't think I can carry you, Bear."

"I can follow you, Katy," Bear said at once. "I can

walk!" It stood up on its hind legs, which made it almost as tall as Katy, took two steps forward, and promptly fell off the counter.

"Bear, are you all right?" Katy knelt down beside it, but it rolled over and got up and its bear-face whirred open into a grin.

"Oops!" it said. "I'm all right, Katy. Let's go home and play!"

"Come on, Bear!" she said cheerfully, and she took her mother's hand and they set off toward the gate through the gathering twilight.

As they left the carnival ground, Bear piped, "Wait for me, Katy!" and Katy looked back and called, "Hurry up, Bear!" then laughed at the way Bear's little stubby legs churned away as though it were running really fast, though it never got any closer. Behind Bear the magical city of rides and games and tents glittered with lights in every color she could think of, and a dozen different kinds of music drifted out of the fairgrounds in competing snatches, and all she could feel from her parents was love and happiness as they laughed and talked over her head, no worries in them at all, no way, and she looked up at the stars twinkling overhead and thought she must be the happiest girl in the galaxy.

And then suddenly the sky went all ripply, and ripped open like a piece of cloth, and filled up with big silvery things.

Mama and Daddy stopped, and Mama's hand tightened on Katy's so hard she gasped. And then Daddy said a word Katy had never heard before and didn't like, and scooped her up right off the ground like she was a baby and started running, and all the happiness was gone and all she could feel from her parents was fear, a big, choking kind of fear she'd never felt before, not ever, and it scared her so much she started to cry, and behind her Bear kept squeaking, "Come back, Katy, come back, Katy, come back . . ." and then she couldn't even hear him any more, and that made her cry even harder.

All around her people shouted and screamed and ran every which way, and a siren wailed from Daddy's building as they passed it, and Katy heard her mother praying, almost sobbing, and she got so scared she couldn't even cry anymore.

They ran down their own street, toward their own house, but now other things filled the sky, black, with wings, and one came right over their heads, high up, except suddenly it wasn't, it got really big really fast, and it had red glittering eyes and big white teeth and it smelled bad and it carried something long and thin in its claws, and now they were on their porch and Katy's father shoved her through the front door so hard she tumbled over and over and hit her head and started crying again, and she scrambled up to run back to her parents, only something flashed really bright just outside the door and her parents fell down funny and *she couldn't feel their love anymore . . .*

And when the Earth marines came looking for survivors two days later, they found Katy sitting on the porch between her dead parents, staring blankly into the blank black glass eyes of a run-down synthibear, barely breathing, hardly blinking; and that never changed, not when the medic bundled her up in a blanket and took her to the makeshift hospital, not when the shuttle took her into orbit, not even when the warship *Frobisher Bay* took her to Earth.

They took the synthibear with them, but halfway to Earth Katy roused herself just long enough to stuff it down a disposal chute.

Chapter 3

For half a year, as the S'sinn struck at human outposts from one side of the Spiral Arm to the other, Jarrikk rejoiced with the rest of the Flock. The humans seemed routed, unable to oppose the lightning-fast attacks of the S'sinn Hunters. The Supreme Flight Leader vowed to drive the naked, four-limbed monstrosities back to their homeworld and keep them penned there forever, freeing the Arm of their foul presence.

But something went wrong. The humans regrouped. They captured a S'sinn ship intact, and from its data banks drew their own list of targets. The return blows were every bit as deadly as the S'sinn strikes had been. Humans proved to be far more effective warriors than the S'sinn had guessed.

Half a year stretched to a year. Fleets on both sides grew larger and better armed. The massive presence on Kikks'sarr, which had been only a tiny, unimportant colony before, doubled, then redoubled. A city took shape, an ugly city designed for only one purpose: to service the ships of war and the Hunters that crewed them. The colony's own long-range plans for a quiet, graceful city, full of the soaring architecture of peace, were indefinitely shelved. Like it or not, they had become the staging and headquarters center for the S'sinn war effort, far in advance of the homeworld of S'sinndikk, whose location had to be kept secret from the humans at all costs. No ship carried *that* information in its data banks. The S'sinn *did* know the location of Earth, but no attack had yet been mounted against its powerful defenses.

Jarrikk regretted that bitterly. He didn't want humans merely pushed back to their homeworld: he wanted them exterminated. As much as he hated the ugly city that had swallowed the tree-houses where they had lived before the humans appeared, he applauded its purpose. But he didn't spend much time there. Mostly, he remained with Kitillikk; since the raid on the human camp, she had taken an interest in him, assigning Ukkarr himself as his tutor. He practiced flying and tracking and shooting and unarmed combat, ate at Kitillikk's side, grew stronger and harder and taller and heavier, until, he realized with a shock one day as he studied his reflection in a mirror, Kakkchiss wouldn't have recognized him. In fact, he looked almost like a full-grown Hunter, though his coming-of-age ceremony was still a quarter of a year away. He stood straight, fluffed his glossy black fur, spread his wings, folded his arms, and stared sternly at himself. "Death to humans!" he growled, trying to sound menacing.

A long, lingering wail from the Tower of Time drove him away from the mirror, through the arches of his room, and into the air above the city. Kitillikk had called him today for one of her periodic examinations of his progress. He wanted very much to please her; she had been hinting at something special she had planned for his coming-of-age, and from the way she'd been looking at him, he'd thought he might know what it was. Coming-of-age usually went hand in hand with First Mating. First Mating with the Flight Leader would be an incredible honor. It would secure his place in the upper echelon of the Flight, ensure that when he joined the fight against the humans, it would be as a wing leader, at least . . . and Kitillikk, he had heard it murmured among the male Hunters, was the kind of mate whole flocks had gone to war over in ancient times on S'sinndikk. His imagination recently had begun to focus less on what mating with her would do for his position in the flock and more on the pleasures of the mating flight itself. Certainly it had enlivened his dreams on several occasions . . .

But as he glided down towards Kitillikk's fortress, something blotted out the sun.

"Excuses waste breath and energy, old one," Kitillikk growled at the factory manager who stood submissively in her audience room, dry, papery wings unfurled and drooping. "You have not met the quota. Those firelances are vital to the war effort."

"Flight Leader—" the gray-furred S'sinn began.

"Silence!" Ukkarr banged the butt of his lance against the stone floor, and the old one subsided, trembling.

"You are relieved of your position," Kitillikk said. "I have already informed your deputy that he is now in charge of the factory. Ukkarr, take his collar."

Ukkarr stepped forward and removed the steel supervisor's collar from the old one's thin neck. Beneath it, his fur had rubbed away in spots, revealing brown-spotted gray flesh. Kitillikk's lip curled in disgust. "Your usefulness is at an end, old one. Remove yourself. The priests await."

The old one looked up at her a moment with rheumy eyes, then bowed his head and trudged from the room, wingtips dragging on the floor. "Will he go?" Ukkarr asked.

Kitillikk had already turned away. "If he does not go to the priests, the priests will come to him." She glanced at the computer by her shikk. "Jarrikk is late."

"Unlike him. Perhaps these rumors you have had me spread of First Mating have frightened him away."

"If they have, he is not the S'sinn I want." Kitillikk smiled at Ukkarr. "Am I really so frightening, Ukkarr?"

"Terrifying," he said with absolute seriousness. "But it is a terror I crave."

"Perhaps you will experience it again sooner than you think," she said. Ukkarr had been a faithful follower, and she believed in rewarding loyalty. Or, in Jarrikk's case, building it. Let him ride her in the air on the night of his coming-of-age, and he would be hers forever. She wondered if Supreme Flight Leader Akkanndikk had sealed a pact with her famed Left and Right Wing in the same way. She doubted it: she doubted the Supreme had that kind of fire in her.

But Ukkarr was right; Jarrikk was never late. "Ukkarr," she began, intending to have him go search for the youngling, but her computer suddenly squawked at her, announcing a message, and she turned to it instead. "Proceed."

The image of Wing Leader Lakkassikk, commander of the military forces on the planet, appeared. "You must come to the spaceport, Flight Leader," he said.

"Must?" Kitillikk bristled at his tone. "Why *must* I, Wing Leader?" She put just a slight emphasis on his lesser rank.

Lakkassikk answered by clearing his image from the screen and replacing it with a view of the spaceport—and the impossibly huge thundercloud of bright metal hovering above it.

Jarrikk gaped at the thing that had appeared in his sky. Hunterships of various sizes had come and gone daily at the port since the war began, but he'd never seen anything like this. It seemed as large as the entire city. *Human attack!* he thought wildly, but the humans had no ships like these, or the war would have long since been over—and lost.

He'd landed outside Kitillikk's fortress without being aware of it; now he saw the Flight Leader leap into the air from her balcony, Ukkarr at her side, and he threw himself after them. "Flight Leader, what is it?" he asked Kitillikk.

"The Commonwealth," she snarled. "Come with me, but keep silent."

Jarrikk swallowed the thousand questions still on his tongue and fell in mutely beside her as, with almost every other S'sinn in the city, they beat toward the port. From the belly of the ship now dropped three small golden flyers—or small Jarrikk thought them until he, Kitillikk, and Ukkarr swept down over the blackened native stone of the landing field. Then he stared up at the descending vehicles in awe: each was almost as large as a Huntership.

At the same moment Kitillikk, Ukkarr, and Jarrikk alighted, the egg-shaped ships touched down with a thunderclap apiece, the sound echoing around the city and back from the high rock cliffs of the mountain above it. *Gravity displacement drives!* Jarrikk thought, awed all over again. He looked around the perimeter of the port. Every one of the heavy weapons that ringed it had swung toward the golden flyers, but no one was foolish enough to fire: not with that impossibly huge ship hanging overhead.

The outer two flyers split open, spilling out phalanxes of soldiers, one group shaped something like wingless S'sinn—or like the despised humans—but much thicker around the middle. Full space armor encased their massive legs and arms, and closed and silvered helmet visors gave no clues to their identities. They carried powerful-looking beamer rifles, pointed down, but ready for use at a moment's notice.

The second group, fanged, clawed, and scaled, moved with a deceptive slow grace that nevertheless brought them lined up, their own beamer rifles ready, just as the last of the other soldiers took his (her?) place. Together the two groups formed a guard of honor for the third flyer, which now opened to reveal three figures: two more reptilians, and—Jarrikk drew in a surprised breath—a S'sinn male, red-furred, with a star-shaped white blaze on his chest and a large silver collar around his neck.

With a rustle of wings, a dozen Hunters landed behind Jarrikk, who hurriedly stepped aside as burly, black-furred Wing Leader Lakkassikk strode forward to join Kitillikk. Jarrikk knew the two of them had had more than one falling out, that Kitillikk resented the Wing Leader's authority over the Hunter fleet based on the planet *she* governed, but they closed ranks now, walking toward the aliens together. Ukkarr started forward, too, and Jarrikk, not wanting to be left standing alone in the middle of the landing field, fell in behind him, feeling terribly conspicuous under the cold gaze of the aliens and the distant stares of the S'sinn encircling the field. Lakkassikk's Hunters remained where they were, forming a single line facing the golden ships.

Kitillikk and Lakkassikk reached the newcomers. One of the reptilians and the S'sinn stretched a thin silvery cord between them, and each touched it to a spot behind one of their ears. Then the S'sinn turned to face Flight Leader and Wing Leader, and the reptilian faced the other reptilian, who said something in a hissing, growling, throat-hurting voice, echoed almost immediately by the S'sinn:

"By decree of the Commonwealth of the Six Races," he shouted, his voice echoing across the landing field, "the war between the S'sinn and the humans is ended."

A shocked silence met that incredible statement. Jarrikk gaped, mouth hanging open, for a full ten beats—and then from somewhere inside him rage reared up and he heard himself scream, "Never!"

Kitillikk whipped around to face him. "Silence!" she hissed, but as though his voice had been a catalyst, the entire assembled city now roared its defiance. The two squads of Commonwealth soldiers fingered their beamers uneasily, glancing around the field. Lakkassikk's Hunters gripped their weapons in a way that wasn't quite threatening, but could easily become so. But the military commander made a sharp gesture in their direction, and Kitillikk turned and raked the crowd with her red gaze, and the shouting died away.

The reptilian spoke again. "This matter is not open for discussion," the S'sinn translated, his voice cold and haughty. "Trade has been disrupted. Innocent ships have been destroyed. Commonwealth Central forecasts serious economic consequences to at least three homeworlds within the next Central year. This places the Human–S'sinn War within the guidelines for military intervention. Commonwealth Central is so intervening. At this moment, the same decree is being issued on the S'sinn homeworld—" more shouts, which went ignored "—at the human forward command center, and at the human homeworld. Terms of the cease-fire are as follows: all hostilities are to cease immediately. Violations of the truce will be met with complete destruction of the attacking force. Continued violations will result in a blockade of the offending race's homeworld.

"Recognizing that the original dispute arose over this planet, the Commonwealth decrees that this military base be immediately downsized to comply with specific limits contained in more detail in the formal Truce documents. Noting that this planet has only one major continent, divided by mountains, the Commonwealth decrees that the S'sinn shall restrict their activities to the southernmost portion of this continent—and that the humans will be granted the right to colonize the northernmost portion, site of their original landing."

The roar of anger from the crowd this time didn't need Jarrikk to start it. He stared at Lakkassikk and Kitillikk. When would they put a stop to this charade? These demands were ridiculous. The Commonwealth couldn't be serious . . .

But there was nothing frivolous about the huge ship hanging in the air above them, or the soldiers on the landing field.

The reptilian wasn't finished yet. "Finally," the S'sinn translated, "the humans are to be granted full membership in the Commonwealth as soon as Translators can be found and trained from among them. In the interim, they are considered associate members, with full trading rights but no seats in the Commonwealth Assembly of Peers.

"This concludes my initial statement. Full details of these decrees have already been downloaded to the planetary data bank. Flight Leader, Wing Leader, if you will come aboard my lander, I can answer any questions you have more fully."

Jarrikk held his breath. *Now,* he thought. Now Kitillikk would answer this ridiculous reptilian. Let those murdering creatures, those humans, back on Kikks'-sarr after what they had done, after Hunters had died to drive them off? Trade with humans, with the enemy, after the destruction of Thik'rissik Station and the slaughter on Unindarr?

The history Kitillikk had made him study came back to him. Once before the Commonwealth had decreed the end to a S'sinn war, the war with the Orrisians that had lasted only a few homeworld days before the Orrisians called for help, the war, just a hundred homeworld years ago, that had brought the S'sinn into the Commonwealth. The memory still rankled. It could not be allowed to happen again.

But, somehow, it *was* happening again. Leaving behind Ukkarr, Jarrikk, and the Hunters, Lakkassikk and Kitillikk followed the reptilian and the two Translators into the central ship; and as time passed and nothing else occurred, the crowd surrounding the field dispersed, until, as the day slipped into dusk and at last the commander and Kitillikk emerged, only Jarrikk, Ukkarr, and the Hunters were left. The Hunters stood in silence, facing the equally silent Commonwealth soldiers, in a staring contest that might have been comical if it weren't so deadly serious.

When Kitillikk emerged, Jarrikk saw at once, by the suppressed anger in her stance and the ridge of raised fur on the back of her neck, that she had acquiesced. The rage that had filled him since the slaughter of his friends drove him forward, despite Ukkarr's angry shouts and the sudden movement of Commonwealth beamers being trained on him.

He faced Kitillikk in the gathering dusk, his hot breath forming clouds of white vapor in the chill air. "How could you? How dare you? The humans are murderers, they killed my friends, they *skinned* them—"

Kitillikk's hand lashed out, claws extended, ripping

fur and flesh from Jarrikk's upper arm. Shocked into silence, he grabbed the wound with his hand and stared at the Flight Leader as blood oozed between his fingers. "You forget yourself, youngling," she growled. "We accept the Commonwealth Treaty because we must, because our destruction hangs over our heads. But the humans remain our enemies. Always."

"You're the youngling whose report started this war, aren't you?" Lakkassikk said in his deep voice. "Be assured, cub, nothing is forgotten. Nothing is forgiven. There will be another day to fight."

"Words." Jarrikk felt dizzy from pain and shock, only a little of it from the wound. "Nothing but words."

"Not words." The Wing Leader opened his wings and his arms. "A promise."

"Ukkarr!" Kitillikk shouted. The Hunter came over to them. "Take Jarrikk back to the fortress. Tend his wound, and see that he's fed. I have matters to discuss with Lakkassikk."

"Yes, Flight Leader," Ukkarr growled. "Come on, youngling. And be thankful she didn't rip off your ear."

Jarrikk followed Ukkarr into the dark, metal-ceilinged sky. Kitillikk could punish him for speaking, but she could not control his thoughts. Humans were coming back. The Wing Leader could talk about fighting in the far future, *when his courage returns,* Jarrikk thought. But he would not wait that long.

When the humans returned, Commonwealth Treaty or no, they would find they still had one enemy willing to fight them.

Kitillikk flew with Lakkassikk to the entrance to his underground headquarters. Despite herself, she shuddered as they rode an elevator to the lowest level, a hundred spans below. The caves they had dwelled in for so long had been bad enough, but to deliberately bury yourself beneath the ground, to cut yourself off from the sky—it was not the S'sinn way. It should not be necessary.

But, of course, it was; the humans had made it so. The inner depths of her own fortress, of every building in the city, were no better, though at least she had some rooms open to the winds. "How well do your Hunters adjust to this place?" Kitillikk asked as at last the elevator stopped and thick steel doors slid open to admit them into a featureless gray corridor.

"Well enough," Lakkassikk growled. "Those few who fail join the Flightless in oblivion."

Kitillikk nodded approvingly. "Their deaths do you honor."

"Thank you." He stopped before a door barely visible in the gray wall. "Open."

"Wing Leader Lakkassikk identified," a male voice replied, and the door swung inward. At Lakkassikk's gesture, Kitillikk entered the sparsely furnished quarters beyond; two shikks and a computer terminal seemed its sole adornments. To her right, an arch led into a waste elimination cubicle; directly opposite, another arch led into a grooming room; and to her left, a third arch opened into a small kitchen.

"Close," Lakkassikk said to the door, and as it complied, motioned Kitillikk to one of the shikks. "Refreshment?"

"Silverwine, if you have it."

"I do—direct from S'sinndikk." He went into the kitchen, and after a few minutes of clinking of flasks and goblets, emerged with two glasses of a thick liquid that glistened like mercury under the harsh white overhead lights. He gave one to Kitillikk, then held his up in a toast. "Death to the humans."

"Death to the humans," Kitillikk agreed, and tipped back her head to let the heavy wine course down her throat, filling her belly with fire and bringing blood pounding to her ears.

Lakkassikk took a deep breath and arranged himself on the other shikk. "You accept my toast," he

said. "I take it then the matter you wish to discuss
with me is our response to this outrageous intervention by the Commonwealth."

"You take it correctly." Kitillikk drained her goblet
and set it aside. "This cannot stand."

"Yet we cannot fight the Commonwealth. Their
technology is overwhelming."

"Give us time, Lakkassikk." Kitillikk looked around
the room. Lakkassikk willingly lived here, like a crimi-
nal, to serve the cause of furthering S'sinn policy. That
bespoke admirable loyalty. She already knew him to
be an able commander; he had led several raids on
human colonies himself, before his promotion to Wing
Leader, by its very nature a more ground-bound rank
in the military, though not in the ancient hierarchy of
the S'sinn. Such a one must chafe at the restrictions
binding him: restrictions strengthened by the Commonwealth's intervention. Such a one was ripe to re-
cruit to a new cause.

"Time for what?" he finally replied, breaking her
long silence. "Time for the humans to return to this
world, foul the air with their cursed flyers and
groundcars, cut down our forests? What good is time?"

"You said yourself we cannot fight the Commonwealth. But what if the Commonwealth were to fight
itself? There are many strains, many stresses. There
are long-buried hurts and fresh new offenses. Race
can be played against race. When the time is right,
the humans will provide us with some new insult, some
new outrage, and the Commonwealth will crack like
a rotten branch. Then we will take our revenge: on
the humans, and on the Commonwealth. Then only
the strongest will survive—and the strongest will be
S'sinn!" Kitillikk waited for Lakkassikk's response. If
she had judged her S'sinn aright . . .

"If this can be done," he breathed at last, "then we
must do it, though it take years!"

"So it will," Kitillikk said solemnly, while inwardly
cracking her wings with glee. "Before we can even

begin, we must enlist allies—powerful allies. The Supreme Flight Leader . . ."

"She will never agree!" Lakkassikk protested. "She has detested this war from the beginning, though she's fought it well enough. She will be glad the Commonwealth has ended it."

"Then she will be glad when the Commonwealth grinds us underfoot!"

"Flight Leader!"

"I'm sorry." Kitillikk put just the right amount of contrition in her voice. "I mean no disrespect. Nevertheless, it will be a challenge to all of us to help the Supreme Flight Leader see the dangers of the course she pursues. As I was about to say, we need powerful allies to accomplish that. I have those I can contact within the traditional hierarchy, but within the military . . ."

Lakkassikk's ears pricked. "I can help there. I know many military Wing and Flight Leaders who will help. They will find this intervention in our affairs as intolerable as I do."

"Then select a few, those you consider most trustworthy and most useful to us. Approach them discreetly. I will do the same within the traditional hierarchy. We will arrange a meeting—somewhere out of the way, and quiet. And thus we will make the first few wingbeats of a long journey."

"My honor is yours, Flight Leader!" Lakkassikk bowed and spread his wings loosely before her.

Kitillikk's blood pounded in her ears again, but not from the silverwine. She had indeed begun a long journey—but longer and far more daring than even Lakkassikk knew, for at its end lay the Great Hall of the Flock: and, clasped around her neck, the Bloodfire Collar of the Supreme Flight Leader.

She slid from the shikk, pulled Lakkassikk to his feet, and pulled him to her, fur to fur, her wings wrapped around his folded ones. "Let us seal our pact, Wing Leader," she breathed into his ear. "Fly with me."

His breath came hard and fast. "It's so far to the surface . . ."

Kitillikk laughed. The military mind was so unimaginative. "There are other ways to fly, Lakkassikk," she said, and proceeded to prove it.

Only three days after the Commonwealth decree, the humans returned. Their ships appeared in orbit, their shuttles descended, and garrisons and guard posts and arms depots went up all along the river that marked the border, matching those the S'sinn had established in anticipation of the humans' return. What the Commonwealth thought of those warlike preparations Jarrikk didn't know, or care. The border was not far from the city, because of the Commonwealth's insistence that the humans be granted the place where their original colony had stood: where, Jarrikk hoped, they had found the unburied skeletons of their original colonists still lying among the burned remnants of their tents and buildings. Across the river's deep gorge, S'sinn and humans glared at each other with mutual hatred.

Among the S'sinn was Jarrikk, in defiance of Kitillikk's direct orders. He didn't care. He despised her for her submissive response to the Commonwealth decree; he only continued his daily visits to her fortress because of Ukkarr's training, training he now wanted more than ever so he could fight the humans as soon as possible. The rest of his time he spent at the border. After being chased off a couple of times by Hunters from the nearest S'sinn garrison, he found a hidden place on the rim of the gorge from which he could watch a human guard post, and for days now he had been returning there to watch them build their ugly buildings, to listen to their harsh shouts—and to dream of flaying the skin from their still-living bodies.

Kitillikk's orders to stay away from the humans had come shortly after he had first started watching them, when he had made the mistake of telling her. "The time will come," she said. "But not for years. Concentrate on preparing for your coming-of-age. Concentrate on becoming the best Hunter you can be. Then, when we strike back at the humans at last, you will be ready."

He said nothing, but he kept going back to the river gorge. By the treaty, the humans could not cross that gorge; if they did, they were fair game. That was what he awaited.

And then one day, as Jarrikk sat on his rocky ledge in the sun and enjoyed the warmth as much as he allowed himself to enjoy anything anymore, he heard the sound of one of the humans' incredibly noisy motors starting up. Then a second motor roared to life, and two brightly colored objects rolled out of one of the guard post's buildings, one blue, one red. Jarrikk focused prey-sight on one of them, but that didn't help much: he still had no idea what it was—until a human climbed into the ungainly harness hung beneath the huge triangle of blue fabric, and the whirling thing on its tail spun even faster, and the whole contraption lifted into the air, followed a moment later by the other.

Jarrikk gaped at them. So these were the artificial wings he'd only heard rumors of before! And then he laughed. If you could call them wings. Powering through the air, pushing aside thermals and ignoring eddies, no grace, no beauty . . .

Unbidden, the memory of his dead brothers rose up, of Kakkchiss riding the air so perfectly in control, slipping aside at the last possible instant as Jarrikk dove on him, and his bitter amusement gave way to a fury and grief that threatened to choke him. The pain of it nestled between his hearts like a knife blade driven to kill. These monsters, these *humans,* dared to foul the air with their choking exhausts and their stiff, unnatural wings, when they had torn from the sky the likes of Kakkchiss?

The Commonwealth and Kitillikk could go to flightless hell: *this could not be borne!*

And with that thought Jarrikk leaped into the sky and rose up over the gorge, high above the humans' crude machines, puttering around in circles far below; and from five hundred lengths above them, he focused his prey-sight on the metal spine of the lead craft, and with a shriek of defiance and rage, folded his wings and dove.

In the few seconds of his descent, he heard humans from the outpost shouting a warning to the circling aircraft, but not even Kakkchiss could have avoided that dive; at the last instant, almost too late, Jarrikk's wings snapped open. He crashed heavily and painfully into the bright blue fabric of the wing, but he was strong, and young, and angry, and he drove upward again with huge rent streamers of cloth in his claws, while below him the wing, its spine broken, crumpled and dropped, tumbling its squalling rider into the thundering white water below.

Jarrikk soared up and over the human outpost, circled once, staring down at the upturned faces of the humans, pink and black and brown, that shouted and screamed at him, and contemptuously dropped the shredded fabric of their crude craft onto their heads. He spread his wings to glide back across the river—and the second machine surged up out of the gorge, and lightning-bright beamer fire scorched across the fur of his belly, a hide's-depth from disemboweling him.

The pain snapped Jarrikk out of whatever world of grief and anger he'd been inhabiting, and he suddenly realized what he'd done: and that below him, a hundred humans were running for their weapons, or already bringing them to bear. He sideslipped as another beamer snapped at him, and dove for the gorge, dipping far down into it to avoid direct fire from the camp, then turning and beating strongly upstream, toward the S'sinn garrison, hoping the artificial wing would follow him. If the Hunters saw another youngling being pursued by the murderous humans, no Treaty would protect the aliens from S'sinn wrath . . .

Jarrikk discovered the flaw in his plan within a hundred beats: the human machine flew faster. And as his wings started to tire, the machine's earsplitting engine roared on unabated.

So he couldn't outrun the machine—so what? He'd bet his fangs he could outfly it.

Another beam slashed by, and he decided he'd better try.

First he swept up and up, then caught himself and dropped, expecting the human to fly right under him. Instead he found himself staring straight into the human's eyes over a hundred lengths as the machine climbed steeply toward him, closer than it had been yet. Jarrikk had to catch air clumsily and snap sharply right to avoid presenting an unmissable target. That gave him another idea and he tried to circle around behind the machine, but it seemed to almost turn in place, though at least for a moment he was far enough behind the human to avoid being shot.

Only for a moment, though. The circling had brought him far over the forest on the human side of the river; he abandoned his turn and dove for the gorge again. There! Up ahead, where it narrowed! His youngflight had flown that rocky maze at speed a hundred times, Kakkchiss always in the lead, laughing as his wingtips brushed rock. No human brute in a clumsy machine could fly through there the way Jarrikk could.

And then something else caught his eye, and he bared his fangs in a ferocious grin. A lone patrolling Hunter wheeled in the air on the other side of the gorge. Just what he wanted . . .

Towering rock walls leaped upward at him, the opening between them looking impossibly small at this speed and distance, but he knew he could fit between it, he'd done it often enough. A beam slashed by on his left, another on his right. *The Hunter will have seen that,* he thought. *The human fool has bought his death—and I'm all but safe—*

Agony lanced his left wing. The stench of burning hair and flesh filled his nostrils, then his wing collapsed, the membrane ripping. He flailed out of control, fluttering down and down until he hit the river in a geyser of spray and pain.

The last thing he saw was the human flyer's bright red wing blotting out the sun.

Chapter 4

Katy sat in the big upstairs playroom of the orphanage, staring out at Earth's strange blue sky, as she had done almost every day for two years.

Every day was just like the one before. In the morning she would get up, and dress and wash herself, and use the bathroom, and eat her breakfast; but she wouldn't talk, not to the other children in the orphanage, not to plump, rosy-cheeked Mrs. Spencer, not to tall, gaunt Mr. Piwarski, not to the various government officials who paid her visits, not to the many different doctors and therapists she'd been carted off to over the months, sometimes spending days or weeks in strange white rooms with mirrors all around. It didn't really matter; wherever she was, she sat quietly, day after day, and stared at nothing.

To Katy, the world all these people moved through seemed a strange gray place that had nothing to do with her. Her world was all taken up by the hole in her heart, by the black pit that had formed the day the bad things came out of the sky and tore away the love she'd always felt flowing from her parents.

"Poor child," she'd heard Mrs. Spencer say once, as she showed yet another child welfare officer the orphanage's saddest case. "She's waiting for her parents to come back."

Katy could have told her she was wrong, if she'd wanted to. Katy knew they would never come back. If she were waiting for anything, it was for the bad things that had ripped her parents from her heart to come and take her away, too. Maybe they would take her wherever her parents were, and the hole in her heart would be filled.

But though she watched the sky every day, not once did she see that funny rippling, or the silver ships, or the bad things with wings. They'd only wanted her parents; they didn't want her.

Still she waited. Most of the time she thought about nothing at all, because without her parents' love, nothing really mattered. Her mind kept swirling aimlessly into the hole their love had left behind, like water going down a black drain. Someday, she thought, she would drop right through that hole and never come back.

Through the window she could see not only the sky, but also the pale gray road that led to the orphanage, a long lane arched over with big trees, all turning gold now as another winter approached. Now a black floatcar came down that lane, circled the drive in front of the orphanage, and settled to the ground.

A figure emerged, taller than most men and much bigger around, wearing a blue spacesuit with a shiny silver backpack and helmet. But it wasn't one of the bad things that had taken away her parents, so Katy ignored it and looked back up at the sky.

A boy playing with magnetic blocks looked out the window just then and jumped up, sending the blocks clattering across the floor, snapping together at random. He ran out into the hall, yelling, "Mrs. Spencer! Mrs. Spencer! There's an *alien* coming up the walk!"

Other children ran after him, pounding down the stairs, their excited voices rising back up in a wash of sound that quit suddenly as Mrs. Spencer said something sharply. And then came a knock on the downstairs door.

Karak-kak-aka-ka-isss ar ?Ung!, Master of the Guild of Translators, 117th leader of the most respected organization in the Commonwealth, one of the most gifted and skilled empaths in the galaxy, tried to re-arrange his tentacles into a non-chafing configuration inside the ridiculous humanoid-shaped watersuit he had to wear on Earth, and wondered if any of the froth-brained humans he could sense inside the orphanage would ever get around to opening the door.

After a lot of scurrying noises transmitted clearly by the helmet's exterior microphones, one of them finally did: a woman he took to be the Mrs. Spencer his research staff had informed him was the orphanage's director. He rather towered over her, and could feel her fear (and more than a little disgust) as she looked up into his beaked, tentacle-encircled face. It was just as well, he thought, that she could only get a hint of it through the UV-shielding faceplate. "I'm here to look at Kathryn Bircher," he said. Ithkarites were the only race in the Commonwealth whose mouth-parts were flexible and ears sensitive enough to allow them to learn the spoken languages of the three races—four, now that the humans had been added—of the Commonwealth that used sound to communicate. It was a skill very useful for running a multiracial organization such as the Guild. Karak wondered, however, if other Ithkarites' mouthparts hurt as much as his did when he spoke a human language—and it didn't seem to matter which one. He'd learned French, Mandarin, German, Spanish, Japanese, and this one they called English, and all of them involved serious strain to his vibratory muscles.

"She's not well," Mrs. Spencer said. "You'll frighten her. Go away."

Karak stuck his three right motive/support limbs (encased in the watersuit, they looked like a single leg) into the door to keep her from closing it on him, then pushed it open with his top left manipulators, the tips of which, encased in the watersuit's glove, gave him the semblance of a three-fingered hand. With his top right manipulators, he opened the carry-pouch on his belt and held out a piece of paper. "I'm afraid I must insist."

While she read the letter from the Director of the Government Services for War Orphans and Veterans' Dependents, he stepped into the wood-paneled hallway and stared back at the wide-eyed children peering at him around the corner where the hallway entered the kitchen. They radiated only curiosity and shyness. He wondered how long it would be before Mrs. Spencer taught them her fear and disgust. And *they* would be the first generation of humans to grow up in the Commonwealth. It made his mission that much more urgent.

Mrs. Spencer, lips tight, held out the paper. "Keep it," Karak said. "It is for your records." He looked around. "The child?"

"This way." Mrs. Spencer tucked the letter into the pocket of her apron and led him up the stairs, which creaked alarmingly under the combined weight of him and the fifty liters of liquid circulating through the watersuit. She showed him into a bright, cheerful playroom. At the window, ignoring the toys all around her, sat a little blond-haired girl, staring out at the sky. "Katy," said Mrs. Spencer. "There's someth— some*one* here to see you."

Karak crossed the floor, its boards groaning under him, and touched Katy's head with his gloved manipulators. Before he even reached her he knew what he would find; the touch confirmed it. She was an empath, all right—an empath locked in feedback, all her abilities turned inward, chasing her own thoughts and emotions around and around twisted neural pathways. The trauma of her parents' deaths had trapped her in an endless emotional loop. And she'd been that way so long that when he touched her she almost pulled him into the black whirlpool inside her head. It was just as well he'd come himself: she was strong enough, and traumatized enough, to be dangerous to a lesser empath.

After a moment he pulled his hand away and turned back to Mrs. Spencer. "Mrs. Spencer, this child is suffering bondcut."

"Nonsense! She's perfectly healthy."

"Bondcut is not a disease; it is a trauma suffered by empaths when someone with whom they are emotionally linked dies in their presence."

"Empaths? Katy's not—"

"Yes, she is. And she must come with me. I've shown you my authorization . . ."

"But if she's not well, she needs—"

Karak would have liked to have let his impatience into his voice, but he still didn't know humans well enough to be able to mimic such emotional nuances. "What she needs, Mrs. Spencer, is the company of fellow empaths, in the Guild of Translators. As the letter states, the Commonwealth Treaty permits us to draft—"

"You mean kidnap!"

"—any individual who shows possibility as a Translator. If you will be so good as to pack her things . . ."

Mrs. Spencer gave him a look he didn't need empathy to interpret, then walked over to Katy, giving him a wide berth, and took the girl's hand gently. "Come along, Katy. You have to go with this . . . person."

"Karak," Karak supplied.

Mrs. Spencer ignored him. "It will be all right, Katy."

She took Katy to her room to pack (with the maximum number of banging noises), and Karak returned to the hallway to endure the continued stares of the other children. He wondered sourly, as he watched them, if, after he'd taken Katy away, Mrs. Spencer would use him as a threat to maintain discipline. *"You do that one more time, young one, and the monster from the stars will come and get you just like he got Katy!"*

Mrs. Spencer came down with Katy and a small suitcase. Karak took the suitcase, thanked Mrs. Spencer just as if she deserved it, and led Katy out.

As they went down the walk he heard Mrs. Spencer remark loudly to someone that if Katy hadn't been happy in the orphanage with other children, she cer-

tainly wouldn't be happy God-knew-where with only
monsters for company, and how could the government
sign a treaty that let *things* like that kidnap little girls,
and as Karak opened the door of the black floatcar
and Katy climbed inside, he heard Mrs. Spencer starting to sniffle about how brave Katy was being . . .

"Spaceport," he told the floatcar, and it lifted and
drove away.

He had what he'd come for—and he was more than
ready to leave Earth and its Mrs. Spencers behind.

Katy heard Mrs. Spencer talk about how brave she
was being, too, but Mrs. Spencer was wrong. Katy
wasn't being brave, because she wasn't scared. She
just didn't care. About anything.

The alien didn't speak as they drove to the spaceport; unlike human adults, he seemed to have no need
to talk unless he had something to say. She liked
that—as much as she liked anything.

At the spaceport, they boarded a ship very different
from the one that had brought Katy to Earth. Inside
the main airlock's massive outer hatch were seven different inner hatches, each a different color and marked
with strange symbols. Karak led Katy through a green
hatch and down a short corridor to a complex of
rooms like the inside of a little house, with a kitchen,
a multileveled living room space without any furniture
but with lots of cushions spread around on the blue-
carpeted floor, and four bedrooms, each with its own
tiny bathroom.

Karak took Katy's suitcase into one of the bedrooms. When he came out he said, in that funny,
squeaky voice of his, "This is where you'll stay for the
next few days. Right now you are the only human on
the ship, so you'll be alone here. The kitchen will
automatically prepare food for you three times a day
in that compartment." He pointed at a shiny black
rectangle in the kitchen wall. "Whatever you don't eat
will be automatically removed from that same compartment." He touched her head again, and when he

removed his three-fingered hand, spoke more gently. "I know none of this matters to you right now. We're going to fix that, Katy. We're going to make you better." He went to the door, turned, and said, "Welcome to the Guild of Translators," then went out. The door slid shut and sealed behind him.

Katy lay down on the bed and stared at the ceiling.

She didn't know, or care, how many days had passed when the door opened again and Karak reappeared. She had eaten several times, and slept, but there were no timekeepers in the apartment.

She looked up at him as he came in, but didn't say anything. He touched her head again, then led her silently out of the ship.

At the top of the loading ramp, Karak stopped and looked down at the small, silent figure by his side. "Commonwealth Central," he told her, hoping for some reaction. Garish lights of pink and blue glistened off the mirror-black wet pavement surrounding the ship, their reflections pockmarked by the icy rain dropping from the night sky. He felt nothing from her in any way related to the excitement he might have expected in a young one brought so many light years from home, but he did sense a faint spark of resentment as rain blew in under the overhang protecting the ramp. *Of course,* he thought; *she's dressed for the warm weather she left on Earth. She's cold.*

The resentment flared and died like a burning bit of straw, leaving her as inert to his empathic senses as a lump of wood, but he had felt it: no doubt of that. "So, there's life in there yet," he said to her. "As I knew. Come; you'll soon be warm." That earned him a faint glimmer of surprise, probably that he had guessed she was cold. Feeling better about the child than he had since he first sensed her pain in the orphanage's playroom, he led her down the ramp as an egg-shaped silver groundcar rolled across the pavement toward them on fat blue wheels.

He felt more surprise from her, as short-lived as her

earlier resentment, when the egg split open to reveal another human in its padded pink interior, a boy a few years older than her. Her reaction pleased Karak, but that pleasure faded as he slid in beside the boy and helped Katy in after him. Jim Ornawka was as strange a case as Katy. He was the only confirmed empath Karak had ever run across, in the Guild or out of it, who had the ability to completely block him out. All empaths could hide their emotions to a certain degree, but never completely, and never from someone with the skill and power of a Guildmaster. But Jim could do it—and did, constantly. Whereas other empaths were normally as open with their emotions as non-empaths, and had to concentrate to block, Jim claimed, and the facts seemed to indicate, that his natural state was blocked and he had to concentrate to open himself up.

So far the Guild researchers had failed to find anything within the structure of his brain or his genetic material that explained his unique ability. A non-empathic S'sinn scientist employed by the Guild had suggested dissection, but of course that was out of the question while the boy was alive; though if he became a Translator, his body would be available for autopsy and further research upon his death. Barring disease or accident, however, that time was yet many years away.

Karak suspected even dissection would not find the answer, that the boy's mysterious ability arose from something in his equally mysterious past. Jim had been found wandering the streets of a very rough port city on a mostly military planet, selling his body for food. His very blankness had drawn the attention of a passing Translator; someone like Jim, who could not be read, stood out in a crowd as much as or more than someone broadcasting the strongest hate or anger.

For more than a year now, Jim had been in training to be a Translator. Karak had heard nothing but good reports about his abilities and commitment. Yet the eerie emotional dead space that surrounded him still bothered Karak every time he had dealings with the boy.

He noticed Jim watching him, and nodded from Jim to Katy. Jim looked at the girl, and showed his teeth in the alarming human expression that Karak still found hard to believe conveyed friendliness instead of aggression. "Hi! I'm Jim," Jim said.

Katy ignored him. The boy closed his eyes for a moment, then opened them and blinked at the girl before looking at Karak. "I can't read her at all. It's like she's not even there."

Now you know how we *feel around you,* Karak thought. "Did you not feel her momentary surprise when she entered the car and saw you?"

"No, Guildmaster . . ."

"You must learn not to let your own emotions cloud your perceptions of others. The surprise was faint, but it was there. And so is she. Deep inside."

The car began to roll, the bumps of the road translating to a slow up-and-down motion inside that always made Karak think of the way his spawnhome swayed when storm-waves lashed the sea-top. "I read all the material you gave me on bondcut, Guildmaster, but I never thought it would be like this," Jim said. "It's—frightening."

"It is. And I hope you will never suffer from it." *Though you may have already,* he thought. *Perhaps that explains what happened to you . . .* "However, it is not always this way. Katy is an extreme case, because she has suffered without any treatment for a very long time. There has been no one to pull her out of the void left by her parents' death. It's like a wound that has abscessed; it has closed up and trapped her inside. It must be lanced: the poison drained, the wound opened to dry and begin to heal."

"But . . . Guildmaster, how?"

"I will show you. You have an important role to play. We will begin the process tonight, when we reach the Guildhall."

Jim turned his gaze back toward the girl, his eyes

bright with . . . interest? Sorrow? Karak wished he knew.

He settled back for the short trip to the Guildhall.

Katy kept her own gaze on the floor, hearing and understanding everything, yet feeling as if they talked about someone else entirely, someone of absolutely no importance. Vaguely, she hoped they might be able to help this Katy they spoke of, but she doubted it, and the hope slid away into nothingness almost as soon as it formed.

Ten or fifteen minutes later they stopped, and the car split open to disgorge them in front of a huge stone building like an ancient fortress, lit by more of the pink-and-blue lights. They entered through an oval doorway that slid up at their approach and down behind them, and crossed a dim hall through which their footsteps echoed, then went down a long, arched corridor of white stone, lit by pink-glowing lamps on long black cords, passing closed oval doors to either side. The chill air smelled faintly of cinnamon and roses.

At a cross-corridor they turned right, climbed a long flight of stairs, and a short distance down another corridor came to a door larger than any they had passed. The spicy/floral scent grew stronger. Karak took something from his watersuit's belt and pressed it to the door's surface, and it opened to reveal another large, egg-shaped chamber, this one lined with black stone pricked with tiny lights, and floored with a glassy substance that glowed pearly white with its own inner radiance.

Encircling it were aliens.

The surprise, and even a little fear, that flared in Katy this time lingered for several seconds before the emptiness smothered it—but she heard Jim, close behind her, draw in a sharp breath. "Guildmaster, I felt her! And then . . . then she just went away . . ."

"We're going to bring her back, Jim," Karak said. "All of her. All of us."

All of us? Katy looked around. Karak, in his blue

watersuit. A thing like a giant insect whose meter-spanning wings filled the air with a thick drone, and whose four golden eyes seemed to glow more than they should be able to just by reflecting the dim light of the room. A trio of tiny winged humanoids, no bigger than Katy herself and much more slender: blue-skinned, naked, and sexless. A reptilian creature with legs as big and gnarled as tree-trunks, who glistened with green-black scales from head to foot, whose hands ended in long, curved claws painted the red of fresh blood and whose slit-pupiled, yellow eyes never blinked. A dull-black four-metre sluglike thing in thick gooey mud inside a big glass-walled aquarium on wheels. And a . . .

. . . a . . .

She hadn't clearly seen the last figure in the dark room when they first came in; darkness seemed to be its friend, almost swallowing it up. But now it stirred, and spread leathery wings, and Katy spoke for the first time since her parents died.

She screamed.

The sound echoed inside the stone-walled room, magnified, and seemed to feed on itself. Katy screamed and kept on screaming, mindlessly, fear rising out of the dark pit in her heart on the black leathery wings that had taken her parents away and *now were in this room with her* . . .

"Quickly!" Karak shouted above the noise. "Jim, you must help us! Reach out to her . . ."

"But I'm not a projective . . ."

"The rest of us are. But we're not human. We need *your* emotion. Katy needs it."

"But what?" Jim cried. "What emotion?"

"Love!" Karak shouted. "Let us feel your human love, Jim, and we will make Katy feel it. Hurry!"

Katy felt herself slipping finally, once and for all, into the black pit of emptiness—and welcomed it. Her own screaming faded to a faint echo in her ears, then disappeared. The room faded from her awareness. Numbness gripped her body. Blackness reached up for her, and she reached out for it. Blackness had taken her parents. Maybe she would find them inside it . . .

But there in the dark, with the last gray light fading around her, something touched her: something not of herself, something that didn't belong in her disappearing world, something warm, and hot, and alive . . .

. . . something human.

Katy didn't want it. She wanted the numbness, the darkness, the nothingness. She didn't want to think, she didn't want to feel. Feelings hurt, not just her feelings, but other people's feelings. She didn't want to hurt. Why couldn't they just leave her alone?

But the faint touch returned, like a gentle caress, and strengthened, and the darkness lightened, at first just a little, and then a lot, and then suddenly it was like the night the bad things attacked and the sky rippled and filled up with bright silver and flashing lights, only this time the light was warm and red, like a campfire. She felt as if she were being buoyed up by a hot wave, a wave that poured into the pit of her soul's emptiness and covered it with steaming water, hiding it from view.

Katy stopped screaming. She stared at the batlike alien that had startled her, and said, "Bad thing! Bad thing! You took my parents!" And then she burst into tears and, without even thinking about it, turned and buried her face in the cool blue fabric of Karak's watersuit.

Jim patted her awkwardly on the shoulder, and she felt the same fiery sense of humanity that had brought her back. Karak touched her head gently. "So," he said. "Welcome back, little one. Welcome to your new family."

Katy wept even harder, feeling everything, feeling too much, feeling not only her grief but Karak's concern, the little winged humanoids' hot bright happiness, the almost frightening single-minded interest of the giant insectoid, the analytical satisfaction of the reptilian, the benign disinterest of the slug in the glass box, and worst of all, the faint, not-quite-hidden distaste and resentment of the bad thing. She didn't want to feel any of it, and she sobbed not just because of the loss of her parents, but because she knew that never again could she hide herself away from her feelings, or anyone else's, that whatever all these monsters had just done to her, she could never change it.

They'd made her one of them.

Chapter 5

Jarrikk flitted in and out of consciousness for a long time—how long, he had no way of knowing. Afterward, bits of memories stayed with him, memories of shouting, of lifting, memories of flying—no, of *being flown*—memories of faces, curious, horrified, angry—and then, memories of dreams, horrible dreams, dreams of Kakkchiss fluttering helplessly into the forest, his chest a smoking ruin; dreams of Yvenndrill spinning down, his lifeblood a trailing red stain against the sky; dreams of Llindarr crashing into the trees, wings ripping, bones splintering and bursting through his skin; and most of all, dreams of little Illissikk, butchered and headless, his skin drying on a rack in the human camp.

In some of those dreams, Jarrikk felt the beam slice through his own neck, and saw his own body violated by the humans' knives, and the agony should have brought him awake screaming and flapping, except somehow he couldn't wake up, and sometimes he thought they had cut off his wings and he would never fly again—the worst nightmare of all.

Finally he did wake up, and found out his nightmare had come true.

He woke over a period of days, coming to consciousness to find himself tended by healers who never seemed to look at him, who treated him almost like the humans had treated Illissikk, turning him on his shikk like a slab of meat, never speaking to him, never meeting his eyes. He tried to talk to them, when the haze of drugs and pain would let him, but they never answered him, never even seemed to hear him, until he wondered if something had gone wrong with his throat and he'd become mute, or if all this were just another bad dream.

But then one day he opened his eyes and felt fully awake for the first time, his wings still immobilized, his body still bandaged and sore in every part, but his brain, finally, in fully working condition, so that he remembered what had happened, remembered the human shooting him, and remembered crashing into the water. *War!* he thought with grim satisfaction. *We must be at war again. Kitillikk, Lakkassikk, they won't have let this go unavenged . . .*

He raised his head from the shikk and looked around the room. To his right, two glowing blue globes on silver pillars pulsed in time with his heart-beats; otherwise the room was empty, a closed door beyond the flashing blue globe the only opening in the blank walls.

A chill went through him. Windowless? Doored? Only prisoners were kept in windowless rooms with doors. But he couldn't be a prisoner, could he?

Could he? For attacking a human?

Space is limited, he told himself. *We must be fighting again. The hospital needs all its rooms for war injuries. Someone had to be put down here, and since I was unconscious . . .*

But if space were that limited, there would be others with him in this large, echoing room, and there was no one; no one but himself.

Then the door opened.

The S'sinn who entered stopped when she saw Jar-rikk looking at her, then nodded once and crossed to him. He stared at her with something approaching dread. He'd been expecting a healer, or, if he really were a prisoner, a Hunter; maybe even Kitillikk her-self, eyes aflame with fury at his stupidity; but not this, not a female wearing a gold collar embossed with the jet-black outline of a S'sinn holding a glowing blue gem in its claws.

Not a priest!

"Jarrikk," said the priest as she came to stand beside his shikk. "I am Iko."

"Am I dying, Mother Iko?"

The priest stared into his eyes. "You are already dead, Jarrikk."

One of his hearts skipped a beat, causing one blue globe to flash briefly red and beep a warning before resuming its pulsing at a much faster rate. "Mother?" Jarrikk said faintly.

"You were badly wounded, Jarrikk. The healers saved your life; they could not repair your wing. You are flightless."

The heartglobe beeped another warning. The blackness he'd just escaped whirled around Jarrikk, threatening to engulf him again. Flightless! *Flightless!* No wonder the healers never spoke to him, no wonder he had been put in this windowless cell, no wonder he shared it with no other patients. Flightless? The healers should have slain him, should never have let him wake up. They had a duty to the Flock, a duty to the S'sinn, they had a duty to him! "Why do I still breathe?" he cried, and would have lunged up and flung himself at the wall to shatter his skull against it if not for the straps that restrained him.

"It was not our doing." Disgust tinged Mother Iko's voice. "The incident you caused brought the Commonwealth meddlers diving in. They prevented us from avenging you. Then, after one of their Translators touched you to see if he could make sense of your ravings, they insisted that we keep you alive. They have monitored every step of your treatment. The healers have had no opportunity to uphold their oaths, Jarrikk. Nor have I. The Commonwealth has claimed you for itself."

Jarrikk strained against the restraints once more. "Mother, you are here, we are alone, kill me, now, quickly! By the Hunter of Worlds, Mother, I beg you—"

The priest backed away. "I cannot, Jarrikk. The Hunter forgive me, I cannot."

"You must! You swore an oath! Mother—"

Iko took a step forward, her hands reaching out toward him—

—and the door crashed inward, admitting two of the reptilian soldiers Jarrikk had seen the day of the Treaty, beamers aimed at the priest. Iko lowered her hands. "I'm sorry, Jarrikk. I truly am. But you are not of the S'sinn anymore."

"Then I am nothing!" Jarrikk howled after her as she turned and fled. *I am nothing!*

A new figure appeared in the door, a male S'sinn, wearing a silver collar bearing a triangle within a circle within a square, all set in blue stone. "Stop that," he snapped. "Of course you are." He nodded curtly to the reptilians, who went out, closing the door behind them.

"I am flightless!"

"So, you're flightless." The S'sinn opened his wings and regarded them. "Most races are, you know. You don't see them swearing at their doctors because they kept them alive."

"We are not 'most races!'" Jarrikk snarled. "We are S'sinn!"

"Yes, aren't we." The stranger came over to Jarrikk's shikk. "There are more ways to fly than with wings, Jarrikk." He put his hand on Jarrikk's head. "Do you feel that?"

"Of course I feel it," Jarrikk snapped. "Who are you, anyway? Why don't you just go away?"

"And leave you contemplating creative ways to suicide? I don't think so." The strange S'sinn continued to hold his hand to Jarrikk's head. "That's quite a block," he murmured, almost to himself. "I never had anything half that strong. Of course, I didn't grow up in the broodhall . . . you'd have to have a strong shield with all those other S'sinn around . . ."

Didn't grow up in the broodhall? Jarrikk stared up at the stranger. "Who are you?" he repeated.

"Quiet," the other said softly. "I've almost got . . . there!"

And with a kind of soundless click, the windowless room seemed suddenly to flood with light, as though open to the sky in every direction. Jarrikk could feel— *feel*—the other S'sinn's mixture of amusement and concern and exasperation, could faintly sense the strange bored intensity of the reptilian soldiers outside his door, could pick up other echoes of emotions from other S'sinn from who-knew-where—but most astonishingly of all, he could feel, really feel, himself, could identify the layers of grief and anger and lust for revenge that colored every thought and action, could almost see the new layer of astonishment and wonder building on top of that, dissolving some of it away—

—dissolving, for example, a little of the wish for, the expectation of, death.

"Ah, I see you feel it now," said the other S'sinn.

"I don't—I don't understand . . ."

"You will." The other S'sinn spread his wings again and made an exaggerated court curtsey normally reserved for the Supreme Flight Leader. "Allow me to present myself. I am Ukkaddikk, of the Guild of Translators."

"Guild of—"

"Translators," Ukkaddikk finished helpfully. "Don't try to take it all in at once," he added, unnecessarily, since Jarrikk was hardly taking anything in at all at that moment, weariness having suddenly washed over him like a bank of gray fog. "Plenty of time. The rest of your life, in fact—which, I'm happy to say, now looks like it should be a long one." He went to the door. "Rest. We'll talk more later, and I'll explain."

He went out, and Jarrikk marveled at the fading sense of satisfaction he sensed from the retreating Translator. Flightless . . . it was still his duty to die, of course, nothing could change that . . .

. . . but the thought trailed him down into sleep that since they insisted on keeping him alive, it couldn't hurt to hear what this Translator had to say, and to explore this strange new sense.

He'd live. *For a while, anyway.*

"A Translator?" Kitillikk stared at Mother Iko. "You're certain?"

"I heard two of the Commonwealth monsters talking, Flight Leader," Iko said. "He is a Translator. Or he will be. He has the gift."

"So that is why they would not let us honor him!" Kitillikk went to the window and looked out over the city, the walls of its ugly buildings almost beautiful in the golden light of the setting sun. A single bright star already shone in the eastern sky. "Ukkarr."

"Flight Leader?" He came out of the shadows to her side.

"It would be a useful thing to have a Translator in our service, would it not?"

"It would," Ukkarr said. "But they swear an oath . . ."

"Jarrikk has already sworn an oath—to me. I think he will be little inclined to break it in favor of the oath of the Translators, which I understand requires a promise to treat all races equally." She ran a claw delicately along the windowsill. "Not when he learns that that promise includes humans."

Ukkarr showed his teeth in amusement. "I'm sure you are right, Flight Leader. What action should I take?"

"Arrange for me to visit Jarrikk. He may be confused about his duty. I must explain to him his responsibility to uphold the Commonwealth Treaty."

"I go, Flight Leader." Ukkarr sprang out the window and away.

"Now, Mother Iko . . ." Kitillikk turned back toward the priest—but she, too, was gone. "Leave it alone, priest," Kitillikk growled to the empty room. "Leave it alone!"

* * *

"The Commonwealth Treaty," Ukkaddikk began, looking out the window of Jarrikk's new room. At his insistence, Jarrikk had been moved upstairs into a chamber with huge arched windows that overlooked a landscaped courtyard with lots of trees and flowers and a delicate fountain that must have been shipped directly from S'sinndikk; there'd been little time for that kind of art on Kikks'sarr. Jarrikk had thought he wanted the window; now he wasn't so sure, as a youngflight soared overhead and he thought again of his slain brothers and his own useless wings. He was in no mood to listen to a lecture on the Commonwealth Treaty, but it seemed Ukkaddikk intended to give him one, nevertheless.

"The Commonwealth is based on the fortunate fact that the Swampworlders communicate with each other telepathically and empathically," Ukkaddikk continued. "When the Hasshingu-Issk—the reptilian race whose soldiers I think you've seen—landed on the Swampworld, the Swampworlders—"

"—captured one that had some natural empathic ability and turned him into the first Translator," Jarrikk finished. "I have had some education, Ukkaddikk. I know the history of the Translators. The Swampworlders, masters of genetic engineering, mutated a symbiotic lifeform native to their planet into a universal nervous system interface that allows telepathic communication between two empaths from any sentient races."

"Well, any that we've come across so far."

"Even humans?"

"Oh, yes—in fact, it took very little work to adapt the interface to humans. According to the Swampworlders, they're very much like us."

Jarrikk growled.

Ukkaddikk half-spread his wings. "I suppose I can't blame you for that. But you'll get over it. You'll have to, if you're going to be a Translator."

"I don't understand that, either," Jarrikk complained. "If I have this natural empathic ability, how come I never knew anything about it until you touched my head yesterday?"

"You grew up in a broodhall," said Ukkaddikk. "Hundreds of other S'sinn surrounding you all the time. You were born with the empathic ability, but your brain shut out the signals it received, the spill-over of emotion from all those other brains all around it. It built shields in self-defense. It took a projective empath—me—to break through. But you feel it now, don't you?"

Yes, he still felt it; had already become used to it, to feeling Ukkaddikk's eagerness and the stolid, bored watchfulness of the Hasshingu-Issk soldiers, just on the edge of his awareness. Sensitivity faded quickly with distance, but doubled or tripled when somebody touched him.

Which meant that he had felt full-force the way the apprentice healers who had moved him to his new room that morning had despised him for still being alive. "How can I ever be a Translator?" he asked, remembering that. "No S'sinn will let a Flightless One speak for them!"

Ukkaddikk came over to his shikk. "They will have no choice. They will need a S'sinn Translator, and you will be provided by the Guild. They can refuse your services, but if so, they forfeit the right to ever again be provided with a Translator. No one in government or business can risk that."

"That won't stop them from despising me. No S'sinn will ever look on me as anything but a freak, an embarrassment." *And I will never look at them without envy and bitterness.*

"Do your job properly, and respect will follow."

"You are not flightless," Jarrikk snapped. "You cannot know."

"Neither can you. You are the first. Perhaps, if you succeed in this, others who have lost flight will find that they can still serve the Flock. Perhaps, if you succeed, you will save the lives of Flightless Ones to follow."

Jarrikk turned his face to the window. A lone S'sinn passed high overhead, momentarily silhouetted against a snowy cloud. "Perhaps they will not thank me for it," he murmured. He closed his eyes, and after a moment heard Ukkaddikk slip out, thinking him asleep.

In another moment, Ukkaddikk would have been right.

Jarrikk woke in confusion, jerked from deep sleep by—something. It took him a moment to realize his new sense had awakened him, to realize that the stolid presence of the Hasshingu-Issk soldiers beyond the beaded curtain of the entrance arch had vanished, and that a new presence approached, hard, determined, deeply impassioned—

The beads clattered aside. Mother Iko swept into the room, wings half-spread, a military-issue stunner in her left hand and a long silver dagger with a black hilt in her right. "Damn the Commonwealth to Flightless Hell!" she shouted, her fanatical devotion roaring in Jarrikk's head like a hot red fire. She tossed the stunner aside and quickly unbuckled the restraints that still held him to the shikk, then pulled him upright. He almost screamed from the agony, and the heartglobe flashed brilliant red and started to beep frantically. "I've come to help you!" Iko cried. "Their treaty means nothing in the eyes of the Hunter of Worlds!" She pressed the silver dagger into his hand. "Now, Jarrikk! Now you can be free!"

Maddening pain, mingled with the heat of Iko's devotion, filled him with confusion. He could be free— free of the pain and the confusion—free of this strange sense the Translator had woken in him—free of a world where humans killed younglings and yet returned to live peacefully on the same blood-soaked ground where they had butchered Illissikk—he lifted the knife, pressed its point to his chest, heard Iko begin the rising, wailing words of a prayer to the Hunter of Worlds to devour the soul about to be delivered . . .

. . . and then he felt a new presence, even stronger than the priest's, heard a shout, and for a moment fell free of both Iko's fiery emotions and the new arrival's force of command and found a quiet space in which to make his own decision.

He lowered the knife. "No," he said to Iko, whose prayer stopped in mid-howl. "I choose to live."

"The choice is not yours!" she hissed. "The choice is the Hunter's, and His choice has been made!" She snatched the dagger from Jarrikk's hand, pushed him back against the shikk, lunged forward—

—and spasmed and collapsed, as though every tendon in her body had been severed, the silver knife thudding against the padded hospital floor. Jarrikk, pain still pulsing through him, looked across her fallen body to where Kitillikk stood, Iko's own stunner grasped in her hand. "I told you to leave it alone, priest," she said to the unconscious body on the floor.

"Flight Leader?" Jarrikk gasped, and passed out.

He came to an indeterminate time later to find Ukkaddikk and Kitillikk standing on either side of him. "I am glad to find you still breathing," Ukkaddikk said. "You may thank your Flight Leader for it."

"I know," Jarrikk said. "Thank you, Flight Leader Kitillikk."

"She wishes to speak to you privately. I leave you in her capable hands." Ukkaddikk bowed to Kitillikk and went out.

Jarrikk looked up into Kitillikk's unreadable face. "I did not expect to see you, Flight Leader. Why are you here?"

"You served me well. I repay loyalty with loyalty."

"But I am Flightless. I am dead to you. I can serve you no longer."

"Perhaps not as you did." Kitillikk spread her wings slightly. "But you can still serve the Flock."

Jarrikk felt something strange in the emotions behind the words. She wasn't lying—he could swear to that, now—but there were depths of meaning he could not fathom, not with his body aching and his head still buzzing from pain and pain-dulling drugs and his new sense only a day old. "I do not understand."

"We need S'sinn Translators. We need them to ensure our words are heard properly in the councils of the Commonwealth. Your talent is too important to be thrown away because you are Flightless."

More complexities. More dizzying doubts. More doubled words. Too much. "I thank you, Flight Leader. I will serve as best I can."

"I'm counting on it, Jarrikk. I have given you your life. Use it well."

"I swear I will, Flight Leader." His eyes closed; he couldn't keep them open. "I swear," he murmured.

He didn't hear her leave.

Chapter 6

Kathryn rubbed her right eye with the heel of her hand and said, "Aga—ah—in." A yawn swallowed the middle of the word.

"Input not recognized," said the computer in its pleasant male voice. "Please repeat."

Kathryn sighed and leaned forward on the desk, resting her head in her hands. "Again."

"Exercise commencing. Name the four major elements of the Treaty of Ha'gr'akas-ee! Explain how the treaty, hailed as a great success at the time, led directly to the Dispute of the Dry Winter. Support your reasoning with references. Begin."

Kathryn closed her eyes, concentrating. "The Treaty of Ha'gr'akas-ee!—"

"Can wait," said another pleasant male voice, behind her. "Computer, cancel exercise."

"Jim!" Kathryn started to turn, but strong hands on her shoulders stopped her.

"How long have you been studying?" Jim Ornawka said. He began massaging her shoulder muscles.

"I don't know, an hour or two—Jim, I'm glad you're back, but I've got to—computer, restart—"

"Computer," Jim's stronger voice overrode hers. "How long has Trainee Bircher been using this study booth?"

"Nine hours, fourteen minutes," the computer replied promptly.

Jim's fingers dug a little deeper into Kathryn's muscles. "Nine hours, Katy. It's enough."

"But the exam—First Translation—I've got to be ready—"

"If you're not ready, you can't learn it all tonight." Kathryn started to protest, but Jim hushed her. "But don't worry. You're ready."

"How would you know? You haven't even been here for half a year!"

"Because I know you. Best human student the Guild's ever seen. You're always ready. Except for one thing."

"What?" Kathryn frantically ran over her preparations for the next day. "What did I forget?"

"To relax." His fingers had never stopped, and despite herself, Kathryn could feel some of her tension slipping away.

"That does feel good," she murmured.

"I know," Jim said, amused. "I am an empath, you know."

"So am I," Kathryn said, a little sleepily now. "But I've never been able to read you, and you've always been able to read me like a giant vidscreen. 'S'not fair . . .'"

Jim laughed softly. "Feeling better?"

"Feel like I've been sitting in this bloody cubicle for nine hours and fourteen minutes," Kathryn admitted.

"Hungry?"

Kathryn thought about that. "Yeah," she said, a little surprised it was true. "I am."

"Good. Because I have prepared a special night-before-the-big-test dinner for you in my quarters."

"Before you even asked me? Sure of yourself, aren't you?"

"You're not saying no, are you?"

Kathryn laughed. "No. It sounds wonderful."

"Then if you will allow me to escort you . . ."

Kathryn let him help her to her feet and take her arm. As he led her out of the study booth and into the broad, bland corridors of the Guildhall's human habitat, she felt her long hours sitting at the computer anew in the stiff muscles of her calves and thighs, and leaned on Jim for support. She'd leaned on him a lot over the years, she thought; ever since she'd been brought to the Guildhall and he'd been the only other human child there. She'd been eight, and he'd been thirteen; now, ten Earth-years later, by the careful count Jim had always kept, he'd been a full-fledged Translator for almost five years and she was about to become one. Tomorrow she would face the by-all-accounts harrowing First Translation, not to mention the (to her way of thinking) even-more-harrowing Final Exam, and he'd made sure he was back to support her once again. "It must have been tough," she said, looking up at his dark, high-cheekboned face.

He glanced down at her, mouth quirking in a smile. "What?"

"It must have been tough for you—first human Translator—going through your Final Exam and First Translation. You didn't have someone who'd been there before, like I do." She gave his arm a squeeze. "You've been like a big brother to me, Jim. I really appreciate it."

His smile faded and he looked away from her. "It wasn't so bad. There'd been one-sided Translations with humans. They knew it wouldn't kill us."

"Weren't you at least a little bit scared?" Kathryn asked. *Because I am,* she added silently. *There have been a dozen human Translators since Jim, and I'm still scared.*

"No," Jim said. "I wasn't a little bit scared. I was bloody well terrified." He stopped. "Here we are. Open!"

The dark gray wall in front of them split apart, admitting them into Jim's quarters, a quintet of rooms: kitchen, bedroom, bathroom, office, and the general-purpose room into which the door opened. Kathryn stopped in the doorway and stared open-mouthed at a table draped in pristine white, the glitter of crystal and silver, the soft glow of tall red candles, the fragrant red flowers (*roses,* the name came to her from somewhere) in a slender white vase . . . and a long-necked bottle cooling in a silver bucket of ice beside the table. "Jim—" Kathryn's throat closed off. "Jim, I—" She had to shrug and finally laugh. "I'm speechless!"

"I'll take that as a compliment," Jim said. "Allow me, Lady Kathryn."

He escorted her to one of the two chairs at the table and seated her with a flourish that made her laugh again, feeling like she was in one of the historical romances currently the rage in the entertainment chips they got from Earth. She'd always thought they were pretty silly. Now she wasn't so sure. "But how—"

"This assignment I just finished was to Earth—"

"You said you were going to Orris," Kathryn said accusingly.

"Security," Jim said. "The whole thing's tied up with this Fairholm mess. Anyway, since I was on our beloved homeworld, I slipped away from the conference for a day when I wasn't needed and took the liberty of picking up a few things the Guild has unaccountably failed to import for us."

"Just for me?" Kathryn couldn't believe it. "That's—incredible!"

"For you—and for me, too." He pulled the open bottle from its bed of ice and poured two glasses full of a golden liquid that bubbled and sparkled, catching the light of the candles.

"For you?" Kathryn breathed. Champagne—it had to be champagne. She'd never tasted it, never even seen it outside of entertainment vids.

"It gave me an excuse to pry you away from the computer—something I haven't been able to do since you started your final training this year. In other words," he handed her one of the glasses, "it has given me the pleasure of your company." She took the chill glass from him, and feeling more than ever like she'd fallen out of real life, clinked it against his, and sipped the pale liquid.

It tasted nothing at all like she'd imagined, and the bubbles seemed to race up into her nose and explode there, tickling, but leaving behind a sharp warmth. She closed her eyes and sipped again, and the sensation repeated itself. "Mmmmm . . . no wonder they drink this for special occasions."

"They also smash it against the bows of ships about to launch on their maiden voyages, which makes it doubly appropriate, since tomorrow you, fair maiden, will be launched on your new life as a Translator."

Kathryn opened her eyes and smiled at him. "Why, Jim, I never knew you were a romantic at heart."

Jim's eyes caught and held hers, glints of candlelight in them. "Far more romantic than you would ever think, probably," he said softly. Kathryn felt heat rise to her cheeks, and looked away, carefully setting down the champagne.

After a moment's silence, Jim said, "I'll get dinner," and went into the kitchen.

"How did your assignment go?" Kathryn called after him, by way of changing the strange, charged mood that had gripped the room—and her. "Or should I ask?"

"My assignment was simply to Translate, which I did successfully," Jim said. "Careful how you phrase things, Trainee."

"You know what I mean."

"You mean, how did the diplomatic mission of which I was a part go?" Jim came back into the room carrying a covered dish. "Depends on who you ask. Certain people on S'sinndikk and Earth were undoubtedly very pleased. The Commonwealth diplomats, however, were not." He set the dish on the table. "No compromises. Earth insists it was on Fairholm first. S'sinndikk claims the same. Both have computer records to support their positions. And meantime, the rest of the Seven Races are taking sides. It was not a particularly pleasant assignment, passing barely-veiled insults from side to side. I'm glad to be back." He paused, his hand on the dish, and smiled at her, teeth flashing white in his dark brown face. "Especially glad to be back with you." His eyes looked into hers, and again she felt that strange, electric tension, mingling with the warmth of the champagne in her brain. This time she didn't look away; Jim did, lifting the lid from the dish and releasing a swirl of steam and mouth-watering, spicy fragrance. "A delicacy of Earth: fettuccini Alfredo. Allow me to serve."

The food tasted every bit as strange and wonderful as it smelled; as strange and wonderful as Kathryn felt. She and Jim ate in near silence, but every time she looked up, there were his dark, liquid eyes, somehow drawing her in. It wasn't her empathic ability—he was as blank to her as ever—but something new. Something—exciting.

When the dinner ended, Jim held out his hand to her. His fingers, warm and dry, touched hers, and she gasped with the sudden shock of being able to read him at last, of being able to read the strength of his desire for her, desire that found an echo in her and resonated with a force that dissolved the distance between their minds, and, within moments, between their bodies.

Kathryn woke slowly, and stretched languidly, then looked up at the ceiling, pale blue instead of her own bedroom's gray, and sat abruptly upright. Daylight flooded the room through the lightubes from the surface far above. Kathryn scrambled out of bed and reached for her clothes.

Jim rolled over and blinked at her. "Katy, what—"

Kathryn ignored him. "Computer, what time is it?"

"0514," the computer answered promptly.

Kathryn stopped with her skirt in her hand. "0514?"

"Now 0515," replied the computer.

Jim levered himself up on one elbow and grinned at her. "You've got two hours before you need to get up," he said. "And the computer wouldn't have let you oversleep. I programmed it last night."

"You—" Kathryn turned toward the bed. "When?"

Jim's grin slipped a little. "When? Well—I don't remember. Sometime before we slept."

"You didn't really have a chance, did you?" Kathryn resumed dressing. "You programmed the computer to wake me, here, before you ever came to get me last night, didn't you?"

"Does it matter?" Jim wasn't grinning at all, anymore.

"It matters. You seduced me."

"I didn't force you to do anything you didn't want to."

"Oh, no?" Kathryn pulled on her blouse, sat down on the bed, and reached for her boots. "You know, I've never been able to read you before when we touched. How come the barriers came down just then, Jim? And just what is your rating on the projective scale?"

"Katy—"

"I've got to go." She stood up, fully dressed, and marched to the bedroom door. "I can still get in a couple of hours of study—"

She heard Jim scramble out of the bed as she entered the dining room, where the congealed remains of the previous night's dinner didn't look nearly as romantic as it had by candlelight, white tablecloth or not. She almost made it to the front door before he grabbed her arm and spun her around.

"Katy, you can't mean that. You can't really think I'd use my ability to—that's like saying I raped you!"

Kathryn opened her mouth, then closed it again. "No," she said. "No, I wouldn't go that far. But you helped things along, didn't you?"

"So what?" Jim sounded angry. "So what? Katy, I've been attracted to you for years, but you've—well, you said it last night. You've always seen me as your big brother. So I decided to change that. I wanted you to look at me differently, Katy. I wanted you to see me as a man, not the boy you grew up with. So I pulled out all the stops, last night, and it worked. You were attracted to me, I could feel it—so I let you feel my attraction to you. And we did something about it. Why are you angry? You can't tell me you didn't enjoy it!"

"I—" Kathryn began, then stopped. No, she couldn't honestly say that. It had been—wonderful. More than she had ever imagined, watching the couples in the entertainment vids. The empathic overtones alone . . . so why was she angry?

She looked at Jim, and realized something. He might be standing naked in front of her, but his mind and emotions were fully clothed. She couldn't read him. She hadn't been able to since she got up. He'd gotten what he wanted, and then closed her out again. Her anger flared anew, and when he flinched, she knew he felt it, and let it burn even hotter. "Put on some clothes," she snapped. "Or go back to bed. Frankly, I don't care which." She swept out, and the door closed behind her.

On the walk back to her own quarters, she reached inside herself and tried to quiet her emotions. Today was the most important day of her life. She couldn't afford to be less than perfectly centered. She couldn't let thoughts of Jim—who'd *known* what day this was and had still—

She cut off that train of thought as quickly as it formed. She would *not* think about Jim Ornawka. Not until this day was over.

Today, all her thoughts had to be on the Exam: the Exam, and First Translation.

Eight hours later, Kathryn stood in the circular Guildheart, the star-filled chamber where she had been brought upon her arrival in the Guildhall ten years before. The Guild Council member for each race formed a semicircle around her. Above them, slowly turning in the random air currents of the Hall, filled today with Earth-normal atmosphere, hung a sphere within a pyramid within a cube, all of gold set with diamond chips that reflected the torchlight in thousands of firefly sparkles: torchlight, because Translation could only take place in an environment shielded from electromagnetic interference, and artificial lighting put out far too much of it.

"Candidate Bircher, you have successfully completed your training and answered the questions put to you by the Guild Councilors. Are you ready to take the Oath of the Guild?" Karak's squeaky, dolphin-like voice filled the chamber with echoes. Today he didn't speak a human language at all, but the *lingua franca* of the Guild, which the Hasshingu-Issk had invented long ago and humans had dubbed Guildtalk. With it, humans, Hasshingu-Issk, Ithkarites, and S'sinn could usually make themselves understood to each other. Kathryn faced Karak's aquarium and looked squarely into his round, dead-black eyes, close behind the thick glass.

"I am, Guildmaster Karak," she said in the same language.

"Then state it."

No repeat-after-me; candidates were expected to know their oath long before they took it—know every word and every ramification that two centuries of Guild experience had brought to light. Much of the Final Exam had centered on exactly that. Kathryn took a deep breath, and continued to face Karak, remembering the day he had taken her from the orphanage, and the day these same Councilors had brought her back from the despairing depths of bondcut. "I renounce all ties to my home planet and species," she said clearly. "I am no longer human, but Translator. I belong to no race, but am kin to all, and I serve the good of all, without bias or prejudice. I surrender my will freely, that others may speak through me. I make this Oath in the presence of Seven Races, and by all that they honor."

Kathryn bowed to Karak, who bowed back, the tentacles around his beaked face weaving a slow pattern.

She turned to the aquarium next to his, filled with a thicker, darker liquid. Dimly visible, a four-metre slug-like body pulsated dreamily. Kathryn repeated her oath to the Swampworlder, though only Full Translation could have made it understandable, then turned to the next Councilor, a single Aza drone, wings humming, and spoke to it, and through it to all the thousands of members of its Swarm, although the Aza, being deaf, couldn't understand Guildtalk either—they (it?) communicated by chemical signals.

Next came the mated trio of winged, child-sized Orrisian "elves" who together were the Orrisian representative on the Council. They understood Guildtalk, she'd been told, but could not reproduce the sounds necessary to speak it: their own speech consisted of ultrasonic chirps.

Then—for a moment her voice faltered. Ten meters away, at the very edge of the Guildheart, but still too close, a brown-furred S'sinn rested on his padded wooden shikk. Kathryn stiffened her resolve and spoke her oath again, but without looking directly at him.

Behind her—she turned and faced Jim, but fought down the tide of memory and repeated the oath once more. He wasn't a Councilor, of course—no human had yet progressed that far in the Guild—but as the first human Translator, he often served as the human representative at First Translations. He bowed gravely to her when she finished.

Finally she turned to the final Councilor, the man-high, reptilian Hasshingu-Issk. Two of them stood there, but she spoke her oath to the one wearing the bright green armband of a Master, vivid against his black scales; the other wore the blue of a medic.

". . . by all that they honor," Kathryn finished, a little hoarsely.

"We have heard your oath," Karak said. "Now demonstrate your resolve. Begin First Translation."

While the Hasshingu-Issk Master watched with unblinking, slit-pupiled yellow eyes, the medic wheeled forward a metal container. Opening it released a sharp, salty smell that mingled with the reptilian's own sulfurous scent, stinging Kathryn's nostrils.

She looked down, knowing what she would see, but still flinching: the slowly-writhing, ropy gray mass nestled in the pink nutrient fluid inside the tank set off ancient primate "snake!" alarms. But mere squeamishness wouldn't keep Kathryn from this climax of her training. At the medic's nod, she lowered her hand firmly into the case, and just as she had forced herself as a child to watch the needle of a doctor's syringe pierce her skin, she kept her eyes on the squirming creature that looped itself wetly around her fingers.

At first nothing happened. But slowly a tingling spread through her hand, which grew peculiarly heavy; and, as the minutes passed in a silence broken only by the thudding of her own heart, the mass of tissue in the case diminished. The tingling moved up her arm, into her shoulder, like an internal itch she could not scratch, but she held perfectly still, though silent tears ran down her cheeks. The Councilors watched impassively, thick solemnity the only emotion she could read from them.

Just when she thought she couldn't stand the horrible crawling under her skin one minute longer, it stopped.

She lifted her hand from the empty container, and sound rumbled around the room as each Witness confirmed that Kathryn had freely accepted the Swampworlder-invented universal nervous system interface, the engineered lifeform that humans called "The Beast." To her right, Jim said, "Amen."

Kathryn felt vaguely disappointed. An alien creature nestled within her, its tendrils infiltrating her entire nervous system, and so far all she'd felt was an unscratchable itch.

But now the Master came forward. He opened a small case of bluish metal, revealing two very different syringes and a coil of silvery cord. The Master took out the smaller syringe and proffered it to Kathryn, who accepted it from his claws, embarrassed by her trembling fingers. Then the Master took out the other syringe, and plunged its dagger-sized needle into his thigh, his eyes never wavering from Kathryn's face. Kathryn, only too aware of the fear she was broadcasting to the Council, put her own syringe against her bare upper arm and pulled the trigger.

A sharp pain, and the liquid surged into her bloodstream. She felt only a faint warmth, but knew that inside her chemicals were programming The Beast, preparing it and her for—

This. The Master uncoiled the silvery cord and touched one end to a matching patch behind his barely visible ear. It clung there as he held out the other end to her.

Kathryn knew some Guild trainees backed out even at this point. Many, like the Hasshingu-Issk medic, served faithfully in non-Translation duties. To withdraw would not shame her; it would simply prove she wasn't suited to be a Translator. You needed utter confidence in yourself to survive First Translation unscathed. Doubt could be fatal . . .

Breathing a prayer to God, who at the moment she very much wanted to believe in, Kathryn took the cord and touched it to the interface that had been surgically implanted behind her own ear a month earlier.

Humans talked of sex as the joining of two people. But the night before, the union she had enjoyed with Jim, even with all its empathic overtones, had been nothing compared to *this!*

She had never been to the Hasshingu-Issk homeworld, but in an instant it surrounded her in all its sun-drenched beauty. She rolled on a baking-hot rock with her mate, fought in the Arena of God for the glory of the Toothed One, ripped out the throat of a magnificent ikisss she had chased for kilometers across a lava plain. She knew the names of the Five Moons of the Gods and the Seven Cities of the Dead; she shed her skin and burrowed in ecstasy in the cooling mud; she understood why imperfect hatchlings had to be eaten and knew that she could explain that custom to the weakling races who called it barbaric, if only she could . . .

. . . could . . .

. . . *if only she could remember how!* She panicked, her mind thrashing in the welter of overwhelming alien images. She was *not* Hasshingu-Issk, she was human, but lost, lost, lost . . .

. . . then she felt the Master lifting her dolphinlike out of the swirling depths, helping her shed him like he shed his skin, until they were linked, but separate; one, but two; a single organism with two minds, two mouths—two languages.

Kathryn opened her eyes and looked around at Jim. Those sweaty, exciting moments they had shared . . . he'd gotten what he wanted. Maybe she had, too, if she were honest with herself. But it meant nothing. This was what she had lived for, trained for, longed for.

The hole in her heart had been boarded over by a decade of empathic help; in Jim's arms she had forgotten it for the briefest moment; but now, in this glorious union with her Hasshingu-Issk comrade/friend/lover, that hole was filled.

Chapter 7

On the vidscreen in the lounge of the Guildship *Dikari,* the pattern of stars suddenly rippled and changed. Moments later, a bright blue-and-green ball moved majestically into view, sailing slowly across the screen until it filled it completely.

Jarrikk sipped his laa'ik tea and contemplated his own emotional state. It seemed surprisingly stable. Ukkaddikk had expressed concern on that score when they parted at the Guildhall, and though Jarrikk had reassured him, still it relieved him to discover that the sight of Kikks'sarr for the first time in ten Guild years did not disturb him.

Of course, he reminded himself honestly, he had yet to land on it.

He wouldn't be landing on it for some time yet, either. The planet, continuing to move across the screen, revealed a widening sliver of blackness. Something glittered in that blackness, and began slowly to swell. Jarrikk set his tea on the polished black pillar beside his shikk, rose, and made his way across the deserted lounge to the arch leading to the passenger quarters. He'd better double-check his documentation before the *Dikari* docked at the Commonwealth peacekeeping station. He might be a Translator, but in his experience (even if that only amounted to four minor assignments) Commonwealth bureaucrats were more concerned with their precious regulations than with the supposed standing order that they were to offer all possible assistance to members of the Guild.

In his quarters, he touched the Guild insignia on his collar, opening a small compartment in which nestled the datachip detailing his identity, his official standing, and his assignment. He popped it into the reader for a final perusal, and his own face stared back at him from the screen, scruffy and wild-eyed, like a Hunter back from a twenty-day hunt, thanks to the Guild's insistence on preparing identchips in the last day or two before Final Examination and First Translation. Everything else seemed in order . . . although he wondered if the Peacekeepers would question him on the one entry on his Planetary Visa request form conspicuously flagged as "incomplete," the line for "Name of Employer, Sponsor, or Host," where the Guild had put CONFIDENTIAL. Guild confidentiality was supposed to be absolute and accepted without question, but bureaucrats were bureaucrats . . .

"Attention. Attention," said a voice seemingly coming from thin air, though in fact it came from the tiny transceiver almost hidden in the fur behind Jarrikk's left ear. It spoke Guildtalk with the unmistakable accent of a Hasshingu-Issk computer. "Docking procedures commencing. Translator Jarrikk, please report to main lock."

"Jarrikk, acknowledging," Jarrikk said. He put the datachip back into his collar, then turned to the blank wall across the chamber from the door. "Mirror," he said, and the wall turned reflective. Jarrikk smoothed the fur behind his ears and gave his snout a quick rub, then spread his wings as much as he could, the familiar tight pulling of his old wound stopping him before he had the left one open much more than halfway. Still, he thought, looking at his reflection, they opened far enough to show their lack of insignia. He thought it was time to do something about that, and he should be able to find a first-rate insignia artist now that he was finally back on a S'sinn world . . .

. . . *half-S'sinn world* . . .

He shrugged that thought aside, annoyed that it even came up. He had seen several humans in the Guildhall over the years, and though he had never spoken to one, much less Translated with one, he hadn't tried to tear their heads off, either. What more could anyone ask?

He closed his wings a little too quickly, causing a sharp needle-jab of pain, and headed for the lock.

Just before he reached it he heard the faint, distant rumbling of docking. "Attention, attention," said the voice again. "Submitting to station gravitational field in five . . . four . . . three . . . two . . . one . . . now." Jarrikk suddenly felt lighter. With a new spring in his step, he entered the lock. The Hasshingu-Issk captain of the *Dikari* raised a clawed fist by way of greeting, and Jarrikk raised his own fist back, but didn't say anything; he could feel the captain's intense concentration and didn't want to disturb him.

The inner lock door suddenly dilated open, letting in a puff of much warmer air carrying a rich assortment of odors that made Jarrikk's snout wrinkle reflexively. He hastily smoothed his expression as an Ithkarite stepped heavily into the dock, wearing a bright green watersuit with the binary-star symbol of the Commonwealth Peacekeepers emblazoned in red on his chest. As most Commonwealth bureaucrats did, he spoke Guildtalk, albeit badly. "Welcome to Commonwealth Station 190-489," he squeaked. "I am Peacekeeper Ishta, Co-commander, Second Class. Captain Hi'i'liss and . . ." Ishta paused, obviously listening to a voice in his own ear. ". . . Translator Jarrikk, please accompany me to my office. In the meantime, Captain, you will open your ship for weapons inspection."

"Certainly," Captain Hi'i'liss growled. "First Mate Jo'a'rimm stands ready to assist."

"Excellent," said Ishta. "Then if you will follow me . . ."

Jarrikk trailed Ishta and Hi'i'liss out through the

lock and down a narrow corridor to another lock, which opened into a huge, echoing space cluttered with loading equipment, cargo containers of every shape and color, and a dozen more Peacekeepers, half Ithkarites and half Hasshingu-Issk, waiting in dual ranks. A sharp stink of ozone and burning metal assaulted Jarrikk's nose from the far end of the dock, where a S'sinn worked on a deck plate with a cutting laser.

Ishta nodded to the Peacekeepers, then led Hi'i'liss and Jarrikk toward one of several doors of various sizes and shapes on the far side of the dock. Glancing back, Jarrikk saw the twelve Peacekeepers filing into the docking tunnel.

A two-tone alarm note sounded, and the station computer said, "Here follows Station Status Update number two-seven for this rotation. Newly docked: Guildship *Dikari,* from Commonwealth Central. Next arrival: *Wings of Blackest Night,* inbound from S'sinn-dikk, now on final approach vector, estimated arrival in one thousand beats. Next departure: *Maishista,* Ithkarite trader, undocking in two thousand four hundred beats. Just arrived: *Sri Lanka,* Earth vessel, still undergoing weapons search. Status unchanged: *Hunter's Claw,* S'sinn trader, awaiting customs inspection. Report ends."

Jarrikk felt a faint prickle of unease. Humans just arrived on the station, and one S'sinn ship already docked and another inbound. If he were the station commander, he'd double his security watch.

The door in front of them irised open, and Ishta motioned Hi'i'liss and Jarrikk through an airlock into a small, oval chamber, its walls glistening with moisture. Jarrikk was glad the Peacekeeper had chosen to wear his watersuit rather than make the two of them suit up; like most S'sinn, he'd had no experience with being under water until his Translation duties had demanded it. He'd learned to control his instinctive panic, but he still hated it.

The Ithkarite's computer terminal, a crystal ovoid, stood on a green pillar in the center of the room. He waved a manipulator over it and it lit up with symbols meaningless to Jarrikk. Ishta studied it. "Yes . . . everything seems to be in order, Captain. No cargo?"

"None," said Hi'i'liss. "Our sole purpose is to convey Translator Jarrikk here for his assignment."

"Translator Jarrikk," said Ishta. "Your identchip, please."

Jarrikk opened the collar compartment and handed over the chip, but almost dropped it when his fingers brushed Ishta's gloved manipulators. Whereas until that moment Jarrikk had felt only the ordinary casual competence and slight boredom of an official doing his job, when he touched Ishta he suddenly sensed suppressed excitement and even a touch of fear—both connected with his presence.

He stared hard at Ishta as the Peacekeeper casually turned and put the datachip into a depression in the base of the crystal egg. "Again, everything seems in order." No questioning of the confidentiality of the assignment, Jarrikk noted; of course, that was how it should be, but now it seemed suspicious. Ishta slipped the datachip out of the terminal and handed it back to Jarrikk, who returned it to his collar. "You may return to your vessel and proceed to the surface as soon as weapons check is concluded and certified. Thank you."

Hi'i'liss nodded once, sharply, then strode out, anxious, Jarrikk could feel, to get back to his ship. Jarrikk followed more slowly, pausing at the inner door of the office's airlock to glance back at Ishta. Now that he'd been sensitized to it, he could still feel the Ithkarite's strange excitement.

He didn't know why, but he knew Ishta had been eagerly awaiting his arrival. Maybe he already knew all about Jarrikk's assignment.

If that were so, Jarrikk thought as he went down the corridor, he wished the Ithkarite would share the information, because so far, its confidentiality extended even to him. As was frequently the case in the

Guild, exactly who he'd be Translating for, and why, wouldn't be revealed until he reached his destination. Which shouldn't be long; the weapons inspectors were already emerging from the docking tunnel into the loading area.

He started toward the tunnel, but a loud, harsh voice startled him. A surge of anger accompanied the noise: only that kind of violent emotion could carry over the hundred spans or more to the mouth of the next docking tunnel, where two Ithkarite Peacekeepers faced one shouting human, whose heavily accented Guildtalk was peppered with other sounds that meant nothing to Jarrikk. ". . . (untranslatable) Guildship is already cleared to leave and we've been undergoing weapons check for half a rotation! You've taken every (untranslatable) thing in there apart and you haven't found anything because there's nothing to (untranslatable) find! I've got delivery deadlines to meet on the surface! This is (untranslatable) harassment and I intend to . . ."

Higher-pitched shouts drowned out the human's voice; shouts from a half-dozen S'sinn, emerging into the loading area from another of the doors behind Jarrikk. "Hey, flightmates, look! A wingless slime grub!"

"A nightcrawling stinkworm!"

"A coilworm turd!"

"No, no, it's even more disgusting—it's a human!"

The human might not have understood the insults, most of which couldn't have been translated into Guildtalk anyway, but maybe he'd picked up enough S'sinn to get the gist of them; he stiffened, broke off yelling at the Peacekeepers, and glanced quickly around the loading area. No other humans were in sight. He glanced at the Peacekeepers again. "I trust you will expedite your search," he said with sudden restraint, then hurried back down the docking tunnel.

Jarrikk's eyes narrowed. The human's anger hadn't gone away; it had just shifted focus to the S'sinn. Jarrikk had the distinct feeling that if the Commonwealth did not confiscate all weapons from ships coming to this world, the human would have very shortly returned with armed friends. As for the Ithkarite Peacekeepers . . . they were difficult to read accurately at that range, but amused contempt suggested itself.

There was nothing amused about the contempt of the S'sinn and, with a shock, Jarrikk realized they'd already forgotten about the human—the contempt was for *him!*

He turned slowly to find a dozen red eyes glaring at him. He folded his crippled wings tightly and said, "Greetings, flockmates. I am Translator Jarrikk."

He received no reply. One by one, they turned their backs on him and strode toward their own docking tunnel, until only the leader remained. Only he spoke, and then only one word. "Traitor," he hissed. He spread his wings, clapped them once, sharply, the blast of air buffeting Jarrikk, then strode after his ship-mates, leaving behind a miasma of utter disgust that Jarrikk could almost feel clinging to his fur like the stench of something dead and slimy.

"Welcome home," Jarrikk growled.

In his quarters, as the ship shuddered and pulled away from the station, he regarded his reflection again. Any other S'sinn could see at a glance he could not fly even when his wings were not spread enough to show the left's scarred membrane; the gnarled muscles of his damaged shoulder made a small but, to S'sinn, obvious and disfiguring lump beneath his pelt. He knew it was difficult for some S'sinn to accept that a Flightless One lived; he'd felt the shock of the S'sinn traders he'd Translated for on his previous missions. He'd warned himself that on Kikks'sarr, divided among S'sinn and humans, his people would find it even more difficult to accept that such a one served the hated Commonwealth. He'd thought himself prepared for that reaction.

Now, he wasn't so sure.

They made planetfall within half a rotation, setting down in the same spaceport where Jarrikk had raged at the Commonwealth delegation when it came to declare an end to the war. His mirror-wall now a vidscreen, Jarrikk looked out across the landing field to the distant lights of the city, barely visible through a driving rain. *Home?* he thought. It didn't feel like it. Not after his encounter in the station.

Now, when he thought of home, he thought of the Guildhall. And maybe that was as it should be. Karak would certainly have said so.

Yet Jarrikk could have wished he felt a little more glad to be here.

The transceiver behind his ear beeped. "Captain Hi-'i'liss here, Translator. We're receiving a vidcall for you."

"Please display it in my quarters, Captain."

"Displaying."

The image of the rain-swept spaceport disappeared, replaced by that of an anonymous S'sinn in front of a blank stone wall. "Welcome, Translator Jarrikk," said the S'sinn.

"Thank you."

"We have contracted for your services on a matter of some urgency," the other continued. "I regret the imposition, but we require your presence at once."

"No imposition," Jarrikk said. "I am entirely at your disposal during my assignment here. Where should I go?"

"A vehicle is already on its way to your ship. It will bring you to us. We look forward to meeting you in person."

"And I, you." The screen blanked. Jarrikk scratched his chest thoughtfully. Not very informative. He'd grown to hate communicating by vidscreen, where his empathy was useless. Maybe someday the Swamp-worlders would come up with a way to transmit emotions over long distances. He doubted it; their peculiar "wet" technology didn't mesh very well with things like vidscreens.

The Captain spoke to him again. "Translator Jarrikk, your transportation is here."

Already? "On my way, Captain." He quickly collected his Translation case from a wall compartment and made his way into the corridor and down it to the nearest liftshaft. "I'm afraid I've had no indication yet of how long this assignment will take, Captain," he said as he sank toward ground level. "You'll just have to stand by until I get more information."

"Understood and accepted. Good luck, Translator."

The lift deposited him at the very base of the ship, in an area inaccessible except when the *Dikari* was on the ground. It contained the *Dikari*'s own ground transports, a large hatch for unloading and loading them, and a small hatch for personnel. Jarrikk removed his transceiver and handed it to the Hasshingu-Issk on duty; the crewman set it aside, then opened the hatch and extended the ramp.

Jarrikk squinted up at the pouring sky, growled deep in his throat, and then stepped out into the storm, moved down the ramp, and splashed through puddles to the groundcar, which he really thought could have been brought much closer to the hatch. "An Ithkarite would feel right at home," he muttered.

A door in the side of the silvery ovoid opened, and he climbed gratefully into the warm, dry interior. A different S'sinn from the one who had called greeted him, physically masking quite well, Jarrikk thought, his shock at the fact that the Translator he had been eagerly awaiting was flightless. "Welcome, Translator," was all the new S'sinn said, as the door closed behind Jarrikk. "I am Yvekkarr. Please make yourself comfortable; the drive will be a lengthy one."

Jarrikk nodded and arranged himself on one of the four padded shikks in the compartment as the computer-driven vehicle accelerated. He couldn't see out through the fully opaque windows, but he said nothing; Translators, by definition, were called in only for very special circumstances—otherwise Guildtalk sufficed, at least among the races that could use it. Quite frequently, those circumstances were very delicate, at least for the parties involved, and required the utmost discretion.

Yvekkarr didn't seem inclined to talk, despite his obvious curiosity about this crippled Translator. They rode in silence for a thousand beats, then a thousand more. Yvekkarr slipped into a doze, but Jarrikk remained wide awake; he'd slept well between leaving the orbital station and planetfall. A Translator had a duty to be well-rested and ready to go to work immediately. He shifted on the shikk, not nearly as comfortable as it had felt when he'd first settled into it, and hoped the drive would end soon.

It didn't. He estimated a full four thousand beats passed before the vehicle, which had been climbing steeply for some time, slowed and stopped. Yvekkarr mumbled, stirred, then suddenly straightened, his wings half-unfurling in startlement. He clapped them shut and turned to Jarrikk. "Translator, I'm sorry for sleeping, it's just—"

"No apology necessary," Jarrikk assured him. "I take it we've arrived?"

"Yes. Please, follow me . . ."

The door slid open and Jarrikk followed Yvekkarr into the stormy night. The rain hadn't let up, and wherever they were, the wind blew much harder than it had on the landing field. Jarrikk did his best to keep his wings tight against his body, but the buffeting still woke twinges of pain in the damaged one. The only lights he could see were the running lights of the vehicle behind them and a dim orange glow, like torchlight, ahead. His claws skittered on wet, black rock. To either side wind rushed through tall trees, bringing to his nostrils the fresh green smell of the forest, and bringing to his mind unwanted memories of the days when he had soared above these same swaying trees instead of trudging among them.

The orange glow *was* torchlight, and the moment Jarrikk stepped into its circle of light, and sniffed the cool, dry air, he knew exactly where Yvekkarr had brought him: the caves to which the colony had fled when the humans first landed, the caves which even before that had sheltered the broodhall.

The caves where he was born.

Seeing the planet from space had had little effect on him; the city had meant nothing; but now, as the scent of his birthplace filled his nostrils, hard on the tail of the all-too-familiar smell of the trees outside, memories rushed over him so suddenly it took all his emotional control to keep his surface composure. He couldn't give in to sentiment, however powerful; he had a job to do.

But he did allow himself to wonder why whoever had contracted for his services wanted to conduct business *here*.

Yvekkarr led him through well-remembered corridors—the entrance they'd used, he realized grimly, was the very one he and the rest of his youngflight had sneaked out of on their ill-fated expedition to the humans' landing place—to a small chamber that, if memory served, had been a meat locker, where the bloody carcasses of prey brought home by the Hunters had been hung to age. Torches lit the way, as they had years before, but the entrance to the chamber was sealed by something the meat locker had never required: a door.

A door meant either special efforts at security, which certainly fit with the secrecy surrounding this whole assignment, or a prison. But it was absurd to conjecture an elaborate plot to capture him. He couldn't imagine a motive, for one thing; for another, Yvekkarr radiated friendliness and respect. So, when Yvekkarr opened the door, he stepped through into the firelit room without hesitation, claws scraping on a stone floor still stained by the blood of all the slaughtered beasts that had hung there so many years before.

A S'sinn female rose from a plain wooden shikk. "Greetings, Translator Jarrikk."

Feeling as if he'd stepped back in time, Jarrikk found his voice. "Greetings, Flight Leader Kitillikk."

Another S'sinn, a powerful male, stepped into the

light from the shadows behind Jarrikk's old leader. "Translator Jarrikk," he said gravely.

"Ukkarr." Jarrikk looked back at Kitillikk. "*You* contracted for my services?"

"Yes. I asked for you specifically, because of your—special understanding of our situation here."

"But why meet here?" Jarrikk gestured at the glistening walls of the cavern. "Surely the city would have been more convenient."

"This place was mine," Kitillikk said. "Mine in a way the city never was and never could be. For the negotiations I am about to undertake, I wish to gain strength any way I can."

Jarrikk bowed his head slightly. "I am at your command. Within the bounds of my Guild Oath, of course. With what race am I to Translate?"

"Ithkarite. Their negotiating team should arrive at any moment. I would offer you refreshment, but—" She gestured at the empty room. "Amenities are limited here."

"I require nothing, assuming the space is free from electromagnetic interference—computers, recording devices, artificial lighting . . ."

"It is." Kitillikk regarded him. "You Translators require a great deal of trust from us."

"In five S'sinn lifetimes, that trust has never been betrayed. Nor will it be tonight. I am ready."

"Then we wait."

Jarrikk stood with his body at ease, but his mind in turmoil. He did not like the eagerness he sensed in Kitillikk and Ukkarr. They had far more at stake than a simple trade deal. The eagerness that filled them felt more like . . . like the bloodlust that had gripped him, when he flew with the Hunters from this very place to take revenge on the humans for the murder of his flightmates. Though what that could have to do with Ithkarites . . .

Yvekkarr, who had left after showing Jarrikk into the room, opened the door. "The Ithkarites are here," he said.

Kitillikk exchanged a look with Ukkarr. Their eagerness intensified. "We are ready."

Jarrikk turned to face the door as the waterbreathers entered. There were three, two in nondescript watersuits of pale gray, unmarked by any ornamentation or insignia, and the third in a dark blue watersuit with the insignia of the Translators on his chest. Jarrikk sensed wariness in the first two, and a blank readiness in the Translator. He didn't seem to have any better idea than Jarrikk what this was all about.

"Let us proceed," Kitillikk said. "Translator Jarrikk, please . . ."

"Yes, Flight Leader." Jarrikk moved to the center of the room and gestured for the Ithkarite Translator to join him. They exchanged silent greetings, then Jarrikk set his case on the floor, took out the Programming injector, and selected the Ithkarite vial from the selection he had brought with him. Across from him, the Ithkarite did the same. Jarrikk connected the vial to the injector and plunged the needle into his arm, barely feeling its ultra-sharp point. He felt the Programming at once as the symbiote woke to its duty, encoded in a complex stew of DNA, RNA, amino acids, proteins, enzymes, and only the Swampworlders knew what else. A warm, tingling sensation spread through him.

The Ithkarite set aside his Programming vial—in his case, the injector was part of his watersuit and he'd had only to slip the vial into a compartment in the suit controls at his waist—picked up his Link, and slipped one end of the silvery cord into a self-sealing valve in the side of his helmet. He offered the other end to Jarrikk, who bowed slightly, took it, and touched it to the silvery patch beneath his right ear.

The Ithkarite's thoughts and feelings flooded him. His mind filled with images of vast underwater cities, glimmering green sunlight, joyful fishing expeditions through jewel-encrusted caves, predators, mates, young, friends, enemies. In an instant, he knew more about the Ithkarite Translator Liska than he had ever learned about any S'sinn, and could feel through the Link that Liska knew just as much about him. They exchanged glances, then together put aside the rush of memory and emotion and turned to their respective races. "Begin," Jarrikk/Liska said.

The Ithkarite delegates began to speak. Their words, inflections, and body language Jarrikk heard, saw, and understood through Liska's eyes, and translated through his S'sinn body. The Programming and the symbiote gave him no leeway for emotional response of his own to what he was saying; that would come three or four thousand beats later, when the Programming's built-in antidote kicked in and the session ended.

Kitillikk timed it nicely; the Ithkarites were just exiting the chamber when suddenly Liska vanished from Jarrikk's thoughts, a feeling like an amputation, and everything they had just Translated hit him in a hurricane rush. He and Liska exchanged horrified glances, then Liska snatched up his case and the Link and dashed after the Ithkarite delegation, while Jarrikk turned on Kitillikk, whose smugness filled him—and sickened him.

"The Guild of Translators may not be used to establish military alliances within the Commonwealth!" Jarrikk snarled. "I cannot believe they agreed to this—"

"They agreed to provide a Translator for trade negotiations," Kitillikk said. "Which we discussed. The military aspects were . . . an afterthought. A prudent afterthought, in view of the situation at Kisradikk."

Now anger kicked in. "Don't lie to me, Flight Leader. These negotiations were well planned in advance. That's the reason for the secrecy. When the Guild hears about this . . ."

"What of the vaunted Guild confidentiality?" Kitillikk mocked. "Or will you betray your precious Guild's principles as readily as you betrayed your species?"

Ukkarr remained impassive, but Jarrikk felt the Hunter's amusement and his feet contracted, his claws grinding against the bloodstained stone floor. "Guild confidentiality does not apply when the Translation is in violation of Guild and Commonwealth Law. The Guild serves the Commonwealth, Flight Leader. It does not serve the S'sinn, or any other race. It serves all Seven Races."

"Even humans?" Kitillikk growled the ugly-sounding S'sinn word for the Earth species. "You disappoint me with this self-righteous ranting, Jarrikk. I knew a Flightless One who continues to live must be without honor, but I did not think even you could forget what humans did on this world that was your home."

"I forget nothing." Jarrikk spread his wings, ignoring the pain, showing the scars. "I forgive nothing. Not while I have *this* to remind me. But the Commonwealth survives only on the willingness of Seven Races to put aside past wrongs. There are still many Orrisians who curse the S'sinn for the burning of the tree-city of Issri-kalung, before we were brought into the Commonwealth, though a hundred of their homeworld's revolutions have passed. We did not enter the Commonwealth under any better circumstances than the humans. Yet the Orrisians accept us."

"Do they?" Kitillikk showed her teeth. "You are naive, Translator. Our information is that the humans have already formed an alliance with the Orrisians. And with the principal swarm of the Aza. The Hasshingu-Issk and the Ithkarites side with us. Only the Swampworlders remain neutral. Your precious Commonwealth is split right down the middle, Jarrikk, like a worm-eaten misska fruit. The day is coming when many past wrongs will be righted, without the interference of Commonwealth meddlers or anyone else. And the S'sinn will regain their honor!"

Jarrikk felt as stunned as when the humans had shot him from the sky. "Impossible. These alliances could not form without Translators . . ."

"There are Translators who put their homeworlds above some empty oath to your precious Guild, Jarrikk," said Kitillikk. "I had hoped you might be one of them, in view of what you owe me—or have you conveniently forgotten *that* oath? But of course the Priest whose knife I saved you from was right—a Flightless One is no true S'sinn. I should have let her kill you." She rose from her shikk and clapped her wings, the blast of air, thick with the smoke of the dying fire, echoing the blast of contemptuous anger Jarrikk had already felt from her, forcing him to painfully spread his own crippled wings again to catch himself. "Go to your Guild. Tell them what you will. The alliance is sealed. The humans will be driven from Kisradikk, and then from this world, and then from the galaxy."

Jarrikk closed his wings and stood his ground. "And do you speak for the Supreme Flight Leader, Kitillikk? Or do your ambitions run even to deposing the Chosen? What will she say when news of this alliance you have negotiated for all of S'sinndikk reaches her ears?"

"I am done talking with you. Yvekkarr!"

"Flight Leader?" The young S'sinn dashed in through the door the retreating Ithkarites had left open.

"Escort the Translator back to his ship. Now."

"Yes, Flight Leader." Yvekkarr took Jarrikk's arm. With a final glare at Kitillikk and Ukkarr, Jarrikk followed him out of the chamber and out of the caves. The storm had ended, and dawn's approach turned the sky a high, deep blue, slowly lightening. In the valley below, the city glowed with light, but Jarrikk looked beyond it, ignoring Yvekkarr's plea to get in the vehicle. He breathed deep the memory-stirring scent of the rain-soaked woods. Out there, not far on wings that worked, humans lived on this world that had been S'sinn alone. Among them might still be the human who had burned him from the sky. He examined his emotions, and found, still buried deep, the ember of his hatred. He had told Kitillikk the truth: he forgot nothing, he forgave nothing. She could kill all the humans she could find, and he would not lift a claw to stop her.

But it couldn't be done this way. It couldn't be done by drawing the entire Commonwealth into war, a war that would destroy it, and with it the Guild that served it—the Guild that had carried him past his first death, his death as a S'sinn. He couldn't allow it!

To Yvekkarr's apparent relief, he started walking again. He had felt Kitillikk's momentary fear when he mentioned the Supreme Flight Leader. She had overstepped her authority, he felt certain, to make this play for power. It made her vulnerable. He would report to Karak as soon as he returned to the *Dikari,* and . . .

He stopped short, ignoring the exasperation he felt from Yvekkarr. "There are Translators who put their home-worlds above some empty oath to your precious Guild," Kitillikk had said. And Karak was Ithkarite . . .

And with that thought, that worm of distrust, though he put it aside as firmly as he could, it occurred to him that the damage done to Guild and Commonwealth might already be past anyone's repairing.

As the door closed behind the crippled Translator, Ukkarr growled. "You wasted your generosity on that one, Flight Leader."

"Did I?" Kitillikk stretched her wings languorously. "I'm not so sure."

"But he refused you!"

"He performed his task well this evening. As for the rest . . . one can never tell what fruit such plantings will yield." She stretched out her hand, admiring the glistening black claws against the background of the chamber's red-stained stone. "More important than whether he agreed to help us or not was to firmly establish his views. In the game to come, Translator Jarrikk will be an important piece. I had to know if he was mine or my opponent's. Had he been mine— and he may yet be—I would have known how to play him. Should he prove to belong to my opponent, I know how to counter him." She clenched her hand suddenly. "Either way, he is trapped in the game—and he cannot escape." Kitillikk leaped to her feet. "Things are moving quickly, Ukkarr!" She moved closer to him, ran her hands through the thick fur of his body, her hearts beginning to pound. "Can you keep up?"

"Always, Flight Leader." Ukkarr bared his teeth. "Always."

"Then catch me!" Kitillikk threw open the door, ran down the corridor, and flung herself into the cool morning air, and as she heard the beat of Ukkarr's wings rising fast behind her, she laughed. *This is my advantage,* she thought. *This is my edge. The Supreme Flight Leader has grown old, and complacent. She belongs to the Commonwealth, not to the S'sinn. This is what it is to be S'sinn! Let passion rule! What does the Supreme Flight Leader know of passion: for sex, for power, for revenge?*

"I'm coming!" she screamed at the sky, at the stars beyond it, at distant S'sinndikk and even more distant Earth; then Ukkarr caught her and she forgot all her ambition in the ancient skydance of the S'sinn.

Sometimes it was best to concentrate on one passion at a time.

Jarrikk stood in his quarters aboard the *Dikari,* facing the vidwall, which displayed a life-sized image of Karak floating naked in the waters of his own quarters in the Guildhall. Free of the watersuit and its exoskeleton, his shape was not bipedal at all; his almost globular, iridescent body, from which writhed six locomotive tentacles and six manipulators, moved through the water with boneless grace, gill-slits pulsating below the fringe of feeding-tentacles that encircled his beak. It seemed odd to hear perfect home-planet S'sinn emerging from that alien mouth. "Your news, while distressing, is not unexpected," Karak said. "The Guild has been aware for some time of the other treaties you mention. Two Translators have been expelled from the Guild for their part in arranging them. Other Translators must have been involved, too, of course, but as yet we have not identified them."

Jarrikk felt a chill. "Master, I—"

"No need to fear, Translator; the two in question were actively involved in the process, not used unknowingly by the perpetrators, as you were. In both instances, we discovered the treaty through other sources and confronted them with the facts. I regret to say they were unrepentant." One of the tentacles at the top of his head snatched a tiny silver fish from the water. It passed from tentacle to tentacle to his beak, which snapped once, devouring it.

"Flight Leader Kitillikk wanted me to join her conspiracy," Jarrikk said. "I refused."

"I almost wish you hadn't. It would have been useful to have a spy within the S'sinn war party. I don't suppose you could convince her you've changed your mind—"

"I do not think so," Jarrikk said stiffly, while several dearly-held notions of the Guild's political purity came crashing down.

"You're shocked, aren't you?" Karak said. Not for the first time in dealing with the Guildmaster, Jarrikk wondered if maybe the Swampworlders *had* perfected a method of transmitting emotions over long distances, after all. "The Guild exists on two levels, Jarrikk, like everything else. On one level, we are an ideal, an ideal of neutrality and cooperation among species. On another level, we are a huge organization with two goals: serving the Commonwealth, and surviving. At the upper level, you can afford to be above all the political maneuvering the Seven Races can muster, which is quite a lot. At the lower, you cannot."

"But such a spy . . . could not survive his first Translation with a Translator sympathetic to the other side," Jarrikk said slowly. "Unless . . ." With all the other shocks he'd been given, who was to say this couldn't be true, as well? "Unless it *is* possible to lie under Programming!"

Karak stopped swimming. "No! Jarrikk, I apologize. I did not mean to shock you into questioning . . . some things are inviolate. The Oath is binding. You cannot lie under Programming. You need not doubt your most basic beliefs. But you must give up one small one. The Guild is not neutral in all political matters. Where the survival of the Commonwealth, and itself, is at stake, it cannot afford to be."

Jarrikk nodded slowly. "I can accept that," he said, feeling as though he'd just been through a minor earthquake and his world was just now settling back into place. "But in any event, I cannot help you now."

"Not with Kitillikk, no, but in another matter, you can." Karak reached for something out of camera range and light flickered in his face. "I have a new assignment for you. On S'sinndikk."

"The homeworld?" Jarrikk's hearts pounded suddenly. "Translating?"

"Yes, and no." Karak held up two manipulators, one high, one low. "Two levels, again. On one level, you will be Translating for a Hasshingu-Issk trade delegation hoping to sell environment-monitoring satellites to the S'sinn government. On the other level, the Council of Masters has need for a reliable source of information on S'sinndikk. Our other S'sinn Translators are far-flung at the moment, and in view of the political situation, I cannot be as sure of their sympathies as I now am of yours."

"You want me to spy on my own people?" Jarrikk said slowly. "But Kitillikk will suspect me . . ."

"Not spy. Simply observe. Gauge public opinion. Once the trade negotiations are finished—and one session may well be sufficient for that—take leave. Tour the planet. Listen to your people and your politicians, and report what you hear to me. That's all."

Jarrikk, in the throes of his new-found cynicism, had his doubts. But it sounded simple—and honorable—enough. And it would give him an opportunity to see S'sinndikk, as he had always longed to, at the Guild's expense. "Very well," he said.

In his water-filled compartment in the Guildhall, Karak looked from the screen from which Jarrikk's face had just vanished to another screen showing a gray-muzzled female S'sinn. "It's arranged. He will be where we need him to be."

"You are certain he is the one? His past . . ."

"I remind you he contacted me with news of Kitillikk's actions. And you saw, probably better than I did, how he reacted when he learned the Guild is not as politically pure as he's always thought. He is the one."

"Very well, Guildmaster. And the other?"

"Not until the formal agreement to negotiate is announced."

"So late?"

"I deem it better that way."

The S'sinn inclined her head. "I bow to your knowledge of your Flight, Guildmaster. I'll contact you again after all is prepared."

"Very well." Once the vidscreen blanked, Karak waved a tentacle to generate the pressure wave that turned the communicator off, then looked back at the screen on which Jarrikk had appeared. "Time to test your wings, Flightless One," he said, then snatched another silverfin from the water by his head and swam back to his sleeping hole.

Chapter 8

Kathryn regarded her standard-issue suitcase ruefully. Whatever Earth company the Guild had contracted to provide its human Translators with luggage had obviously been more concerned with aesthetics than practicality. Sure, the slim blue case looked terrific; trouble was, it only held about two changes of clothes, some toiletries, and a handful of datachips—and the datachips were pushing it.

She sighed. It didn't seem like very much to take with her on her first off-planet mission, but she supposed she'd manage. The Guildship, after all, would be well-stocked with anything else she might need for her three-month stay on Inikri-Ossong, the Orrisian world that had suddenly discovered a taste for chocolate and wanted to find out if the human predilection for munching on Orrisian prejilli sticks matched it enough to form the basis for profitable trading.

The initial thrill of receiving her first assignment had been tempered somewhat by the less-than-thrilling nature of it, but trade held the Commonwealth together and the Guild of Translators served the Commonwealth. She supposed it was unavoidable that a great many assignments would deal with trade.

The two "practice" assignments she'd already undertaken, working with a seasoned Ithkarite Translator and even a Swampworlder in accurate simulations of past Translations, had been special cases; for simulations, they chose the most complex and interesting situations possible, negotiations relating to humanity's initiation into the Commonwealth at the conclusion of the Human–S'sinn War. Obviously, such negotiations didn't come along very often—and when they did, the Translator of choice was the most experienced, Jim Ornawka.

She envied him; he'd been back to Earth twice more for mysterious negotiations related to the Fairholm/Kisradikk Incident, as it was beginning to be called in the Earth news services. Kathryn couldn't really see what all the fuss was about. So humans and S'sinn had tried to colonize the same planet at the same time, again. Surely all that had been settled when the Commonwealth ended the last war. Put up another station and let both of them have the world . . . although, to hear Jim tell it, there was no doubt the humans had been there first.

Anyway, it wasn't worth arguing about, although Kathryn would have loved to have been involved in talks on the subject. It sure sounded more interesting than the relative worth of prejilli sticks and chocolate . . .

She went over to her dresser mirror to check her hair and uniform, patted at them unnecessarily for a few seconds, started to turn back to the bed, and stopped, caught by the glint of light on the jeweled eyes of the tiny ceramic cat, just five centimeters tall, that sat, its tail curled neatly around its feet, on one corner of the dresser. She caressed its glassy back with a finger. Jim had given it to her after his last trip to Earth. Since that night before her First Translation he had persistently pursued her. She'd kept her distance; since experiencing the true union of Translation, she'd told him, she'd put sex behind her. It was part of her old self. Besides, she'd also told him, she still hadn't forgiven him for the manipulative way he'd gotten her into bed in the first place.

He apparently didn't believe her, which probably wasn't surprising, considering her pulse still quickened every time he walked into the room; there had been nights when it had been all she could do not to call him—and he'd always been able to read her feelings with ease.

"Thinking about me?" said a familiar voice from the open doorway. Kathryn's head jerked up and her eyes met Jim's in the mirror.

"Any reason why I should be?" she said as casually as she could. But she could feel her face flushing—not that Jim needed that tell-tale sign.

"You tell me." Jim came into the room. "Close," he said over his shoulder, and the door slid shut.

"Jim, I've got to get down to the spaceport . . ."

"Your ship doesn't leave for two hours yet. I checked." He crossed over to her and stood very close, the sandalwood scent of his favorite cologne filling her head with memories of their night together. Her heart pounded so hard she thought even he must be able to hear it.

"I like—" She cleared her throat. "I like to be early." She brushed past him, went to the bed, and started to close the lid of the suitcase.

"Aren't you forgetting something?"

She turned around to see him holding the little ceramic cat. "Limited space," she said weakly. "You know how it is."

"But don't you want something to remember me by?" He set the cat down. "Of course, I could give you something even better." He moved close again, and ran a finger down her arm. She shivered, and cursed her body's weakness. "Something to remember humans by, when you're out there all by yourself for three months with nothing but bird-aliens for company . . ."

She pulled away, disturbed. "Bird-aliens? You mean the Orrisians?"

"Whatever."

"Then call them by name. The Oath says—"

"I know, I know, 'I renounce all species ties . . .' " Jim leaned back against the dresser and picked up the cat again, tossing it from hand to hand. "Don't be too quick to take those words to heart, Katy. 'Species ties' are going to be pretty important if this Fairholm business blows up."

Shocked, she could only stare at him.

"Oh, don't get all holier-than-thou." He looked hard into her eyes. "If war comes, will you side with aliens against your own kind?"

"Jim, you've Translated with all these aliens, you've lived their lives and their thoughts! As Translators, they're our kind, too!"

"Even S'sinn?"

She tried desperately to read him, then, and failed as always. But she knew her own reaction to that name had been nakedly obvious.

"Thought so." Jim tossed her the cat, and she caught it automatically. "Take it with you. Remember what I said." He went to the door. "Open." He glanced back. "Have a nice trip." He left.

Kathryn stared after him, then realized she had a death-grip on the little ceramic cat and opened her hand to look at it. It seemed to wink at her condescendingly, and in sudden anger she threw it at the wall, smashing it into shards and powder. From the wreckage, the two eyes still glittered. She turned her back on them, slammed the suitcase shut, and left the room that had been her home for more than half her life without even looking back. *I'm better than that,* she thought. *I* meant *my Oath.*

And if Jim Ornawka thought he'd ever lay a hand on her again . . .

Even for the speedy Guildship *Senti-or-noss* the journey to Inikri-Ossong was a three-jump trip, with two ship days—each about thirty-two hours long—between jumps for recharging, plus a day on either end for maneuvering around the planets. More than one hundred ninety hours in all, Kathryn had figured before she left, and just past the halfway point, she found herself thoroughly bored with her first mission before she'd even properly begun it. Translators served not only to Translate but also to advise negotiators, when asked, and she was fed up to her eyebrows with reading about the principal exports of Inikri-Ossong, and especially fed up with prejilli sticks and chocolate. Given a choice between starving and eating either, she would have had to think long and hard.

She sat in front of her computer terminal, idly scrolling through information she'd already read twice, occasionally sipping from a hot cup of *iss,* a sweet Orrisian concoction that gratefully neither tasted nor smelled at all like chocolate or prejilli, when suddenly the screen blanked, turned bright red, then displayed blazing yellow Guildtalk script: "URGENT MESSAGE INCOMING FROM COMMONWEALTH CENTRAL. STAND BY."

"Sure thing," Kathryn said. She leaned back, stretched, and was in the middle of a yawn when the screen cleared to reveal Karak's tentacled, beaked face. "What's up, oh mighty Guildmaster?"

"I'm afraid you'll have to postpone your current assignment," Karak said. His dolphinish voice wasn't much good at inflection, and of course her empathic ability was useless over a dimspace communicator. She couldn't tell his mood.

Wondering, not for the first time, how non-empathic humans ever communicated anything, she said, "All right by me. I take it you've got something more urgent for me to do?"

"I do. Extremely urgent. Full briefing materials are already being uploaded into the *Senti-or-noss*' computer, but the salient points are these: you are ordered to proceed at once to S'sinndikk, where you will Translate for Earth Ambassador Carlton Matthews as he and the Supreme Flight Leader of the S'sinn attempt to negotiate a way out of the Fairholm/Kisradikk impasse."

Kathryn felt as if he'd slugged her. "Me? On . . . S'sinndikk? But that means . . ."

"Translating with a S'sinn," Karak said. "I am aware of your history, Translator Bircher, and I know that I have previously told you that your first Translation with a S'sinn would happen only in the Guildhall under my personal supervision. This, however, is an emergency. The humans have issued an ultimatum to the S'sinn to leave Fairholm or face attack. The S'sinn have countered with their own ultimatum. Both sides, in defiance of Commonwealth Law, have established military alliances with other races. Should either race fire on the other, war, engulfing and destroying the Commonwealth, is almost inevitable."

Kathryn swallowed. "This isn't exactly explaining why you chose me."

"Necessity, Translator. Necessity. The Commonwealth, too, is under an ultimatum. Both sides have agreed to these last-minute talks, but both insist that they happen before the ultimatum expires. You are the only suitable human Translator close enough to S'sinndikk to make it there in time. Therefore, you will have to do the job." He glanced to one side. "Briefing upload is complete. Good luck, Translator. I have every confidence in you."

As Karak disappeared and the briefing information filled her screen, Kathryn was glad for a moment she hadn't been able to read Karak's emotions.

This way, she could only *guess* that that last comment had been a lie.

Once again, Karak turned from speaking with one of his Translators to face the image of the gray-muzzled S'sinn. "I do not like misleading her," he said. "She has suffered much already."

"It is necessary. You and I are both agreed on that."

"Yes. But it still does not please me."

"A great many things do not please me, Karak. But we deal with the universe on its terms, not our own." The S'sinn female glanced to one side, then back at the screen. "So. We have set something in flight, you and I. Let us hope it flies true. Farewell, Guild-master."

The screen blanked, and Karak floated silently for a long moment, remembering the strange, silent little girl he had brought from Earth.

He hoped she would forgive him.

Two ship-days later the *Senti-or-noss* arrived at S'sinndikk, and rendezvoused with the Earth Planetary Government diplomatic ship *Geneva*. As she watched the docking maneuver on a vidscreen in the crew lounge, Kathryn's attention was less on the swelling teardrop shape of the *Geneva* than on the vast blue-green curve of the planet below. So beautiful, so peaceful-looking, so Earth-like: hard to believe it could be the homeworld of the demons of her childhood, the winged monsters who had murdered her parents . . .

Her breath caught in her throat. So much anger, so much buried hatred; she could feel it inside her, infusing all of her emotions. How could she Translate with a S'sinn—and under such conditions, with war threatening again?

Yet, how could she not? Karak had said she was the only Translator available. Had there been another, she was quite certain he would not have chosen her. He knew her inner emotional landscape as well as anyone who had not Linked with her, and possibly even better than some who had: his own unaugmented empathic abilities, she'd been told, were easily the equal of what most ordinary Translators managed under full Programming.

He knew her fear of the S'sinn, but he had sent her anyway. She really must be the Commonwealth's last hope. *Which means you have no choice,* she thought bleakly. *No choice but another war. Remember what the last one cost. Remember what it cost* you.

Yet the thought of landing on S'sinndikk, of being surrounded by S'sinn, of Linking with one, mind to mind, feeling that hateful alien presence in her very soul . . . terrified her. She picked up her cup of *iss* from the low table beside the backless stool on which she sat, then set it down again abruptly when she saw how much her hand shook. *Get a grip, Katy,* she scolded herself. *This Ambassador Matthews you're about to meet is going to expect a cool, calm professional. Whatever you feel inside, at least look the part.*

She closed her eyes and concentrated on the calming exercises she had learned in the Guildhall, visualizing her emotions as her own tangled hair which she had to brush, slowly and carefully, into shining smoothness.

When the time came to transfer to the *Geneva,* she walked calmly through the docking tunnel, her slim blue suitcase in one hand and her silver Translator's case in the other, and nodded gravely to the man who greeted her in the lock.

"Translator Bircher?" he said. She pegged him at about fifty Earth years, with steel-gray hair, eyes to match, and the kind of fashionably pale, never-touched-by-ultraviolet skin that could only be obtained artificially. He wore an impeccable black business one-piece with the Earth Planetary Government symbol, a slim blue crescent, stitched neatly over his left breast pocket. He was, in fact, the very model of a modern elder statesman, and she would have found his appearance immensely comforting if not for the utter lack of compassion or concern beneath that carefully cultured surface. All she could feel from him was an eager, almost bloodthirsty desire to accomplish . . . something.

So he's dedicated, she told herself. *That's good.* "Ambassador Matthews?"

"At your service." He somehow managed to convey the impression of clicking his heels together without actually doing it. "We will be undocking at once and landing within six hours. In the meantime, may I offer you some refreshment?"

"That's very kind of you." He took her arm and led her graciously out of the lock and down richly appointed corridors complete with dark wood paneling, thick red carpets, marble sculptures in little wall niches, and the occasional oil painting. A faint hint of lilac suffused the air. Kathryn felt as if she'd stepped into a historical romance, just like she had when Jim had prepared that dinner for her the night before First Translation . . .

Hmmm. And maybe this is just another kind of seduction.

They ended their tour in a neo-Victorian lounge that made Kathryn appreciate the benefits of traveling in a human-crewed ship; she'd been a giant aboard the Orrisian ship and it felt good to sit in a proper, if overstuffed, human chair and accept (from a white-coated steward, no less) a proper human drink: coffee, in a Wedgwood cup. "We have a fine selection of wines, too, my dear," Matthews said.

Don't call me "dear," Kathryn thought, but all she said was, "I'm afraid the Translator symbiote does not like alcohol. Fortunately, caffeine is . . . acceptable." She hesitated over the last word, surprised by the momentary, but very real, sense of distaste she had received from Matthews at the mention of the symbiote. Well, she could hardly blame him for that; the notion of accepting a squirming mass of alien tissue into her body hadn't exactly thrilled her the first time she'd heard about it, either.

"I'm curious about your . . . profession," Matthews said. "I've had occasion to work with one or two other Translators, and was most impressed with their dedication to a goal I confess I find a little unclear."

Here it comes, Kathryn thought. Matthews' attention had sharpened on her like a hungry hawk's on a gopher. "Perhaps I can clarify it for you," she said carefully. "What did you find hard to understand?"

"Well, in conversation with them, they left me with the impression that they no longer considered themselves human." Matthews spread his hands. "Yet they were obviously as human as I am—or you are."

"I suppose it depends on what you mean by human." She sipped her coffee; set it down again on the antique rosewood table beside her chair. "Of course we are still physically members of the human species, but intellectually—or maybe spiritually would be a better word—we are not. We are Translators. We belong to all Seven Races of the Commonwealth."

"But surely the Commonwealth is only a political entity," Matthews protested. "You may serve it, but you can't really belong to it—not in the sense you belong to the human race." She sensed satisfaction from him as he spoke, like a game player scoring a major point.

A point Kathryn was willing to concede—if it would help her find out where he was heading. "I suppose that's true. Nevertheless, that belief is the basis of the Guild of Translators. We have to be separate from all the races, no matter what our own biological makeup, in order to do our jobs effectively. There must be no hint of bias on the part of Translators, or it could be suggested that the Translation was less than perfect." She laughed lightly. "The fact that it is absolutely impossible for a Translator to falsify Translation under Programming would not in itself be enough to offset that suggestion. Mere scientific fact is no match for suspicion, especially not when you mix in the liberal dose of superstition empaths are still subject to in many cultures."

"Is that really true?" Matthews said.

"Oh, I assure you, it is. The Orrisians, for example, used to exile empaths to a particularly nasty swamp infested with—"

A flash of irritation from Matthews confirmed this was more than idle conversation, though he tried to cover it with a laugh. "No, I meant, is it really true that it is impossible to falsify Translation? I'm sure I heard somewhere that—"

Kathryn let a little irritation of her own into her voice. "I assure you, Ambassador, Translators cannot lie under Programming. Ever."

Matthews wasn't about to give up. "I find that hard to believe, Translator Bircher. There must have been occasions when it would have been advantageous for . . . oh, I don't know, for a negotiator to make a prior arrangement with a Translator so that the negotiator could say one thing out loud, for his own people to hear, while the Translator delivered quite a different message. You could save face and achieve a hidden agenda at the same time." He shrugged. "Despicable, of course, but I have been a diplomat long enough to know that there are many despicable people who might take advantage of just such a situation."

And you're one of them, aren't you? Kathryn thought. She couldn't believe the gall of the man, practically spelling out what he wanted her to do. As though she would violate her Oath for *him.* "Whether you believe it or not, Ambassador, it is the truth. Programming submerges self-will. No matter what the Translator's determination beforehand, she couldn't possibly carry out such a plan. And the other Translator would know immediately upon Linking that she had such a plan in mind. By even discussing such a plan with a Translator, the negotiator would effectively tip off the other side that negotiations were not proceeding in good faith." *Take that,* Kathryn thought, enjoying Matthews' sudden uncertainty. No need to tell him that the other side wouldn't hear of it from their own Translator, because such information was protected by privilege.

Unless, of course, the other Translator was not as Oath-upholding once self-will reasserted itself, Kathryn thought, and immediately hated herself for thinking it. Blast Matthews and his devious little mind for contaminating her. And the S'sinn Translator would know she had thought it—that much of what she'd told Matthews was true.

Of course, that little doubting of his sincerity shouldn't bother the S'sinn very much, what with all the loathing and hatred of him that would already be swirling around . . .

Matthews smiled, once again suavely in complete control. "Well, the question was, of course, purely theoretical. I am relieved to know that this vital mission is in such good hands."

Oh, sure, Kathryn thought, *a Translator with a phobia about the S'sinn and a diplomat with a secret agenda of his own.*

Really *good hands.*

Chapter 9

The trade negotiations for the Hasshingu-Issk satellite system that were Jarrikk's ostensible reason for visiting S'sinndikk did indeed take only a single session; much of the work had been done ahead of time via Guildtalk, and Jarrikk's presence was really more to satisfy Commonwealth legal requirements than anything else. He immediately took advantage of his suddenly unlimited funds to travel, not just around the capital city of Kkirrik'S'sinn but around the world, just as Karak had suggested—and everywhere he went, he found hatred for the humans, anger at the Commonwealth for supporting the new upstart race at the expense of one that had been a part of the Commonwealth for a hundred S'sinndikk years, and an almost universal desire for revenge on both of them: directly on the humans, through war, and indirectly on the Commonwealth, by showing its leaders that it could not dictate to the S'sinn.

He also found a wide range of reactions to his disability, from simple curiosity to disgust to embarrassment to outright hostility. Twice he had to retreat from flocking halls to avoid a brawl with intoxicated Hunters. There were, he gathered, other disabled S'sinn still alive on S'sinndikk, where rigid belief in the traditional practices of religion had softened in the face of exposure to so many other races and belief systems, but they were still rare and lived mostly in seclusion. Certainly he was the first living Flightless One most S'sinn had ever seen.

He had a feeling reactions would have been even stronger if he'd let them know he was also a Translator for the despised Commonwealth, so that was one fact he kept to himself on his flocking-hall forays, leaving his distinctive collar at his lodgings.

Every couple of days he reported to Karak, who in turn kept him apprised of the worsening situation on Kisradikk/Fairholm. In the coastal city of Ukkill Nek-kassik, home of the magnificent Floating Gardens built a thousand years before by the Supreme Flight Leader Ittikk the Red-Clawed for her mate, Karak's report brought both good news and bad, inseparably intertwined.

War seemed imminent—but a final round of negotiations had been arranged by the Commonwealth, on S'sinndikk. "And you, Translator Jarrikk," Karak said, "will be Translating for the S'sinn."

Jarrikk's foot-claws clutched the thick black floor-pad of his luxurious inn-room. "I? I know of at least two other Translators currently on S'sinndikk, Guild-master. Why me?"

"I can trust you."

"With a human?"

"You are a Translator. You've already shown your loyalty is to the Guild. I am confident you can overcome your distaste for humans."

I'm not, Jarrikk thought, but out loud he only said, "Understood . . . and accepted."

"Good." Karak picked up something that looked like a porous rock and poked his manipulators into various openings. "I'm uploading the necessary information to the *Dikari*. Return to Kkirrikk'S'sinn at once to review it. The human negotiating team will arrive with their Translator in two days."

Half a day later, wearing his Translator's collar again for the first time in days and still groggy from a sub-orbital flight halfway around S'sinndikk, Jarrikk wearily entered his quarters on the *Dikari* to find two messages flagged for his attention: the briefing material from Karak, and one other.

He keyed it up, stared at it for several seconds, then cleared it bemusedly and touched his collar, dimly thinking he should see about having it polished and that he should definitely take time to have his wings properly tattooed.

One wanted to look one's best before appearing before the Supreme Flight Leader, after all.

Jarrikk had already visited the Great Hall of the Flock once in his guise as a tourist; it was quite a different matter arriving on official Guild business, collar shining, claws buffed, right wing newly emblazoned with the Guild symbol, and fur carefully groomed, and to enter, not through the towering arch used by the general public, but through a much smaller arch at the other end of the building. On entering as a tourist, one was impressed by the sheer size and magnificent design of the soaring building, with its fine pillars of polished bloodwood and gleaming floor of black marble. On this side of the building, one was impressed by something quite different: the grim-looking, heavily-armed, black-furred Hunters whose red eyes raked over Jarrikk like beamers before one of them escorted him into the quietly opulent vestibule beyond.

A grizzled female rose slowly from a shikk behind an electronic desk to greet him. "Translator Jarrikk. The Supreme Flight Leader is pleased you could come."

"I am honored to be asked," Jarrikk said.

"This way." The old female led him through another arch into a short corridor of gold-stippled black marble, where another black-furred Hunter even more grim and deadly-looking than the ones out front met him.

"I am Her Altitude's Left Wing," the black S'sinn

said. "Please proceed ahead of me into the audience chamber. You will spread your wings and kneel. You will not speak until spoken to. You will—"

"I am aware of the proper protocol for a Translator meeting the Supreme Flight Leader of the S'sinn," Jarrikk said briskly. "May I proceed?"

He felt the Left Wing's cold anger, but the black S'sinn stood silently aside.

Jarrikk walked the final few steps to the end of the corridor and rattled through the curtain of obsidian beads that covered the arch into the Supreme Flight Leader's audience chamber. Though only a few dozen spans in diameter, the oval room's walls soared up much further to a distant opening in the ceiling. A bright white shaft of sunlight stabbed down from it, illuminating the unadorned bloodwood shikk of Supreme Flight Leader Akkanndikk and her Right Wing, a female version of the Left Wing.

Jarrikk spread his wings as best he could, displaying the Guild symbol, but he did not kneel. Despite the pounding of his hearts, he no longer served the Supreme Flight Leader of the S'sinn; as a Translator, he served only the Guild, and through it, the Commonwealth.

He hoped Supreme Flight Leader Akkanndikk appreciated that. Even more, he hoped the Left and Right Wings appreciated it.

Left Wing growled behind him, but Akkanndikk raised one hand in a gesture of peace. "Translator Jarrikk is no longer, strictly speaking, of our flock. Do I read your actions aright, Translator?"

"Yes, Your Altitude. I do you honor, but I am not, I fear, at your command."

Left Wing growled again, but said nothing. Akkanndikk motioned for Jarrikk to come closer. He did so, stepping into the beam of light from above. Akkanndikk's eyes moved to his crippled wing, then back to his face. "I am pleased to meet you, Translator. I have heard a lot about you from a variety of sources."

"Your interest does me honor," Jarrikk replied cautiously. Akkanndikk's interest in him certainly was

keen—far too keen to be mere idle curiosity. He also
sensed great dedication and purpose, plus worry and—
perhaps strongest of all—weariness. Akkanndikk was
tired, to the core of her being.

Not that it showed outwardly. "May I offer you
refreshment? Hus'staan nectar, perhaps?"

"Thank you, Your Altitude."

Akkanndikk raised her hand, and after a moment
the Left Wing stepped into the circle of light, bringing
with him two silver goblets on a tray. The Supreme
Flight Leader took one and motioned to Jarrikk to
take the other. As he sipped the tart, icy liquid within,
its fruity aroma filling his nostrils, the Left Wing disappeared again, returning an instant later with another
bloodwood shikk. Akkanndikk indicated Jarrikk should
rest on it, which he did. But he didn't relax, sensing
Akkanndikk was about to come to the real purpose
of the meeting. She didn't disappoint him.

"No doubt you are curious as to the reasons for my
invitation to you," the Supreme Flight Leader said.
"There are two. One was simply to help prepare myself for the negotiations tomorrow. I wished to see
through whom I would be speaking." She sipped her
nectar, but Jarrikk tensed, sensing her interest sharpen,
like a Hunter focusing prey-sight on a fleeing jarrbukk.
"The other reason was to ask you about your meeting
with Flight Leader Kitillikk on Kikks'sarr."

Jarrikk took another drink from his goblet to cover
his shock. "I'm surprised you heard of that," he finally
said. "But I'm afraid there is little I can tell you about
it. Guild Law is very strict about confidentiality."

He sensed amusement. "I'm not asking for information about what you Translated," Akkanndikk said.
"I already know what transpired. Kitillikk negotiated
a separate treaty with Ithkar. In the event of war with
the humans, the Ithkarites will support us."

Jarrikk didn't even try to hide his shock this time.
As a Translator, he had every right to be shocked.
"Separate treaties are forbidden by Commonwealth
Law. How could you know about this unless—did you

authorize this? Your Altitude," he added hastily as he
sensed both Wings' quick anger.

Akkanndikk's own anger flashed beneath her words.
"I did not. But Kitillikk is not without support—
powerful support—among Flight Leaders here on
S'sinndikk whose support I must also have if I am to
remain Supreme Flight Leader. I fly through turbulent
air, Translator. War is not my choice, but it is the
choice of a great many of the S'sinn who elevated me.
They have been taking their own actions to make war
more likely. I have countered when and where I could.
These final negotiations are my best and last attempt.
If they fail, I will have no choice but to take military action."

"Then *I* fail to understand what information you need
from me concerning the meeting with Kitillikk, Your
Altitude," Jarrikk said. "If you already know all about
it—"

"My sources could not tell me one thing: one very
important thing, Translator. Were you a willing partic-
ipant in those negotiations?"

Jarrikk felt himself gripping the goblet so hard that
had it been glass, it would have shattered. He carefully
relaxed his hand. "No, Your Altitude. I was not."

"So you would say, even if you were." Akkanndikk's eyes bore into his. "I find it a distressing coinci-
dence that you were Translator at that illegal and
clandestine meeting and are also to be my Translator
for these negotiations. How do I know you are speaking the truth?"

"I am a Translator."

"And Translators do not lie," Akkanndikk said. "So
the Translators say. But that statement itself could be
a lie." She handed her goblet to the Left Wing, who
had somehow appeared at her elbow without any signal being given. "I am sorely tempted to reject your
appointment to these negotiations. Considering your
past, and your injury—inflicted by humans—I do not
see why I should take the risk of trusting you."

"That is your privilege," Jarrikk said. "The Guild

would have no choice but to accept your decision. But it would be a mistake, Your Altitude."

"Convince me."

"I have no love for humans, it's true. But consider this: I live only because of the Guild of Translators. I am flightless. Who is more likely to be working for those who want a war that could destroy the Commonwealth and with it the Guild of Translators: those S'sinn who are whole and long for revenge and glory, or me? Destroy the Commonwealth, destroy the Guild, and you destroy me. I have no part in the glory of the S'sinn race; I died to that race the day the human beamer crippled my wing." He stood and spread that wing to the limited extent he could. "My scars are proof of my loyalty—not to you, and not to those who want war, but to the Guild of Translators. I will do nothing to hinder these negotiations, and everything in my power to facilitate them. I have sworn an Oath to the Guild, Your Altitude, and now I swear that oath to you. You *can* trust me."

"I believe you," Akkanndikk said after a moment, and Jarrikk could feel that she spoke the truth. "Very well." She stood, and the Left Wing moved forward, taking Jarrikk's goblet from him. "The humans are already in orbit. Negotiations will proceed on schedule tomorrow morning. I look forward to working with you, Translator."

"And I you, Your Altitude."

Akkanndikk nodded, then snapped her wings open and leaped into the air, climbing toward the opening high above with strong, sure beats. Right Wing followed at once; Left Wing, disposing of the goblets somewhere in the shadows, sprang after them a moment later.

Jarrikk clamped his own wings tightly closed and walked slowly out of the audience chamber.

"Akkanndikk did *what?*" Karak stared at Jarrikk's image. A silverfin swam in front of the screen and he snapped at it irritably.

"Called me to her," Jarrikk repeated. "To be certain she could trust me."

Karak could do nothing about the angry writhing of the feeding tentacles around his beak, but hoped that Jarrikk didn't know what the motion meant. "Most unusual," he said. "*Most* unusual. It could be construed as questioning the choice of the Guild."

"It could be," Jarrikk said; ironically, Karak thought. "Translations have been canceled for less."

"But not this one?"

"Of course not." *Though it would serve that arrogant S'sinn female right.* Unfortunately, far more was at stake here than just some minnow-sized trade deal. Negotiations had to go ahead. As Akkanndikk, of course, had known. "You did well, Jarrikk," Karak said, and meant it; the young S'sinn had kept his head and the honor of the Guild and not retreated to his species' usual near-superstitious reverence of the Supreme Flight Leader. Although it sounded like *Kitillikk* certainly didn't reverence her, come to think of it. Perhaps attitudes had changed since Karak had last Translated with a S'sinn. They had been very new to the Commonwealth all those decades ago . . .

Maybe Kitillikk's right, he thought. *The Commonwealth* is *corrupting the S'sinn. They're learning politics.*

Jarrikk still watched him. "Thank you for your report, Translator," Karak said. "Nothing has changed. Translation proceeds as planned tomorrow."

"Yes, Guildmaster." Jarrikk's image vanished.

Whereupon Karak immediately turned to another long-established dimspace communication link, and waited impatiently for a response. Impatience did no good; Karak thought he could have swum to Ithkar and back before his call was accepted, and the screen finally blinked, then filled with the grizzled muzzle of a S'sinn Jarrikk would have recognized at once, having just faced her in her own hall: Supreme Flight Leader Akkanndikk.

The long delay in contacting her had served one useful purpose: Karak, with a day-tenth's worth of deep-water meditation, had regained his usual level of calm. "I do not understand what you hoped to gain by calling Jarrikk to you," he said. "You could have upset his mental balance to the point where he would be useless. And there is no backup plan, should this one fail."

"I was willing to accept your judgment concerning the human," Akkanndikk said, "but not concerning one of my people."

"I have been S'sinn," Karak said. "And human, and Orrisian, and all the other races. That's what it means to be a Translator."

"Perhaps. I confess I do not fully understand *what* that means. But whether you have been S'sinn or not, you are not S'sinn now. More particularly, you are not Supreme Flight Leader of the S'sinn, chosen by the Hunter of Worlds to guide and protect the People. I had to judge Jarrikk myself."

"Even if it meant risking everything."

"Not making that judgment would have been just as great a risk."

Karak understood her point of view. Understanding alien points of view was also what it meant to be a Translator. That didn't mean he had to like them. "I wish you had consulted me first."

"It was not a matter for offworlders."

Karak relinquished the argument. He'd never change the mind of a stubborn old predator like Akkanndikk with mere words. "What's done is done. In any event, I understand you confirmed my judgment."

"Jarrikk is suitable," Akkanndikk said. "I trust him."

"Then everything is ready."

"The humans are here. The Great Hall is prepared."

Karak wove his upper manipulators into the sign for completion—not that Akkanndikk would know that. "Then it is in the tentacles of the Great Swimmer."

"The Hunter of Worlds holds all in His claws," Akkanndikk replied, and cut the connection.

"Not a very comforting image," Karak murmured, and swam away.

Chapter 10

And so, the next day, they came together: Translator Kathryn Bircher of Earth and Translator Jarrikk of the S'sinn. Before the dais in the Great Hall of the Flock, before the Supreme Flight Leader, as Matthews and Kitillikk and a thousand S'sinn looked on, they Linked, souls and memories bared to each other in the blink of an eye, their doubts overcome and absorbed. Together they fought their way back to selfhood, turned outward, and stood back to back as one unit, Kathryn/Jarrikk, facing their respective delegates.

"Begin," they said in unison.

Akkanndikk, as host of the conference, spoke first. She reeled off a long list of grievances dating back to the war. Kathryn saw, heard, and understood through Jarrikk's eyes and ears, and faced the humans with a sneer in her voice and a challenge in her stance, the closest human equivalents to the haughty contempt of the S'sinn leader.

Matthews responded with his own list, from the original S'sinn attack on the human colony on Kikks'sarr— no mention of Jarrikk's murdered flightmates—to "this most recent outrage of landing colonists on a world already inhabited by humans"—no mention that the two colonization attempts occurred simultaneously.

Charge and counter-charge flew, perfectly communicated by Kathryn and Jarrikk. Locked in the unity of Translation, they felt no emotion of their own. All that changed when, four hours after Translation began, the timed-release antidote to the Programming kicked in and severed the Link.

Both of them staggered a little, feeling for a moment as if half of themselves had suddenly died. Kathryn took a deep breath, pulled the Link free, and stopped Matthews in mid-speech. "I'm sorry, Mr. Ambassador, but this session is ended."

Matthews glared at her, glared at the S'sinn, then bowed stiffly, gathered his papers, and led his aides off the platform and out of the hall, footsteps clattering. Akkanndikk and her Left and Right Wing stalked off in the other direction, showing their contempt by staying on the ground, although Kathryn knew Matthews would never understand that unless she told him. Since she knew from Jarrikk's memories that Akkanndikk's contempt was mostly feigned for domestic consumption, she wouldn't tell him. She shivered, chilled through and bone-weary, and rubbed her throbbing temples. "I love being a Translator," she muttered.

Jarrikk cocked his head at her. She felt his own weariness and a concern that warmed her. "Sleep well, friend," she said in Guildtalk. "Until tomorrow."

"Tomorrow," he replied. "Fly safely in this night's dreams." He closed and locked his case and trudged after his Supreme Flight Leader—but Kathryn knew that *he* stayed on the ground not from contempt, but because of that tragic childhood contact with humans.

She picked up her own case and turned to go; then stopped, feeling the red gaze of the hundreds of watching S'sinn and the weight of their massed emotions. Instinct urged her to run for the distant exit, but mindful of the Guild's reputation, she walked slowly and deliberately across the space-black floor.

"Translator," Matthews greeted her coldly when she entered the windowless human quarters. Another deliberate insult, implying they were prisoners or animals; another bit of information she wouldn't tell Matthews. Her duty was to Translate and provide any other assistance she could toward the success of the negotiations; telling Matthews the S'sinn were insulting him didn't seem likely to be helpful.

Of course, that didn't stop *him* from insulting *her,* in his own oblique fashion. "I see I needed to have no fear about the veracity of your Translation; it seemed obvious enough that you had great sympathy for the S'sinn point of view. No doubt you've learned to look at the issue from both sides in that alien-run Guildhall of yours."

Kathryn sighed. He wasn't the first client to mistake accurate Translation for some bias on the part of the Translator. She'd been taught that such confusion was the sign of excellent Translation. She didn't feel like explaining that to Matthews. So what if he thought of her as a traitor? She thought of him as an idiot. "I have indeed, Ambassador. A trait I've always assumed would also be useful in a diplomat. Perhaps I was wrong." She smiled inwardly at the flash of outrage that elicited; she would have smiled more if it had also raised at least a tinge of guilt. "I believe I'll retire to my room for the rest of the evening. If you could see that supper is delivered there . . . ?"

"Of course, Translator," Matthews said in his most formal voice. "No doubt you will sleep well after this day's work."

"No doubt I will, Ambassador. Until tomorrow, then."

"Good night."

Supper, provided by the S'sinn, proved palatable enough: a kind of thick meaty stew and odd vegetables which combined the texture of packing foam with a strong, yeasty taste. Kathryn downed every bite, "eating for two," as the joke among the human Translators went; the symbiote, too, required nourishment.

But when she settled into bed, sleep eluded her; her mind kept running over what she had seen in Jarrikk's memories. He had as much reason to hate humans as she had to hate the S'sinn. Today both had Linked, for the first time, with the creatures of their nightmares, and overcome those nightmares to work together: proof, if only those they were Translating for could see it, that humans and S'sinn need not be enemies.

But the blind fools couldn't see it, or didn't want to. To most of the S'sinn, like Jarrikk's old Flight Leader Kitillikk, the humans were brutal child-killers, and to most of humanity, like Matthews, the S'sinn were hideous batlike monsters, and neither could wait to rid the galaxy of the other.

Kathryn's nightmares that night were of burning flesh and broken wings.

Jarrikk stood by the high arches of his ground-floor apartment in another wing of the Great Hall, looking up at the constellations of S'sinndikk, constellations he had learned in the broodhall on a planet where S'sinndikk's sun itself was barely visible in the night sky. Most of them were named after the near-mythical Hunters and Flight Leaders of the days before the S'sinn knew the stars were other suns and thought of them as the eyes of the great black beasts that accompanied the Hunter of Worlds on his midnight rides across the heavens. S'sinn heroes had always been warriors and Hunters. And now, it seemed, his people wanted a new war to create a whole new crop of heroes.

Maybe they can rename the constellations after them—if there's anybody left to look up, Jarrikk thought.

Surprised by his own bitterness, he stepped back from the arch and returned to the warmth of his sleeping pit, curling in among the pillows, automatically forming himself into the one position in which his damaged wing did not ache. He'd discovered something that day, when he Linked with the young human female. Rather than what made humans so different, he'd discovered how much alike they were: two races with violent pasts, only recently expanding into the galaxy and still carrying the baggage of their pre-space history with them.

He'd discovered something else: that humans were not a faceless mass of wingless murderers, but individuals. He'd met many through Kathryn's memories, but most of all, he'd met her—and uncovered the wound of her loss, a wound as deep and crippling as his own.

He'd thought it hard, with his history, to make the Link with a human. Knowing what he did now, he thought he'd had the easier part of the arrangement.

He sighed and closed his eyes. It would be a lot harder for Kitillikk and the other S'sinn who wanted war to hate humans if he could somehow share what he had learned. It was a lot easier to hate a race than an individual.

In Kathryn's case, he couldn't do it at all.

The walk across the black basalt floor between the blood-red pillars wasn't any easier or any warmer the following morning. Kathryn covered a yawn with one hand and flexed her other shoulder. After a night of reliving Jarrikk's childhood terrors, she not only felt exhausted, she felt pain in body parts she didn't even have. No other Link had ever affected her this deeply.

Then again, few Translators brought to the experience emotions as deep as those she and Jarrikk had shared. She yawned again. Just as well; otherwise, Translators would spend all their time between Translations trying to catch up on sleep.

"You seem tired, Translator Bircher," Ambassador Matthews said from behind her. "I'm sorry you found it harder to sleep than you supposed."

"I slept fine, Ambassador," Kathryn snapped. "Bad dreams."

"I'm not surprised," one of Matthews' aides muttered, glancing up at the massed S'sinn watching them approach the dais. "All these bats are enough to give anyone nightmares. Not to mention the stench. It's like a zoo . . ."

"My nightmares weren't about the S'sinn," Kathryn said sweetly. "They were all about humans."

"Quiet," Matthews ordered. "They'll hear us."

Kathryn forbore telling him that S'sinn hearing was so keen everyone in the hall had heard everything they'd said since they'd entered.

Jarrikk stepped forward to meet her, spreading his wings, as she climbed onto the dais. She opened her arms in the best approximation of the S'sinn greeting she could manage, being one set of limbs short, then extended her hand in the human greeting, trusting Jarrikk to remember the custom from her memories. He hesitated, then held out his clawed right hand. She shook it firmly, his leathery palm warm against hers, his claws pressing lightly against the back of her hand and the fur on the back of his hand tickling her fingers.

Today neither of them hesitated to Link. In fact, she eagerly took her syringe and stabbed it into her arm. Jarrikk's was the only friendly presence she could sense in the entire room, and that included the three humans behind her.

After a brief rush of fresh memories from their respective evenings, Jarrikk/Kathryn faced their delegates again. "Begin."

If anything, this second session was worse. Neither side offered any compromise on Fairholm/Kisradikk; the entire four hours passed in useless reiteration of claims already made and demands already rejected. The S'sinn demanded humans withdraw from the planet; humans demanded the same of the S'sinn. Stalemate.

Except that, unlike a stalemate in chess, this stalemate would end nothing; it would only precipitate a far nastier game. And when Kathryn severed the Link at the end of the session, her stomach churned as the realization hit home that the next morning there would be only one thing to Translate: the human declaration of war on the S'sinn—war, which had slain her parents and so many others on both sides; war, which had crippled Jarrikk. She felt his own dismay, but aside from a faint echo of that dismay in Akkanndikk, any other peace-loving feelings were lost in the tidal wave of avid hatred from all sides.

It seemed that only she and Jarrikk truly wanted the negotiations to succeed, but though they were right in the middle of those negotiations, crucial to them, in fact, they were in the worst position of all to influence them. Neither carried any weight with their respective delegates; had effectively denied the possibility by emphasizing so strongly that Translators served the Guild and the Commonwealth, and could not Translate falsely. They could do nothing; nothing but Translate the end of the . . .

Kathryn froze, the silvery cord of the Link dangling in her hand, her mouth suddenly bone-dry. The idea that had just come to her, unbidden, would violate her Oath. It could mean expulsion from the Guild, loss of a second family . . .

. . . but it might just stop a war.

She touched Jarrikk's wing before he could leave the dais. He turned his ruby eyes on her, and she sensed his puzzlement. "We need to talk in private," she murmured in Guildtalk. "Where . . . ?"

For a moment he regarded her, puzzlement growing; then he flicked his ears forward and back, and said, "My quarters. This way."

As they crossed the floor together the hostility of the gathered S'sinn increased tenfold, and buried faintly within it, like a hint of vinegar in a spicy food, she felt the humans' hostility as well. In fact, she felt like a mouse at an owl convention, but she kept her even pace. Jarrikk couldn't move any faster anyway.

He led her through a ten-meter-high arch into a long hall with smaller arches leading off at three levels. They passed through the third ground-floor portal on the right into a high-ceilinged, airy room with enormous, glassless windows opening onto the gardens outside the Hall of the Flock. Rough-woven tapestries hung from the other three walls above padded shikks of polished, multicolored woods, and a sweet-smelling bluish vapor rose from a censer over the Guild-standard computer terminal.

"It's beautiful," Kathryn said.

"Thank you."

As she moved around the room, afraid to speak her thoughts, now that the moment had come, Jarrikk watched her with the natural stillness of a waiting predator. What if he reported her to the Guild, had her removed?

Then war would come, and she would have lost nothing. The Guild would die with the Commonwealth.

Hesitantly, she began.

Despite all he now knew about Kathryn Bircher, despite all he had shared with her, the sight of a human in his quarters, among his familiar objects, troubled Jarrikk deeply. Echoes of the hate he'd thought he'd buried, at least where Kathryn was concerned, rang in distant corners of his mind. He clamped down on his emotions forcefully: he couldn't have Kathryn sensing those ghosts from his past. He didn't want to wake the ghosts from her own.

Though perhaps they were already awake. He sensed unease from her; unease and distress, but also strange exhilaration, determination, and maybe even fear. Intrigued, he listened closely as she finally began to speak. "We work well together."

No argument there. Surprise that it should be so, maybe, but no argument. "Agreed."

"Our negotiators do not."

No argument there, either. He'd seen more amicable negotiations between mating-frenzied jarrbukks. Whatever Akkanndikk's true feelings about the possibility of war were, she had set them aside to play directly to public opinion. He didn't know why that disappointed him; he'd thought he was past looking for heroes, except among the constellations. "True."

"They do not want peace."

He agreed, of course he agreed, but that simple statement took them winging into unstable air. Guild rules strictly forbade Translators to discuss ongoing negotiations between themselves. But he had to know where she was going . . . "Also true," he said after a moment.

"So—we need new negotiators."

What? "We have no say. The human and S'sinn governments chose—"

"Perhaps they chose badly."

He clamped down on his outrage and turmoil, blocking her completely, as he had blocked so successfully most of his young life, until Ukkaddikk discovered his talent. She flew them straight into a hurricane with such a statement!

But she rushed on. "We serve the Guild. The Guild serves the Commonwealth. War will destroy the Commonwealth and the Guild. Our loyalty to the Guild demands we prevent that."

All the warnings he had heard about Translators who did not Translate honestly, who somehow worked for one side or another, came rushing back—but no, that didn't fit; Kathryn challenged the Oath to preserve the Guild and Commonwealth, not to shatter it.

He wondered if such a challenge might not be the most insidious of all.

She waited, staring up at him with those odd, white-rimmed blue eyes. "We can do nothing," he said emphatically. "Nothing!"

"We can," she insisted. But then she hesitated. He could still read her clearly, and he felt her determination suddenly run headlong into some final, almost insurmountable barrier. Almost as though she were in pain, she grated out, "We can fake the Link."

Jarrikk's blocks crashed down, and he stumbled back from her, his denial and outrage flowing out of him full-force. "No! No, no, no!" This was worse, far worse, then, than just Translating for illicit negotiations. This was heresy!

"We must!" Her determination roared up in response to his denial. "We must negotiate for them!

We must find the compromise they will not! We must—"

"Lie! Break our Oaths! Dishonor the Guild! Dishonor ourselves! Ruin everything!"

"War will destroy the Guild, destroy honor, destroy everything!" Kathryn moved after him, and he backed away until he found himself trapped in the corner by the windows, wings half-spread against the walls. "War killed my parents!" She pointed at his scars. "War made you *walk!*"

Jarrikk turned his head away, looked out the window, frightened not by Kathryn but by the echo of support her words found in himself. He thought of his dead flightmates, and of that day in the gorge. How many other young S'sinn would face terror and pain if war came? What good was honor to the dead?

He could almost see a priest rearing back, wings extended, clawing the sky, howling, "Heresy! Heresy!" at such a thought. Those who died with honor received more honor yet as a flightmate of the Hunter of Worlds in the next life, and the most honorable death of all was death in war.

But the honor the priests touted sprang from the tales of the ancient Hunters after whom the stars were named, Hunters who knew only one world and one race and who fought their battles with spears and clubs and claws and teeth, not firelances and neutron bombs and planet-cracking asteroids and city-slagging satellites and brain-rotting viruses and all the other terrible weapons invented by the military minds of the Seven Races. Death came from such weapons to both the brave fighter and the helpless youngling, to both the Huntership and the broodhall. Surely the greatest honor of all would be to prevent such horrors. Surely even the priests would agree: weren't the most honored of all the ancient Hunters those who fought to protect the innocent?

A flight of S'sinn soared overhead in perfect diamond formation, and Jarrikk's wings twitched. Even if it were heresy, this new definition of honor, it could be no more heretical than his very existence: a living, breathing Flightless One. He looked back at Kathryn and said, very slowly, "It's dangerous. You cannot know what will happen. Without Programming . . ." He could not imagine what it might be like, but the thought terrified him: the Link would open their minds to each other without the interface of the symbiote, flood their brains with alien neural impulses. It could kill them—or drive them mad.

"I know what will happen if war comes," Kathryn said. "And so do you."

Jarrikk looked at his crippled left wing. "Yes." He met her eyes. "Yes."

But with his capitulation, he felt her determination dissolve into renewed uncertainty and fear that she tried unsuccessfully to hide from him. It didn't matter; he knew she felt his own.

"I'll prepare a proposal and send it to you before the morning session," Kathryn said hastily, and hurried out.

Jarrikk watched her leave, and despite his recent thoughts of heresy, said a prayer to the Hunter of Worlds.

Chapter 11

The crowd in the Great Hall of the Flock had lessened somewhat; the hostility had not. Kathryn hurried to her own quarters, relieved to find Matthews and his aides in conference, sequestered in Matthews' room. She didn't particularly fancy trying to explain to Matthews just what she had been doing in the S'sinn Translator's private apartment . . .

She sat at her computer terminal, trying to compose her thoughts, to recall all she had learned of Commonwealth Law, former treaties, and the current dispute. They would need a truly workable compromise to pull this off, and she only had a few hours . . .

. . . only a few hours to come up with the solution that had escaped every diplomatic mind in the Commonwealth until now? Who was she kidding?

She wrenched her mind away from that train of thought. She would not give in to defeatism; she couldn't afford it. A solution had not been found because no one really wanted a solution: no one, at least, who had been in a position to implement one. The politicians and generals had their own reasons for wanting war, which had nothing to do with the reasons people like her and Jarrikk and the millions of others who would suffer had for not wanting one.

But despite the importance of beginning work, or maybe because of it, her mind kept going back to that moment with Jim, before she left on the assignment that had been aborted to bring her here, when she'd been so shocked to hear him talk about "species ties." She'd been so determined to uphold her Oath—yet now that same determination to treat aliens as her kin was leading her to *break* that Oath.

She wondered what Jim would have said, and was glad he wasn't there to read her confusion.

She turned to the computer. At least she was doing *something* to try to stop a war, she thought fiercely. Even if she'd failed, at least she would have *tried*. That was more than Jim would be able to say. Or Matthews.

The key to a compromise, she felt sure, lay in Commonwealth history. There must have been similar disputes between other races. What had *they* done?

An hour later, the beep of her terminal brought her out of the depths of research. She had an incoming message; she punched "receive."

Words scrolled by in Guildtalk. "Researched matter. Found following: 'Attempts to Link without Programming produce severe pain; one Orrisian volunteer suffered respiratory and circulatory arrest and narrowly escaped death. In all cases, the Translator symbiote died, and volunteers required long periods of convalescence due to immune-system rejection of the symbiote's dead tissue. All recovered, but were no longer able to function as Translators; their bodies rejected all attempts to introduce a new symbiote. Native empathic abilities survived, but augmentation became impossible.' Jarrikk."

Kathryn read the message, read it again, read it a third time, then blanked the screen and stared blindly at the gray, windowless wall. Pain she could face—*had* faced, over and over—but the rest . . . "No longer able to function as Translators . . ."

It would be like bondcut all over again. A part of her would die.

But millions of others would die—fully—if she *didn't* take the risk. And Jarrikk didn't say where he'd gotten the information. Maybe he was having second thoughts, and was just trying to frighten her out of her scheme.

Well, he'd frightened her, all right—but not enough to make her quit. To prove to herself she meant that, she got up, took an empty Programming vial, filled it with water, then colored the liquid pale pink with a drop of blood from her finger, drawn with the point of a syringe. She placed the vial in her Translator's case, but stared at it a long time before slowly closing and latching the case and returning to her terminal.

Near dawn, when sleep could no longer be denied, she felt she had barely begun—but she could do no better. She sucked her sore finger and studied the proposal on the screen before her. Drawing on two previous cases from a century before, one a dispute between the Hasshingu-Issk and the Orrisians and the other between the Ithkarites and the Aza, she had cobbled together a compromise that would see the colonization rights to Fairholm/Kisradikk awarded on the basis of a competition adjudicated by an impartial panel chosen from the remaining five races, all individuals to be acceptable to both humans and S'sinn. The planet would be awarded to whichever race could demonstrate both the most need and the best plan for its colonization. The loser in that competition would receive special trading privileges on the planet for a period of fifty planetary years and other rights to be negotiated separately. The arrangement had the twofold benefit of at least giving the loser something, so he didn't go away empty-handed, and fostering more negotiations and cooperation between the competing factions. Kathryn knew, from Translating with Jarrikk, that humans and S'sinn were very much alike, with more in common than either had with many of the other Commonwealth Races; once they began to develop normal relations, especially trade, the hostility would ease, cooperation would blossom, peace would be ensured, the Commonwealth would survive . . .

"And everyone will live happily ever after," Kathryn muttered, and rubbed her eyes hard with the heels of her hands. Maybe all she had written was an elaborate fantasy, a fairy tale with a happy ending. Maybe she was throwing away her career, her life, on nothing more than wish-fulfillment.

Maybe. But then again, maybe there were worse things to risk your life for than the chance for a happy ending.

She keyed up Jarrikk's address and punched SEND, then fell fully clothed into bed and instant sleep.

The high-pitched squeal of his computer brought Jarrikk instantly awake and to his feet, wings half-spread and claws ready. An instant later he recognized the sound for what it was and went to the computer stand. "Display," he said.

The holographic tank clouded, then displayed Kathryn's proposed compromise, written in Guildscript, fully annotated with notes and references to previous Commonwealth treaties of similar form. Jarrikk ignored the peripherals, concentrating on the main proposal. When he'd finished reading it, he felt slightly more confident—slightly. Deciding he might as well start the day, he went to the censer, placed a fresh rod of incense in the burner, and pushed the button to light it. As the fragrant blue smoke rose to his nostrils, he breathed deep, clearing the last fog of sleep from his mind.

Certainly Kathryn's proposal was a good one, one that should be acceptable to both sides, one they might have come up with themselves if they were negotiating in good faith. But they weren't. To date, they had only been posturing for their respective populations. Would that change, even if they suddenly heard a reasonable proposal apparently offered by the other side?

Jarrikk considered that very carefully as he turned from the computer to the printout he had made of what he had discovered about attempts to Link without Programming. There had been strange hesitation on the dimspace link to the Guildhall when he had asked for that information, the kind that often preceded a message that access to the requested data was restricted. But just when he'd decided that must be the case, the data had appeared.

Could the warnings of danger be false information, planted to preclude any attempt by the Translators to take matters into their own hands?

No way to tell. If so, it hadn't worked; Kathryn remained committed, or she wouldn't have sent him the proposal.

He turned back to it. His questions had no answers; certainty eluded him in every direction except one: Kathryn. In the face of her commitment, he could not renege on their agreement.

He pored over her proposal more closely, made a few minor suggestions, and sent it just as Akkanndikk's Left Wing appeared at his entrance. "Her Altitude invites you to eat with her before this final session," said the Left Wing. "I will escort you."

"My thanks," said Jarrikk. He blanked the screen and followed.

It seemed to Kathryn she had barely closed her eyes when someone knocked. "Duty calls, Translator Bircher," Matthews said through the door. "One hour. We're all anxious to conclude this."

I'll bet you are, Kathryn thought. She splashed cold water on her face, surveyed herself in the mirror, shuddered, then returned to the computer to review her creation. Jarrikk had sent it back with a few eminently sensible changes. *We make a good team,* she thought as she read them—but if the information Jarrikk had sent her were true, she'd never Link with him, or anyone else, again.

She cleared the computer and picked up her case. If Matthews had done the work she had just attempted, she would have been able to hold to her Oath. But if her darker suspicions were correct, and war had been intended from the moment Earth colonized Fairholm/Kisradikk, how would Matthews react when this proposal surfaced?

She paused at the door. *Earth depends on its allies,* she told herself. *They'll pressure it to accept anything reasonable that preserves the peace. Even Matthews is enough of a diplomat to understand that.*

She hoped.

The anger of the S'sinn who packed every recess of the Great Hall beat down on Kathryn like a desert sun as she followed Matthews to the dais. The air felt colder than ever, but the distinctive musky scent of the assembled S'sinn was hot and troubling. She saw Jarrikk, trailing the Supreme Flight Leader, approaching from the other side. Keeping a tight rein on her own emotions, she could feel nothing from him. Ritualistically they made their preparations, but when Kathryn pressed the injector to her arm, she felt nothing but the sting of the needle. The Beast inside her slumbered on. She took up her end of the Link—and froze.

She could feel the ravenous attention of S'sinn and humans, could almost hear them saying, "Do it! Link! Give us war!"

She could. She could make some excuse, return to her quarters, inject the real Programming, and Translate perfectly, as her Oath demanded. War would come, but she would still be a Translator, still have that wonderful union with other races, the only thing that could fill the void left by her parents' deaths.

Her parents . . .

They'd left Earth for Luckystrike, dreaming of building a new and better world. War had snuffed out those dreams. What she was about to do would destroy *her* dreams just as surely—but maybe, just maybe, it would ensure that millions of others could keep theirs.

She pictured her father standing in her place, and her hesitation vanished. She touched the cord to the patch behind her ear.

Agony ripped her open, screamed through every nerve, as The Beast woke to alien, untranslatable signals. Her vision grayed and the world spun around her, roaring, but she clung grimly to consciousness, fighting for control, fighting to hide her suffering from Matthews and all the gathered S'sinn watching her like vultures, and gradually, oh-so-gradually, the pain subsided, leaving her nauseated but functioning—and, abruptly, terrified. *She'd gone empathy-blind!* She could sense nothing, not the hostility of the assembled S'sinn, not Jarrikk's worry, not Matthews' impatience.

She had killed the Beast, and in so doing, she had killed her own abilities.

Feeling blind, deaf, and desperate, she nodded tersely to Jarrikk, and the S'sinn delegation began.

Kathryn heard only the same growling gibberish as Matthews, but she began talking, reciting the speech she had written the night before. "Upon consideration, the First Flight of S'sinndikk has realized that our mutual recriminations have been of little benefit to ourselves or to our allies. In the hope that these negotiations may yet produce a fruitful and lasting accommodation between us concerning the planet Fairholm/Kisradikk, we propose the following compromise . . ."

Matthews' aides exchanged surprised glances, but Matthews' expression never changed. Kathryn's inability to perceive his emotions unnerved her. How did non-empaths communicate? She might as well be talking to herself.

The S'sinn stopped. She hastily summarized what remained of her proposal, and concluded, "Do you have a response at this time?"

One of Matthews' aides whispered something into his ear. He whispered something back, then said, "We will study your remarks and make a counterproposal at our next session. Tomorrow morning?"

Jarrikk began speaking, and Kathryn held her breath. If he now Translated truly, as his Oath demanded, there would only be confusion on the part of the S'sinn—confusion and, very shortly, suspicion; suspicion that the human Translator had, unthinkably, lied. And the mere fact a Translator had lied could destroy the Guild and Commonwealth as thoroughly as any war . . .

Matthews frowned as the translation of his simple remark went on for an inordinate length of time, but there had been similar differences before. Besides, Kathryn thought, what could he possibly suspect? *Translators don't lie. Everyone knows that.*

Another thought struck her, and she groaned inwardly. What would happen at the "next session" if she couldn't Translate?

One thing at a time. There might not even be another session. And if the S'sinn did agree to it, how was she to know, empathically maimed as she was?

Jarrikk found a way around that. As the S'sinn finished speaking, he nodded—a human gesture meaningless to his own people. "Agreed," she told Matthews.

The delegates departed, and the galleries buzzed as the news spread among the S'sinn that negotiations would continue. Kathryn's knees buckled unexpectedly and she would have fallen if Jarrikk hadn't caught her. He gently tugged the Link free and she leaned against his broad, furry chest for a moment. "Thanks," she murmured, then, wary of how the crowd might react, straightened hurriedly and stepped back. She knew Jarrikk wouldn't take it amiss; after two full sessions of Translation, they knew each other as well as anyone could ever know another person, better than she had ever known another human—certainly better than she had known Jim, whose image came to her unbidden, standing in her room, suggesting she break her Oath . . .

Which she had. She shook her head, confused. "I'm blind," she told Jarrikk. He would know how she meant it.

"You were very brave," he said. "Tomorrow both sides will present modifications to your proposal, but I expect ultimate success."

"How?" Kathryn whispered. "I can't Translate." A lump in her throat choked her; she swallowed angrily. She would *not* cry, not in self-pity: never!

"Would you please come to my quarters?" Jarrikk cocked his head to one side, watching her.

Kathryn blinked. "Why?"

"Please. We must talk—to Karak."

Karak. She closed her eyes for a moment. Of course, he was right; Karak would know if there were another human Translator close enough to be of assistance, and if there weren't, Karak could arrange a non-inflammatory delay in the negotiations.

But talking to Karak meant telling him what they had done. And she thought that might hurt as much as the death of the Beast, but in a far deeper way.

"All right," she said.

In a way it was a relief not to feel the crowd's hostility as she walked with Jarrikk to his sunny apartment. She sat on the closest thing to a human stool in the room, although she suspected the round, truncated pillar was actually a waste disposal unit, and watched as Jarrikk keyed his computer to call the Guildhall. She breathed the sweet smell drifting from the censer and for a moment felt almost tranquil. The thing was done, the decision made, the action taken. She would not second-guess herself: whatever the consequences, she would accept them and deal with them.

Karak appeared on the screen. "Translator Jarrikk," he squeaked. "Is Translator Bircher with you?"

"I'm here," Kathryn said, standing and stepping into range of the computer's vid pickup.

"Translator Bircher, Translator Annette Ursu is en route to S'sinndikk and will take your place in the morning session." Karak's tentacles wove a slow dance around his beaked face as he spoke.

"Annette—" Kathryn stared at Karak, then turned furiously on Jarrikk. "You told him!"

"No."

Kathryn spun back toward the computer. "Then how—" Another thought struck her. "You said no other Translators were near enough—"

"I said no *suitable* Translator was near enough. You were the ideal choice, therefore Translator Ursu, though relatively close in distance, was unsuitable for the task." Karak ignored Kathryn's glare, if he even knew how to interpret it. "The Guild Council felt that if you and Jarrikk, with your unfortunate personal histories, could overcome your mutual distrust and successfully Link, it would demonstrate graphically the possibility—and need—of humans and S'sinn working together. As well, both of you have recently demonstrated your unswerving devotion to the good of the Guild and the cause of peace. With that in mind, we worked within the Commonwealth to arrange these negotiations, and insured you were the Translators: the only people, other than the negotiators, who might be able to arrive at a peaceful solution, because both of you so desperately wanted it." He raised a manipulator and moved it in a small circle. "It worked."

"It worked—" Kathryn stopped, took a deep breath, and repeated, "It worked because I broke my Oath."

"All unfolded as anticipated."

"Anticipated!" Kathryn's face flamed. "You *expected* me to break my Oath?"

"You did not break it," Karak said. "You upheld it. Your Oath states that all races are your kin. You kept your kin from destroying each other."

"But Translators—can't lie. If the Seven Races knew—"

"Please see they do not find out."

"I need to sit down." Kathryn's stomach churned and a hot steel band seemed clamped around her forehead. She leaned against one of the padded wooden shikks. Jarrikk moved close beside her. "Why me? Why not Jim?" Did Karak know what Jim had said to her before she left? she wondered, suddenly worried for him.

"Translator Ornawka we felt to be unsuitable," Karak said.

"Why?"

Karak said nothing more, which didn't make Kathryn feel any better. In fact, she felt rather worse. She shook her aching head and coughed. Jarrikk placed one clawed hand on her shoulder and she leaned gratefully back against his warm bulk. She looked at Karak again. "There's something else," she said hoarsely. "I'm empathy-blind. I'm not—I'm not a Translator anymore."

"True," Karak said simply, and Kathryn closed her eyes. She'd hoped, with the illogical hope of a child, that Jarrikk's information had been wrong. "However," Karak continued, "your natural empathic ability will slowly recover."

Kathryn's eyes flew open. "Truth?"

"Translators do not lie."

Kathryn grimaced. "So what happens now?"

"You may soon be feeling rather ill."

Kathryn laughed, which turned into an aching cough.

"This will provide the perfect excuse for you to withdraw. The ship delivering Translator Ursu has an unusually well-equipped medical bay. Its personnel will take care of you."

Jarrikk moved around in front of her, blocking her view of Karak. "Until then, *I* will take care of you," he said.

She wished she could read his emotions; at least he could read hers. She let her gratitude flood her. He patted her knee clumsily, and she laughed, knowing he had drawn the gesture from her memories. He moved around behind her again. Karak watched them both. "So it all worked out the way you predicted," she said. "But you couldn't *know* I'd do—what I did. I almost didn't. I almost backed out. The thought of no longer being a Translator . . ." Her throat closed on the words.

"We didn't *know*," Karak said. "One can never *know*. Nor did we know what Jarrikk would do—until he initiated his library search for information on the effects of Linking without Programming. Such information is normally restricted, but I personally cleared it for him. The decision, however, was entirely yours—and his."

"Both?" Kathryn twisted around to stare at Jarrikk. *"Both?"*

Jarrikk met her shocked gaze steadily. Every joint in his body ached and the old wound in his shoulder seemed to be on fire, along with his blood. He hadn't wanted her to know he was sick; she'd soon be gone and he knew she would worry about him, which, in view of the circumstances, was a singular waste of energy. But of course he'd had no way of telling Karak that. "Both," he said.

"Why? There was no need . . ."

"But there was. The S'sinn would be shamed if a human took a risk a S'sinn did not. Such shame could poison relations."

"But they'll never know!"

"Someday, they may." Someday, he might be known as the Flightless One who saved S'sinndikk, if S'sinn prejudice against the Flightless were ever overcome to that extent. He touched Kathryn's forehead gently. "You're a very brave human. I couldn't let you risk what I would not."

"But if you didn't Program . . . you're as blind as me!" Kathryn whispered.

"As of today, two fewer Translators," said Karak. "Two new names in the Hall of Honor. And a new hope of peace."

Kathryn put her hand on Jarrikk's chest. *"You're* a very brave S'sinn," she said softly. "And a very kind one."

He touched her forehead again, moved by her compassion for him, remembering the hatred that she'd held for his race. "And you're my very good friend."

"Yes," she said. "Oh, yes." She kept her eyes on him, but spoke to Karak. "What use are we to the Guild now?"

"When your natural abilities return, you will still be able to seek out new human and S'sinn Translators. We will now need many more."

Kathryn's eyes lit up and she turned toward the computer. "I'd like that. I'd like that very much."

But Jarrikk, the fever burning hotter and hotter inside him, lifted his hands in denial. "No. I cannot. The S'sinn will not accept such judgment from a Flightless One." *Not yet, anyway,* he thought.

"Then what will you do . . ." Kathryn began, turning toward him, and stopped, the color draining from her face. He knew that the knowledge gleaned from his memories had just given her the answer.

Flightless, no longer a Translator, he had no useful function on S'sinndikk or any other world of the S'sinn. Today he had wiped out all the years that had passed since Ukkaddikk had come into his healing room. Without Translation, they meant nothing.

Unflinching, he answered Kathryn's question. "I will die."

Chapter 12

Kathryn stared at Jarrikk, stunned. That part of her that had *been* S'sinn warmed with pride that at last Jarrikk would follow the traditions of his people, uphold the glory of his race, but the human part of her went cold as the depths of space. She wanted to scream at him, to reason with him, but, at war with herself, all she could manage was a choked, "No!"

"It is our way," Jarrikk said. "As you know."

"Karak . . ." Kathryn turned pleadingly toward the terminal.

"It is the S'sinn way," Karak said, and his image vanished.

Kathryn faced Jarrikk again. "But—there are other Flightless Ones who still live on this planet. You don't—I don't want you to die!" The words exploded out of her.

Jarrikk opened his scarred wing. "Only in Translation am I free of pain. I no longer have that freedom. Death is my friend."

"I would not sentence you to a life of pain," Kathryn whispered. "But *I* will not be free of pain. Not if you die."

Jarrikk touched her cheek. "You will remember me. You will remember my memories. In you, I will live on."

Kathryn had no more arguments to give him. She gazed mutely at his face, the face she had thought horrible only a few days before, but that now seemed sadly beautiful. She reached up and ran her fingers along the furry curve of the underside of his muzzle, and breathed in his warm, living scent. A gaping black hole seemed to have opened in her heart, or maybe it was the same bottomless pit left by the death of her parents. Strange that the death of one of the aliens that killed them could tear open that old wound.

Blackness now seemed to be leaking from that hole into her vision. The room had started to turn slow circles around her. "When?" she whispered.

"Soon. When you are gone."

"Gone?" His words seemed to be coming from far away. "When I am . . ."

The hot steel band that seemed to encircle her head suddenly clamped tight, and she crumpled into darkness.

In his quarters in the Guildhall, Karak killed all lights and floated in silent water, black but for the faint phosphorescence of the microscopic creatures that kept it clean and oxygenated. When the call came from Akkanndikk, he left the lights off, confronting the Supreme Flight Leader with a blank screen.

"Equipment malfunction?" the S'sinn leader asked.

"I mourn the death of a Translator," Karak said. "As should you."

"Jarrikk?"

"He and Translator Bircher found a way for you to preserve peace and keep your honor and title. But they gave themselves. Now Jarrikk says he will die as a Flightless One. For this, I mourn."

"That is where we are different, Guildmaster," Akkanndikk said. "I rejoice! As Translator, he lived with honor. As Flightless One, he dies with honor."

"I think your people worry too much about honor, Supreme Flight Leader. Would this sacrifice by those who are more my flightmates than yours have been necessary if not for the need to preserve your precious honor?"

"My honor preserves the peace," Akkanndikk growled.

"If my honor is impugned, I will be overthrown, and those most likely to replace me want war. They could still find a way to get it."

"All this, I know," Karak said wearily. "It is why I agreed to this plan. I accept the necessity of this sacrifice. But still I mourn its cost."

"Mourn, then. But maintain vigilance. I do not believe we have achieved final victory yet. The enemies of peace will regroup. They will try again. Do not let your sorrow for this sacrifice weaken your resolve, Guildmaster. There may yet be greater sacrifices to be made."

"My resolve is strong. But I have a question for you, Akkanndikk, you who talk so well of sacrifice. What if, in the end, the sacrifice required is that of the very honor you value so greatly? Will you still rejoice?"

Only silence replied, then the beep that signified the end of the connection. And that gave Karak things to worry about as well as mourn.

Kathryn struggled up from the sucking depths of a deep black nightmare to wakefulness, her heart racing and her pulse pounding in her temples. "Jarrikk!" she cried at the last moment, and her eyes flew open.

They focused first on the Guild insignia, then on the immaculate uniform it was stitched to, and finally on the smiling face of the wearer—Jim Ornawka. "Not furry enough," he said. "How are you?"

"Jim?" Kathryn licked dry lips with a dry tongue, and found it unexpectedly hard to draw air into her lungs. It sighed in listlessly and wheezed out. "Where—"

"Sick bay. Human-crewed Guildship *Unity.*"

Jim poured a glass of water from a pitcher on a small table beside her bed and held it to her lips. She drank it gratefully, and then, in a stronger voice, asked, "How long . . . ?"

"You've been unconscious for three days."

"Three—" Kathryn turned her head from side to

side on a neck so stiff she expected grinding noises. On her left an IV fed something into her arm. On her right a scanner monitored her vital signs. Beyond it, over the water pitcher Jim had poured from and three empty beds, she could see a glass wall and, behind that, a woman in a green medical tunic talking to another patient hooked up to a bewildering and intimidating array of equipment. To the left of the glass wall the room's only door stood open, revealing the empty corridor beyond. The air smelled of antiseptic and the faint piney scent humans pumped into the air on their spaceships to more-or-less mask the unavoidable personal odors that accumulated during recycling. "Are we still on S'sinndikk?"

"We are."

"The negotiations?"

"Proceeding." His smile slipped a little. "You shouldn't have done what you did."

"Couldn't let war . . ."

"Yeah, well, there's still no guarantee there won't be one. And look what it cost you—"

"No guarantee?" Kathryn tried to struggle up, and fell back, barely fighting off an urge to start a cough she was afraid she might never be able to finish. "You said negotiations are proceeding—"

"They are. But S'sinn and humans, working together peacefully?" Jim shook his head. "It will never happen."

"It already has," Kathryn said, remembering. "Have you—have you heard about Jarrikk?"

"Heard what about him?" Jim didn't sound particularly pleased to be asked.

"Is he . . ." Kathryn swallowed.

"Dead? No more than you are. He collapsed not long after he carried you back to the human quarters. But I hear he recovered more quickly. In fact, he's been asking to see you."

"Please!" Kathryn tried and failed again to sit up. "I've got to talk to him." Maybe she could still change his mind.

"Kathryn." Jim took her hand. "Let it go. We'll be off this planet in a couple of days and you'll never have to set eyes on a S'sinn again. They've caused you enough grief. First your parents, now this stupid scheme. You could have died, you know. You almost did. Forget the S'sinn. You're not a Translator any more; concentrate on being human." He ran one finger along her cheekbone. "I could help you . . ."

Kathryn remembered Jarrikk touching her face just that way. "Jarrikk is my friend, Jim," she whispered through the heaviness in her chest. "He's planning to kill himself because he feels he's worthless now that he can no longer Translate. I have to stop him. Please tell him I'll see him."

"You shouldn't interfere. You'll only get hurt. The S'sinn aren't like us. Their traditions are different. If he feels he has to kill himself, you'll only be hurting him by arguing against it. Let him go, Kathryn."

"He asked to see me, remember? Please do as I ask, Jim. Or I'll simply get the doctor to do it for me."

Jim dropped her hand. "All right. But I still say you're making a mistake. I'll be back later."

He strode out, passing the doctor at the door. "Translator Bircher, nice to see you awake," she said, coming over to Kathryn's bed and putting her small, cool hand on Kathryn's forehead.

"Nice to be awake."

"I'm Doctor Chung. How are you feeling?"

"My lungs . . ."

"A little leftover congestion."

"Left over from what?"

Dr. Chung took her hand from Kathryn's head. "Immune system rejection of the Translator symbiote," she said as she checked the IV. "You slept through the worst, but you're going to feel lousy for a while yet."

"The worst?" Jim had said she'd almost died . . .

"Raging fever, dehydration, vomiting, diarrhea, lungs filling with fluid . . . your body's been doing everything it can to rid itself of that dead symbiote." She rounded the foot of the bed to look over the scanner readings.

That dead symbiote, Kathryn thought. Not much of an epitaph for her life as a Translator. "Not much company in here," she said to change the subject.

"Nobody except poor Garth in intensive care." Dr. Chung pulled an electronic notepad and stylus from the pocket of her dark green lab coat and made a few notes.

"What's wrong with him?"

"Accident in the cargo bay. A programming fault in an automated loader. It ran out of control and pinned him against the bulkhead."

Kathryn winced. "Bad?"

"Crushed his legs. Double amputation." The doctor reattached the stylus to the notepad and replaced it in her pocket. "He may still be all right, though; I've talked to Doctor Kapusianyk at EarthMed Orbital and he feels Garth is a perfect candidate for regeneration therapy."

"Regeneration? They can regrow his legs?"

"Well, it's still experimental, but they've had some remarkable successes and they're looking for subjects. Garth's agreed to try it." Dr. Chung smiled sadly. "What does he have to lose, after all?" She patted Kathryn's shoulder. "You should try to get some sleep."

Kathryn, her mind racing, hardly heard her. "Doctor Chung, could I get a computer terminal in here, please? I need to do some research."

"You should rest. I'm not sure it's a good—"

"Please, Doctor!" Her urgency almost brought on the coughing fit she'd successfully avoided until then. "It's Translator business," she managed to choke out. A Translator claiming Guild business, Kathryn knew, outranked even the captain of a Guildship.

Dr. Chung stiffened. She obviously knew it, too, and didn't care for being clubbed with it. Kathryn regretted that, but she had to find out a few things before

Jarrikk arrived, and she had no idea how soon that might be. "Very well," Dr. Chung said flatly. She went out, and returned a moment later with a small, thin-cased voice-activated terminal.

"Thank you, Doctor Chung. I promise, I'll be as quick as I can, and I'll rest as soon as I've finished." The doctor thawed enough to give her a small smile before going out.

Kathryn opened the terminal and got to work.

Jarrikk contemplated the knife. Two hand spans in length, it glittered coldly in the artificial light of his quarters. His breath fogged its silver blade as he held it close to his muzzle, but even so he caught a reflected glimpse of one red eye, staring back at him.

He grasped the knife's black, leather-wrapped hilt and swung it experimentally. Badly balanced, but then, it wasn't meant for fighting, only for killing the one target he could hardly miss.

He'd gotten it at the Temple of the Hunter of Worlds, where a silent priest had handed it over upon his request. No payment had been offered or required; providing such knives was just one of the many tasks the priests performed in the service of the Hunter. Without his empathic abilities, Jarrikk had been unable to tell if the priest had recognized him as the Translator who had been a part of the negotiations with the humans that had taken such an unexpectedly peaceful turn. He supposed it didn't matter, but it did concern him that his decision to accept the Knife of the Hunter might call into question exactly what had happened in those negotiations.

He'd been tempted to use the knife that very evening, but he had promised himself he would not until he had final word on Kathryn's fate. She had been far more ill than he from the death of the symbiote; ironic, since he intended to die anyway, but she wanted to live.

She wanted him to live, too; of course, but that was impossible. He had nothing to live for, and though, as he had found, a few other Flightless Ones still maintained their existence on S'sinndikk, mere existence didn't interest him.

"Nice knife," said a voice from the archway, speaking Guildtalk, and Jarrikk spun reflexively, earning a twinge of pain from his crippled wing.

A male human in a Translator's uniform stepped into his quarters. "Is that any way to act?" the human said. "And here Kathryn seems to think you're such a nice person—for a S'sinn."

Jarrikk set the knife carefully down on a table. "Who are you?"

"Translator Jim Ornawka, at your service." The human bowed slightly.

This man figured prominently in Kathryn's memories, Jarrikk recalled, though she had seemed ambivalent about him. And Karak had mentioned him, too. But Karak hadn't said anything about him coming to S'sinndikk. In fact, he'd said Ornawka "was not suitable." "Why are you here?"

"To see you."

Jarrikk growled again, and rephrased the question. "Why are you on this planet?"

"To see Kathryn." Ornawka walked slowly around the room, examining the furniture and decorations, fingering each piece. "To make sure she was all right." He paused by the censer, sniffed the pale blue smoke, then coughed, waving it out of his face.

Jarrikk found it unsettling to face this human while still empathically blind. "Karak did not mention you."

"I'm not here officially. I'm on leave."

"You are in uniform."

Ornawka laughed. "I wasn't about to wander around S'sinndikk *without* identifying myself as a Translator." Ornawka stopped in front of one of the wall-hangings. "Very nice work."

"What do you want with me?"

"Kathryn sent me."

"She's awake?"

"Yes. And recovering nicely. Of course she asked about you, and I told her what the Guildship crew told me; that you had already recovered, and were asking for her."

"What did she say?"

Ornawka picked up a corner of the tapestry and examined its weave, rubbing the cloth between thumb and forefinger. "She said she didn't care. She doesn't want to see you again." He dropped the tapestry and carefully smoothed it. "I got the feeling she blames you for what happened to her."

Jarrikk felt as if a heavy weight had suddenly been tied around his neck. He turned back to the table, and picked up the knife again. "I will not trouble her," he said, his back to Ornawka. "Please tell her I am pleased she has recovered, and I wish her well."

"Certainly." Ornawka strode briskly toward the door. "Well, I've done as she asked. I'll be going."

"Wait, please." Ornawka stopped, and Jarrikk put down the knife, then reached up and took off the metal collar that identified him as a Translator. He held it out. "Please give this to her. To remember me by."

"I'm not sure she really wants to remember you," Ornawka said. "But I'll give it to her." He took the collar. "Good-bye."

As Ornawka left, Jarrikk picked up the knife again. He had no reason to wait, after all. At the turn of the night, he would go to the Temple and make his sacrifice.

But that was still several thousand beats away. The priests would say he should meditate until then, he supposed, but whenever he'd tried that as a child he'd always fallen asleep, and he didn't want to sleep away his last few heartbeats.

He put down the knife again, and crossed to his computer. Ornawka had made it clear Kathryn didn't want to see him. Perhaps she had nothing left to say to him. But he still had things to say to her. After what they had shared and accomplished, he could not die without saying good-bye.

"Translator Kathryn Bircher, Guildship *Unity*," he

began dictating. "At the turn of the night, I will make my way to the Temple for my sacrifice. Your friend Jim Ornawka has told me you do not wish to see me, but I hope you will accept this small intrusion. I would not leave without saying good-bye . . ."

Kathryn's research turned up tantalizing hints that her wild notion could work, but nothing concrete. So new were Earth's links to the Commonwealth and its other races that very little Earth technology of any sort had yet been disseminated, much less highly experimental medical techniques like Dr. Kapusianyk's. Yet, from her limited understanding, there seemed no reason it *shouldn't* work. Human and S'sinn were both DNA-based life-forms, after all, and Dr. Kapusianyk's work involved direct manipulation of DNA. And S'sinn scientists, like human scientists, had long since sequenced and deciphered their race's entire genetic code. Dr. Kapusianyk should be able to access all the information he needed.

If he would agree to do it.

Jarrikk still hadn't arrived, and local time was approaching midnight. Kathryn hoped that meant she had a few hours yet before he came to see her. She composed a letter to Dr. Kapusianyk explaining her idea and quickly fired it off via dimspace transmitter, praying his scientific interest would overcome any reluctance he might have to apply his technique to the hated S'sinn.

She'd barely transmitted her message when the little terminal's screen filled with the image of a young woman. "Sorry to bother you, Translator Bircher, but we've received a message for you. Normally we'd just hold it until morning and send it down to sickbay as hardcopy, but since you're online, would you like it now?"

Kathryn yawned. Her message sent to Earth, she felt as tired as the doctor obviously thought she should have felt all along, although her breathing had eased. "I don't know. Is it urgent?"

"It's not flagged that way, no."

"Where's it from?"

"From on-planet . . ." The young woman glanced down at something. "Translator Jarrikk."

Jarrikk! Kathryn sat up a little. "I'll take it now."

"Sending . . . you've got it."

"Thank you."

"Don't mention it."

The screen cleared; Kathryn pressed RECEIVE.

Five minutes later she pulled the IV out of her arm, threw off the covers, and struggled to her feet while the scanner beside her bed screamed alarms. The room spun; she stumbled against her bedside table, sending her water pitcher and glass crashing to the hard white floor, and clutched at the scanner for support.

"Translator Bircher!" Dr. Chung burst into the room. "What are you doing?"

"He's going to kill himself!" Kathryn shouted. Coughing racked her. "I've got to stop him!" she wheezed out.

"Stop who? You must go back to bed—"

Kathryn threw off the doctor's hands. "No! Don't you understand, he's going to kill himself!"

"Translator Bircher—"

Stifling the cough, ignoring the weakness that threatened to floor her, Kathryn drew herself up and drew a ragged breath. "Doctor Chung, this is a Guild emergency. I'm releasing myself from your care. Bring me my clothes!"

"You're in no condition—"

"Guild emergency, Doctor!"

Dr. Chung glared at her, then turned and strode to the wall beside Kathryn's bed. "Open!" she snapped at the featureless white metal, which split apart to reveal a closet and Kathryn's Translator uniform, neatly pressed. Kathryn pulled off the hospital gown and reached for the uniform. "I must formally protest, Translator," Dr. Chung said, making no move to help. "Your well-being is my responsibility. You are endangering your health, possibly your life, by leaving my care."

"I'm not leaving it." Her uniform seemed to be fighting her; she had to sit down on the bed and blink away purple spots before she could get her legs into it. "I want you to come with me."

"Come with you?" Dr. Chung stared at her, obviously caught off-guard yet again.

"Come with me," Kathryn said, zipping up her uniform and reaching for her boots. "And bring your medical kit."

"Translator, I insist—"

"Please hurry, Doctor Chung!"

The doctor glared an instant longer, then turned and dashed out. Kathryn finished with her boots and clung to the bed for a moment. The still-open terminal showed her the local time: about half an hour to midnight, or as Jarrikk called it, "the turn of the night."

Half an hour to stop Jarrikk's suicide.

"Doctor, we're leaving *now!*" Kathryn shouted, and ran-staggered to the door.

A thin, dank mist shrouded the grassy lanes that threaded through S'sinndikk, collecting in cold droplets on Jarrikk's fur as he trudged toward the dark bulk of the Temple that crouched like some huge sleeping beast by the river. Its ancient architect, ever mindful of tradition, had thoughtfully provided a place, a ground-level platform overhanging the water, for sacrifices such as Jarrikk's.

He moved through deep silence, in solitude, the black-hilted knife carried loosely in his right hand. He felt at peace, at one with the thousands of Flightless Ones who had made this journey before, to turn at the end of their brief lifetimes and face the Pursuer who eventually caught everyone, the Hunter of Worlds, to be devoured by Him, to become part of Him, and therefore of the entire universe.

He could smell the dank green scent of the river now, and hear it gurgling its slow way through the city: and there, dimly visible through the mist, stood the two giant statues of wingless S'sinn that marked the Place of Flightless Sacrifice. Despite the damp cold, Jarrikk's mouth suddenly went dry; he lifted the knife and licked the moisture from its icy blade.

Eighteen steps ascended to the Place of Flightless Sacrifice, eighteen steps much higher and narrower than normal, forcing a painful, struggling climb on a flightless S'sinn, emphasizing his incompleteness and unworthiness. At last, however, muscles aching, he stood on the platform itself, circular, bounded by a railing carved in the shape of sharp, curving thorns, pointing inward. At the center of the platform, a small hole waited to drain his lifeblood into the river.

Jarrikk felt doubly glad he had not taken the knife from the priest on his homeworld when he'd first been injured. He had had many more years of purposeful life, true; but more importantly, this was where such things should be done, not in some sterile, windowless room, but here, in holy Kkirrikk'S'sinn, the most ancient city of his kind, in the place where so many others had made the same sacrifice and preserved the honor of the S'sinn.

He spread his wings as best he could and lifted up his hands in prayer to the Hunter, the knife pointed downward toward his breast, soon to be its final resting place.

Kathryn had commandeered one of *Unity*'s small ground vehicles; she and Dr. Chung raced through the wet night along the slippery grass-covered lanes that were all S'sinndikk had for streets. Who needed good roads when the entire population had wings?

"Where are we going?" Dr. Chung demanded. "You still haven't explained any of this."

"Translator Jarrikk plans to . . . suicide at midnight," Kathryn said. The congestion in her lungs had intensified again since she'd left her bed; she had to stop frequently and gulp air. "I have to stop him."

"Suicide? But why—"

"Because of . . . what happened to us. Because he is no longer a Translator. Because tradition demands it." Kathryn pounded on the controls. "Can't this thing go faster?"

"I'm glad it can't." Dr. Chung clutched at the dashboard for support as the car careened around a corner. "If it's S'sinn tradition, how can you talk him out of it?"

"He's only doing it because he's flightless," Kathryn cried. "And he doesn't have to be! He can regain the use of his wings. Just like Garth—"

"Regeneration therapy? But that's never been tried on non-humans—"

"All the more reason to try it now. If we get the chance—there!" Kathryn braked the scooter to a stop. "Up there, that platform."

"It's already past midnight."

"I know!" Kathryn cried desperately. She flung open the door of the scooter and stumbled out, falling onto the grass. "Jarrikk!" she yelled, her voice echoing back from the stone wall of the Temple, but nobody responded.

Coughing, almost choking, she scrambled on her hands and knees up the tall, steep stairs, her heart pounding in her chest. Terrible waves of weakness crashed over her, turning her limbs to lead, but Dr. Chung, after a moment's hesitation, grabbed her under the arms and helped her climb the final few steps.

There was Jarrikk, standing with wings outspread, arms stretched out above him, hands clutching the hilt of a knife that glittered wickedly even in the dim, mist-diffused light from the city behind them.

She opened her mouth to scream at him, to tell him she was there, to stop him, but before she could utter a sound, his arms jerked down and the knife's glitter vanished as it plunged into his chest.

With a soft, moaning sigh, Jarrikk folded his wings and crumpled gently onto the ancient stones.

Chapter 13

"No!" Kathryn screamed, the sound echoing back from the walls of the Temple. Shaking off Dr. Chung's restraining hand, she clambered up the final awkward steps and dropped to her knees beside Jarrikk, whose eyes were closed and whose hand still gripped the knife buried to the hilt in his chest. A thin but widening trickle of blood flowed down his flank, onto the stone, and dropped soundlessly through the hole in the center of the platform to the slow-moving river below. Feeling as if a second knife had been driven into her own heart, Kathryn reached out and touched Jarrikk's damp fur—and felt the flutter of a heartbeat.

"Kathryn?" Dr. Chung called softly.

"He's not dead!" Kathryn yelled back in a sudden agony of hope. "Doctor Chung, hurry!"

The doctor scrambled to her side. "I don't have any training in S'sinn physiology—"

"Doctor, he's a Translator, he's dying, you've got to do something!" Kathryn reached out to touch the knife, but Chung stopped her.

"No. That could be all that's keeping him from bleeding to death. Leave it until we know what we're doing."

"But—"

"Go back to the car, call for help. I'll do what I can."

Kathryn gulped a breath of much-needed air, said "Thank you," and dashed for the car, adrenalin winning out over weakness—for the moment, at least. The communicator lit up at her touch. "Emergency!" she gasped. "Translator Jarrikk's hurt. We need medical help—someone trained to help S'sinn!" A fit of coughing shook her.

"Understood." The comm operator on the Guild-ship sounded perfectly calm; Kathryn wanted to shake *him*. "Where are you?"

"The Temple—by the river," Kathryn choked out between coughs.

"Activate your homing signal. It's the switch just in—right, got it. Help's on the way. Guildship *Unity* out."

Kathryn fought down the coughing, took a few deep wheezing breaths, then crawled back out of the car. She started toward the platform, but froze as something huge and black swept low over her head, landed in front of her, and shrouded itself in leathery wings. Memories of her parents' deaths made her cringe back; then she straightened, angry at herself. "Who are you? What do you want?" she demanded in Guildtalk.

The S'sinn's eyes narrowed: it said something in its own harsh language. It wore a gold collar embossed with an intricate design, and the jeweled hilt of a dagger protruded from its leather belt. When Kathryn started forward again, it snapped open its wings and growled something indecipherable but unquestionably hostile. Kathryn stopped. "My friend's hurt! You've got to—"

The S'sinn's left arm swept down across its body to its belt and came back up holding the dagger. Kathryn's breath caught in her throat. She couldn't talk to the alien, couldn't even feel it empathically. Had they broken some religious taboo by coming here?

If they had, and this guardian or whatever it was felt so strongly about keeping Kathryn from approaching the platform, what would it do when it realized Dr. Chung was already on it, helping Jarrikk?

Kathryn hoped help wasn't far away.

The communicator in the car beeped. The S'sinn didn't move, but its eyes, glowing faintly red in the light from the car's interior, tracked Kathryn as she backed up to the vehicle, reached into it, and touched the controls. "Guildship *Unity*," said the voice of the comm operator. "Translator Bircher, are you there?"

"Bircher here," Kathryn said. "I hope you have good news."

"There's a fully equipped human medical team en route from the *Unity*—but we've had a problem getting help from the S'sinn."

"A problem? What kind of problem? There's a Translator dying out here!"

"Maybe they didn't understand Guildtalk very well, I don't know but . . ." The comm operator hesitated. "They refused to come. Translator, they said Jarrikk has been dead for years."

"I'm sure that's exactly what they said," Kathryn said bitterly. "And I've got my own little problem here. There's some kind of warrior-priest standing between me and Jarrikk, and she doesn't look friendly. Warn the medical team, and then forget trying to get a S'sinn doctor here—get that S'sinn Translator who's taken over the treaty negotiations. I don't think this whatever-she-is is going to let us anywhere near Jarrikk."

"Yes, Translator."

As Kathryn eased back out of the car, another S'sinn swept overhead so close the wind from its passage ruffled her hair. A third followed close behind. They wore dagger-belts and gold collars like the first, and looked no friendlier. Six red eyes watched Kathryn as she straightened up and faced them. "That's right," she said softly. "You just keep watching me. I'm the one you're interested in."

A short eternity passed, or maybe just a century or two, then lights swept over the scene as the medical van from the *Unity* pulled up. Without looking away from the S'sinn, Kathryn raised her hand in warning, and the personnel in the van took the hint and stayed put, though they kept their lights on, which suited Kathryn. The S'sinn were slightly—very slightly—less intimidating when she could see all of them and not just those glowing red eyes.

The standoff, long though it seemed, ended far too soon: Dr. Chung appeared on the platform, her face a pale blotch against the black sky behind the S'sinn, and called, "Kathryn!"

The S'sinn whirled as one: then two of them launched themselves at the platform, the blast of air from their wings driving Kathryn back against the cold, dew-misted metal of the car. "Doctor Chung, get down!" she screamed, as the third S'sinn, the one that had landed first, turned on her, dagger flashing in the headlights of the medical van.

Kathryn heard the van's doors open, heard the medical team rushing toward her, but she knew they couldn't reach her before the S'sinn did, and she crossed her arms over her face as the S'sinn lunged forward—

—and stopped, wings spread, dagger scant centimeters from Kathryn's throat, as an angry screech split the sky like fingernails dragged across metal amplified a thousandfold. The S'sinn's head jerked back and she stared up as two more S'sinn passed overhead, then she spun to face them, her right wing slapping into Kathryn's side, knocking her half-breathless to the ground. She scrambled up, helped by a frightened-looking young man from the medical van, then shoved him aside and dodged around the priest to see the new arrivals.

One S'sinn wore the collar of a Translator, the other—she almost sobbed with relief—a collar bearing the green circle of a Commonwealth medic. Behind them, she saw the two S'sinn who had flown at Dr. Chung returning to the ground, and on top of the platform, Chung reappeared. "Kathryn! What's happening?"

"I'm not sure. How's Jarrikk?"

"Alive. Stable, I think. But I can't be sure. I don't know enough—"

The S'sinn wearing the medic's collar slipped past Kathryn's attacker, who gave him one smoldering glance before returning to her argument with the Translator. "The injured one is on the platform?" the medic asked Kathryn in passable Guildtalk.

"Yes," she replied. "A human doctor is with him."

The doctor launched himself toward the platform, ignoring the outraged shrieks of the two S'sinn he flew over to get there. Kathryn saw Dr. Chung raise her arms reflexively, then relax when she saw the medical insignia—and plunge at once into animated conversation. The two medics bent over Jarrikk, disappearing from sight.

Kathryn turned her attention back to the argument between the Translator and the S'sinn who had attacked her, which seemed to be reaching a climax. Her attacker growled something, snapped an angry gesture at her underlings, whirled and gave Kathryn one more hate-filled glare, then disappeared in a blast of musk-scented air.

The S'sinn Translator approached Kathryn. "Greetings, Translator Bircher," he said. "I am Translator Ukkaddikk. I came at once when I received word, and fortunately the medic who accompanied me was nearby. We are old friends—as are Jarrikk and I." He spoke Guildtalk far more fluidly than even Jarrikk.

"You know Jarrikk?" Kathryn said, then felt foolish. Of course the S'sinn Translators would know each other, just like all the human Translators knew each other.

But Ukkaddikk didn't seem to find her question odd. "Search those memories you retain from your Link with Jarrikk. I think you will find me there."

Most shared memories faded quickly after the Link ended, but some of the strongest lingered. Kathryn closed her eyes, called up those images that had flashed through her mind when she and Jarrikk first

Linked—and her eyes flew open again. "Of course, Ukkaddikk! You brought Jarrikk into the Guild."

"I stopped him then from taking the Dagger of the Hunter. I hoped he had learned that in this new age there are new possibilities. But he has always had a thick skull."

Kathryn smiled ruefully. "I know," she said. "But so do I. We are . . ." She stopped. "We *were* a good team."

"Perhaps you will be again. Let us see what the medic has to say."

What the medic had to say was grim. Jarrikk had plunged the dagger into one of his two hearts. The other still beat, raggedly, keeping him alive, but blood loss and shock threatened to drive it into fibrillation at any moment, and it alone could not provide the necessary blood flow to his brain. If they did not get him connected to artificial life support within a matter of minutes, he would suffer irreparable brain damage. Yet moving him could kill him.

"We have no choice," Ukkaddikk said, and Kathryn agreed. "We must move him." He turned to Kathryn. "Have your personal empathic powers returned?"

"No."

"No? But I sense . . ." So quickly Kathryn flinched, he reached out one hand and touched her left temple. He closed his eyes and cocked his head to one side momentarily—and suddenly Kathryn could sense him, warm and concerned, and the cool professionalism of the Commonwealth medics, and Dr. Chung's slightly flustered excitement, and the welter of emotions from the humans gathered by the medical van, and she gasped, feeling as if she'd been encased in a thick, deadening gel that had suddenly been flushed away.

"Thank you," she breathed. "I was afraid it was gone forever!"

"Now you can help."

"How?"

"Hold Jarrikk's head. Will him to live."

"But I'm—" *not a projective empath,* she wanted

to say, but Ukkaddikk had already leaped from the platform, gliding down to the ambulance to prepare them to receive Jarrikk.

Kathryn crawled across the rain- and blood-slicked stones and lifted Jarrikk's head. It felt light, fragile, and frighteningly cold, and the fur behind his wolf-like ears was sticky with blood from a cut he must have suffered when he fell. Kathryn closed her eyes and tried to sense the tiny spark of life still flickering inside her friend, deep within, past the layers of darkness and pain. Somewhere . . .

There. She could feel him, faint, oh-so-faint, like a candle at the bottom of a mineshaft guttering in an icy downdraft. She concentrated, pushed harder. She no longer felt the cold night air, no longer felt the stones of the platform bruising her knees, no longer felt anything but that faint presence, that last flicker of life. She folded her mind around it, cupped it, tried to shield it from the deadly wind howling through his damaged body.

Far away, like a distant shout, she felt messages from her own body, that both she and Jarrikk were being lifted, carried, that her hands still cradled his head. But she shut that out of her mind, concentrating on Jarrikk, on keeping him alive.

She drew closer and closer to the heart of his dim presence, and as she did so she began to feel new sensations—the messages of his body: no agony, only a terrifying numbness radiating from the wound in his chest, and the frantic, uneven spasming of his remaining heart. She turned to that sensation fiercely, trying to strengthen the beats, to smooth the rhythm—and slowly, slowly, she felt it working, felt his body respond, felt the frightening cold gripping him lessen somewhat. The flicker of life strengthened, steadied: and then, just for a moment, she felt Jarrikk's consciousness, dazed, lost, wondering, but definitely there. She sent him a wave of reassurance—then, suddenly, it all vanished, darkness crashing down on her.

She screamed, certain Jarrikk had died. Her eyes

snapped open and she tried to jump up. Something stopped her, and she struggled against it for a moment before realizing Dr. Chung stood over her, gentle hands restraining her. "It's all right," Dr. Chung said soothingly. "It's all right. They've taken Jarrikk into surgery. He's on life support."

"He's alive?" Kathryn gasped. Her own heartbeat felt none too steady at that moment.

"He's alive."

Kathryn looked around. She sat on the edge of her old bed in *Unity*'s sickbay. "How did I get here?" she asked, amazed.

"Once you took hold of Jarrikk's head, you slipped into a kind of trance—you were practically catatonic. I wanted to try to bring you out of it, but Ukkaddikk touched both of you and said to leave you. We brought the two of you back here in the medvan, and just pulled your hands free of Jarrikk as the S'sinn medic took him into surgery."

Kathryn looked at her hands. Jarrikk's blood had stained them with dark brown patches that flaked off as she clenched her fists, dusting the blue cloth of her Translator's uniform with rusty brown. "I don't even know what happened. I've never made a connection like that before . . . not even with the symbiote."

"Ukkaddikk was certainly excited about it. He wants to talk to you as soon as you're able."

"No," Kathryn said instantly. "Not until we know about Jarrikk."

"I'm glad you feel that way, because . . ." Dr. Chung held up the medical gown Kathryn had flung off earlier. ". . . as your doctor, I'm ordering you back to bed—the perfect place for you to wait."

Kathryn started to protest, then thought better of it as the protest turned into a cough. When she'd mastered it, she said meekly, "You're the doctor, Doctor."

"I am indeed," Dr. Chung said briskly. "First, let's get you cleaned up . . ."

Kathryn waited until she'd washed and changed and Dr. Chung had taken her temperature and reconnected the monitors and pumped her arm full of drugs before asking the question foremost on her mind. "Doctor Chung, all of this effort tonight was pointless if we can't get regeneration therapy for Jarrikk. He'll just try to kill himself again."

"I'm aware of that. I've sent my own recommendation to Doctor Kapusianyk as a follow-up to your message to him. I don't expect a problem. In fact, I wager they'll jump at the chance to try regeneration therapy on a non-human. Now get some sleep." Dr. Chung went out, dimming the lights on her way.

Sleep? Kathryn thought. How could she sleep when not a dozen meters away the medics fought to save Jarrikk's life? She closed her eyes, trying to remember her own part in that fight. What exactly had she done? It had been almost like Linking with the symbiote's help—almost, but different. Deeper. Had Jarrikk been conscious, she felt she might almost have been able to understand his thoughts, not just feel his feelings. But that shouldn't be possible without Link, and symbiote, and Programming.

Ukkaddikk had seemed to know something about it. She'd have to ask him.

Tomorrow. When Jarrikk was out of danger.

Her eyes still closed, she tried to reach out to him on the operating table . . . but all she accomplished was putting herself to sleep.

Kitillikk commiserated with the priest who brought her the news. Yes, it was a terrible thing when a Flightless One was prevented from dying an honorable death. Yes, she was appalled that the Commonwealth could interfere even in the worship of the Hunter of Worlds. No doubt He would rise up and take vengeance. "No doubt at all," Kitillikk said as the priest took flight. She watched the Hunter's servant soar into the graying sky of morning, then dive toward the black bulk of the Temple, where no doubt the discussion of the night's events would rage for days.

That was the trouble with priests, and why she'd

never been able to make much use of them, Kitillikk
reflected as she stepped back through the arched windows into her quarters in a minor tower of the Hall
of the Flock. They talked and talked and talked some
more; they rarely acted. And when they did, they were
quite unpredictable. One could never tell how they
would interpret the Hunter's will.

She preferred to rely on her own will. Her goals
required no interpretation, and she couldn't see how
Jarrikk's continued survival would affect them, much
though she would have enjoyed killing him herself that
day in the Hall when peace had suddenly broken out,
against all odds. With the odd symbiote technology of
the Guild precluding any electronic recordings of exactly what had been said on that dais, she couldn't
prove it, but she was convinced the Translators had
somehow cheated, no doubt with the connivance of
their spineless, limp-winged excuse for a Supreme
Flight Leader.

No matter. There would soon be a new Supreme
Flight Leader, and war between Earth and S'sinn, an
end to the meddling of the Commonwealth and their
thrice-cursed Guild of Translators, and well-deserved
glory for the S'sinn—and herself. She grinned a savage
grin and swept aside the beaded curtain that had hidden her other guest from the priest. He came out
warily, and she grimaced as she caught a whiff of his
scent. She'd have to sleep elsewhere; no doubt her
sleeping chamber now reeked of him.

"So, human," she said in Guildtalk, though the
Commonwealth's pidgin always left a bad taste in her
mouth. "You heard?"

"I do not understand your tongue."

Of course not. "Translator Jarrikk still lives. Your
Translator Bircher saved him after he attempted to
give himself to the Hunter—though I do not think he
will thank her for it."

The human's eyes narrowed and his mouth grew
tight. "I am sorry Jarrikk did not die."

"So am I. But there is time enough for that. We

have a more important matter to discuss." She settled herself on a shikk, fully aware he could not sit comfortably on anything in the room, and showed her teeth again. "A human and S'sinn working together have temporarily staved off this war. Ironic that a human and S'sinn will now work together to ensure that it comes about as originally intended."

"For the destruction of the Commonwealth, I would work with the devil himself."

"Appropriate, since I understand your human devil is supposed to look a lot like a S'sinn." Kitillikk picked up a scarlet-hilted dagger from the table by the shikk and toyed with it idly, admiring the watery play of light on its silver blade. "Have you chosen your method?"

"Method, and time, and place." The human showed his broad, flat teeth. "None of which I will tell you, of course."

"Of course. Mutual distrust can only carry a relationship so far." She held up the dagger and squinted down its length at the human's hideous hairless face. "But you realize your secrecy means I won't be able to help you escape."

"I can look after myself." More teeth. "I could kill you, now, after all, and no one would be the wiser."

"Could you?" Kitillikk purred. A flick of her wrist, and the knife in her hand suddenly sprouted in the bloodwood floor a centimeter from the human's booted foot. The human didn't even flinch. "I am no coddled palace quisling, human. I am a S'sinn Hunter, and Flight Leader. You would do well to respect me."

The human bowed slightly. "Oh, I do, Flight Leader, I do. As I respect those who guard the Supreme Flight Leader. But you must also give me *my* due. Akkanndikk will still die, and I will escape—and there will be no doubt in anyone's mind that a human assassinated her. Kathryn Bircher is no longer a Translator. Nor is Jarrikk, even if he still lives. The peace plan they have Translated will vanish like a dream, like smoke in a hurricane. War will come . . ."

"And I will lead the Hunters as Supreme Flight Leader!" Kitillikk breathed, wanting to shout it but not quite daring to: not yet.

"I must go." The human went to the arch that led into the corridor where Ukkarr stood watch. "I will not see you again. But the deed will be done soon; I promise you that." He pulled the hood of his black cloak over his black-furred head, and slipped out.

Kitillikk waited, held it in as long as she could, then laughed, a roaring sound of pure triumph that brought Ukkarr dashing into the room, wings spread and weapon drawn. He pulled up short at the sight of her, and holstered his fireblade with a bemused look.

"A human, Ukkarr," Kitillikk said. "A human is going to help make me Supreme Flight Leader!"

"I . . . don't see the humor, Flight Leader."

"Me, Ukkarr! The fools actually want this war, and they want me leading the Hunters against them. And I—I will wipe them from this galaxy as though they never existed, starting with their Translators, starting with Translator Jim Ornawka, who is going to assassinate the Supreme Flight Leader and hasten my ascension! It is a joke of cosmic proportions, Ukkarr!"

Ukkarr smiled, but barely, and that sent Kitillikk off again into fresh paroxysms of merriment.

Poor old Ukkarr, she thought. *He never did have a sense of humor.*

Chapter 14

The cold, the damp, the acidlike, icy burning of the knife plunging into his chest, the impact of his body on the old stones, and then the growing numbness . . . these things Jarrikk remembered, and that was wrong.

It was wrong, because he shouldn't be remembering anything at all.

He felt the padded slats of a shikk beneath him where there should only have been cold, wet, stone, and when he opened his eyes—*he opened his eyes!*—he saw a white metal ceiling where there should have been only black sky.

The S'sinn built nothing out of metal but their spaceships.

Where was he?

Why was he alive?

Slowly he turned his head, fighting stiffness and a grating, throbbing pain. A small metal room. To his right, a door. To his left . . . medical monitors. Not S'sinn technology—Commonwealth.

A ship. He was on board a Commonwealth ship . . . the *Dikari?* No, the *Dikari* was long gone . . . the *Unity*. It had to be the *Unity*.

Who had brought him here? Why hadn't they let him die?

Anger woke, matching its heat to the warm throb of pain in his chest, which matched the beat of his hearts. *Karak.* After all he had said about letting Jarrikk choose his own path, he had ordered the Guild to step in, ordered them not to let Jarrikk die. Politics or propaganda. He wanted Jarrikk as a figurehead, a hero to inspire other Translators, or promote the new Earth–S'sinndikk treaty . . . whatever. It didn't matter. Two levels to everything, Karak had said, the ideal and the pragmatic, and Ithkar's Great Swimmer forbid the Guild should choose the higher path when there was so much to be gained on the lower. The Great Swimmer forbid the Guild should let honor interfere with politics.

Jarrikk wouldn't let it happen. He didn't belong to Karak, and he no longer belonged to the Guild: he belonged to the Hunter of Souls, and he intended to join Him.

He pulled at the constraints, but they held firm. Frustrated, he subsided and glared at the white ceiling. Sooner or later they would have to release him. Sooner or later, he would give himself to the Hunter, and complete his sacrifice.

And the Hunter did not stipulate *how* a Flightless One should die . . .

He would wait.

Six days after the night by the Temple, Kathryn, still recuperating in sickbay, woke to the good news that Jarrikk was awake—and the bad news that all he did was stare at the ceiling. He wouldn't speak to Dr. Chung, to a nurse, or even to Ukkaddikk, who brought Kathryn the word as she ate breakfast.

"Has Doctor Chung had a reply to her request for the regeneration treatment?" Kathryn gulped the fresh-squeezed orange juice that had accompanied her French toast and sausage. God bless human-crewed ships.

"Yes," Ukkaddikk said. "Doctor Kapusianyk is eager for the opportunity, and Commonwealth Central is anxious to see the experiment proceed, as well, feeling it offers great hope for S'sinn and may help smooth acceptance and implementation of the new peace agreement. The Guild has approved the use of the

Unity to ferry you and Jarrikk to Earth in five days' time—"

"Five days?" Kathryn stopped a forkful of sausage halfway to her mouth. "Why not at once?"

"Doctor Chung feels it best to remain here, where there are S'sinn medical experts, until Jarrikk is further along the flight to recovery," Ukkaddikk responded. "But this slight delay should not be your main concern. Doctor Kapusianyk, Commonwealth Central, and Karak are all adamant that this procedure can only take place with the full and informed consent of Jarrikk."

"Didn't Doctor Chung tell him that he could be healed—that he could fly again?"

"I asked her not to."

Kathryn stared at him. "What? Why?"

"I believe that you, and only you, should tell Jarrikk. You are the one closest to him."

"We've only known each other for a few days . . ."

"But you Translated together. More than that, you sacrificed your Translation ability together. And more than that, there is what you did for Jarrikk between the Temple and here."

"I don't *know* what I did."

"Nor do I," Ukkaddikk said. "Nor does anyone else in the Guild I have talked to. Somehow you achieved a bond, similar to the Translation Link, without symbiote or Programming. Such things have been known within races—the Swampworlders, for one, are said to join minds, and of course the Aza Swarms are group minds. But such a natural linkage between two races has never been observed before, even between powerful empaths. We must know more about how it happened . . ."

". . . so the Guild can figure out how to use it," Kathryn finished, and surprised herself with the bitterness she felt, knowing that Ukkaddikk would feel it, too.

"You and Jarrikk serve the Guild," Ukkaddikk

said. "Surely you will be happy if this phenomenon proves useful to the Guild."

Kathryn said nothing. She wanted time to work through exactly *what* she felt about the Guild. Something, unexpectedly, had changed.

Ukkaddikk, being a good empath, didn't press the debate. "In any event," he said, "this unique link between you and Jarrikk may help you convince him to take part in the experiment."

There was no question about Kathryn's support of *that*. "I'll try." She pushed aside her breakfast tray. "Take me to him."

Several hours had passed since Jarrikk woke. He had endured the ministrations of the human nurse who had changed the dressing on his chest, but he had not acknowledged her presence in any way, even when, with something of a shock, he realized he could sense her empathically, that his ability had returned.

He ignored Ukkaddikk just as thoroughly when he entered later. Jarrikk heard and felt Ukkaddikk's concern, but he sensed something else, too, an odd eagerness that made him suspicious. *Ukkaddikk serves the Guild,* he reminded himself. *He stopped me from taking the knife the first time because the Guild needed me. I've been stopped again because the Guild needs me. Ukkaddikk cares nothing for my sacrifice. He cares only for the Guild.*

I served the Guild well. I do not regret it. But I did it by choice, and now I have made a different choice.

He was through letting the Guild use him. He was all used up.

Then came Dr. Chung. He could sense her, too, professionally concerned, but with that same strange eagerness underneath. Suspicion that had budded with Ukkaddikk's appearance blossomed now. He was not being told everything.

But then, as she talked about his wound and how they had treated it, she told him one thing he had not expected—one thing that made his ears roar and the room spin around him.

She told him it had been Kathryn who had saved him—*Kathryn* who had stopped his sacrifice! Karak, Ukkaddikk, the Guild itself, had had nothing to do with it!

And so when Kathryn herself appeared, and he felt that same strong undercurrent of eagerness beneath her open concern and happiness, a bitter anger such as he'd never felt before welled up in him, and if not for the constraints, he would have hurled himself at her.

As it was, he had to be content with keeping his gaze fixed firmly on the ceiling, though with an intensity that should have burned a hole right through it.

The cheerful greeting on Kathryn's lips died as she came into Jarrikk's room and felt a sudden blast of hatred and fury from the furred figure on the shikk. She staggered back against Ukkaddikk, whose strong, clawed hands grabbed her arms and held her upright. She turned to him almost blindly. "Did you feel—"

"Yes. Your task will not be an easy one. I wish you luck." He slightly opened his wings in salute to her, then went out.

Kathryn turned back to Jarrikk. "I . . . I am glad to see you awake," she said uncertainly. "I was afraid I'd brought help too late."

A renewed surge of fury left her gasping. That had obviously been the wrong thing to say. But why . . . ?

Another good thing about human-crewed ships was that they put real chairs in rooms. Kathryn took one near the door and moved it beside the shikk. She couldn't force Jarrikk to meet her eyes, but he couldn't stop her from talking.

If only he would listen . . .

"Jarrikk, I know why you did what you did. I felt it inside you, when we Translated . . . I didn't want to accept it, but I knew it was your way. In your mind, you had no choice, and I respected that."

No change in her sense of his feelings.

"But now you have a choice." Not a flicker of interest. She pressed on. "There is a human doctor, a brilliant man, who has developed a technique for regenerating damaged limbs and organs. It's very new, very experimental—it's only been used on a few humans. But it has worked, almost every time." She paused. "Jarrikk, he thinks it can be used on S'sinn, too."

Still no change. Had he even heard her?

"Jarrikk, don't you understand? Doctor Kapusianyk could heal you—not the wound in your chest, that's healing anyway—but the real hurt. Your wing." She reached out hesitantly, then touched the upturned palm of one of his restrained hands. "Jarrikk, you could fly—unnh!"

With lightning speed, his hand snapped shut. Kathryn snatched her fingers back reflexively, but not before a dagger-sharp claw sliced a three-centimeter gash in the back of her right hand. She clapped her other hand over the wound and, as blood welled between her fingers, stared at Jarrikk, who finally turned his open eyes toward her—and let her feel his fury full-force.

Jarrikk saw Kathryn's blood dripping from her fingers with grim satisfaction heightened by her sense of shock and violated trust. Let her understand what it felt like to be turned on by someone she had counted as a friend—as he had counted her a friend. And now he knew why she had done it—they wanted an experimental animal. They would take away from him the one meaningful act he could still perform as a S'sinn, they would cut him off completely from his people, make him a freak, a scientific subject, nothing more than an exhibit in the Commonwealth's ongoing attempt to prove how benign it was, how it served all races. And when he was still a Translator, he might even have volunteered—but he wasn't being asked to volunteer. He wasn't being asked anything at all. They had stolen his choice from him. A dark, brooding pride that Kitillikk would have recognized instantly swelled up inside him. Who were these furless monstrosities, these murderers of the young and helpless, to choose the fate of S'sinn? He glared at Kathryn with black rage. How could he ever have thought of her as "friend"?

I once swore an oath to Kitillikk to use my life well, he thought. *I should have used it to help her destroy all humans!*

He screamed the Hunter's challenge, struggling uselessly against the restraints that were all that kept him from Kathryn's throat.

Kathryn clapped her bloody hands over her ears as Jarrikk's piercing shriek filled the tiny room, and staggered up and back from the shikk, the chair clattering to the floor. She could feel nothing now but his hatred and rage and wounded pride. *He's gone mad,* she thought. *The shock . . . he's insane!*

He pulled at the straps so hard she feared he'd hurt himself, then harder yet, until she feared even more he might break free. She edged around the wall of the room toward the door, leaving a trail of smeared red handprints, then stopped with her hand on the door controls.

If she left that room, Jarrikk would die, sooner or later, by his own hand. There would be no miracle cure, no hope, and everything she had done to offer him that hope would have been futile.

But he wants to die, she argued with herself. *He wants to die!*

He wanted to die before, she answered. You knew that. Yet you stopped him, to give him this choice.

He's made his choice. Look at him! He's made his choice.

He hasn't even considered it. He may not have even heard you. He's too full of anger and wounded pride to think. What kind of choice is that?

But what can I do? I can't make him think . . . or can I?

She remembered holding his head as he lay in his blood in the Place of Flightless Sacrifice, reaching inside him, touching more than just emotions. Deep under layers of thickening darkness, she had connected with something else, with his self, his mind. Like Translation, Ukkaddikk had said, but it had been something else, something that went even deeper than Translation's joining of knowledge and memory.

If she could re-create that bond now, here, with his waking mind, if she could contact that inner core of his personality beneath layers of rage just as she had beneath layers of pain-filled darkness, maybe she could make him think, make him see that she had done what she did because she cared so deeply about him, because she didn't want to lose him . . .

The thought terrified her. How could she bear his hatred if it were a hundred or a thousand times more intense than she already felt it, when even now her stomach churned with it?

How can you not face it? a sterner part of herself argued. *Actions have consequences. What he feels now is a direct result of what you did. If you abandon responsibility now, you also abandon him. Do that, and his won't be the only inner self you're afraid to face.*

She took a step away from the door, toward the shikk; then another, and another. The shock of the cut on her hand had made her dizzy; she staggered the next two steps and had to cling to the back of the chair until the spinning fuzziness in her eyes and the roaring in her ears went away. Jarrikk screamed again, so loudly she expected nurses and doctors to come running, but the door behind her remained sealed. She probably had Ukkaddikk to thank for that.

Her next step brought her to the shikk itself. She took a firm grasp of one of its solid metal supports with her left hand and stretched out the still-bleeding right toward Jarrikk's forehead.

Jarrikk howled his hunting cry again as Kathryn approached, and tried to turn his head away from her touch, but the restraints wouldn't let him. He could smell her blood, a smell that fed his rage and made his upper lip curl back from his fangs, then he felt her strange, blunt fingers in his fur . . . and then he screamed again as he felt her enter his mind . . .

. . . and this time Kathryn screamed with him, though she didn't know it. The room vanished. She could see nothing but darkness, could feel nothing but hatred and anger surrounding her, pressing in on her, trying to smother her, to force her out again—but she wouldn't give in. She growled deep in her throat, though she didn't know that, either, and pushed with her mind, hard and then harder, pushed in the way she had pushed when she fought herself free of the mind of the Master during her First Translation, only this time in the other direction . . . deeper into Jarrikk's mind.

Emotions, emotions, she could feel nothing but his emotions. What had been darkness when he lay unconscious now took shape all around her, shifting all the time: bursts of flame, swords and spears, smothering darkness, and howling gray fogs. She pushed harder yet, as hard as she thought she could, and then even harder, and all she found was more chaos and rage and . . .

. . . and then, glimmering among the emotions, the beginnings of thoughts. Memories she recognized from Translation flashed past. She fell inward, faster and faster, memories streaming by so quickly she could no longer recognize them, emotions struggling to cling to her, to slow her down, but being stripped away by the speed of her passage, and there, ahead of her, grew a white light . . .

Jarrikk screamed a fourth time, but was no more aware of it than Kathryn. He stared sightlessly at the ceiling, but the images in his mind were not of bare white metal. Instead, it seemed to him he crouched once more on the rim of the chasm marking the border between the human sector and the S'sinn sector of Kikks'sarr, that once more he watched the humans launch one of their horrible little flying machines, only this time, instead of flying out to it, he started pelting it with everything that came to hand, rocks and knives, torches and twigs, but nothing stopped it, it just came closer and closer until he could see the pilot, could see her familiar, once-loved, now-hated face, could see a strange white light in her eyes . . .

. . . and then that white light swallowed . . .

. . . white light swallowed . . .

. . . him . . .

. . . her . . .

. . . whole.

Disembodied voices in the white void. They needed no images to recognize each other.

Why have you come here? I don't want you here.

You must listen to me. You must think about what I say. You must make a choice.

I made my choice. You took it away from me.

That choice is still yours. I have given you another option.

You want me for the Guild. You want me for the Commonwealth. But I have chosen. I will be S'sinn!

I don't care about the Guild, or the Commonwealth. I care about you.

You defiled my Sacrifice. You made a mockery of my gift to the Hunter. This is how you care for me?

I am human. I did not understand your Sacrifice.

You understand now. Leave me. Let me complete my gift to the Hunter.

I do not understand. Does the Hunter desire death?

Death serves the Hunter. All things serve the Hunter.

Then life also serves the Hunter.

Useful life. I gave my usefulness to the Guild.

Did that not serve the Hunter?

All things serve the Hunter.

Then live.

I have lived too long already. I am flightless! Humans made me so!

Then let humans change that. Fly again. Serve the Hunter again. Surely He prefers living servants to dead sacrifices.

I have made my decision.

But now you have new information. Make your decision again.

I HAVE MADE MY DECISION!

S'sinn pride. Does pride serve the Hunter?

All things serve the Hunter.

But what do you have to be proud about? You are flightless.

I served as a Translator. Now I would make my Sacrifice!

Still not much to be proud about. Service as a Translator for a handful of years, then death.

It is all I can offer.

It is not. Be the first Flightless One to regain flight. Find pride in blazing a trail for the others who have only been able to serve the Hunter by their deaths. Dedicate your new life to the service of the Hunter. Let those who follow dedicate theirs. Surely the gift of many new living servants is a greater gift to the Hunter than your death?

You twist my thoughts! You come into my mind and twist my thoughts!

Do I? Then come into mine . . .

Rushing. A storm of emotions, memories, thoughts, a whirlwind of sensory information, the thunder of a living mind.

The light changes, takes on a bluish tinge.

See it all . . .

You . . . do care. You . . . did not do this for the Commonwealth, or the Guild. You . . . did it for me.

Yes. Yes!

I . . . must . . . think . . .

Think. Choose wisely . . . but the choice is still yours. It always has been.
I . . .

Darkness.
Light.
Kathryn opened her eyes and looked at Jarrikk, unconscious on the shikk, his forehead slick with the blood from her hand. She pulled it away. Her fingers trembled.

"Ukkaddikk . . ." she whispered, turning toward the door . . . and then her knees buckled.

Darkness.

Chapter 15

Kitillikk stood looking out over Kkirrik'S'sinn as the sun westered toward night. Days had passed since Ornawka had fouled her quarters with his presence, promising to strike soon against the Supreme Flight Leader. Days had passed, and nothing had happened. Time, place, and method—he'd said all three were chosen. "Twenty years hence, in her sleeping pit, of old age," Kitillikk snarled out loud. What if his whole approach had been part of some Commonwealth scheme to uncover her plotting . . . ?

But no. Her sources on Commonwealth Central had assured her that Jim Ornawka was as committed to his humans-first philosophy as she was to the honor of the S'sinn. She smiled, showing teeth, as she thought of her "sources." They were far more than that, as the Commonwealth would discover when the time came to act, but they were also absolutely reliable, and she believed them without question. No, Ornawka was no spy; no doubt he was just being cautious.

Besides, had he been a Commonwealth spy, she would already have been arrested. They would never have left her free to act as she had been acting since her arrival on S'sinndikk, meeting quietly with the powerful S'sinn of the Supreme Flight, sounding out which would back her claim when Akkanndikk fell, making promises, making bribes, doing whatever she had to to win support.

She supposed in some ways she should be grateful that Ornawka delayed his strike: it had given her time to firm up some of that support. As she would be doing tonight.

As if cued by her thoughts, Ukkarr appeared in the arch behind her. "Ikkilliss of the Supreme Flight is here to see you, Flight Leader."

"How very punctual of him." She'd told him to come at sunset, and the sun had just touched the horizon. "Just this side of eager."

"I confess I am surprised he is here at all, Flight Leader. In the Supreme Flight no one has been more constant or vocal in support of Akkanndikk than Ikkilliss."

"There are ways and ways, Ukkarr. Please show him in to me. Then you will leave. Enjoy a night free from your duties."

Ukkarr hesitated. "Flight Leader, is that wise? You have not won Ikkilliss to your side yet. If he should accuse you of plotting against the Supreme Flight Leader . . . he could have you arrested."

"He will not have me arrested," Kitillikk growled. "He is not even here to discuss politics. Or at least that's what he thinks."

Ukkarr blinked at her. "Flight Leader?"

"Show him in, Ukkarr! Then leave! At once!" Kitillikk put wing-snap in her voice, and Ukkarr jerked to attention, then turned in a swirl of leather and hurried back into the apartment.

Kitillikk looked back out over the city, calming herself. Ukkarr was invaluable as aide, bodyguard, military leader, and occasional enthusiastic lover, but he could also be annoyingly naive about some things. She doubted he would approve of her method of winning some of the male members of the Supreme Flight to her side, but as far as she was concerned, sex was just one more tool to use to build her future success. She would rule the S'sinn, and she would put up with the fumbling fingers and trembling wings and tiresome moaning and gasping of the oldest and most decrepit of the Supreme Flight if it meant they would vote for her when the succession became a question. She grinned. Ukkarr would be even more shocked if he knew that sometimes she hadn't even had to fake her enjoyment of these political liaisons.

Ikkilliss, for example, was a magnificent Hunter in the prime of his life . . . and a great believer in the new philosophy that it was the duty of leaders of the S'sinn to disperse their genetic material as widely as possible, improving the breed. Kitillikk rather thought that "new philosophy" was nothing more than a modern excuse for ancient vices, but it had made it easy for her to convince Ikkilliss to come tonight.

"Flight Leader Kitillikk?" His voice was as smooth and powerful as the rest of him, and Kitillikk grinned another grin of pure, savage glee before smoothing her face and turning to graciously greet her prospective ally.

This was one politician whose support she eagerly looked forward to firming up.

After all, nobody said politics couldn't be fun.

Kathryn came out of her faint to find herself sitting in the chair beside Jarrikk's shikk, Ukkaddikk and Dr. Chung both bending over her, Chung's fingers busy bandaging her hand. She blinked at them. "Hello," she ventured. "How's Jarrikk?"

"I'm surprised you care," Chung snapped. "He did this, didn't he? Is this the thanks you get for risking your life to save him?"

"How are *you,* Translator Bircher?" asked Ukkaddikk. Kathryn sensed his question went deeper than her physical state.

"It happened," she replied. Chung glanced at her sharply, but kept working.

Ukkaddikk drew in a quick breath. "As before?"

"Different. He was conscious." She looked straight into Ukkaddikk's eyes. "We exchanged thoughts."

"Translation?"

"Different. Stronger, but more focused. We carried on a conversation, first in his mind, then in mine."

She felt his sudden excitement. "Incredible!"

"Yes." It had been. Even better than the Translation union she'd thought she'd never feel again. She glanced at Jarrikk, and was surprised to see him staring at her. Ukkaddikk followed her gaze, and leaped to Jarrikk's side. Jarrikk replied to his questions in short growls, but he did reply. And Kathryn no longer felt the same hatred and hostility from him. Now she sensed . . . confusion . . . uncertainty . . . and maybe, just maybe, a little . . . hope? She reached out her free hand to him and touched his shoulder, closing her eyes to try to read him better, and suddenly, with no warning at all, she was back in the white void with him.

Impossi . . .

. . . ssible . . .

Telepathy!

Telepathy!

Kathryn's eyes flew open. The white void vanished, but Jarrikk was still there inside her mind. Chung stared at her, and dimly Kathryn realized she'd clenched her wounded right hand into a fist, but even its throbbing didn't break the connection. She met Jarrikk's wide, startled eyes.

"Incredible!" Ukkaddikk said. "I sense . . . I sense something . . . like a Translation bond, but . . ."

He reached out, touched Jarrikk, and Kathryn gasped and stiffened as suddenly there were three of them in the Link. She could read Ukkaddikk's emotional state stronger than ever before, but more than that, she knew exactly what he was thinking, could trace the pattern of his thoughts as he searched through memories of the studies he had made into mind-to-mind contact, could even retrieve those memories, she felt sure, if she tried hard enough . . .

. . . no, if *they* tried hard enough . . . she couldn't direct it. The power, this amazing power, came from the bond between herself and Jarrikk. They could only wield it together . . . and Ukkaddikk?

Ukkaddikk? she tried. No reply. No indication in his thoughts that he was aware of her—of them—at all.

He cannot hear us. Jarrikk's "voice." **We are reading his mind and he is unaware.**

Then he's not part of the Link?

No. The power comes from us, from our minds combined . . . maybe from changes that occurred when our symbiotes died. It is ours alone, Kathryn. Together, we are greater than one of us could ever be. We are something new.

But what are we?

Telepath. Not empath. *Telepath.*

Telepathy between races is a myth . . .

Not anymore. Not anymore!

You're fading.

So are you.

Tired . . .

. . . so tired . . .

"Unh." Kathryn slumped in the chair, the room spinning around her and a buzzing in her ears. Chung took her pulse, lifted her eyelid. "I'm . . . all right, Doctor," Kathryn said irritably. But she wasn't. She felt nauseous, and tired . . . and scared.

She looked at Jarrikk again. His eyes were closed and his bandaged chest rose and fell in great gasps. Ukkaddikk pulled back from him, frowning, and turned to her. "What happened? You must tell me."

"Not now," Dr. Chung snapped. "She's still my patient, and she's going back to bed." Ukkaddikk growled at her, but she ignored him, reaching up to the intercom above the shikk. "Nurse Altman, this is Doctor Chung. Please bring a wheelchair to Jarrikk's room."

"Kathryn?" Ukkaddikk pleaded. But for once Kathryn was happy to let Dr. Chung cart her off to bed. She closed her eyes and kept them that way until the wheelchair arrived, then climbed gratefully into it . . .

and all the time, she could feel a faint tendril of Jarrikk's presence in the back of her mind.

Before she talked to Ukkaddikk—before either she or Jarrikk let the Guild find out about what they had achieved—they had a lot of talking and thinking to do.

Of course, now maybe that amounted to the same thing.

Oh. There was one thing, though. "Doctor," she said over her shoulder as the burly and bearded Nurse Altman pushed her toward the door, "you can take the restraints off Jarrikk."

"Are you sure? We still can't be certain what his state of mind is . . ."

"I can. Release him." She stopped and had Altman turn her around. "Please, Doctor."

Chung looked at her, then at Ukkaddikk, who hesitated, then said, "Do it."

"Very well. I hope you're right."

I am, Kathryn thought, but didn't say it. *Jarrikk knows he has other options now. He promised me he would consider them.* She smiled a small, slightly dazed smile. "And I'd know if he were lying," she murmured.

"Translator?" Nurse Altman said.

"Nothing, nurse." She leaned back in the chair and closed her eyes. "Please take me back to bed."

"Translation bonding without the symbiote?" Karak floated in his quarters, staring at Ukkaddikk's image. A school of silverfins gathered curiously in front of the screen; he flicked a manipulator at them irritably and they darted away. "Are you certain?"

"As certain as I can be without having experienced it myself. Translator Bircher described it as being even deeper than the Translation bond, in fact."

"This must be studied! The *Unity* must bring them back to Commonwealth Central at once!"

"It's not that simple, Guildmaster. Officially, Jarrikk has not rescinded his decision to take the knife. And politically, the Guild's position here might be strengthened more if he chooses to return to the Place of Flightless Sacrifice than if he chooses to live and leave the planet. The priests have been stirring up public sentiment against us for defiling a sacrifice to the Hunter of Worlds."

"I know all that," Karak said impatiently. "And under other circumstances, I would reprimand Translator Bircher severely for interfering, however much I might secretly applaud her. But this changes everything. If we can eliminate the symbiote from Translation, we could revolutionize the process. No more need for electromagnetic shielding, no more time limits on Translation . . ."

"I'm not so sure of that. They seemed exhausted when they finished, and they were only linked for seconds."

"That's why we need more study. Jarrikk cannot be allowed the luxury of choosing for himself whether or not to take the knife, Ukkaddikk. He must return to Commonwealth Central. As Guildmaster, I order it."

Ukkaddikk replied only after a longish pause. "I'm not sure ordering Jarrikk is the best way to gain his cooperation at this point in time, Guildmaster."

"Explain."

"I sense . . . doubts. In his hearts and Translator Bircher's. They seem to feel they have been manipulated by the Guild—manipulated to come together here and do what they did. I think, to a certain extent, they both feel betrayed."

"Nonsense," Karak said, but he said it uncomfortably. The Guild Council had known exactly what it was doing. He and Akkanndikk had both known exactly what they were doing. They *had* manipulated the two young Translators, played on their loyalty to the Guild to obtain the necessary results. But surely that same loyalty would help them understand . . .

"Perhaps," Ukkaddikk said. "But that is the way they feel. And Kathryn, I think, feels that the Guild was too willing to let Jarrikk die after he was no longer of any use as a Translator. You know how humans are always so quick to judge the actions of other races by their own moral standards."

In this case, a standard Karak shared. But he had a duty to seek what was best for the Guild and the Commonwealth, not for specific individuals. And that duty still drove him. "However they feel, they must return to Commonwealth Central," he said slowly. "But perhaps we can convince them of the necessity without putting it in terms of an order. Tell them that there are still strong factions on both Earth and S'sinndikk clamoring for repudiation of the treaty, that the Guild fears for their safety and the safety of the humans with them on the *Unity,* and that the *Unity* has therefore been ordered to return to Commonwealth Central and I hope they will come with it. Leave them the appearance, at least, of having a choice—but, Ukkaddikk, I am counting on you to insure that the 'choice' they make is the correct one."

"There is also the matter of the experimental regeneration technique the humans are anxious to try on Jarrikk, Guildmaster. If he is to make the right choice, that procedure must still be carried out."

"It will be, it will be," Karak said irritably. "But this new linkage takes precedence. I'll look into having this human doctor transfer his equipment to Commonwealth Central—I'm sure the Commonwealth medical college will want to observe the procedure in any event. None of that need concern you. Just get the pair of them off that planet as soon as you can and safely on their way here."

"Yes, Guildmaster Karak. Ukkaddikk out."

Karak waved a manipulator to kill the transmitter, then snagged one of the curious silverfins, bit it in two, and gulped down the head. There was a lot of truth in what he had just told Ukkaddikk, he reflected. The Humanity First party on Earth and the faction led by Kitillikk on S'sinndikk *were* still fighting to have the agreement overthrown. Akkanndikk seemed confident she could manage the situation on S'sinndikk and the Earth government seemed equally confident, but Karak did not share their confidence.

All it would take at this point is one small rupture in the wall we have built against the current for war, he thought. *One tiny crack, and we'll all be swept into the ocean depths.*

All he could really do was pray to the Great Swimmer that the wall held firm.

He let the tail of the silverfin settle to the floor for the scuttlers to eat, and swam back to his sleeping cave.

With a hundred thousand others, Kitillikk roosted near the Temple. Unlike most of those others, no one crowded her, thanks to Ukkarr, who even when weaponless, as now, could intimidate most lesser S'sinn.

Like everyone else, Kitillikk gazed skyward, toward the topmost Temple tower, where three S'sinn circled on artificial thermals generated by heating vents in the Temple roof. Kitillikk kept her expression carefully neutral, but deep in her throat she growled. "Look at her," she muttered to Ukkarr. "How dare she!"

The "she" in question was the Supreme Flight Leader, circling in formation with her Left and Right Wings. The thousands gathered below and the millions more watching on planet-wide vidcast had come to celebrate the most holy day in the worship of the Hunter of Worlds, the day when the Supreme Flight Leader symbolically brought, to feed the Hunter, the blood of all the Hunters who had died in the previous year.

Akkanndikk's wings flashed scarlet in the sunshine, covered from shoulder to tip with blood-red paint. The thousands with Kitillikk gazed raptly as somewhere a priest intoned a description of the ceremony, but Kitillikk preferred her own commentary. "In her reign Hunters die of old age, not in battle," she growled. "When I am Supreme Flight Leader, the Hunter of Worlds will feast on the ugly flesh of humans and the sweet blood of our strong young warriors!"

Ukkarr gave her a sideways glance. "I confess surprise at this sudden surge of piety, Flight Leader."

"If piety is necessary in a Supreme Flight Leader, then I will be pious, Ukkarr." She sharpened her vision, bringing prey-sight to bear on Akkanndikk, now circling downward toward the platform that crowned the tower. Some time later she would emerge, supposedly having sacrificed to the Hunter in a ceremony only she and the High Priest would attend. Kitillikk sometimes wondered if they really just sat and passed a bottle of silverwine back and forth for a few hundred beats. Next year, she intended to find out in person.

The Supreme Flight Leader spread her wings to land—and Kitillikk stiffened. In her prey-sight, all was clear, and the sudden outbreak of shouting all around her indicated the crowd saw, too, as a shape suddenly sprang up on the platform. "Ukkarr, the time is at hand!" Kitillikk breathed. "Human, I salute you!"

A flash like lightning. The Supreme Flight Leader's wings collapsed and she dropped, crashing onto the next platform down on the tower, one scarlet wing draped over the edge. The Left Wing dove toward her, while the Right hurled herself at the human. The beamer lashed out again, and the Right Wing snapped into a fluttering spin that ended when one of the upthrust "fangs" of the Temple wall impaled her. Blood streaked the stones. Her wings jerked twice, then fell limp.

The thousands roosting around and below Kitillikk surged this way and that in confusion and shrieking horror. Some tried to fly and collided with others, sending both crashing into the S'sinn on the ground. There would be more dead and wounded in the crowd, Kitillikk thought. All of which could be laid at the human's feet. She raked her prey-sight over the spire again, but the human had vanished.

No matter. Jim Ornawka was the least of her concerns. She turned to Ukkarr. "Now," she said. "Send the signals. First to our supporters in the Temple. Have them meet me where the Supreme Flight Leader lies. Then call Ikkilliss. The Supreme Flight must meet at once to discuss the succession. Go." Ukkarr snapped his wings in salute and went.

Her hearts pounding fiercely with anticipation, Kitillikk threw herself into the air, climbing quickly to the tower platform. As she swept in, the Left Wing swung toward her, teeth bared. "Kitillikk," he snarled. "Come to survey your handiwork?"

"Mine?" Kitillikk feigned astonishment, careful not to get too close to the angry bodyguard. "I was in the crowd at the base of the tower."

"One of your assassins—"

"It was not her doing," Akkanndikk whispered, and this time Kitillikk's astonishment was unfeigned, and followed quickly by anger. Bloody incompetent human—couldn't even kill a single unarmed S'sinn!

Instantly the Left Wing turned to his mistress, his wings blocking Akkanndikk from Kitillikk's view—which allowed her to shift her gaze to the only door into the Temple. They were certain to be inundated with priests at any moment—would have been already if not for the symbolic importance of the Supreme Flight Leader making her descent from the Tower unaided and alone. But which priests? Much depended on that—and that, in turn, depended on how quickly Ukkarr had gotten his message to her supporters.

Left Wing straightened and turned back toward Kitillikk. "My apologies," he said stiffly. "Her Altitude tells me her attacker was a human."

"May the Hunter spew him out of his mouth!" Kitillikk said fervently.

"Nevertheless, Flight Leader Kitillikk, I must insist that you stay back from Her Altitude until the priests arrive. You have made no secret of your enmity toward her."

"There is a difference between political enmity and attempted assassination, Left Wing," Kitillikk snapped. "In this hour, there is only the good of the S'sinn to consider. We must rally together. I came out of concern, not ambition." She didn't really expect the bodyguard to believe her, but it never hurt to make the right sounds. You never knew who might be listening.

"Your concern is noted. I still will not let you near the Supreme Flight Leader."

"As you wish." Kitillikk heard the snap of wings from below; a moment later three priests popped into view and landed beside her, and she carefully kept from smiling: they were hers. Unreliable over the long term, like all priests, but certainly ready to seize the moment—which they did, no doubt thanks to Ukkaddikk's instruction:

"Quickly!" said the first. "We must move her inside! The human has been spotted nearby—he could fire at any moment!"

"Where?" Left Wing sprang up. "I will rip out his heart!"

"East Tower!" the priest said, and Left Wing, with a final glance at the Supreme Flight Leader, already surrounded by the other priests, flung himself into the air.

"Excellent," Kitillikk said. "Get her inside and hide her."

The priests who had been "treating" the Supreme Flight Leader straightened. "You want her alive?" said one in surprise. "It would be an easy matter to—"

"I want her alive." In the few moments she'd had to think about that prospect, Kitillikk had seen how it could be used to her advantage. "It will keep her supporters off-balance, while we act. Now move her, before Left Wing comes back!"

Without further argument, the priests picked up Akkanndikk, who moaned and tossed her head, and carried her through the door. Kitillikk followed, pausing only long enough to scan the rooftops around them. "I hope Left Wing finds you, Jim Ornawka," she said softly. "It will save me the trouble."

Inside, a staircase spiraled down—a rare architectural feature in most S'sinn buildings, but common in the Temple; remaining on foot was a powerful symbol of humility before the Hunter. The Supreme Flight

Leader would have been expected to descend the entire height of the Tower on foot; now she descended instead in the none-too-gentle grasp of the priests. They had not gone far when they heard a shriek above them—no doubt Left Wing had returned to find his mistress gone. "Move!" Kitillikk snapped, and they redoubled their efforts.

They reached what must have been ground level, judging by the size of the chamber into which they emerged, but instead of going out through one of the four large doors spaced equidistantly around it, the priests instead stepped off the staircase and turned sharply left, toward a small black door underneath the stairs. They carried the now limp Akkanndikk through it, and Kitillikk, following, closed it behind them—and, finding a bolt, bolted it.

Now they descended in utter blackness, but sound gave Kitillikk all the information she needed. The stairs continued spiraling down, and down, until she judged they must be forty or more spans beneath the surface—and then, finally, they came on light, a large, round torch-lit chamber with a half-dozen shikks scattered around it, a table in the center on which rested the day-old (at least) remnants of a meal, and nothing else.

"This is where we meet," said the lead priest. "In darkness and dampness. We've suffered much to return our race to greatness, Flight Leader." Unspoken, she heard his challenge: *do not disappoint us.*

Unreliable, she thought again. *Priests are unreliable.*

It seemed, though, that with the Supreme Flight Leader unexpectedly alive, she would have to rely on them at least a while longer. "You have done well. And I promise I will remember your sacrifices when I am Supreme Flight Leader. But I must ask you to use this chamber a while longer. Keep her," she gestured at the unconscious figure of Akkanndikk, "hidden down here, for now. Treat her wounds, but answer no questions, should she recover enough to ask them. She won't know where she is, or who you are, unless you tell her. Should I need her, I will tell you. Should I decide I do not need her, I will tell you that, as well, and . . ."

"We understand and obey," said the priest, the traditional response of a lower priest to the command of a higher. Kitillikk rather thought she might adopt it in her court when she was Supreme Flight Leader.

Which she had better get busy arranging. "How can I get out without being seen? If I go back up the stairs—"

"There is another exit." The lead priest showed her an arch into deeper darkness. "This passage slopes gradually up and emerges near the river in a place well-screened from view. Should you wish to visit your captive, you should enter that way."

"My thanks," Kitillikk said, and went out.

A hundred damp, slippery spans later, she emerged onto the muddy river bank, beneath an overhanging platform with a hole in its center . . . the Place of Flightless Sacrifice, she realized, and smiled, thinking of Jarrikk. Very soon she would be in a position to pay back a lot of old debts—including that one. Maybe she'd bring him back here and use the knife on him herself . . .

But for now, her business lay with the Supreme Flight. Splattering mud, she launched herself into the air.

Chapter 16

Kathryn woke uncomfortably, all at once, to a harsh buzzing that brought her upright in bed, heart pounding. "Stand by for the captain," said a disembodied voice.

"I'd rather go back to sleep," Kathryn muttered, lying down again.

That, unfortunately, didn't appear to be an option: the door opened and Dr. Chung came in, her electronic notebook clasped protectively to her chest with folded arms and her lips pressed tightly together.

"Jarrikk?" Kathryn said anxiously, sitting up again, but even as she asked, she knew he was all right; she could tell by the—feel, she guessed was the word—of the tendril of his mind in hers. Something else, however, obviously *wasn't* all right.

"He's fine," Dr. Chung said. "For the moment. I'm not sure about the rest of us."

"What?"

"Listen." Dr. Chung pointed to the speaker overhead.

As if cued by her finger, a new voice came over it. "This is Captain Hall. A situation has arisen that may threaten the security of this ship. These are the facts as we know them: shortly after dawn this morning, someone attempted to assassinate the Supreme Flight Leader of the S'sinn during a religious ceremony at the Temple. She hasn't been seen since.

"The attacker escaped, but there are literally thousands of witnesses, backed up by vidrecords, who swear that he was human."

Kathryn gasped. Captain Hall carried inexorably on, his voice calm but tense. "The Supreme Flight met in emergency session almost immediately, and shortly thereafter announced that though still alive, the Supreme Flight Leader is grievously wounded and unable to carry out her duties. They claimed she has been sequestered in a secure place, then announced that, until she recovers—and there seems considerable doubt that she will—her duties will be assumed by Flight Leader Kitillikk."

Kathryn gasped again. "Kitillikk!"

Dr. Chung stared at her. "You know this S'sinn?"

"Through Jarrikk's memories . . . shhh!"

". . . not a universally acceptable choice, apparently. We have reports of fighting in the streets among unidentified factions. Communications, datalinks, and transportation are all under the control of armed Hunters. The Spaceport has been sealed. We were able to report to Commonwealth Central what has happened, but since then a scrambler field has been set up, blocking all off-planet communications. No S'sinn has contacted us directly since the assassination attempt, nor have we had any word from Translator Ursu, Translator Ornawka, Ambassador Matthews, or any of the other humans currently in the city.

"All we can do for the moment, ladies and gentlemen, is sit tight behind closed hatches. As a Commonwealth ship, we are theoretically inviolate—but whether the new leader adheres to that theory remains to be seen.

"I'll keep you posted as I learn more."

The shipcom clicked off; Kathryn's feet hit the floor a second later. "I must see Jarrikk."

"Kathryn—" Dr. Chung began.

"I feel fine. Perfectly healthy." Still very tired, actually, some of the good a week's rest had done undone by the stress of her meeting with Jarrikk the day before, but Dr. Chung didn't need to know that. "This is an emergency, Doctor."

"I'd stop you if I didn't know you'd pull 'Translator business' on me again," Chung grumbled. She flipped open her notebook, unclipped the stylus from its side, and scribbled something with unnecessary force. "Very well. You're released. Go wherever you like, do whatever you want."

"Thank you." Kathryn was halfway to the door before she looked down at her flimsy hospital gown, stopped, and turned sheepishly back to Dr. Chung. "Uh . . . maybe I should start with clothes."

As Kathryn strode down the corridor toward Jarrikk's room a few minutes later, wearing her freshly pressed Translator's uniform, with a jacket over the sleeveless top, she sensed the tendril from Jarrikk's mind growing stronger. *So distance matters,* she thought. *Ukkaddikk will be interested to hear that—if we ever decide to tell him.*

By the time she reached Jarrikk's door she could even sense that he still slept, and she hesitated for a long moment before deciding it was more important to tell him what had happened than to let him rest. He was still S'sinn, after all, and it was his leader who had almost been killed—and he also had a long personal history with her successor, Kitillikk.

Somehow, Kathryn doubted he would be pleased at the news of his old Flight Leader's promotion.

Jarrikk woke swiftly, all at once, as she entered, and at the same moment his presence in her mind quadrupled in strength, so suddenly she gasped and staggered back a little. It wasn't telepathy—that seemed to require touch—but it was far stronger than any empathic bond she'd ever experienced or heard of outside of Translation.

She told him swiftly and succinctly what she had heard the captain say, and had to grab the back of the chair by his bed for support as his outrage and shock crashed through her. "Kitillikk is behind this," he snarled.

"They said it was a human . . ."

"Then she arranged it."

"But . . . from what I know from your memories about her, she hates humans. She would never align herself with one . . ."

"That's what makes it so perfect. No one will suspect that Kitillikk would use a human. But she would. She'd use and do anything to become Supreme Flight Leader."

"And now she is," Kathryn said slowly.

"Exactly."

"Then the next step . . ."

"War." His bitterness made his words burn like acid in her mind. "She'll ruin everything we accomplished. She'll already be gathering the Hunterships, calling her old friend Lakkassikk to mobilize the attack troops."

Kathryn took that in. "Then—then what will happen to us? We're trapped here!"

"She'll need all her Hunters to quell any budding rebellions—but the moment she has any to spare, we'll be next on her list."

"They can't get in . . . can they?"

"This is nothing but a glorified yacht. It's not a warship. They can get in."

The speaker overhead crackled to life again. "This is Captain Hall," said the familiar voice, now drawn as tight as a bow string. "Our outside cameras show armed S'sinn Hunters moving onto the Spaceport landing field.

"Ladies and gentlemen, I'm afraid we're surrounded."

Jarrikk heard the captain's voice, but didn't understand it. What he did understand was the sudden surge of fear in Kathryn. "What is it?" he asked in Guild-talk.

"S'sinn Hunters surrounding us." Kathryn looked at him. "Kitillikk?"

"Who else? She wants us, Kathryn."

"Us, specifically, or humans in general?"

"Us. Specifically."

"Why?"

"She may know by now how we salvaged the peace treaty. Even if she doesn't, she knows we were the ones Translating when the agreement was reached. We're visible symbols of the Commonwealth. Plus, simply by being alive, I'm a symbol of how S'sinn culture has been corrupted by contact with the Commonwealth—and you're a symbol of that corruption, having defiled my sacrifice to the Hunter." He couldn't help the bitterness that seeped through him at that, though he no longer intended to finish the job at the first opportunity. Kathryn had given him an option and he had yet to consider it carefully. Yet if even he, the beneficiary of it, could feel anger at the human's arrogance in stopping a sacrifice to the Hunter of Worlds, how would more traditional S'sinn react?

By tearing any convenient human apart, he thought— *and Kathryn would be the most convenient of all.* He reached out and took her hand, feeling her concern more strongly than ever and letting her feel his. He wouldn't put it past Kitillikk to try to pin the assassination attempt on her, instead of on whatever pathetic human traitor she had actually used. What better way to destroy sympathy for the Commonwealth than putting it out that a Translator had been the assassin, absurd though that was?

Kathryn had pulled her hand away again, and he realized he had almost dozed off. He looked at her with some alarm. How much of what he had just been thinking had traveled over the intangible link between them?

Enough, it seemed. She looked visibly scared for the first time—if he were reading her strange human face aright. But then the speaker crackled again, and this time Jarrikk understood two words perfectly: "Translator Bircher . . ."

*   *   *

". . . report to the bridge. Translator Bircher, please report to the bridge."

Kitillikk, was her first thought. *Kitillikk has demanded they turn Jarrikk and me over to her, and . . .*

. . . and what? a derisive inner voice spoke up. *Do you really think the captain is just going to hand you over?*

He's Guild. Not a Translator, but still part of the Guild. And the Guild has already sacrificed me once— or at least set me up so I would sacrifice myself. She smoothed wrinkles out of her uniform. *Well, only one way to find out.* "Summoned to the bridge," she told Jarrikk. "I'll be back." She felt his concern and curiosity follow her as she went out.

Having already decided she knew why she was being summoned, she was totally unprepared when the door to the bridge slid aside to reveal Jim Ornawka.

He sat in one of the swinging crewchairs at an unmanned station, and looked like he'd crawled through a hundred miles of mud and barbed wire to get there. Brown water tinged with red dripped from the tattered black cloak he wore, dirt smudged his face, and one cheek bore a red, blistered streak. But he managed a smile when he saw her. "Hello, Katy."

She didn't smile back. There'd been only one thing she'd wanted to say to Jim Ornawka for days; she said it now. "You lied to Jarrikk. You told him I didn't want to see him. He almost died because of you."

"I'm sorry," Jim said, but empathically he was as blank to her as ever. "I only did it to protect you— and honor Jarrikk. I knew he wouldn't thank you for interfering with his Sacrifice. You think too much like a human for your own good, Katy. The S'sinn may be a lot like us, at least compared to races like the Swampworlders, but they're not *human.*"

Kathryn said nothing. The captain, who had come up behind Jim while they were talking (and while the other half-dozen crew on the bridge very carefully didn't look at them), cleared his throat. "Translator Ornawka made it through the blockade around the Spaceport. He says he can take you out the same way."

"Take us out?" Kathryn stared at him. "Why would we want to leave the ship?"

"It's not safe," Jim said. "It's only a matter of time before they move in and take it. And with all due respect to the captain and crew of the *Unity,* they're not what Kitillikk really wants. She wants Translators. She's announced that it was a Translator who tried to kill the Supreme Flight Leader."

It was so much like the fears she had read from Jarrikk while he held her hand that it startled Kathryn. "Then what about Annette Ursu? She's in the Great Hall with Matthews—"

Jim didn't say anything, but the captain cleared his throat and, sensing his grimness, she knew what he was going to say before he said it. "Translator Ursu and Ambassador Matthews are dead. We presume the others in the diplomatic mission are dead, too, although some may have escaped to other Commonwealth embassies."

"Matthews and Annette were torn apart by a so-called 'mob,' " Jim said. "Kitillikk's doing, of course. I'm sorry, Katy."

Katy hadn't had much use for Matthews, but the news of his death still shocked her deeply. And though she'd never met Annette Ursu, the violent death of any Translator should have been unthinkable. "But if the people are against us . . . where would we go?" she whispered. "It's not our world."

"They're not all against us. They're fighting each other in the streets. There must be Commonwealth sympathizers who could help us—and maybe Jarrikk knows who they are." Jim got to his feet slowly. "Shall we go see him? I think it's about time I went to sick-bay anyway."

Kathryn tried to read him one more time—and one more time, she failed. Maybe Jarrikk would have better luck. "Let's go."

*   *   *

Shortly after Kathryn left Jarrikk's room in response to the call from the bridge, Ukkaddikk came in. He greeted Jarrikk solemnly. "Grim news," he said, his words underscored empathically by deep concern. "Kitillikk is tightening her hold. There is no word of Akkanndikk's whereabouts, and Kitillikk has said it was a human Translator who tried to kill her."

"In other words, Kathryn," Jarrikk said.

"Translator Ursu is dead. With Ambassador Matthews and others. No doubt I would be, too, had I not been on the *Unity*. But this is only a temporary refuge, Jarrikk. This ship cannot be held against the Hunters."

"We don't seem to have much choice." Inwardly Jarrikk seethed with anger at Kitillikk. *May the Hunter gag on that female's soul!* he thought. *How many lives will she spend in her ambition?*

"No," Ukkaddikk agreed gloomily. "If we were anywhere but the Spaceport, I might be able to find us refuge, but the Spaceport is designed to be easily defensible—which means it's just as easily besieged." He gave Jarrikk a curious look. "I don't suppose this new link of yours with Translator Bircher could help us?"

"How?" Jarrikk asked, instantly wary. Even now, Ukkaddikk was fishing for information. *Ever the true Guild loyalist. Anything for the good of the Guild.*

Well, he still wasn't prepared to tell the Guild exactly what he and Kathryn had achieved. Not yet.

"Obviously I don't know, since I know very little about what you're able to do. I do know Translator Bircher is a projective, at least a little bit. Could the two of you, working together, plant a suggestion in a third person's mind?"

"I don't think so," Jarrikk said. "No. We couldn't." But inside, he wondered, and a part of him began worrying at the problem, trying to remember how that link with Kathryn felt and what could be done from it. But he didn't get far before the door opened and Kathryn came in—with Jim Ornawka.

Jim's face glistened with synthiskin bandages, beneath which Jarrikk could still dimly see a variety of nasty cuts and bruises. "Translator Jarrikk," Jim said. "Translator Ukkaddikk."

Jarrikk glared at him. Jim Ornawka had lied to him about Kathryn. She *had* wanted to see him before he took the knife. He felt he had ample reason to dislike and distrust the man.

So why is he here?

Kathryn's own emotions felt similarly tangled—yet she had entered with Ornawka. Somehow, Jarrikk sensed, Ornawka had convinced her to trust him, at least a little.

"Jim got through the blockade," she said tensely. "He thinks he can get all of us out—if we want to go."

Ukkaddikk glanced at Jarrikk. "We were just discussing the matter. We did not think it possible."

"It might not be," Ornawka said. "They may find the route I used at any time and plug the hole. But it's the only hope I see. They've got major military hardware piling up outside. They can take this ship any time they want."

"Then what are they waiting for?" asked Kathryn.

Jarrikk knew the answer to that. "The right moment," he said. "Kitillikk is using everything to strengthen her position as interim Supreme Flight Leader—a position she will make permanent when she is certain that she can. She is keeping us in reserve. When she feels she needs to boost popular support, or distract the public's attention from something, then she will take us. We're just being used." *Again.*

"But if we escape, it backfires," Ornawka said. "If we escape, and she is not aware of it, and strikes at this ship anyway—"

"No," Jarrikk said emphatically. "If we leave, we must let Captain Hall tell Kitillikk we have escaped as soon as the Hunters move in. They will search the ship, of course, but they will not need to take it by force. We cannot ask the crew to die to cover our escape."

"They serve the Guild. They should be prepared to die."

"I agree with Jarrikk," Kathryn put in hurriedly. "We must do what we can to protect them."

Ornawka shrugged, but Jarrikk felt his irritation: the first emotion Ornawka had let leak through his shield.

"Whatever we do, we must do quickly," Ukkaddikk said. He gave his wings a nervous shake. "There is another question. Jarrikk, are you well enough to travel?"

"Yes," he said, hoping it was true.

"We should ask Doctor Chung," Kathryn said. "I'll go." She slipped out.

Jarrikk looked at Ornawka. "There's no point in running if we have nowhere safe to run to."

"I hoped you could help there," Ornawka said.

"He can't, but I can," said Ukkaddikk. "A powerful family with strong pro-Commonwealth sentiments has a jarrbukk ranch not far from here. We will go there, away from prying eyes. They will also have news of what's really happening, news that isn't filtered through Kitillikk."

"Excellent," Ornawka said. "We're agreed, then."

"Agreed," said Ukkaddikk.

"Agreed," Jarrikk said, but he kept his eyes on Ornawka, the Translator who hid behind an impenetrable empathic block, the Translator who had lied to a fellow Translator, the Translator who would willingly have sacrificed the crew of the *Unity* to make Kitillikk's grab for power just a little more difficult.

Dr. Chung, after considerable argument, finally admitted that Jarrikk could probably travel without risking permanent damage. But she was adamant about one thing: "I must come with you."

"No. Doctor, I put you at risk once, dragging you off to the Place of Flightless Sacrifice. I can't—"

"It's got nothing to do with you, with all due respect, *Translator* Bircher. In Translator business I am at your command, but this is medical business. *My* business. And Jarrikk is *my* patient. I'm coming." She picked up her medical bag and brushed past Kathryn without looking at her.

So there were three humans and two S'sinn in the party that gathered in one of the auxiliary airlocks twenty minutes later. Jarrikk leaned heavily on Kathryn, but though she could feel his mind, she didn't try to link telepathically. They both needed all their energy—especially Jarrikk. Chung hovered near him, playing the flickering blue beam of a medical scanner over his chest, watching its readouts with lips pressed and eyes narrowed.

The humans all wore packs—there had been nothing that would fit S'sinn and Jarrikk was in no condition to carry extra weight anyway—and all of them except Dr. Chung wore Commonwealth-issue beamers holstered at their waists. The unfamiliar weight at her hip bothered Kathryn. She couldn't imagine actually firing the thing, but the captain had insisted and Ukkaddikk had thought it a good idea as well. Certainly Jim had taken his with no qualms. Chung had refused as a matter of ethics.

"I hope your ethics don't come with too high a price," Jim said to her.

"No price *could* be too high," Chung replied quietly.

Jim and Ukkaddikk were already in the airlock when the others arrived. The open outer door revealed, not the landing field, as Kathryn had expected, but a strange, tubular corridor. Dim blue lights every metre or so glistened off walls of black plastic. "This is how I got to the ship without being seen," Jim said. "It's a maintenance tube; provides easy access for Spaceport crews and a handy source of compatible power for their tools."

"Where does it go?" Kathryn asked.

"All the way back to the maintenance shop in the main terminal. And the maintenance shop has a loading dock opening onto a lev-line outside the Spaceport's perimeter fencing."

"Kitillikk wouldn't miss something that obvious," Ukkaddikk growled. "Surely it's guarded."

"It's guarded—but it's also crowded with boxes and barrels and half-a-dozen lev-cars. Lots of shadows. We can slip through it without being seen. I proved it."

"I hope you weren't just lucky," Kathryn said.

They moved through the eerie black tube in silence, its padded floor, designed to provide traction to clawed S'sinn feet, muffling their footsteps. Periodically they passed joints between sections of tubing, but every section looked just like every other. Kathryn had no idea how far they had come or how far they still had to go when, suddenly, they arrived at an open hatch.

Jim drew his beamer, motioned the others to keep silent, then edged forward to look through the hatch. He turned his head this way and that, looking, listening, and, Kathryn realized, reaching out with his empathic sense. After a moment he gestured for them to follow him.

Work platforms hung from metal beams at apparently haphazard heights above them in the circular, high-ceilinged shop. Metal shutters secured several large windows or doors right under the ceiling, and closed hatches like the one they'd just come through circled the room at floor-level, presumably linking the shop to other ships on the landing field. A sharp, metallic scent hung in the chill air, and odd-shaped, inscrutable pieces of large machinery stood around like silent sentinels, the light from the three floodlights spaced equidistantly around the shop throwing some areas into high relief and others into pitch-black shadow.

"Spooky," Kathryn whispered, hugging herself against the chill, glad she'd thought to wear the jacket.

"But empty," Jim said briskly. "Unless you can sense something I can't."

Kathryn closed her eyes for a minute and concentrated, focusing her empathic sense, and quite unexpectedly found herself in momentary linkage with Jarrikk and at the same time suddenly aware of a much larger area than she'd ever been able to scan before—and aware of a single S'sinn presence, not in the room, but somewhere nearby.

She opened her eyes again. "I thought I felt someone," she said, glancing at Jarrikk, then back at Jim. "Outside the room."

"Outside . . . ?" Jim frowned at her. "Since when have you been able to sense . . ."

"It doesn't matter, does it?" Kathryn snapped. "I'm just telling you what I felt. Or thought I felt. Maybe I'm wrong."

"No," Ukkaddikk said. "I feel him, too. But I don't believe I would have if you hadn't told me he was there."

"Probably just someone cleaning up," Jim said. He sounded unreasonably irritable. "Shouldn't even know we're here. Let's go."

He led them through the maze of machinery toward a hatch on the far side of the room, larger than any of the others, large enough to admit a transport.

They were only halfway across the floor when the hatch started to rise.

Chapter 17

The party from the *Unity* scattered like quail into the shadows of the shop. Peering cautiously around the base of the lathelike machine behind which she hid, Kathryn saw a S'sinn, carrying a firelance, duck under the still-rising hatch into the room—and at the same time sensed him empathically, this time without Jarrikk's help. Jarrikk hid behind her, not quite touching her; but then he did touch her, placing his hand lightly on her calf, and suddenly she could sense the strange S'sinn with shocking strength, as though he were standing right next to her: and knew at once that, as long as they didn't show themselves, they had nothing to fear. She sensed nothing from him but boredom, not a hint of suspicion, and was certain that after he completed his desultory inspection of the room from the hatchway he'd go back out again—a certainty heightened as he paused to stretch, wings rustling as he spread them wide, and yawned hugely, revealing alarmingly sharp white teeth.

Kathryn could also sense Ukkaddikk's anxiety, Dr. Chung's fear, and even—for the first time she could remember—a hint of something from Jim, though the emotions roiling beneath his thick shield remained too complex to read clearly. Most of all, of course, she could sense Jarrikk, strong and surprisingly calm. But then, she supposed, if you had the courage to stick a knife in your own heart, a little thing like a firelance wouldn't bother you.

Jim judged the location of the Hunter, then crawled quickly across open space to join Kathryn and Jarrikk. "Only one," he mouthed. "I'll take care of him."

"No," Kathryn whispered back. "Can't you sense him? He's not suspicious. There's no need—"

But Jim was already scooting away on his belly, wriggling out of sight behind a long bench that stretched almost to the big hatch.

Kathryn looked at Jarrikk and Ukkaddikk and Chung, but none of them said anything. There was really nothing they could do.

With great relief, Kathryn saw the Hunter turn back to the still-open hatch. *He's going,* she thought pointlessly at Jim, wishing she could contact *him* telepathically. *He's going. Let him go . . .*

But Jim didn't. He rose silently from behind the bench, and without a sound, without a warning, he raised his beamer and fired a single pulse.

The white beam slashed across the S'sinn Hunter's back, severing his spine and cutting his wings in half. Kathryn cried out as the Hunter's agony exploded in her own mind, then he vanished from her awareness and collapsed in a smoldering heap.

The severed tip of one wing burned with sharp popping sounds, a thin tendril of smoke curling up from it, for several more seconds.

And Kathryn, to her horror, felt one undisguised, unblocked emotion from Jim: pleasure.

Jarrikk also felt Ornawka's sick satisfaction, so forcefully he almost vomited. Nauseated and enraged, he staggered to his feet, his mind filled with unwanted images from years past of his youngflight brothers, shot from the sky by humans. He lunged at Ornawka as the human Translator walked nonchalantly back, but Ornawka raised the beamer again.

"Don't," he said.

"Murderer!" Jarrikk snarled in Guildtalk. "There was no need—"

"There was every need," Ornawka replied, his own

voice calm and controlled. "It would be much harder to slip past him outside than in here."

"You didn't have to kill him!" Kathryn cried. She, too, Jarrikk knew, must have taken the full empathic force of the Hunter's death.

"What would you have suggested? Unarmed combat? He'd have taken me apart."

"As I yet may!" Jarrikk growled.

"You? You can hardly walk."

Jarrikk's claws dug hard into the padded floor, but Ukkaddikk stepped between him and Ornawka with spread arms and half-spread wings. "This gets us nowhere," Ukkaddikk snapped. "I would have preferred to avoid bloodshed, but it is Kitillikk who chose the path of war. The next blood to be shed may be our own if we do not escape the Spaceport!"

"My point exactly." Ornawka holstered his beamer and turned away. "So let's go."

Promising himself there would yet be a reckoning, Jarrikk accompanied the others to the hatch, passing within a span of the dead S'sinn's charred corpse and the slowly spreading dark red pool around it. Jarrikk saw Kathryn look away, but he stared long and hard. *I will remember you, brother,* he thought fiercely. *You may have stood against me, but I do not call you enemy. May the Hunter avenge your death—with my help!*

Outside the hatch, as Ornawka had said, supply boxes and parked lev-cars provided cover, and beyond them rose dark forest. Even when Jarrikk touched Kathryn again and once again staggered slightly under the impact of the vastly more powerful empathic sense they shared together, he could sense no one but his companions within five hundred spans. They crossed the silvery surface of the lev-line between two crate-piled cars, and plunged in among the trees.

Ukkaddikk seemed confident of their goal, but the walk, first through the woods, stumbling over roots and pushing aside undergrowth, then over a mercifully narrow, muddy, plowed field where muck mixed with manure sucked at their feet and choked them with sour fumes, and finally through a seemingly endless waist-high crop of green fedra, drained Jarrikk dry. Kathryn supported him, and he could feel her soul-warming concern, and Dr. Chung soon joined her on the other side, but still his energy deserted him, and the almost-healed wound in his chest began to throb, a throbbing that grew into a stabbing pain—and if anyone should know what a stabbing pain felt like, Jarrikk thought half-deliriously, it was him.

Dr. Chung played her medical scanner over his chest, frowned, and said something in her own language to Kathryn, who went up to talk to Ukkaddikk. Jarrikk couldn't hear clearly through the pounding in his ears, but he thought she was asking how much farther they were going. He didn't hear Ukkaddikk's reply, either, but when Kathryn came back he sensed her relief.

"We're almost there," she said in Guildtalk. "This field belongs to the Commonwealth sympathizer he expects to take us in. I hope he's right about that part," she added in a low voice to Dr. Chung.

"He'd better be right about the first part," Chung replied acidly. "Jarrikk will collapse if we go on much farther. And it hasn't been all that long since you were bedridden, either. How do you feel?"

"I feel fine," Kathryn said, but Jarrikk knew she lied. He thought that from now on he would always know.

Yet she continued to support him, and with her help and Dr. Chung's he made it to the edge of a farmyard, and sagged gratefully against the wall of the house, an ancient structure made in the traditional fashion: a high circular dwelling tower atop ground-level rooms used for keeping animals. There might be a stair leading from the stables to the dwelling rooms, to make it easier to move large objects from one to the other, but the main entrance would be four or five spans above the ground, and Jarrikk, whose eyes had closed of their own free will, heard the rush of air as Ukkad-dikk took wing to investigate.

He also heard the crunch of boots on cobblestones and sensed Ornawka's approach. "Is he dying?"

"Of course not," Kathryn snapped. "He's perfectly all right. Just tired."

You're lying again, Jarrikk thought dreamily, and slept.

Karak, clad in the bulky watersuit he hated, slowly and heavily climbed the stone stairs to the Guildheart. Not all the weight he carried was in the form of water or the machinery to circulate and oxygenate it: a lot of it came from the news he had just received from two fronts.

The other Councilors awaited him in the star-spangled room, one representative from each race except the humans, seated, sprawled, or entanked around the circular council table moved into the room for these meetings. It was a cross-section of a huge tree from the Swampworlders' planet, in honor of their creation of the Translator symbiote. Pinpoint-sized lights embedded in its black, non-reflective surface created an almost perfect illusion of an impossible view of Commonwealth Space, the home stars of the various races given rather greater magnitude than justified by astronomical fact.

Karak gravely greeted each of the Councilors, then took his place at the head of the table, not far from the light representing his own homeworld of Ithkar, and checked to make sure that the computerized translation system necessary for the non-Guildtalk-speaking races was activated. It was irony itself that the greatest Translators of the Guild could only talk to each other through a pidgin language and crude machines, but though the Swampworlders had been working on the problem for years, they had yet to devise a way to Link more than two minds at once. Three-way Linkages had been tried: the results were hidden deep in the Guild Hall, cared for by machines as their vegetative lives slipped away.

Without formality, Karak made his report. "Kitillikk has firm control of S'sinndikk. There have been various attempted uprisings, but all have been crushed by the Army of the Hunter, commanded by Flight Leader Lakkassikk. Supreme Flight Leader Akkanndikk is still sequestered, supposedly in hospital, but no one seems to know exactly where or what her condition is." He drew in an extra gillful of the suit's stagnant-tasting water before continuing. "Worse: Kitillikk has announced that the assassination attempt was the work of a human Translator."

That brought pandemonium, ear-piercing peeps from the Orrisians, a room-vibrating hum from the Aza, and a much-faster-than-usual burbling from the Swampworlder, all accompanied by an overwhelming surge of empathically felt outrage. But Karak wasn't finished. "Translator Ursu and Ambassador Matthews are dead. Translators Jarrikk, Ukkaddikk, and Bircher we believe to be on board the Guildship *Unity,* which is trapped at S'sinndikk spaceport and surrounded by Hunters. Translator Ornawka's whereabouts are unknown. We predict that Kitillikk will not wait long before attacking *Unity.* After that, the captured Translators will probably be subjected to a show trial, to build public support for the new regime, and then executed, probably as a send-off for the Hunter Fleet, which Kitillikk is rapidly mobilizing. We cannot be sure what her target will be."

Karak looked down at the star-studded tabletop. "I also have news from Earth. The pro-war Humanity First faction that was temporarily silenced by the apparent success of Matthews' so-called peace mission has suddenly gained the ascendancy with his death at the claws of the S'sinn. The people of Earth are demanding immediate retaliation, and the Earth government is responding. Earth, too, is mobilizing its fleet."

"Can't the Commonwealth stop this?" the computer

said on behalf of the Orrisians. "The Hasshingu-Issk
have ships that cowed both sides once before—"

Karak raised his head again. "The Commonwealth
is split along exactly the same fault lines as before
Matthews' mission. Commonwealth Central dares not
intervene for fear of being seen to favor one side or
the other. The governments of the other races are, in
some instances, under severe pressure from their own
people to uphold the illegal treaties they signed before
the peace agreement was reached. Any move by the
Commonwealth could topple some of those governments, and the Commonwealth would fall with them.
The war that would destroy everything, including this
Guild, would follow inevitably."

Silence. Finally the old Hasshingu-Issk Master, who
had initiated Kathryn Bircher and so many other
young Translators of all races, asked in his soft, hissing
voice, "Then what does this Council do to stop it?"

More silence followed, and as it deepened and remained unbroken, Karak turned and left the chamber.

Kitillikk surveyed Kkirrik'S'sinn from the topmost
spire of the Great Hall. There, from a round platform,
she could see all of the city, and the countryside for
thousands of spans in all directions. And all of it, she
thought with great satisfaction, belonged to her: the
riots quelled with club and firelance, her opponents
driven underground (though she was still determined
to root the last of them out), the priests receiving
nothing but favorable omens from the Mouth of the
Hunter. The old, weak order had been swept away.
The days of glory were just begun: and Kitillikk, not
one given to fancy, nevertheless allowed herself to
imagine, just for a moment, that the statues of the
great Supreme Flight Leaders from S'sinndikk's bloody
past gazed at her with satisfaction from the memorial
towers all around her.

Ukkarr came winging up toward her, circled the
tower once below her as a gesture of respect, then

flew up onto the platform. "News," he said brusquely. "News that will not please you, Your Altitude."

What could fail to please me today? she thought magnanimously. Sometimes Ukkarr was an old worrier. "Tell me this news."

"*Unity* has opened its hatches to us."

Kitillikk almost laughed. "Why should this displease me, Ukkarr?"

He said nothing, just gazed at her steadily, and suddenly she realized what his news really meant, and her good mood fell away as though it had never been. "Hunter's spew! The Translators have escaped!"

"We have searched the *Unity*. They are not there, and the crew willingly admits that they fled overnight through a maintenance tube."

"Which would have led them to the maintenance shop, which was guarded, of course?" Kitillikk said icily.

"It was guarded. The guard is dead. A beamer wound in the back."

"One guard? Incompetence!" Kitillikk glared across the city to the spaceport. She had been planning to order the attack on the *Unity* for that evening. The escaped Translators could do her no real harm, but she did not appreciate the setback to her public relations plans. And there was still the matter of revenge. Revenge was a duty of every S'sinn, the priests said, but for Kitillikk, revenge against Jarrikk and Bircher and especially Ornawka was more than a duty—it would be a pleasure. "Find them," she snarled. "They can't have gone far. They'll be hiding, probably in the countryside. Search every farm in the vicinity."

"I obey, Your Altitude. Will that be all?"

"No. How stands the Fleet?"

"Ready."

"Order them to the marshalling point. I will join them in two days with final instructions. And then, Ukkarr, then the humans will feel the full power of the S'sinn!"

"Yes, Supreme Flight Leader."

"Go."

Ukkarr flung himself into space and swept away. Kitillikk took one more look around at the city in the gathering dusk, then descended into the depths of the tower, to the communications room. Most of the dimspace coordinates she had found preset in its transmitter matched those she now input: Akkanndikk had been talking to someone at Commonwealth Central, though not, she felt certain, the same someone she was about to contact.

The screen filled only with static, no image of the S'sinn to whom she spoke, a function of the extremely narrow bandwidth of the dimspace channel they were using, intended to minimize the already vanishingly small chance it would be intercepted. But she knew well the voice that answered, having hand-picked this Hunter and all the others in his secret little group from the rather large delegation the former Supreme Flight Leader had sent to Commonwealth Central as part of the official diplomatic corps.

"Two S'sinn days," she said crisply. "Exactly. From now. Whatever time that translates to locally. You'll be ready?"

"Ready since the first day we got here," the Hunter replied. "This planet takes its security for granted."

"Not for long," Kitillikk said. "Not for long. When you've accomplished your mission, report to me. I'll be on board the *Bloodfeud*. You have the coordinates."

"Understood."

Kitillikk broke the connection. *Revenge,* she thought. Glory to the Hunter; if the priests had it right, glory to her and to the S'sinn race, whatever. They would have revenge—on the humans, on the Translators, and on the Commonwealth.

She grinned savagely at her reflection in the dark screen of the transmitter, then went to find something to eat.

Chapter 18

Dozing beside Jarrikk, Kathryn jerked fearfully awake as half a dozen S'sinn winged down from the dark sky to light in the farmyard, but the empathic resonances were, if not exactly friendly, at least non-threatening, and a moment later she recognized Ukkaddikk, who came over to her, ignoring Jim. "Jarrikk?"

Kathryn looked at Dr. Chung. "Asleep," the doctor said. "Exhausted. He needs rest."

"As do we all," said Ukkaddikk. "These are friends. They will take us in."

"Give them our thanks," Kathryn said.

"I already have." Ukkaddikk turned and said something to the other waiting S'sinn, two of whom moved forward and gathered up Jarrikk. He stirred, but did not wake, as they carried him inside toward the wooden stairs, past massive six-legged beasts that grumbled in deep, growling tones at having their slumber disturbed. Kathryn and the other humans followed on their own, with Ukkaddikk; one of the remaining S'sinn remained on the ground at the stable entrance, while the other two exchanged rapid-fire words, then leaped into the sky.

Kathryn found the muttering of the animals, and their warm, musty smell, oddly warm and comforting. The brief surge of adrenalin from the arrival of the S'sinn had already faded, and she yawned hugely.

The stairs led to an open cellar-type door that let them into a semi-circular kitchen. Two big arched windows looked out into darkness, and at a fireplace in the flat wall a gray-muzzled female S'sinn coaxed embers into flame with wood taken from a big pile to one side. She didn't look up as they passed by her into a smaller room that Kathryn judged to be a dining area, furnished with a chest-high table surrounded by well-worn shikks of blood-red wood. They trudged on over scarred floors of dark brown planks into a hallway with arches to the left and more stairs going up at the end; went up those stairs into a windowless, circular chamber with six arches opening off of it, and went through one of those arches into a room with a padded, shallow circular pit in its centre, into which the leading S'sinn lowered Jarrikk, who stirred and muttered, but still did not wake.

Ukkaddikk spoke softly to the S'sinn, who growled something in return and went out. "I have asked them to bring cushions for you to sleep on," he told the humans.

"Thank you," Kathryn and Dr. Chung replied together.

"Yeah, thanks," Jim said. "But what happens next?"

"I suggest we discuss that in the morning."

"I suggest we discuss it now."

"In the morning." Ukkaddikk spread his wings and dove out the window.

"I don't like this," Jim said. "We don't really know what's going on here."

"You can sense as well as I can that these S'sinn aren't hostile," Kathryn said.

"And you can sense as well as I can that they're on edge. They're up to something."

"Of course they're on edge. They're harboring fugitives."

"There's more to it than that." Jim sat down against the wall, arms folded, beamer cradled in the crook of his left elbow. "I'm keeping watch."

"Suit yourself." Kathryn yawned again. "As soon as they get back with those cushions—ah, here they are!"

Their S'sinn hosts entered with a stack of thin cushions like the ones in Jarrikk's sleeping pit, little more than pads, really, but better than bare wood. She nodded her thanks; the S'sinn exchanged glances and left. Kathryn and Dr. Chung spread the cushions and lay down on them, but tired though she was, Kathryn didn't sleep for several minutes.

Blast Jim for putting the thought in her head, but . . . these S'sinn *were* up to something. Something involving them. She'd have to ask Ukkaddikk . . .

In the morning.

Jarrikk woke to the sounds of falling rain and two S'sinn arguing. Not quite sure where he was, he blinked open gritty eyes and saw Ukkaddikk, framed by an arch-window filled with soggy gray sky. ". . . name won't protect you against Kitillikk's search."

"She wouldn't dare!"

"She dared to move against the Supreme Flight Leader."

Jarrikk looked from Ukkaddikk to the second S'sinn, someone he'd never seen before, but who wore the red-gold collar that bespoke a place in the Supreme Flight. "She thinks I support her," the stranger said. "And Lakkassikk's army knows that. They will not search here."

Jarrikk remembered now . . . fleeing the *Unity,* Ornawka shooting the guard in the back, the painful trudge across muddy fields, the ancient farmhouse. "But we can't stay here forever," he said, his voice grating in his ears.

Both S'sinn looked down in surprise. "Good, you're awake!" Ukkaddikk said.

"How could I sleep with people arguing over my sleeping pit?"

"Translator Jarrikk, I am Pikkiro," said the stranger. "We are honored by your presence."

"I'm honored by your hospitality," Jarrikk said. "And grateful. But, Ukkaddikk, I mean what I say.

Even if Lakkassikk's Hunters do not find us here, we cannot stay. We have to try to stop Kitillikk."

"I am glad to hear you say so," said Pikkiro. "Because I think I know how we can."

"Not now," Ukkaddikk said. "Later. When we are all as sure as you are that the search will pass us by. If we are taken, the less we know about the opposition to Kitillikk the better."

Pikkiro bowed his head slightly. "Agreed. In any event, it is a discussion your human friends should also be a part of, and they still sleep. Tonight, over meat." He looked at Jarrikk. "I am sorry we woke you. Please rest as long as you like."

"I doubt we have that much time," Jarrikk said. "But thank you."

Pikkiro and Ukkaddikk left, arguing again, but in low voices. Jarrikk raised his head above the edge of the pit and looked around the room. Somebody had brought cushions for the three humans. Dr. Chung and Kathryn slept soundly, but Ornawka sat against the wall, cradling the beamer with which he'd killed the guard. Jarrikk exchanged a long, cold look with him, then settled back again. Outside the rain intensified, its steady patter soon lulling him back to sleep.

He felt almost like himself again that evening when all of them gathered in the dining room downstairs: Pikkiro, his brother Tillikk, Ukkaddikk, Jarrikk, Kathryn, Ornawka, and Dr. Chung. Pikkiro's prediction had proven correct: Lakkassikk's Hunters had accepted without question Pikkiro's assurance he had searched his land himself and found no fugitives. That gave them a little breathing space—but not much, Pikkiro said. He paused as the elderly female servant brought in platters of raw, fresh-killed meat for the S'sinn and (well-hiding the distaste that was clear in her mind) cooked meat for the humans. Salty lukka bread, tangy mukkuro cheese, and a selection of raw fruits and vegetables rounded out the repast, which Jarrikk fell to with a vengeance. The humans ate heartily, too, though they avoided looking at their more carnivorous companions.

"Kitillikk has mustered the Fleet," Pikkiro continued when the servant had left. "It gathers above us now. It launches tomorrow."

"What target?" Ukkaddikk asked, as Jarrikk stopped eating to translate what was being said into Guildtalk for the humans' benefit. "Kisradikk?"

"No. Kikks'sarr. Where the War began."

Of course, Jarrikk thought. Where Kitillikk suffered the indignity of seeing half the world that should have been hers given over to the humans by the Commonwealth.

"We'll have to start calling it the First War if she succeeds," Ukkaddikk said grimly. "She must be stopped. The Fleet must be stopped. Now, Pikkiro. Now, tell us this plan."

Pikkiro nodded to his brother, who got up to close and bolt the door and the shutters on the windows, shutting out the dying light of the gray day and leaving the room lit only by the fire that blazed behind Pikkiro. "I know where the Supreme Flight Leader is," he said in a low voice. "We must rescue her."

As Jarrikk repeated that for the humans, he caught a surprising flood of satisfaction from Kathryn, and looked at her. "I knew it," she said. "I knew they were planning something!"

Ornawka, as usual, was an empathic blank, but he absently rubbed his hand over the beamer at his belt.

Pikkiro continued. "The priests have only supported Kitillikk because they believe Akkanndikk is really dead, and that Kitillikk has said she is alive only to keep the populace in line. That's what Kitillikk has told them. But an acolyte in the Temple has told me that he has seen priests who are fanatical supporters of Kitillikk carrying food into the depths of the Temple, through a door that is used by no one else, and always locked. He also tells me that he has no doubt that if those priests found him spying on them, he would be killed, so he has made no attempt to find out what lies through that door."

"Then you're not sure."

"As sure as we can hope to be. And if we are wrong, then all is lost, because if Akkanndikk is not there, either she really is dead, or at the very least we have no hope of finding her before the Fleet breaks orbit."

"The Temple," Ukkaddikk said slowly. "A difficult place to sneak into. How can we hope to make this rescue?"

"It will be all but deserted tomorrow. Every ship in the Fleet must receive the blessing of the Hunter before setting off to war, and Kitillikk is in a hurry. Every priest that can be spared will be pressed into that service."

Ukkaddikk looked at Jarrikk. "What do you think?"

Jarrikk finished translating for the humans and turned to the other two S'sinn. "We must try," he said quietly. "Or our escape from the *Unity* served no purpose—as did all our efforts to avert war."

Kathryn spoke up in Guildtalk. "We must try, or everything we've done here has been wasted," and Jarrikk laughed to hear her echoing his words so closely, then had to quickly explain his amusement to her when she frowned at him.

Ornawka didn't smile at all. "Sounds like it's a good thing I hung on to this," he growled, and patted the beamer.

Pikkiro's plan, Kathryn judged as she listened to Jarrikk's translation of it, was simplicity itself, though it promised to be more than a little uncomfortable. As a member of the Supreme Flight, Pikkiro had access to a private area of the Temple for meditation and worship. Ukkaddikk and Jarrikk could both enter as members of his entourage. The difficulty, obviously, lay in getting the humans inside. Pikkiro's plan was to offer sacrifice to the Hunter and ask His blessing on the Fleet. He would bring in a large, living animal on a heavily decorated cart—and the humans would be hidden in the cart.

Once inside, they need only find the door the informative acolyte had told Pikkiro about, rescue the Supreme Flight Leader, and then take her to the priests, who, Pikkiro seemed confident, would immediately call a halt to blessing the Fleet and demand that Kitillikk return.

Kathryn wasn't so sure, but she said nothing about her doubts. After all, what else could they do?

So it was that, before dawn the next morning, she found herself flat on her back in pitch blackness, her right arm pressed tightly against Jim and her left against Dr. Chung, and her nose just a centimeter away from a false floor of rough wood that Pikkiro and Tillikko had built into a cart the night before. Above that, she knew, a jarrbukk contentedly munched fedra inside a gilded cage. The jarrbukk, a gorgeous golden hexaped, might have been taken intact from some ancient pastoral frieze if not for the incredible, eye-watering stench that accompanied it and had already thoroughly infiltrated their enclosed hiding space.

At least the journey would be a relatively short one: no more than four thousand beats, Pikkiro had said, which Jarrikk had explained meant between two and three hours. They planned to arrive at the Temple just as the priests' shuttle left the spaceport, shortly after sunrise.

The cart jerked and began to roll. One good thing about being so tightly packed into their hiding space, Kathryn reflected as they jounced out of the farmyard: it saved them from bouncing around as the unsprung cart transmitted every irregularity of the ground perfectly to their bodies. Above them the jarrbukk brayed harshly, obviously unhappy about this sudden change in its fortunes.

Without even trying, Kathryn could sense Jarrikk, not five meters away, behind the cart and off to the right. Since their strange linking, he had never been so far away that she could not feel his presence at least a little bit in the back of her mind. But even with Jim closer to her than he had been since that night in his quarters in the Guildhall—centuries ago that seemed, now—she could not penetrate his shield. By contrast, she could read Dr. Chung's emotional state—dominantly apprehension—easily.

But it was Jim's emotions she really wanted to be able to read, and if empathy couldn't do it for her, she'd have to fall back on that poorest of all substitutes: words.

She turned her head the little bit toward him she could, and whispered, so that Dr. Chung wouldn't hear, "Jim, what's wrong?"

She felt his body stiffen. "Nothing. Why?"

"You've been . . . hostile. Ever since you made it back to *Unity*. Especially to Jarrikk and Ukkaddikk."

"S'sinn killed Matthews and Annette. I'm just having a little trouble being friendly right now."

"But Jarrikk and Ukkaddikk are Translators . . ."

"They're still S'sinn. And I don't want to talk about it anymore."

Kathryn turned her face upward again, remembering that conversation she'd had with Jim before she left the Guildhall, remembering how Jim had told her not to take the words of her Oath too much to heart, remembering how he'd said "species ties" were going to be important, and especially remembering his last question: "If war comes, will you side with aliens against your own kind?"

And then she also remembered that one brief glimpse beneath Jim's shields that she and Jarrikk had achieved in the maintenance room, the horrifying pleasure that had been Jim's reaction to his killing of the guard, and despite the sweltering confines of the cart, she felt very cold.

Jarrikk had never before worn the enfolding cloak of a Temple Penitent, and he found it uncomfortably warm and confining, even in the damp pre-dawn gloom.

At the same time, he could appreciate its value as a disguise, especially when, after an hour's easy walk along muddy but well-maintained roads, they saw ahead, in the growing twilight, a checkpoint guarded by two huge, firelance-toting Hunters. Two others circled overhead. "I'll take care of this," Pikkiro said. "Stop the cart." He went ahead as Ukkaddikk calmed the two horned kaxxa that pulled the cart.

Jarrikk sensed Kathryn's questioning uneasiness at the halt, but dared not speak to her out loud. Instead, he tried to reach out telepathically, but with no success. That particular link still seemed to require touch. Still, she relaxed a little, and he hoped that at least some reassurance had seeped through.

He couldn't do anything about Dr. Chung's equal uneasiness, and as for Ornawka . . .

Pikkiro came back. "There are two more checkpoints between here and the Temple," he said calmly, "but I've cleared us through both of them. It would appear I am still one of the most trusted members of the Supreme Flight."

"Not for much longer," Ukkaddikk said dryly.

"Only if we fail. If we succeed, my position will be stronger than ever with the true Supreme Flight Leader. Heek!" He chirped at the kaxxa, and they climbed up from their knees and started forward again.

Jarrikk kept his eyes down as they passed the Hunters, but he sensed no suspicion from them, only boredom. The same held true at the remaining two checkpoints. And then they were into the city, where the crowds seemed sparse, even for early morning. Normally the city bustled from dawn to dusk and from top to bottom, with carters and merchants hauling or hawking large or bulk wares on the ground, specialty merchants selling smaller personal or luxury items from the balconies and perches that thrust out at all levels of the city's towers, and eating and drinking establishments thriving among the spires. But today only a few carts like their own and even fewer powered vehicles trundled along the grassy lanes, and no

merchants seemed to be about at all. Nor did the res-
taurants and bars seem to be doing much business,
those that weren't shuttered. If there were S'sinn
about, they were keeping a low profile and keeping
quiet.

"Kitillikk," Pikkiro growled as they rolled down one
empty lane past closed shop after closed shop. "She
forbids assemblies of more than five S'sinn, forbids
flights above a limited distance, forbids this, forbids
that. She has strangled the city half-unconscious so she
need not fear an uprising while she is off fighting her
war. Then, when she has won, she will return and
celebrate her victory by freeing her own populace,
who will be so grateful to her, and so pleased that she
has destroyed the hated humans, that they will flock
to her side and her ascension to Supreme Flight
Leader will be made permanent. At which time, no
doubt, the true Supreme Flight Leader really will suc-
cumb to the injuries she suffered in the assassination
attempt, just as the priests already think she has."

They could be right, Jarrikk thought as the black
towers of the Temple rose in front of them. *We could
be on a fool's errand.*

To their right rose the wingless statues guarding the
Place of Flightless Sacrifice. Jarrikk ignored them.
Ahead gaped the Hunter's Maw, the main gate into
the Temple courtyard. Normally the grassy space beyond would be crowded with worshippers and tourists
from around the world and even off-planet, but today
it was empty. They rolled into it beneath the impassive
stone eyes of ancient High Priests, carved in holy
poses atop the Temple walls.

When Jarrikk had come into this courtyard as a
tourist himself, before the peace conference with the
humans, he had next mounted the twenty-nine well-
worn black stone steps directly ahead that led into the
main worship hall, the Hunter's Heart, one of the few
times in his life his flightlessness had gone unnoticed,
since all S'sinn entered the Hunter's Heart on foot.
But Pikkiro led them instead to a closed gate in the

courtyard's left wall. He knocked, and after a few moments a small panel in the middle of the gate swung inward. The grizzled gatekeeper who looked out nodded to Pikkiro in recognition and unbolted the gate for them.

Beyond stretched a long, narrow path of yellowing grass, hemmed in by black stone walls. At its end, the path turned sharply right, revealing another gate, smaller than the public one leading into the Hunter's Heart but also far more ornate, its arch of black marble shot through with fiery red streaks. A blood-red flame burned in a torch at the arch's peak.

This time they had to open the gate themselves. "A sign of humility," Pikkiro said. "Like walking up the stairs to the public gate. It also means we can enter without alerting anyone inside."

Apparently the S'sinn of the Supreme Flight didn't like to carry humility to extremes: the finely balanced, well-oiled doors practically opened at the first touch of Pikkiro's finger. They urged the kaxxa through the arch and into a large round worship chamber (though much smaller than the Hunter's Heart), where more of the scarlet-burning torches struggled but failed to lift the gloom clinging to the dead-black walls. Pillars shaped like huge interlocking teeth encircled the chamber, and at its center reposed a round slab of dark red stone; reaching down from the ceiling above it, a clawed stone hand crooked its fingers to take what was offered.

"Help me unload the jarrbukk and move the kaxxa out onto the grass," Pikkiro said. "Then I will make the sacrifice while you free the humans."

From the change in the sound that penetrated their dark hiding place, Kathryn presumed they had entered the Temple, and it was with relief that she heard the jarrbukk's hooves clattering above her as it was led from the cart, and with much greater relief that she gulped fresh air as the first of the planks disappeared from over their heads.

The first thing she did when she could sit up was scratch her nose; then she climbed out of the cart, groaning, and turned to help Dr. Chung. She had hold of the doctor's hand and was helping her from the cart when something screamed behind her and she almost pulled Dr. Chung down on top of her.

She spun to see the jarrbukk drop to its knees, blood from its slit throat pouring down over the red altar. Its eyes glazed, its tail twitched spasmodically, then it fell on its side and lay still. Behind it, Pikkiro held aloft a curved, bloodstained blade, and shouted something to the giant clawed hand descending from ceiling. Kathryn felt his fervor and devotion, and it terrified, thrilled, and troubled her all at once. The knowledge they would face that same fanatical devotion in the priests who held Akkanndikk captive terrified her; the sheer, blazing heat of the emotion that filled Pikkiro thrilled her—and the realization that she no longer believed in anything with that kind of fervor troubled her. Once, maybe, she had given the Guild such devotion: no longer. And she wasn't even sure if that were good or bad.

"Barbaric," Jim muttered, then drew his beamer and turned away, surveying the encircling giant teeth as though expecting hostile S'sinn to pop out from behind them at any moment. Dr. Chung, on the other hand, seemed more fascinated than horrified.

"A sacrifice to the Hunter," the doctor breathed. "I've read about it, but no offworlder has ever been allowed to see the ceremony performed. Next should come the flame . . ."

"Flame?" Kathryn looked back at the altar. Pikkiro had backed away, wiping the blood from the knife on a clean white cloth, which he then threw onto the animal's carcass. As the cloth touched it, the carcass burst into flames. Kathryn's ears popped and a powerful breeze tugged at her clothes. The flames, smoke, and sparks raced up into the Hand of the Hunter. In seconds, all trace of the jarrbukk had vanished, leaving the altar clean and blank as before.

Kathryn looked at Jarrikk. "Impressive," she said. He half-spread his wings in a S'sinn shrug.

Pikkiro came back to them. "I have asked the Hunter's favor on our mission. Let us begin it." He tossed the sheathed sacrificial knife down into the cart, and in its place drew out a long black firelance. Jarrikk and Ukkaddikk pulled firelances from the cart as well; they had left their Commonwealth beamers at the farm. Kathryn checked the hilt of her own beamer to make sure the weapon was fully charged, but did not draw it from its holster.

Pikkiro silently held out an extra lance to Dr. Chung, but she refused.

Behind the altar, an open arch led out of the worship chamber. Pikkiro took them through it into a long, dark corridor, punctuated by other arches at regular intervals. Only their footsteps on the well-worn stone floor broke the deathly silence that otherwise gripped the Temple, as though it had been abandoned for a thousand years. Kathryn glanced through each of the arches they passed, but always saw the same thing: a dark, empty stone chamber, unrelieved even by windows.

"Penitence chambers," Jarrikk explained before she even asked him. "The priests consider it good to occasionally shut themselves away from the sky and meditate on their service to the Hunter."

They came to a rising flight of stairs, down which poured daylight. Pikkiro climbed them cautiously, looked around, then motioned for the others to follow. They emerged into a grassy courtyard surrounded by towers and walls, filled with gaping black arches glaring down at them. They stood there in plain sight for an agonizingly long time, while Pikkiro slowly turned in place, but at last he gestured and pointed to a ground-level arch almost directly opposite the stairs they'd just ascended, and they scurried into it like roaches surprised by a midnight light.

This corridor ran for a much shorter distance before ending in a door. Pikkiro said something, and Jarrikk translated for the humans. "Beyond this door is the base of the Great Tower," he said. "Supreme Flight Leader Akkanndikk, if she is here, is being held in a chamber beneath the Tower. Across from this door is another door, beneath a flight of stairs. That door leads to Akkanndikk's prison. Pikkiro does not expect to find guards on this level; the strength of this chamber as a prison is that it has been unused for so long its existence is all but forgotten. But he admits he is not positive, so he asks that you have your weapons ready."

"My weapon's been ready since we left the *Unity*," Jim said.

"We noticed," Kathryn said. "But I don't sense anybody except us. The chamber must be empty." Nevertheless, she drew her own beamer for the first time. It felt awkward and unpleasant in her hand. She wondered if she could actually bring herself to fire the thing, and hoped fervently she wasn't about to find out.

Pikkiro opened the door. Kathryn tensed, but nothing happened as he eased it wide, then stepped through. One by one, they followed.

Beyond lay a huge, circular chamber, floored by an intricate red-gold mosaic showing the snarling face of the Hunter, glowing in the light of thousands of candles—the priests, Kathryn had already noted, did not go in much for modern technology. There were four large doors, including the one they had just come through, set equidistant around the walls—and then there was the fifth door, small, black, and almost invisible, underneath the staircase that climbed up through the ceiling. Pikkiro pointed at it unnecessarily.

At least there was no one to shoot at, Kathryn thought—and better yet, no one shooting at them.

They crossed the chamber. Pikkiro stopped by the little black door and spoke again, in a near-whisper. Jarrikk translated in the same low voice. "He says he is certain there will be guards in the chamber below, and possibly on the stairs. He says we must rush down as quickly as we can, because he is afraid Kitillikk's orders are to kill Akkanndikk if anyone attempts a rescue. He says—"

Kathryn sensed S'sinn outrage behind her, and at the same instant someone screamed harshly at them. She whirled to see a priest standing in one of the doorways, carrying a silver tray with a glass pitcher and goblets on it. Jim spun and fired almost at once, but the beam went wide, slicing through a rack of candles by the door and sending them clattering to the floor. The tray crashed down after them as the priest screeched and ran, the pitcher and goblets shattering into a thousand glittering shards and the pitcher's dark red contents flaring as it poured out over the fallen candles, so that for a moment the doorway was blocked by a pool of fire.

"Damn!" Jim pushed past Ukkaddikk and Jarrikk to face Pikkiro. "Now! We've got to go in *now!*"

Pikkiro backed up from the door and sliced open its lock with a single quick bolt from his firelance. Then he pushed the door open, folded his wings tightly and dashed through. His lance fired again almost at once as he plunged out of sight.

Jim followed him, then Ukkaddikk, Jarrikk, Kathryn, and finally Dr. Chung, whose fear Kathryn sensed clearly—not that it was any greater than her own. Kathryn could see only Jarrikk's scarred wings as they dashed down the circling stairs, passing the decapitated body of a S'sinn and, several steps later, his still smoldering head. Kathryn swallowed hard and kept moving.

More flashing red firelance bolts silhouetted Jarrikk, then the more sustained white light of a beamer ray. Kathryn sensed four strangers ahead of them, three terrified and angry, and one barely even conscious; then a S'sinn screamed and she sensed only two terrified and angry strangers—and then Jarrikk reached the bottom of the stairs and leaped to one side as the beam from a firelance lashed the wall above his head. Kathryn flung herself on the cold stone floor. Dr.

Chung, she noted briefly, had wisely decided to hang back in the stairwell.

Jarrikk had crawled behind an overturned shikk; she followed him. The guards were barricaded behind a table; behind them, chained to another shikk, hung a female S'sinn: Supreme Flight Leader Akkanndikk, Kathryn supposed. A dead S'sinn lay near her.

Jim lay behind another overturned shikk to their right; Pikkiro and Ukkaddikk had ducked into the archway of a corridor leading off to their left. Pikkiro shouted something; Jarrikk touched Kathryn's arm, and suddenly they were Linked.

He says we must attack together, that we are spread out enough that they cannot fire at all of us at once; that when they rise to fire, another of us can kill them. I think he hopes they will surrender rather than fight to the death.

I thought S'sinn always fought to the death.

There is a difference between legend and reality. Jarrikk tensed. **He says—now!**

Kathryn intended to leap up, beamer blazing, but in the aftermath of telepathic contact her muscles refused to respond for just a moment, and in that moment, empathy still heightened by her contact with Jarrikk, she sensed for only the second time something beneath the surface of Jim's empathic block, something that confused, then frightened, then enraged her; and when she did leap up, she didn't face the overturned table, she faced Jim, and ran across the chamber floor through the strobe-like flicker of the firelances, jumping toward him, hitting his outstretched arm just as he fired his beamer—

—so that the ray slashed only across the stone beside the Supreme Flight Leader and didn't rip through her hearts as he intended.

Kathryn crashed to the floor, stunned and breathless. Dimly she sensed that the guards behind the table had died, that Ukkaddikk had been wounded, but more strongly than anything else she sensed Jim's pure hatred for all aliens, his feelings for once naked and unshielded, as he lifted his beamer again—and this time aimed it at her.

Jarrikk, too, sensed Ornawka clearly, and his hand tightened on his firelance. But Ornawka's beamer snapped up from Kathryn to Jarrikk, then back down to Kathryn, then suddenly he turned and ran toward the archway where Pikkiro and Ukkaddikk had taken shelter—except Ukkaddikk lay smoldering in his own blood, wounded and unconscious, and Pikkiro the non-empath, oblivious to all that had been going on, was checking the guards to make sure they were dead.

Jarrikk whipped up his lance and fired a single bolt after Ornawka, but it only scored the ceiling of the tunnel above and behind the human's head just before he ran out of sight. Pikkiro spun from his examination of the Supreme Flight Leader, firelance snapping up. "What . . . ?"

"Ornawka was the human who attempted to assassinate the Supreme Flight Leader," Jarrikk snarled. "He just tried again."

Kathryn got to her feet, breathing hard and feeling her ribs gingerly. "Doctor Chung," she shouted up the stairs, "Ukkaddikk is hurt!" No reply. Kathryn started toward the stairs as Jarrikk crossed to the older Translator. "Doctor Chung?"

A flash of light—and Dr. Chung's scorched body came tumbling down the stairs. Kathryn screamed, then turned and ran toward Jarrikk as more S'sinn burst into the room. The first fell to Pikkiro's beam, but the second's firelance cut Pikkiro almost in half. Jarrikk gave a despairing look at Ukkaddikk, then grabbed Kathryn's hand and almost dragged her along the corridor after Jim.

Ukkaddikk . . . Doctor Chung!

We can't help them.

Who . . . ?

I don't know. Renegade priests or loyal priests. It doesn't matter. We've failed.

Where are we going?

I don't know.

Neither one of them could afford to spend any more energy on telepathy. They simply ran, sensing their pursuers racing after them, and finally burst out through an opening on the river bank—

—just as eight armed priests alighted above them in the Place of Flightless Sacrifice.

Chapter 19

Kitillikk saw the High Priest off her flagship *Bloodfeud* with barely disguised impatience. The priests' silly blood-sprinkling ceremony had wasted several thousand beats, and it wouldn't surprise her if it had gummed up some vital piece of equipment, too. But if it made her Hunters fight more fiercely, she supposed she had to put up with it.

The moment the airlock door closed behind the High Priest and her entourage, Kitillikk spun and plunged into the gravity-shielded central shaft that provided zero-G access to all the decks of her huge, cylindrical ship, and flew up it toward the bridge. She alighted neatly on the access balcony, her claws digging deep into its padding to stop herself from bouncing away again, and, after a momentary pause while the computer identified her and activated the balcony's artificial gravity, the airtight door slid aside to admit her.

Ukkarr greeted her, rising from the Fleet Commander's shikk, which overlooked the sunken area where the bridge crew labored. "Final preparations have been completed on all but a handful of ships, and even those vessels are at least flight-ready," he said. "The Fleet awaits your orders, Your Altitude."

"Then I'd better give them, hadn't I?" Kitillikk slid onto the shikk that Ukkarr had vacated, slipped her hands into the control gloves, and lowered the helmet over her eyes. The virtual-reality command space encompassed her: she could see the location of any ship at a glance, zoom in on it for a closer look, even reach out with her hands and mold the Fleet into whatever formation she desired, the computer then translating that formation into detailed maneuvering orders for each ship. She savored the feeling of complete control for a moment, then said, "Computer. Voice-link, all vessels."

"Voice-link activated," the computer responded.

"This is Acting Supreme Flight Leader Kitillikk," Kitillikk said, imagining her voice echoing through all the hundred ships of the Hunter's fleet. "Greetings, Hunters! We have received the blessings of the Hunter of Worlds. We have prepared ourselves, body and spirit. Our ships are ready, and we are ready. Now is the time. Now is the time to avenge Supreme Flight Leader Akkanndikk, to take back our stolen worlds, to redeem our honor, to release ourselves from the shackles of the Commonwealth and once more fly free. The time is now, brave Hunters! Captains, acknowledge!"

A tumultuous roar of voices came back as every ship's captain responded, their ships glowing blue in her display as they spoke. When the entire Fleet shone blue, Kitillikk said, "You have your orders. Execute!"

The mass of ships began to move. *The War of Independence,* Kitillikk thought with great satisfaction, *has begun.*

She freed herself from the controls and glanced at a chronometer on one of the bridge panels as the *Bloodfeud* broke out of orbit with the rest of the Fleet. Ukkarr followed her glance. "The delay was insignificant, and the symbolism important," he said.

"You misunderstand me," Kitillikk replied, but she did not explain.

The War had indeed begun: the first shot, at that very moment, was being fired a thousand light years away.

Kitillikk's only regret was that she could not be there to see the humiliation of the Guild of Translators.

Karak once more climbed the steps to the council chamber, even more slowly than the last time. The watersuit had certainly grown no lighter, and neither had the news from S'sinndikk. *Unity* had been taken by Kitillikk's forces. Now an ominous silence wrapped the Guildship. No word on the fate of the Translators that had been aboard it. *No doubt Kitillikk is saving them for something special,* Karak thought bitterly.

Worse, the S'sinn fleet had launched. Even now it was on its way to its target, no longer a secret: Kikks'-sarr. Where the last war had begun and ended. Already fighting had broken out there among the human and S'sinn colonists. Casualties were reported heavy on both sides, despite the lack of heavy armament, prohibited by the last treaty. Karak doubted there would be anything at all left of the planet in another few days: Kitillikk's Fleet and the Earth Fleet would arrive at the same time.

Meanwhile, the Commonwealth did nothing. Fractured along a dozen internal faults, it waited only for the blow that would shatter it.

This was the news he brought to the Council: and this was the news to which, once again, they would have no response. Like the rest of the Commonwealth, they waited helplessly for the end.

As Karak's watersuit-encased right locomotors fell on the last step of the staircase, the building shook so hard that he grabbed the railing for support with all his manipulators, then stood stock still. *Earthquake?* But Commonwealth Central had been deliberately built in a geologically stable area . . .

A deep gonging began, itself loud enough to shake the building. It took a moment for Karak to recognize the sound: the only other time he'd heard it had been during his investiture ceremony, when he had pledged that as Guildmaster he would defend the Guild against any and all enemies that might arise.

The Guildhall was under attack!

Galvanized by the realization, Karak hurried down the short corridor at the top of the stairs and pushed through the Guildheart doors to find the other Councilors—those with eyes, anyway—staring at him. "Computer—video!" he snapped, and the surface of the star-studded table opened up. A quartet of vid-screens lit as they rose into position. "The Guildhall is under attack. Show me!"

Instantly all of the screens filled with the same image: a gaping, smoking hole in a wall of one of the Guildhall's central towers. They'd chosen well, Karak thought grimly. The topmost part of that tower had been deserted for generations, but three levels near its base remained in use: the lowest housed the central computer, the highest communications, and sandwiched in between—the Guildheart.

No wonder the whole building had seemed to shake.

"Show me the intruders," he commanded, and the screen flickered, revealing six shadowy figures flitting down the tower stairs—shadowy, but unmistakable: S'sinn.

Already the intruders were nearing the entrance to the communications room. "Voice-link to communications!" Karak cried, but too late: one S'sinn tossed something at the door, which burst inward in a camera-blinding flare of white light. Then the image switched to the inside, where a dozen Guild workers, Hasshingu-Issk, Orrisian, and human, knocked down by the concussion, were just picking themselves up when the S'sinn burst in among them.

Firelances flashed red, and the workers dropped, disemboweled, cut in half, or burning alive. Communications equipment exploded in flame and smoke.

The ceiling of the Guildheart shook. The Council itself would be next, then the computer and its irre-placeable records, and the Guild would die. That he would die, too, hardly even registered on Karak in that moment.

"Councilors!" he cried. "The Circle! Form the Circle!"

Whatever their personal fears at that moment, they were all masters of the Guild: the most powerful empaths in the Commonwealth. More than that, the most powerful *projective* empaths. They could not Link, but they could project an emotion, fine-tuning it by sensing the emotions being projected by their neighbors. As Guildmaster, Karak was the key, providing the core emotion for them to sense and duplicate, and the emotion he drew from them now was fear: utter, unnerving, heart-stopping terror.

It poured into him so strongly that he almost lost control of it, almost succumbed to it himself, but the knowledge of what would happen if he did enabled him to hold on, to channel the terror not into his central being, where it would destroy him, but through his own projective ability. He held it there, building and building in intensity, like water piling up behind a dam: then when he sensed the S'sinn terrorists outside, as the vidscreens showed one raising another grenade to hurl against the door; he released it all, pouring the full power of the Circle directly into the minds of the S'sinn.

They screamed, the sound so shrill and high that it filled the Guildheart even through the heavy doors. One dropped senseless, unconscious or dead; two others flung themselves at the stairs they had come down, ripping bloody strips of flesh from each other in their blind struggle to escape, two more fought madly in a paroxysm of violence, howling at the top of their lungs, and the last . . .

. . . the last one started shaking violently, and dropped the primed grenade.

The shaped charge, designed to explode inward through a yielding surface, instead blew downward against the solid stone of the floor, which directed all of its force, and a spray of needlelike stone shards, upward and outward.

The room shook. The screaming stopped. The vid-screen went blank.

The Guildheart doors rattled but held . . . and thin rivulets of red ran beneath them onto the white stone floor, slowly forming a scarlet pool.

Karak found himself flat on his back, the watersuit's stabilization systems having been unable to cope with the sharp shock of the explosion. The Circle broke apart. His ears rang, and exhaustion gripped him like the deadly pressure of the ocean's black depths. But he could not rest yet. They had to check for wounded, remove the dead, restore communications. And then . . .

"Computer," he said, climbing to his "feet" with a whirring of motors. "Record all images of the attack. Transmit to Commonwealth Central." He looked around at the other Councilors. "If we're fortunate, Kitillikk just made her first mistake."

Jarrikk looked around the circle of armed priests and said quickly to Kathryn, "Don't move."

"I don't intend to," she replied softly.

The fact they weren't dead already gave Jarrikk hope that these priests were not renegades, and might not even be aware that Akkanndikk was being held prisoner in the Temple. Although they'd find out soon enough: four of them pushed by Jarrikk and Kathryn and started back up the tunnel from which they'd just emerged.

The leader of the priestly party, a young male wearing a more ornate collar than the rest, snapped, "Bring them," to his subordinates, and flew off toward the Great Tower.

Four large male priests spread their wings and leaped down to the Translators' level, while the remaining two stayed above with weapons ready. Prodded by firelances, the Translators clambered up the slippery river bank and, spattered with mud, trudged back toward the Temple they had just fled.

Kathryn glanced at Jarrikk, but he shook his head;

no conversing would be permitted, and he didn't want to do anything to antagonize their guards, not until he'd had a chance to try to explain to the priests what had really happened in the room beneath the tower.

This time they entered the Temple through a door used only by the priests, in what he judged by the stonework to be the oldest part of the building, and climbed well-worn steps to a long corridor lit only by narrow slits on one side. They must be inside the defensive wall around the Temple, Jarrikk realized, approaching the thick, squat tower on its northeast corner: the dwelling of the High Priest—the same High Priest who earlier that day had been in space blessing the ships about to start the war against the humans that would destroy the Commonwealth.

The question Jarrikk was afraid he and Kathryn might die to answer was whether the High Priest had conspired with Kitillikk to trigger war by having a human kill the Supreme Flight Leader. Considering the fact that Jim had conveniently escaped before the priests arrived at the tunnel exit, that seemed a very real possibility.

The corridor ended in a strong wooden door and a strong armed guard. Jarrikk sensed her utter contempt as she opened the door to admit them to the chamber beyond.

There, in a circular room lit only by more of those narrow slits and a few flickering candles, the High Priest waited on her throne of stone, a shikk carved from a sacred rock the Hunter had spit down to S'sinndikk a millennium ago, blackened and scarred by the heat of His fiery breath. Or so Jarrikk remembered being told as a child. Whether the shikk was truly carved from a meteorite or not, it impressed with both its immense size and its great age. Even more impressive was what it portended: the High Priest considered the matter coming before her now to be of the utmost importance.

Jarrikk made the traditional bow of respect, but without the additional wing-spreading that signified submission. As a Translator, he would no more serve

the High Priest than he served the Supreme Flight
Leader. If he served anyone, now, it was the Guild
and the Commonwealth.

Or maybe he served only himself and his own conscience. Maybe that was the way it should have been
all along.

He felt certain the High Priest's piercing red gaze
noted his lack of obeisance, but she said nothing about
it, nor did any flicker of annoyance flare in the overall
sense of grave determination he read from her. Instead she spoke to another S'sinn, the one who had
led the party that had arrested them. "Recount the
facts."

"Yes, Your Eminence." Jarrikk felt his eagerness—
and, as he looked at Kathryn and Jarrikk, his hatred.
"Yssiddrikk, an Acolyte of the Third Wing, reported
to the Temple Guard shortly after noon that he had
surprised an armed party of S'sinn and humans in
High Tower. We sent a force there. On arrival, they
killed a female human they found in the stairwell.
Priest Skarridd died honorably seconds later at the
hands of Pikkiro of the Supreme Flight, who was then
slain in turn. We found four other dead S'sinn and a
badly wounded S'sinn who died shortly thereafter."

Good-bye, Ukkaddikk, old friend, Jarrikk thought
numbly.

"In addition, we found Supreme Flight Leader Akkanndikk, who is now undergoing medical treatment
and for whom the prognosis remains guarded. Another S'sinn and a human were glimpsed fleeing down
a tunnel, and accessing the Temple database revealed
that it emerged under the Place of Flightless Sacrifice,
although the database indicated the tunnel had been
sealed. I took a force there, and captured this S'sinn
and this human as they emerged.

"We have identified the dead S'sinn as the Priests
Mikkarr, Dekkarriss, Kkillikki, and Akkarramm, all
Acolytes of the Third Wing. The wounded S'sinn who
died was the Commonwealth Translator Ukkaddikk.
These two," he gestured at Jarrikk and Kathryn, "our

computer records identify as Translator Jarrikk and Translator Kathryn Bircher, who escaped from the human-crewed Guildship *Unity*. Acting Supreme Flight Leader Kitillikk has issued a standing order for their arrest, on the grounds of conspiring to assassinate the Supreme Flight Leader."

The High Priest's eyes had never left Jarrikk's face during the recital. "And tell me, Hunter-Priest Rikkarrikk, what interpretation you place on these facts."

"I think there can be only one," Rikkarrikk replied. "Acting Supreme Flight Leader Kitillikk sequestered Supreme Flight Leader Akkanndikk here in secret because she feared there would be more attempts on the Supreme Flight Leader's life—and she was right. These so-called Translators, with the help of the traitorous Pikkiro, discovered the Supreme Flight Leader's whereabouts, escaped their Hunter-surrounded spaceship, and came here to finish the job they started. Our Acolytes surprised them and died trying to save the Supreme Flight Leader's life. Had Yssiddrikk not stumbled on the assassination party, the Supreme Flight Leader would now be dead."

The High Priest already believed in just some version of events, Jarrikk could tell—but he could also detect, deeper within her, a shred of doubt. Would he have the opportunity to try to strengthen that doubt?

It appeared he would. The High Priest spoke to him, now. "And what have you to say, Translator Jarrikk? Do you admit your part in this attempt to kill the Supreme Flight Leader?"

"I do not," Jarrikk said. "We had nothing to do with it."

Rikkarrikk spun on him and lashed out with his claws, stinging his cheek. Jarrikk heard Kathryn gasp and felt her shock at the sudden violence. "How dare you lie to the High Priest!" Rikkarrikk hissed.

Jarrikk didn't even raise his hand to the spot, though he could feel the hot blood oozing through his fur. "I do not lie."

Rikkarrikk lifted his claws again, but the High Priest

stopped him. "Peace, Rikkarrikk. I will hear his interpretation as I heard yours."

Rikkarrikk growled, but stepped aside. Jarrikk mar-
shaled his thoughts. "High Priest, I do not deny that
a human attempted to kill the Supreme Flight Leader,
as Kitillikk has said. I do not even deny that that
human was a Translator: to my horror, I have only
just discovered the truth of that claim.

"Nor do I deny a conspiracy with roots in the Supreme Flight itself. But the details of that conspiracy
are not as Hunter-Priest Rikkarrikk has interpreted
them." He took a deep breath. "Translator Jim Ornawka attempted to kill the Supreme Flight Leader.
He acted with the help of, and in support of, Acting
Supreme Flight Leader Kitillikk. He did so in order
to trigger the war which we are even now on the verge
of beginning." The air in the chamber was thick with
disbelief, including the High Priest's, but he pressed
on. "The other Translators on S'sinndikk at the time
of Kitillikk's coup did not know of Ornawka's involve-
ment. We escaped from the spaceport with his help,
and sheltered with Pikkiro of the Supreme Flight.
Translator Ukkaddikk knew him to be a loyal sup-
porter of the Supreme Flight Leader and hoped he
would help us. Pikkiro had learned that the Supreme
Flight Leader still lived, and was being held in the
Temple by a small group of young priests who were
fanatical supporters of Kitillikk. He hoped that if we
rescued her, she could regain control of the Supreme
Flight and call back the ships before the war began.
Unfortunately, one of the renegade priests discovered
us before we could rescue the Supreme Flight Leader.
We made the attempt anyway. Several of the renegades died. In the confusion, Ornawka tried to kill
the Supreme Flight Leader again, but Kathryn," he
indicated her, "stopped him. He escaped ahead of us
down the tunnel. Rikkarrikk's force must have just
missed him. The rest you know." He stopped, meeting
the High Priest's gaze squarely—and reading clearly
that she did not believe him.

Nor did anyone else in the room, especially Rikkar-rikk. "Give the word, Your Eminence, and they both die now, before you, like the dung-crawlers they are."

"No," the High Priest said. "All must be done as tradition demands—and the Supreme Flight must be involved in the final disposition of this matter. Skkarrissa . . ." She turned to an aide and began talking to her in a low voice.

Jarrikk looked at Kathryn, who looked back at him. Even though she couldn't have understood the words, the emotions in the room must tell her clearly how bleakly things stood. Unless they could make the High Priest believe . . .

The Link, Jarrikk thought. *We need to Link with the High Priest, to show her the truth. But that's impossible . . .*

Or was it?

Together he and Kathryn had already done the impossible: faked a Link, aborted war, Linked without the symbiote, achieved telepathy, read Ukkaddikk's mind without his awareness, sensed minds at an impossible distance. They both had some projective ability; Ukkaddikk had said so. Usually that meant some slight ability to influence another person's emotions—not much help when the emotions were as strong as those in this room.

But together, they weren't just empaths, they were telepaths. Did their projective ability extend to that? Could they, as Ukkaddikk had wondered and Jarrikk had denied, project their thoughts into another's mind?

Only one way to find out . . .

Kathryn stood only a hand-span away. As inconspicuously as possible, he edged over to her. Rikkarrikk watched, but made no move to stop him. He knew they were both unarmed. What difference could it make if they touched?

A great deal, Jarrikk hoped.

His hand brushed Kathryn's. Everything that had

just been said, and what he had just thought, flashed between them.

This time there could be no holding back. This time neither of them could conserve energy, or keep any part of themselves to themselves. This time, they had to Link as completely as they had ever done, and somehow they had to draw in the High Priest, as well.

The room dissolved around Jarrikk as he released his senses, plunging his mind into Kathryn's. The sensation was like falling, like that terrifying plunge into water and pain that had ruined his wings and set him on the path that had led, maybe inevitably, to this time and place—but this plunge didn't end in agony, but in a sudden explosion of new sight and sound and smell and taste. For a moment he *was* Kathryn, sensing every square centimeter of her inside and out, then he was himself, then he was Jarrikk/Kathryn, and his/her mind looked around him/her to find the thoughts of every S'sinn in the room nakedly exposed—but only one mind of interest. The High Priest's mind beckoned like a fire on the other side of a black chasm. Jarrikk/Kathryn gathered his/her incorporeal muscles, and mind-in-mind, leaped into the flames.

Chapter 20

From the moment she and Jarrikk emerged onto the river bank until they stood before the High Priest in the inner sanctum, Kathryn had to take her cue from Jarrikk. Obviously the priests who had captured them were not the renegades who had taken the Supreme Flight Leader prisoner, because they were still alive. But they didn't exactly seem friendly, either. It wasn't until Jarrikk touched her hand and explained in a telepathic flash what he wanted to try that she understood. She agreed instantly: they had everything to gain and nothing to lose.

Linked, they plunged into the High Priest's mind, brushing aside the barriers of shock and denial that rose before them and pouring into her brain the truth as they knew it to be, of Kitillikk's part in the assassination attempt on the Akkanndikk and her subsequent imprisonment.

The High Priest believed them. She had to: in the intimate embrace of the telepathic contact, there could be no lying. She felt that as clearly as they did.

And then, abruptly, the contact ended as Rikkarrikk, sensing something strange, seized Kathryn and pulled her away from Jarrikk. Her mind snapped back into itself like a released bit of elastic, and she staggered and slumped in Rikkarrikk's grasp from the shock, almost blacking out.

Jarrikk, with no one holding him up, dropped to his knees and then fell forward onto his hands, panting—

and the High Priest gave a strange little sigh and fell sideways off of her shikk in a flutter of wings.

Pandemonium ensued as priests rushed to her. Rikkarrikk roared something and tossed Kathryn to one side, where another priest seized her roughly, claws leaving fiery, bloody welts on her arms, the fury that filled him stunning her further. *They think we've killed her,* Kathryn thought numbly, looking at the still figure of the High Priest. *Maybe we have.*

Jarrikk climbed slowly to his feet, looked at the High Priest, then glanced at Kathryn. But nothing of the telepathic link remained. She could sense weariness that matched her own, and concern for the High Priest, and that was all.

Rikkarrikk straightened abruptly, and she half-expected him to turn around and execute them on the spot. But in his emotions she read fury giving way to surprise. He glanced in their direction, then turned back to the High Priest, and Kathryn realized that the High Priest had said something to him. She lived, then: and it seemed Kathryn and Jarrikk would continue to, as well, because Rikkarrikk suddenly turned and snapped an order, and the priest holding her, after a moment's surprise as great as Rikkarrikk's had been, released her reluctantly.

Kathryn went to Jarrikk and took his hand. **Keep holding on,** he said telepathically. **I'll translate.**

What did she say to him?

She told him to release us, that we are not their enemies. I don't think he believes her.

Kathryn leaned gratefully against Jarrikk's warm flank. Why was every building on S'sinndikk so cold, cold, cold? Sensing her discomfort, he enveloped her shoulders with his wing while continuing to hold her hand, and she was momentarily reminded of her father putting his arm around her when she was a little girl—but remembering her father led inevitably to other memories she didn't want to recall just now.

The High Priest straightened and spoke. Through Jarrikk, Kathryn understood her—and sensed her growing anger, no longer directed at them, but at a most unexpected target.

"Kitillikk," the High Priest said. "Kitillikk has used us. Kitillikk arranged the assassination attempt against the Supreme Flight Leader to further her own ambition. Kitillikk swayed some of our own brothers and sisters to keep the Supreme Flight Leader imprisoned here so she might have free reign. Kitillikk lied to us about Akkanndikk being dead."

"Your Eminence," Rikkarrikk said, "I don't understand why you have suddenly decided to believe these two—" he gestured at Jarrikk and Kathryn.

"Are you questioning me, Hunter-Priest?"

Rikkarrikk drew himself up straighter. "It is my duty to do so if I believe you err, Your Eminence. And so I believe."

The S'sinn in the room exchanged uneasy glances, and Kathryn sensed them shifting position: through her Link with Jarrikk, could almost see the battle lines being drawn between Rikkarrikk and his Hunter-Priests and the priests surrounding the High Priest. For a moment she thought violence would erupt then and there, but the High Priest had a better idea.

"Translator Jarrikk," she said. "I think it would be most expedient if you would simply explain matters to Rikkarrikk as you explained them to me."

"Yes, Your Eminence."

Jarrikk squeezed Kathryn's hand by way of preparation. She closed her eyes, and this time the linkage came at once, much more easily, so easily that Kathryn/Jarrikk realized that it would never be difficult again, that they could call on this melding whenever they needed it. They made the projective leap into Rikkarrikk's mind, pushed down his barriers, showed him what they knew, and leaped out again cleanly, this time ending the Link on their own. Simultaneously drawing deep breaths, they opened their eyes to see Rikkarrikk staring at them, looking dazed. "How . . ." he whispered.

"You were saying, Hunter-Priest?" the High Priest said dryly.

Rikkarrikk growled deep in his throat. "Kitillikk must pay for this outrage."

"Indeed she must. But she is momentarily out of our reach. S'sinndikk, however, is not. Her rule here must end at once. Contact Central Communications. Tell them I wish to address the people of S'sinndikk, within two thousand beats. Skkarrissa," she continued, turning to the aide by her side once more, "arrange a preliminary broadcast to all our Temples. All priests to listen and attend. Ikkillikk . . ."

The High Priest's orders went on for several more minutes, but Kathryn quit listening. She snuggled close to Jarrikk, her head against the kitten-soft fur of his flank, the slow throbbing of his right-side heart filling her ear, and all-but-dozed until Jarrikk suddenly stiffened and she straightened up herself, confused until she realized the High Priest had called his name.

"Your Eminence," he replied.

"Rikkarrikk will accompany you to the Guildship *Unity*. You are free to go. I leave to you and your companion," she *almost* managed to hide her distaste for Kathryn, "dealings with your Guild and the Commonwealth. Report to them what you must; let them take what action they will."

"Your Eminence, what about the Hunter Fleet?"

"I can do nothing to stop them."

"But if you contacted—"

"I *will* do nothing to stop them." The High Priest looked steadily at Jarrikk. "Kitillikk has done wrong. Akkanndikk must be restored to her rightful position. If she chooses to call back the fleet, that is her choice. But it would not be mine."

"But—"

"It would not be mine, Translator."

Kathryn felt Jarrikk's anger, and understood. The High Priest would end Kitillikk's rule, because Kitillikk had transgressed against the Law. But she would do nothing to prevent the war Kitillikk had sought to trigger, because she wanted it, too. And the Supreme Flight Leader might not regain consciousness for days—if she ever did.

We've got to get in touch with Karak, Kathryn urged Jarrikk. *Immediately. We've done all we can.*

She **hasn't,** Jarrikk thought, but out loud he said stiffly, "Thank you, Your Eminence."

Rikkarrikk and two other Hunter-Priests moved up beside them. "This way, Translators," Rikkarrikk said, and though this time he served as honor guard rather than prison guard, all Kathryn sensed from him as he led them through the Temple was the same old hatred.

Karak stood on a balcony high up on the central tower of the Guildhall, the same tower through which the S'sinn terrorists had entered two days before, and looked across the gray roofs that lapped like waves at the Guildhall walls to Commonwealth Central's huge main spaceport. Another transport, fat and shiny like a dead, bloated fish, rode white fire into the sky—the fourth in the last twenty rotational degrees, and at least the tenth since the sun had risen that morning, and Karak's dawn flotation-meditation had been interrupted by the raucous signal of his comm.

He'd grown so used to bad news that it had been something of a shock to hear what the Translator who served as the Guild's Ambassador to Commonwealth Central had to report. "It worked," Translator Shakik, a fellow Ithkarite, said, the high pitch of his voice betraying his excitement. Karak had chosen another Ithkarite as Ambassador precisely so that, for once, he wouldn't have to guess the emotional state of someone on the other end of the commlink. "The attack had precisely the opposite effect to what Kitillikk intended. The delegates—not to mention the people they represent, thanks to that video you sent out— suddenly realized, when they saw the Guild attacked, what it would really mean to allow the Commonwealth to splinter over this human/S'sinn question.

They agreed that the Commonwealth must end this war before it begins. Orders have gone out; the Fleet is being mobilized."

Karak had thanked Shakik for his report, but though he shared Shakik's relief, that relief was tempered by knowledge of a single dreadful fact: somewhere out in space, the Earth Fleet and the S'sinn Fleet were already bearing down on each other.

The Commonwealth fleet, with all its mixed crews with varying loyalties and beliefs as to the rights and wrongs of the conflict, might emerge from dimspace in the middle of battle already joined.

How well would this new-found resolve for unity hold up then?

Kitillikk paced the bridge of *Bloodfeud,* claws stabbing into the padded flooring with every step, breath smoking in the chilled air, wings swirling and snapping as she turned at each end of the Captain's Walk. In the pitlike control room below, surrounding her currently unoccupied command's station, the crew dared not look up at her; even Ukkarr had busied himself elsewhere.

Half a day had passed since the time she had expected to hear from her strike force on Commonwealth Central. Half a day since she should have received word of the destruction and humiliation of the Guild, of the first cut in the campaign that would bleed the Commonwealth to death. Half a day—and she had heard nothing. Nothing!

She growled deep in her throat, and a helm officer who had tentatively glanced her way suddenly found his controls of far greater interest.

Something had happened: of that Kitillikk was sure. Commonwealth space normally buzzed with an omnipresent dimspace static, the background roar of countless communications. It had ceased. A silence as deep as the one gripping the bridge now lay over the Commonwealth. But did the silence bode good or ill for the Hunter Fleet?

Civil war might account for it: relay stations abandoned or destroyed by racial factions striking blows for their own independence in response to the proof her strike force had given them that the Guild and Commonwealth were not invulnerable.

But as much as she wanted to believe that explanation, she couldn't. No, this felt more like a deliberate blackout, an attempt to prevent valuable information from leaking into the wrong hands. And those hands, she was almost certain, were attached to her own arms. She stopped pacing and extended those arms, flexing her clawed fingers, then suddenly snapped her wings wide and leaped down from the walkway, alighting beside her command station.

My Hunters must have succeeded, she thought as she settled onto the shikk. She drew on the VR helmet. The ships of her fleet, recharging after their first dimspace jump, hung around her like crystals mounted in a web of silver, the *Bloodfeud* a diamond at its center. Of course it was only a computer simulation, but she drew strength from it.

Yes, she thought. *My Hunters succeeded. The Guild has been hurt badly, perhaps even destroyed. The Commonwealth is starting to break up. Why else black out communication? Commonwealth Central is trying to keep the news from the populace. But it's hopeless. The whole unnatural alliance is dissolving, as I always knew it would. From now on it will truly be a galaxy for Hunters!*

She suddenly laughed out loud, ignoring the startled looks of the bridge crew, and pulled off the helmet. "How long to Kikks'sarr? How long to battle?" she asked the helm officer.

"Two more jumps, Your Altitude. Less than two ship-days."

"Excellent." Kitillikk stretched, relaxed, and closed her eyes, and like any good Hunter trained to take advantage of any opportunity, instantly slept . . .

. . . and woke just a few hundred beats later, sensing someone beside her. "Hmmm?" she said without opening her eyes.

"A communication from S'sinndikk, Your Altitude," Ukkarr said.

Kitillikk opened one eye and looked up at him. "Yes?"

Silently he handed her a short printout. She scanned it, stiffened, and read it again, slowly and carefully. Then she ripped it into shreds and threw it on the floor. "Dungsucking priests!" she screamed, as the bridge crew hunched their wings and studiously ignored her. "Turning on *me* now . . ."

"They found Akkanndikk," Ukkarr said. "You should not have left her alive."

"How dare you question my—" Kitillikk stopped in mid-rant and took a deep breath, then slowly opened and folded her wings. "You're right, of course, Ukkarr. I should not have. I have paid for that mistake."

"What will you do?"

"I will do nothing. Communication from S'sinndikk can only be received by this ship. We will not receive anymore. The Hunter Fleet goes on—and once I have destroyed the humans, and the S'sinn learn of it, and of the crumbling of the Commonwealth, Akkanndikk will have no more power than she did as my prisoner beneath the Temple." She settled herself on her shikk once more. "To the victor goes the prize, Ukkarr. And *I* will be the victor."

"Of that, Your Altitude, I am certain." Ukkarr bowed, gathered up the torn pieces of the message, and left the bridge.

Escorted by Hunter-Priests, Kathryn and Jarrikk walked slowly back to the spaceport, while overhead the sky grew crowded. S'sinn flitted from tower to tower, some furtively, some frantically. Firelances sizzled somewhere in the distance, and once an explosion shook the grassy ground. But no one troubled them.

They reached the Spaceport to find the Hunters who had surrounded it gone and the *Unity,* unguarded, almost alone on the field. Rikkarrikk bowed stiffly to Jarrikk, ignoring Kathryn, then snapped an order to his guards. Instantly they sprang into the air, pelting the two Translators with a stinging hail of grit stirred up by the wind of their wings.

Kathryn took Jarrikk's hand again as they trudged across the duracrete to the *Unity*. *It looks undamaged.*

They had no reason to damage the ship. I wish I were as certain about the people.

Humans. Kathryn tugged Jarrikk forward. *Can't you go any faster?*

No, Jarrikk replied, but he did, a little. In the end it was too much for Kathryn and she broke free of him to dash the remaining fifty meters to the ship.

The hatch stood open and unmanned. After running as fast as she could to get there, Kathryn climbed the ramp tentatively. "Hello?" she called. "Is anyone . . ."

A half-familiar face appeared in the hatchway, and broke into a huge grin at the sight of her. "Translator Bircher! We thought you were dead!" The crewman—Peters, that was his name—looked past her. "Jarrikk, too!"

"What happened here? Is everyone all right?"

"Oh, yeah, they didn't bother us much: searched to make sure we weren't hiding you—and made a mess of the ship in the process—then left us to stew. Cut off spaceport services, of course, but we were already fully supplied, so we just switched to internal power. But what's been happening outside?" He scanned the spaceport over her shoulder. "And where are the others?"

The others. Dr. Chung, who wouldn't even lift a weapon, who had nursed both her and Jarrikk back to health. Jarrikk's mentor, Ukkaddikk. And Jim . . .

"What's wrong?" Peters said. More crew were appearing in the hatchway behind him, now, smiling and pointing and listening, waiting to hear her story. Jarrikk reached her, and took her hand.

The captain must know first, he thought to her. **And Karak.**

I know. Kathryn squeezed his hand. "I'd better report to the captain, first," she said. "Translator business." Those magic words backed Peters up, and cleared the hatchway, but it felt as if a lead curtain had descended between the two Translators and everyone else. "I'm sorry," she said awkwardly.

"I understand, Translator." She could sense that he did—he served the Guild, after all—but she could also sense a touch of hurt. But there was nothing she could do about it. "The captain knows you're back by now, of course, but I'll just call the bridge to let him know you're on your way up."

"Thank you," Kathryn said, and she and Jarrikk left him in the open hatch.

The captain met them at the door to the bridge. "Translators, I'm thankful you're alive—"

"Not all of us," Kathryn said. "Translator Ukkaddikk is dead. So is Doctor Chung." She felt his shock.

"What about Translator Ornawka?"

Kathryn took a deep breath. "He's a traitor," she said flatly. "He made a deal with Kitillikk to kill the Supreme Flight Leader. When we attempted to rescue her, he tried to kill her again. He's at large somewhere on S'sinndikk."

"We've got to find him, then—" The captain half-turned, as if to give an order, but Kathryn stopped him with a hand on his arm.

"No. We've got something more important to do." She still held Jarrikk's hand, and felt his support. "First, Jarrikk and I must contact Karak and tell him what has happened. And then, Captain, you must take us—"

"Back to Commonwealth Central? That course is already plotted, Translator—"

"Captain, please listen." *He won't like this,* she thought to Jarrikk.

He has no choice. Translator business.

Translator business. I'm starting to hate that phrase. "You must plot a course to Kikks'sarr."

"But that's where the Hunter Fleet has gone." The captain stared at her as though doubting her sanity.

"I know, Captain. We're going to stop their attack."

Chapter 21

Jarrikk wanted nothing more than food and sleep, not necessarily in that order. But instead he stood with Kathryn on the bridge, facing Captain Hall.

"That's absurd. I won't do it."

"You have no choice," Jarrikk said. "Translator business. This is a Guild ship and it, and you, are at our complete disposal."

"Guildmaster Karak—"

"Will certainly confirm that for you."

"We'll find out about that." Captain Hall turned. "Communications!"

"Sir!" A young man spun his chair smartly around.

"Contact Guildhall. Urgent priority message for Guildmaster Karak."

"Again, sir?"

"Yes, again."

"Again, Captain?" said Kathryn.

"I contacted him the moment the communications blanket lifted, but I wasn't able to tell him much."

"I see."

"Dimspace penetration achieved," the communications officer announced. "Waiting carrier pick-up . . . carrier accepted. Communication with Guildhall now open, sir. Guildmaster Karak online."

"In here," the Captain said, and ushered Kathryn and Jarrikk into a small adjoining room, where a dozen blank vidscreens stared down at a small desk and chair. Captain Hall offered the chair to Kathryn, who shook her head, though Jarrikk knew she was just as weary as he. The captain touched a control panel on the desk. One of the screens lit up with Karak's glistening gray face.

"More news, Captain?" said Karak. Then he screeched something in ear-splitting Ithkarite, followed by, "Translators! You're alive!"

"Not all of us, Guildmaster," Kathryn said, sensing, perhaps, that Jarrikk didn't want to talk to Karak. The ambivalence that had been with him since he unexpectedly awoke after attempting his Sacrifice came back full-force as he looked at the master of the Guild he now felt had been manipulating him all his life. Kathryn reported quickly and succinctly. When she had finished, Karak was silent for a long moment. "Jim Ornawka, a traitor," he said finally. "This is grievous news, Translators. This will be a serious blow to the credibility of the Guild, by itself, never mind the more broad-ranging consequences . . ."

"We'll worry about the Guild when we have time," Kathryn snapped. "It's one of those broad-ranging consequences we're a little more concerned about now. Namely, the war."

"The Commonwealth Fleet is mobilizing. It will attempt to once again stop the warfare between humans and S'sinn . . ."

"It can't make it to Kikks'sarr in time!"

Again Karak was slow in replying. "No. No, it cannot."

"We can, Karak."

"It's madness, Guildmaster," Captain Hall exploded. "They want me to take my ship into a battle zone. Our screens will barely stop a beamer, much less a Huntership bolt!"

"We're not asking you to fight, Captain," Kathryn said.

"Perhaps," Karak said, "you will be so good as to explain what you *are* asking."

Kathryn touched Jarrikk's hand. *What do I say?* she telepathed. *We don't really have a plan, yet.*

I think I have a youngling one. Tell him this . . .

"Kitillikk's hold on this planet is finished, at least for now," Kathryn said, Translating for Jarrikk, though Karak couldn't know that unless they told him—and neither of them felt any inclination to tell the Guild yet what they could do. Karak might just decide it was more important to save them and their unique ability for study by the Guild than to allow them to go on a probably futile and possibly fatal peace-making mission. "The High Priest has denounced her, and broadcast the details of her scheme.

"The *Unity* is smaller, lighter, and much, much faster than the Hunterships. We won't have to take as long between jumps to recharge. We should be able to reach the Hunter Fleet before its final jump, and transmit the High Priest's message to all the ships. We believe that most of the ships will abandon Kitillikk and return to S'sinndikk. That will leave Kitillikk with too small a force to face the Earth Fleet, and force her to abort the attack. The Commonwealth can then track her down at their leisure and return her to S'sinndikk for trial."

Sounds plausible, Kathryn telepathed when she'd finished talking.

Sounds weak as a day-old jarrbukk to me. But it's the best chance we have.

"Madness," the captain repeated in a growl. "Seconds after we start transmitting, they'll blow us out of space."

"We'll rely on you, Captain Hall, to outmaneuver them until the message is sent," Kathryn said.

Apparently despairing of talking sense into her, the captain appealed to Karak. "Guildmaster . . ."

"I think we must try this plan, Captain," Karak said. "For the moment the Commonwealth is united here, because of Kitillikk's attack on the Guildhall . . ."

What?

Obviously we have some catching up to do.

". . . but the Fleet will arrive either during or after the battle between the S'sinn and the humans. Either side might fire on the Commonwealth ships, and tear the Fleet itself wide open along wounds this latest show of unity has just scabbed over. I fear civil war."

"Guildmaster, I must register the strongest possible protest!"

"Protest noted. Nevertheless, you will follow the instructions of Translators Bircher and Jarrikk—and keep me informed. Guildmaster Karak out."

Karak's image vanished. Jarrikk looked at the captain, who scowled back. "Now, Captain," he said, "please prepare the *Unity* for launch."

As Peters had noted, the *Unity* already operated on internal power. Only two thousand beats after Captain Hall ungraciously accepted his orders, the *Unity* lifted from the spaceport and bore into space, speeding after the Hunter Fleet.

Jarrikk and Kathryn stood on the bridge hand in hand, watching the home planet of the S'sinn dwindling behind them. *Will this really work?* Kathryn telepathed. *Will the Hunter Fleet really turn on Kitillikk at the word of the High Priest?*

Funny how comfortable they had become with something that had been incredible only yesterday, Jarrikk thought. Now they preferred telepathy to Guildtalk, even when it wasn't strictly necessary. He stretched his crippled wing, trying to ease the persistent ache that always grew worse when he was tired. **Many individual S'sinn will,** he replied. **The question is how loyal the captains are to their Flight Leader— or how loyal they were to Akkanndikk. If only a handful turn against Kitillikk, the others will crush them, and we'll be no better off.**

How long?

One ship-day, no longer. The *Unity* recharges very fast compared to the slowest transports in the Hunter Fleet. By this time tomorrow, we should have caught them at the second jump point, and be in range to transmit.

If Kitillikk doesn't blow us out of space first.

Jarrikk made no reply, but he kept holding Kathryn's hand. They no longer grew weary after just a few seconds of telepathy; their neural pathways, altered who-knew-how by the deaths of their symbiotes, seemed to be adapting to the strange signals very well. Now, when he touched Kathryn, he felt only a sense of deep completeness, both from her and because of her, a feedback loop in which it was impossible to tell where she began and he ended. He wanted to touch her even when there was no need for telepathy, and sensed she felt the same. There was nothing of the mating urge about it; it went far deeper than that, even deeper than the Link of the Translators. This was something new, and wonderful—and he had no intention, when whatever was about to happen had finished, of letting the Guild tear apart what he and Kathryn had forged, just to see how it was made.

And if they succeeded, he thought, surely the Guild would owe them that much, at least. Even Karak would set aside the so-called "good of the Guild" this once, at their request.

Wouldn't he?

"I'm tired," Kathryn said out loud suddenly. "I'm very, very tired."

So was he, Jarrikk realized. They yawned simultaneously, laughed together, and went from the bridge hand in hand—sensing as they did so the avid curiosity of every one of the bridge crew.

They think we're having some bizarre form of interspecies sex, Kathryn thought to Jarrikk. *They don't understand the truth.*

How could they? No one but us has ever experienced anything like this.

They walked in warm companionship to Kathryn's door. She paused there and looked up at Jarrikk oddly. *Could there be anything to what they think?* she thought. *Could we ever . . .*

No. Search your S'sinnish memories. With our species, the female controls the mating urge of the male. A S'sinn male can only be aroused by the presence of female pheromones you do not produce—which is

good, I think, since I understand to the human olfactory system they are quite unpleasant.

Good, Kathryn thought, then blushed, even as Jarrikk felt her embarrassment. *I mean, I don't feel anything like that when I'm with you, but if you did, I might be willing—I mean . . .* her thoughts faded off in confusion.

I don't. Though I thank you for your willingness, and I admit my curiosity. But even were it possible, I would not satisfy that curiosity in trade for this bond we have formed. Would you?

No. Never.

They smiled simultaneously, then Jarrikk let go of Kathryn's hand and walked away.

The telepathic bonding ended instantly, but the warmth of her regard followed him up the corridor.

Kathryn, savoring that same warmth from Jarrikk's retreating presence, slept almost instantly, then woke to alarms.

An instant later a huge jolt flung her violently out of her bed. The alarms reached new levels of hysteria, then cut off.

Captain Hall's voice came on, harsh and strained. "This is the captain. We have been intercepted by a Huntership at the second jump point. It has grappled with us and is now rotating us to bring hatches in line in preparation for boarding. The Huntership's Captain has made it clear that if we attempt to resist, he will destroy us. Do not offer resistance. I repeat, do not offer resistance.

"Translators Bircher and Jarrikk, please report to the bridge."

Intercepted? Boarded? How . . . ?

Still groggy from being woken from the deepest pit of sleep, Kathryn stumbled to the door and stepped into the corridor just as Jarrikk approached. He seized her hand.

Kitillikk must have heard about the priests' coup on

S'sinndikk—put scoutships along her back trail, he telepathed.

Then what—?

If we get to the bridge, we may be able to broadcast to the fleet before we're cut off.

Are we close enough?

I don't know. We'll find out.

They raced to the bridge, or raced as fast as Jarrikk could when his clawed feet skittered and slipped with every step on the hard, slick floors. *At least the Hunters won't be able to move any faster,* Kathryn thought.

They sensed Captain Hall's fury long before they reached the bridge door. "I told you this was madness, Translators!" he snarled as they came into the red-lit bridge, filled with the screaming alarms of outraged systems. "My ship is in the grip of S'sinn Hunters and soon will be dragged into the heart of the Hunter Fleet—if they don't just destroy us out of hand!"

Kathryn's annoyance and Jarrikk's peaked in perfect synchronicity. "Captain, shut up," she snapped for both of them. "Communications officer!"

He looked up, blue eyes wide in his pale white face. "Translator?"

"Are we in range to broadcast to the Hunter Fleet?"

"Most of it, Translator."

"Call up the recording of the High Priest's announcement of Kitillikk's treachery. Broadcast it."

"Belay that order!" Captain Hall snapped. "Send that, Translators, and you sentence all of us to death!"

"Fail to send it and you sentence the entire Commonwealth to death—and the Guild you serve with it! Communications officer—"

The young man looked from her to the captain. "Captain?"

The captain stared at Kathryn defiantly, but she could feel his anger slipping away as the truth of her words sank in, and finally he dropped his gaze. "I'm sorry, Translators. Communications officer—"

A bolt of eye-searing red light snapped across the bridge, slashing across the young officer's spine. He jerked crazily up from the smoking ruin of his chair, like a marionette with tangled strings, then crumpled and fell, smearing dark blood across the communications panel. The smell of burned cloth and flesh drifted with a cloud of blue smoke across the bridge.

Through her link with Jarrikk, Kathryn understood the snarling words of the black-furred S'sinn who blocked the door into the bridge: "I take this ship in the name of the Hunter of Worlds, and Supreme Flight Leader Kitillikk!"

Kitillikk bared her teeth with such savage delight upon receipt of the news that the young officer who had brought it to her took a step back. "Fetch Ukkarr," she said to him, and he vanished as though pursued by the Hunter Himself.

She put the VR helmet on again and studied the sensor readings transmitted via dimspace from the last probe she had sent ahead on the final jump to Kikks'sarr. The human Fleet was there, no doubt about it, behind Kikks'sarr, though the probe had been found and destroyed before it could transmit details of its size and disposition. No matter; when she emerged above Kikks'sarr the furless cowards would have to round the planet to face her or she would slag their cities to the ground while they dithered on the dark side.

One way or another, she thought, battle would be joined by the time Kikks'sarr completed another rotation. And now she learned that the last feeble attempt by the Guild of Translators had been foiled, and that at last she had the traitorous Jarrikk and the interfering Kathryn Bircher in her claws.

Was it any wonder she showed her teeth so widely?

Ukkarr entered the bridge. "Yes, Your Altitude?"

"You've heard?"

"Yes, Your Altitude."

"Please take my place on the bridge. I wish to meet our new guests in person."

"Yes, Your Altitude."

Just because she was in a playful mood, and because
Ukkarr was always so solemn, she trailed the edge of
her wing sensuously over his as she passed him, and,
feeling him tremble at her touch, was filled suddenly
with a powerful lust. "Later," she whispered, and he
nodded almost imperceptibly.

Once off the bridge she launched herself into the
zero-G tunnel, savoring the brief moment of flight that
took her to the observation chamber overlooking the
cavernous main landing bay, where the flagship's four
scoutships docked when they weren't on patrol. As
she watched, the scoutship that had captured the *Unity*
floated into the bay and stopped with a small puff of
glittering silvery fuel from its maneuvering rockets. It
settled slowly to the deck as the artificial gravity gen-
erators beneath the floor of the bay, turned off for
docking, eased back up to full power.

An indicator lit on a communications panel set in
the wall. Kitillikk touched a key. "This is Supreme
Flight Leader Kitillikk," she said. "Congratulations,
Captain. How are your prisoners?"

"Silent," the scoutship captain said. "Standing here
holding hands like thunder-spooked younglings."

"Perhaps they'll speak to me," Kitillikk said.
"Please have them escorted to the security level as
soon as pressure has equalized in the docking bay.
Tell them I'll meet them there. I'm sure that will cheer
them up."

"I'm sure it will, Supreme Flight Leader."

"Kitillikk out."

She broke the connection, and called up a view on
the vidscreen of the *Unity,* connected to *Bloodfeud* by
flimsy umbilicals, docking tubes—and the computer-
enslavement of her drive system. Kitillikk rather
thought the Guildship would break apart under the
stresses of combat. Until then, though, she made a
fine shield for that side of *Bloodfeud.* Kitillikk showed
her teeth again. Especially if the humans recognized
Unity as one of their own and realized she was still
crewed . . .

Appreciating the irony of a human-crewed Guild-ship sowing disorder in the ranks of the human fleet, she made her way to Security.

Jarrikk stood stolidly with Kathryn, clasping her hand, though neither had thoughts to share at that moment. They could only draw strength from each other—what little strength they had to share—and try to ignore the hatred and contempt inside the heads of their two armed guards, one just inside and one outside the locked door of their stark metal cell. *Just like Rikkarrikk,* Jarrikk thought.

Just like Rikkarrikk . . . ?

Flightless fools, both of us!

Kathryn, he telepathed. **These two guards. Just like Rikkarrikk—**

I know. They hate us, she replied.

But we changed Rikkarrikk's mind.

He still hated us. All we did was make him listen to the truth.

I think we could have destroyed his hatred, too. I think we could have made him do anything we wanted him to.

Her hand tightened on his. *But these are Hunters. And they're loyal to Kitillikk—*

I don't think it matters. I think we can change that, too. Remember how it felt, inside the High Priest's mind, inside Rikkarrikk's? They had barriers of doubt and mistrust. We just brushed them aside—easily, like cobwebs. These guards aren't even priests, just ordinary Hunters. They can't keep us out. We can implant any idea we want into their brains, true or not, get them to do whatever must be done. We can use them, Kathryn—use them to escape, to take us to communications, to get our message to the entire fleet . . .

But that's—an assault. A rape!

It's a weapon. And this is a war.

No!

Kathryn—

Are you trying to change my mind, too? Suddenly

she jerked her hand free and backed away from him. The guard's firelance snapped down and he motioned her back toward Jarrikk. She returned, but she wouldn't touch him.

And then the door opened and Kitillikk entered.

Her self-satisfaction preceded her like an honor guard. "Jarrikk," she almost purred. "My old pupil. How pleasant to see you again."

"How pleasant to have me in your talons, you mean," he growled back. "Don't try to lie to a Translator, Flight Leader. You want both of us dead. Your only concern is orchestrating our executions to achieve the maximum effect."

"That doesn't mean I'm not happy to see you, Jarrikk. Quite the opposite." She looked at Kathryn. "And your human friend. Parents killed on Luckystrike, I understand, during the First War. How appropriate that she should join them to start the second and final one." She showed her teeth. "And you're a little behind the times, Jarrikk. My title is Supreme Flight Leader."

"Akkanndikk doesn't seem to think so."

The bared teeth went from a grin to snarl. "Akkanndikk is probably dead by now."

"The priests have renounced your title." Jarrikk said it loudly, hoping for a reaction from the guard at the door, but he seemed not to hear, or care.

"If the priests had really renounced me, they would have sent a scoutship after the Fleet to call it back," Kitillikk said. She spread her wings, showing a new insignia emblazoned on the leather: a spiral crossed with a lightning bolt, the emblem reserved for the Supreme Flight Leader. "They know the S'sinn people are on my side. They know the people cry out for the blood of the humans, for the shame of the First War to be wiped away. They know the S'sinn are no longer content to be kept down by the Commonwealth, to be treated as second-class primitives by the decadent older races. They have a law to uphold on S'sinndikk, and so they have said the words to renounce me, and they set you free, but their hearts are not in it. Their hearts, and the hearts of all the S'sinn, belong to me." She snapped her wings together, the blast of air ruffling Jarrikk's fur and driving Kathryn back a stumbling step.

"Brave words. But if they're true, why don't you tell the Fleet yourself what has happened on S'sinndikk?"

"I have no wish to confuse my Hunters on the eve of battle. When the victory is mine, rest assured, they will hear all." Teeth again. "Perhaps I will tell them at your trial, before you are executed for treachery and spying along with your human mate." Kitillikk reached out and ran the point of a claw along Kathryn's chin; Kathryn flinched but held her ground. "An astonishing perversion, that; though for a Flightless One so bereft of honor he refuses to take the Dagger of the Hunter, I suppose no sewer is too foul to crawl in."

Jarrikk tried hard to quell the slow, seething fire of hatred kindled in his hearts. Violent emotions muddied the mind, and he needed a mind as clear and sharp as a dagger of ice. He reached out and took Kathryn's hand, and this time she grasped it eagerly, her revulsion at Kitillikk's touch threatening to spill over into his mind and derail his concentration. He had to keep Kitillikk there, keep her talking, and at the same time convince Kathryn to—

But the opportunity passed as a klaxon sounded, a harsh blatting noise repeated over and over. Elation rushed over Jarrikk and it took a moment to recognize it not as his own, but Kitillikk's.

"Final jump," she said. "Battle begins!" She strode to the door; paused there. "When I return, the S'sinn will be able to hold their heads high for the first time since the humans slaughtered your youngflight, Jarrikk. I will expect your gratitude." The door slid shut, and the guard faced them again, firelance held lightly across his chest.

Chapter 22

Kathryn's mind roiled with confusion, and she pulled her hand free of Jarrikk's once more. She understood what Jarrikk wanted her to do, what she supposed they must do, but it appalled her. To take the link that had always provided her with such joy, which had filled the aching wound of bondcut when she was a girl, which had given her family and friends and now, more than either, Jarrikk—the thought of taking that link and turning it into a weapon almost physically sickened her. It was exactly the kind of thing she was afraid the Guild would use this gift for, if they could duplicate it: realpolitik, wasn't that the old Earth term for it? Do whatever must be done to achieve the desired ends.

Such thinking had a long and dishonorable history among humans, from the firebombing of Dresden to the defoliation of Vietnam to the decompression of the Jacobian far-side dome. Maybe sometimes the ends did justify the means—but you still had to live with the consequences, with the dead children and the cancer-ridden veterans and the Lunar Rebellion. Could she live with the consequences of using the gift she and Jarrikk shared in such a fashion?

Could she live with the consequences if she didn't?

He looked at her steadily, his mind filled with understanding and pity but also a hint of desperation. The guard watched them both, his mind filled with contempt, disgust, and hatred. And somewhere beyond the door Kitillikk hurried to give the orders to attack the fleet from Earth and doom the Commonwealth.

She'd chosen the hard path once before to prevent war. This path seemed harder yet: but she reached out and took Jarrikk's hand.

What do we do?

He flooded her with a momentary surge of gratitude, though it failed to warm the lump of ice that seemed to have formed in the pit of her stomach. **We must change our guard's mind about us,** he telepathed. **Then we must convince him to take us to communications. We must get the truth out to Kitillikk's fleet.**

Will that stop them? she wondered, though the real question, hidden in the still-private depths of her mind at this level of linkage, was, *Is it worth it?*

It will slow them down, Jarrikk replied.

That's not what I asked. But she had already made the choice.

She opened herself fully to him, felt him flinch when he encountered the depth of her doubts, but felt slightly better herself as she discovered that he shared them to a degree. Then all individual thought once more melted away into Kathryn/Jarrikk, and together they plunged into the disturbing darkness of the mind of their guard.

They destroyed his doubts in seconds, filled his mind with the thoughts they wanted him to think—that he had come to rescue them and take them to communications, and could let nothing stand in their way.

Kathryn/Jarrikk withdrew, thinking to conserve their strength to repeat the process with the guard in the hall, whom they could sense clearly through the intervening bulkhead, but their new convert didn't wait for them: he opened the door, and before his colleague could turn around, burned him through with a burst from his firelance.

Kathryn/Jarrikk fell apart into jointly horrified Kathryn and Jarrikk as the inside guard peered both ways down the corridor beyond, then motioned them out.

"That wasn't necessary," Jarrikk said, his voice echoing in translation in Kathryn's head. "We would have dealt with him."

"Your way's too slow," their guard growled. "My way is better. Come on—communication's this way."

They'd dealt the cards, now they had to play the hand, Kathryn thought. *We've created a monster,* she telepathed to Jarrikk.

Maybe, he sent back. **But he *has* saved us time. Come on.**

Their erstwhile guard dragged his dead friend inside the cell, closed and locked the door, then motioned them off, taking up a position behind them, firelance at the ready, in case they met someone—which they did, at the first intersection, a short, thin Hunter with patchy brown fur. He scuttled past them, pausing only long enough to give Kathryn a bloodthirsty glare quite surprising in such a scrawny specimen.

In the clear again, their guard talked. "There's a communications officer on the bridge, you realize. The instant you start broadcasting from down here, he'll know about it."

"We won't need long," Jarrikk said. "The vidchip record is hypercompressed. It will go out in a single burst."

Ask him how many S'sinn will be in communications, Kathryn telepathed.

Jarrikk put the question. "Three, I think," their guard replied. "Unarmed. I'll make short work of them."

No!

How else—

We've got to find a way. Can't we do what we did to this guard?

I thought you considered that a form of rape? an inner voice asked her, but she ignored it. It had to be better than seeing more S'sinn sliced apart by a firelance.

Three of them?

We have to try.

Reluctant agreement. Jarrikk looked around at their escort. "No. Leave them to us."

The guard growled, but said nothing.

The floor trembled beneath them, some residue of a maneuver violent enough to get through the gravity-and-inertia damping fields. *Kitillikk moving in for the kill,* Kathryn thought. *We're running out of time.*

They met no one else as they descended three decks via maintenance ladders, emerging into a short corridor with a door at its end. The guard pointed to it. "Communications," he said.

Jarrikk led Kathryn to the closed door. **Ready?**
Ready, she replied.

Like planets colliding, they plunged into each other's minds.

Instantly they could sense the three S'sinn inside the communications room, as well as the mind of the guard, still slightly confused, like a pool into which someone had dropped a large stone, stirring up mud and sending ripples chasing each other to and fro across the surface. It was an unsettling sensation, but Jarrikk/Kathryn could not spend time worrying about it; they tuned it out and concentrated on the three minds beyond the closed steel door.

This was different than changing a single mind. The three held similar loyalties and beliefs and those loyalties seemed to set up a kind of reinforcing field around each mind. The Guild said that any race which could produce Translators must have some innate empathic ability in all its members, a subconscious ability that did much to explain mobs and riots and politics. Here they could see proof of that. Karak would be fascinated, but it made their task much harder.

Instead of crashing through each mind's barriers as they had with the guard and, before him, with the High Priest and Rikkarrikk, they had to proceed cautiously, slowly, pushing a thought there, prodding an attitude here. It felt like turning the tuning pegs of a three-stringed musical instrument, trying to produce a particular chord. It seemed to take forever, though it must only have been a few beats. They almost had it, almost had the three minds to the point where they could safely open the door and walk in, when something new ripped through their consciousness, like a cymbal crash in the middle of a string sonata.

With a blood-chilling scream, the guard rushed forward, pushing them apart, sending Kathryn crashing against one corridor wall, where she crumpled to the floor, and smashing Jarrikk into the other wall, setting his crippled wing throbbing. But he hardly noticed that in the whirlwind of disorientation that filled his mind from the sudden cessation of his link with Kathryn. He clung to the wall for support, his mind barely registering the sound of the door opening: when it did register, he whirled and lunged for it, but he was far too late. As Kathryn pulled herself up beside him, the guard's firelance sliced through each of the three S'sinn. The room filled with the stench of burned flesh and fur, and the three minds Jarrikk and Kathryn had moments before been delicately tuning fell silent forever as their owners slumped to the floor, hands dropping lifelessly from blood-spattered consoles.

The guard screeched again, not the sound of a rational S'sinn at all, but the sound of a wild carnivore, his mind filled with insane rage. As Kathryn gripped Jarrikk's hand once more, he could sense the guard's mind more clearly. The mud and ripples from the stone they had thrown into it hadn't cleared at all; they had turned into a black whirlpool that had sucked him down into bestiality.

He turned now and saw them. **Down!** Jarrikk cried mind-to-mind to Kathryn, flinging a wing over her protectively and pulling her to the padded floor. An energy-bolt sizzled through the air, but he felt nothing—nothing but the sudden ending of the guard's shattered mind.

Slowly Jarrikk raised his head, as did Kathryn. The guard lay in the center of the room, the firelance clutched in his hand, his head a shattered, smoking ruin, the tip of one wing still jerking spasmodically.

Unintended consequences, thought Kathryn. *Jarrikk, what have we done?*

Jarrikk didn't reply. Kathryn had been right. They had raped the guard's mind, and they had destroyed it. With the priest, and Rikkarrikk, they had just provided information. With the guard, they had deliberately erased whole structures of thought, structures which had held his mind intact. With the communications personnel, the result might have been less traumatic—or maybe not. They'd never know, because of what they'd done to the guard.

He had telepathed none of that, but Kathryn's thoughts obviously echoed his own. *This power we have,* she sent. *I'm not sure I want it. I'm not sure I want anyone else to know about it, either.*

Neither am I. But this isn't the time to sort it out. He looked around the room. **I think I can operate this equipment. Close the door.** He let go of Kathryn's hand and made his way to the nearest console, trying not to look at the dead S'sinn at his feet or the blood now clotting on the controls.

As he had hoped, the flagship had a channel already set up which would allow Kitillikk to speak directly to every Hunter in the fleet. **She's probably already used it to make a morale-building speech about the imminent attack on the human Fleet,** he thought savagely. **I hope she appreciates this irony as much as I do.**

He slipped the datachip out from under his Translator's collar, plugged it into the console, and activated the transmission.

Kikks'sarr now filled the vidscreens on the *Bloodfeud*'s bridge. Kitillikk's control helmet showed the Fleet's course, an atmosphere-skimming trajectory that would help foul the human's scanners and accelerate the Hunterships at the same time. She'd changed her mind; rather than lure the human Fleet out by attacking Kikks'sarr's cities—cities she hoped to make her own—she'd decided instead on a bold, preemptive move, taking the Fleet straight through the center of the human Fleet at far higher speed than was strictly practical for combat, hitting whatever they could hit on that first pass and, she hoped, destroying the cohesion of the humans' formation. Then the Hunter Fleet would split and double back, attacking the disorganized humans from two directions at once.

The humans had rarely fought a pitched fleet battle in space. The S'sinn had been doing it for a century. She intended to show the humans exactly how it was done—and destroy them in the process.

Sudden movement at one of the control consoles caught her peripheral vision. She glanced to her left, Ukkarr following her gaze. "Communications, report!"

"Your Altitude, we've just sent an uncoded, unguarded hypercompressed databurst to all ships."

"I ordered communications silence!"

"Yes, Your Altitude, I know, but—Your Altitude, it went out over your personal channel. It will be automatically broadcast to all crews!"

"Countermand it!" In her fury Kitillikk lifted from her shikk and flew the few steps to the communications console.

"I can't, from here—it's being sent from the main communications—"

The planet and the fleet's trajectory vanished from half of the vidscreens. In their place appeared the familiar, grizzled face of the High Priest of the Hunter of Worlds, and her voice boomed out. "All S'sinn, hear my words," she said. "We have discovered that the plot to kill Supreme Flight Leader Akkanndikk was instigated, not by the Guild of Translators, as you have been told, but by Acting Supreme Flight Leader Kitillikk, in conjunction with a renegade human Translator. For this transgression of the Laws of the Hunter, Acting Supreme Flight Leader Kitillikk is hereby renounced by the Priests of the Hunter. She is stripped of all rank and privilege, and her life is forfeit upon her return to S'sinndikk. All those who serve her are called upon to renounce that service, on pain of death. You will—"

Kitillikk slapped the communications officer away from the console with her right wing and slashed her hand down over the controls, blanking all the comm vidscreens—but even as she did so, she knew she could not stop the damning message from reaching the eyes and ears of every Hunter in the fleet. Even with the bridge screens silenced, she could hear a faint echo of the High Priest's voice from the interior of her own ship.

The bridge crew stared at her. The officer she had knocked to the floor scrambled away from her, clutching his arm. She turned and looked at Ukkarr. He shook his head slightly and pointed at one of the screens that still showed the Fleet.

Most of the ships were still on course, still hurtling toward the planet and the waiting human Fleet: a fleet, she thought angrily, which must have received the open transmission as readily as her own had, if they had a probe anywhere above the horizon of the planet. But a few of the Hunterships had broken formation. More followed. Slowly at first, but faster and faster, the Fleet was unraveling.

If any ships continued on, the humans would devour them like ripe fruit. The Hunter Fleet would be destroyed and with it all hope of ever salvaging S'sinn honor.

Despite the burning fury in her hearts, she managed to keep her voice calm and businesslike as she spoke to the cowering communications officer. "Send this message to the fleet: abort attack. Break formation. Return to S'sinndikk." She growled something that wasn't really a laugh. "You'd better not put my name on that. Sign it, Acting Fleet Commander Tikkivv." She turned and looked at the *Bloodfeud*'s captain. He bowed to her slightly. Then, as the communications officer, after a glance at Tikkivv, warily approached his station again, she looked at Ukkarr. "I think you and I should go down to communications," she snarled.

"An excellent suggestion," he replied, and in his tone she heard the same suppressed rage that burned inside her.

One of the security guards at the door made a half-hearted attempt to block their way, but Captain Tikkivv snapped, "Let them go," and he fell aside, offering no resistance even when Ukkarr reached out and took his firelance from him.

Everyone in the ship was still battened down in battle stations: the corridors and zero-G flight tube were empty. Kitillikk and Ukkarr said nothing as they flew down to the communications deck, taking a brief side trip to confirm what she already knew: the cell where she had locked the two meddling Translators stood empty, one dead guard inside and no sign of the other one. Ukkarr looked at the guard. "Firelance," he said.

"I underestimated our supposedly non-violent friends," Kitillikk growled. "I should have executed them the moment I had them in my claws. This way."

In communications, they found more of the same: four dead S'sinn, including, judging by his insignia, the missing guard from the cell, his head blown off. Ukkarr looked around in amazement. "I don't understand how they did it."

"Does it matter?" Kitillikk strode to the console that had broadcast the High Priest's message, ripped out the vidchip and smashed it against the floor, then pulled the dead guard's firelance from his death-grip and fired it point-blank into the console. The blast ripped open its cover: sparks flew and acrid black smoke began to pour out.

Ukkarr watched silently. When Kitillikk turned back to him, he said, "The *Unity?*"

"The *Unity.*" Leaving behind the wreckage of the room, matching the wreckage of her dreams, they stalked toward the docking bay.

*   *   *

As screens in the communications room began to play the High Priest's message, Jarrikk crossed over to Kathryn and took her hand. *That's it?* she asked.

That's it.

How will we know . . . ?

What effect it's having? We can't, from here. But we can't stay here anyway. I think we should go back to the *Unity*.

Won't it be guarded?

Depends on how much confusion we've managed to sow. But there's nowhere else to go.

They proceeded cautiously through the ship, but saw no S'sinn until they reached the docking bay itself. From the observation deck they watched three Hunters arguing heatedly among themselves beside the hatch that opened into the docking tunnel linking the *Bloodfeud* and the *Unity*. One of them shouted something and turned to go; when one of the others grabbed him he lashed out, ripping a chunk of flesh from his attacker's arm and breaking free, then flung himself into the air toward one of the upper entrances.

The remaining, uninjured S'sinn raised his firelance, but the wounded one shoved the weapon down with his good arm and gesticulated. Together they went out, leaving the hatch unguarded. Kathryn started toward the door.

There will still be cameras watching, Jarrikk cautioned her.

But will anyone be watching what the cameras are watching? It looks to me like we've sowed confusion pretty well.

Maybe. Maybe not.

The ship shuddered beneath their feet. *Another violent maneuver,* Kathryn thought. Were they attacking the Earth Fleet despite the broadcast? Had all their efforts failed?

Had they destroyed that poor S'sinn's mind for nothing?

They had to get into the *Unity* and find out.

Inside the docking bay, empty now of all scoutships,

Kathryn glanced up at the observation deck from which they'd watched the S'sinn guards scuffle. Was that movement up there, behind the half-silvered glass? But nobody tried to stop them. She also felt nervous about the huge hatch to their right, which must open directly into space, but if someone decided to open it, she supposed they'd know little enough about it.

When they got to the docking tunnel's hatch, it opened easily. They passed through the airlock, then the gravlock, feeling their weight shift slightly to match the *Unity*'s Earth-normal, and then they were back inside the Guildship.

Captain Hall met them. "Security told me you were coming in," he said in Guildtalk. "I couldn't believe you were still alive."

"I have a little trouble believing it myself," Kathryn said. "What's happening?"

"A S'sinn transmission came on, the two S'sinn on board—there were only a couple, they seemed confident we couldn't break free of their flagship anyway— listened to it, and then they left, just like that."

"Has the Hunter Fleet attacked the human Fleet?"

"My sensors aren't operating. They're being suppressed by the flagship."

Kathryn felt Jarrikk's frustration. "Maybe you should try to bring them online again," he said. "There should be a lot of confusion on board the flagship right now. You might get away with it."

"Then that transmission—"

"Was what we came out here to send. Captain Hall, please, the sensors?"

"Of course." Kathryn and Jarrikk followed him out of the lock. Just at the door, Kathryn glanced over her shoulder as an odd popping noise from down the open docking tunnel caught her attention, but seeing nothing, she dismissed it as the ping of contracting metal and put it out of her mind.

"Safety locks disabled," Ukkarr said. "Along with the drive enslavement. The umbilicals will hold the

Unity through ordinary maneuvers, but a sharp outward boost should easily tear her free."

"Excellent." Kitillikk raised her borrowed firelance and inspected it with a practiced eye. "Well-kept," she said approvingly. "Come on, Ukkarr."

"At your service, Flight Leader."

On the bridge, a young woman now sat in the charred chair in front of the communications console. She didn't glance up as the captain entered with the Translators, but others did, and exchanged surprised looks among themselves. The captain went at once to the sensor console. "Initiate restart," he said.

"But, Captain . . ."

"Just do it, Ensign!"

"Yes, sir!" The young woman bent to her controls. Blank blue screens flickered, went white, then black, then suddenly started scrolling reams of numbers. Intent now, the ensign sent her fingers dancing over the console. The numbers gave way to visuals, and with a triumphant flick of a final switch, the ensign brought the main vidscreens to life. "Sensors back on line, Captain!"

Kathryn leaned forward eagerly, trying to make sense out of the cryptically-notated dots and multicolored vector lines, with little success. "Captain, what's happening?"

He turned to her with fierce glee. "The Hunter Fleet has broken off the attack! It's breaking up and heading for home!"

Kathryn let out a whoop that startled even herself, and turned and flung her arms around Jarrikk, never mind how the bridge crew stared. *We did it!*

So it would appear.

Kathryn drew back. *You don't seem too certain.*

Kitillikk, he reminded her. **We don't know what *she* is doing.** He nodded at the screens. **And we don't know what the Earth Fleet will do.**

Kathryn looked over her shoulder. "Captain, what about the Earth Fleet?"

"It's not doing anything. If it were going to attack

the Hunter ships, I'd have expected it to do so by now. If they wait much longer, they won't be able to catch any of them before they jump."

Kathryn sensed faint disappointment from him; well-hidden, probably subconscious, but there nonetheless. Well, she supposed she couldn't blame him. She put her cheek against Jarrikk's furry chest again. *You see?* she said. *We did it!*

But Jarrikk stiffened. **Wait! Wait, I sense—**

Kathryn sensed it, too, with their jointly heightened empathy. Two S'sinn, moving toward them fast, purposefully, two S'sinn—

Wait, she knew that one, it was—

Jarrikk spun around. "Kitillikk!" he growled out loud, as the deposed Flight Leader burst through the door to the bridge and snapped her black wings wide, firelance aimed right at the two Translators.

Chapter 23

Kitillikk took in the bridge of the *Unity* with a single glance around, then focused on the two Translators and the captain. Behind her she heard Ukkarr, and knew he would make sure none of the other bridge crew did anything stupid. "I should kill you now, Jarrikk, and your human mate," she snarled. "But I need both of you. I know you and your pet can Translate without all that rigmarole of the Guild. Do it. I have orders for the captain, and I refuse to speak your pidgin Guildtalk."

"Kitillikk, this won't accomplish anything," Jarrikk said quietly. "Your scheme is over. You will never be Supreme Flight Leader. You will never lead the S'sinn Fleet in battle."

"I didn't come here to discuss my future. Translate!"

"I already am."

"Good." Kitillikk shifted her gaze to the human captain, who stood stiffly to one side of Jarrikk. "Captain, I have disabled the systems holding the *Unity* to my flagship." Kathryn Bircher began speaking along with her. Just as she'd thought: the two *could* provide Full Translation without the Guild's symbiotes. "You will initiate a full-power boost at a right angle to the long axis of the *Bloodfeud,* and continue this full-power boost until you are out of range of the flagship's weapons, though I do not believe she will fire on you—Captain Tikkivv is, by this time, fully aware of my presence on this ship, and he is not like the rest of these milk-spewing younglings who call themselves Hunters, to be led by that hag of a High Priest. He will allow us to escape."

The human captain said something in his squawking human tongue. "And if I refuse?" Jarrikk translated.

Kitillikk fired an energy bolt into the empty chair at the sensor console, narrowly missing the young ensign, who stared down with wide white-rimmed eyes at the smoking ruin on which she had been sitting seconds before. "Then I start killing your crew. In any event, Captain, why should you refuse? I assume you want to escape from my ship as much as I do."

The captain growled something in reply, then turned and started giving orders. "Translate," Kitillikk snapped at Jarrikk.

"Captain Hall said it wasn't your ship he wanted to escape," Jarrikk said. "It was you."

Kitillikk showed her teeth. "That will not be easy."

The captain faced her again. "We're ready," Jarrikk said.

Kitillikk kept grinning. "You think I'm a fool? Ukkarr, brace yourself." She wrapped one arm around a nearby support and spread her wings. "Unless the three of you like bouncing around the walls . . ." she said to Jarrikk.

He met her gaze for a moment, then led Kathryn Bircher to an empty chair, and, as she strapped herself in, braced himself as Kitillikk had, though he kept one hand on Bircher's shoulder. The captain strapped himself into his own chair in the center of the room, but swung it around to look at Kitillikk instead of facing the sensor screens.

"Now, Captain," Kitillikk said. Bircher translated, and the captain barked an order.

The boosters fired, unheard but felt as a deep vibration in the bones of the ship, and the *Unity* lifted away from the flagship. Tortured metal shrieked and the ship bucked and jerked as it ripped apart the docking tube. Three sensor screens flickered and went dark as their antennae fragmented; another console exploded in sparks and smoke as fractured conduits shorted out; then they were free. *Bloodfeud* dwindled rapidly in the surviving sensor screens, and made no attempt to fire on them or pursue. Nor did any other ship.

Kitillikk released her hold on the brace. If she hadn't gripped it, she knew she would have been full-length on the floor—precisely, she suspected, what the captain had hoped. Now she pointed the firelance at him again. "Now, Captain. About our course—"

Something buzzed behind her. "Ukkarr?" she snapped.

"Someone wants access to the bridge." A pause as he presumably scanned security screens. "It's the human Ornawka, Flight Leader."

"Ornawka? Here?" Kitillikk shifted her focus to Jarrikk. "Why didn't you tell me he was here?"

"I did not know," Jarrikk said. "I do not know how he *could* be here."

"Let him in," Kitillikk said to Ukkarr. "But watch him."

"Yes, Flight Leader."

Jim? Here? How? Kathryn couldn't believe Jarrikk had translated correctly. *Why?*

I don't know. Jarrikk seemed as bemused as she did. **He must have stowed away . . .**

He had help, Kathryn thought. *Of course he had help. Sympathizers. This is a human-crewed ship. A certain percentage—*

None of that matters, Jarrikk sent back. **More important is why is he *here*, on the bridge?**

*He hasn't given up. Jim Ornawka never *gives* up.*

There he is.

It was Jim, all right, looking calm and collected, though as always, his feelings were unreadable behind an empathic shield, a shield even stronger than before. Even in contact with Jarrikk, Kathryn could not penetrate it this time. She suspected they could if they made full Linkage—but after their experience with the guard . . . no. Not even Jim deserved that.

"Kitillikk," Jim said in Guildtalk. "It has been a long time."

"You have joined your friends to die?" Kitillikk said, spitting the Guildtalk words as though they left a bad taste in her mouth.

"Me? Die? I don't think so." Jim looked over at Kathryn and Jarrikk. "Besides, I doubt they really consider me a friend anymore." He smiled the smile that had once charmed Kathryn, but now seemed flat and lifeless. "I'm here to help you."

"Help *me?*" Kitillikk laughed the harsh S'sinn laugh. "You have never done anything that didn't serve yourself. You hate all S'sinn."

"Exactly. And I told you so. That's why you can trust me, Kitillikk. I've always told you the truth." He came a little further forward, until Ukkarr's firelance, pressed into his back, told him he'd gone far enough. "We can still salvage this situation, Kitillikk. But we have to get the human fleet to attack now, while there are still Hunterships adrift in confusion. Most of your fleet will escape intact. You'll be able to rally your people around you, no matter what the High Priest says, if the humans have precipitated another war. They know you're their best fleet commander."

"My people may yet rally around me," Kitillikk said. "But I will not sacrifice a single Huntership to arrange it."

"Don't give me that. You were willing to kill your own Supreme Flight Leader—"

"I will not waste the lives of Hunters. And I will not listen to you any longer. Ukkarr, put Ornawka with the others."

Ukkarr pushed Jim forward, toward the three steps that led to the lower level of the bridge. Jim's right foot found empty space; he stumbled forward, fell— and then suddenly came rolling upright, something tiny and metallic in his hand that flashed once, twice—

—and Ukkarr fell, his head neatly separating from his body and thumping down the steps to lie in a spreading pool of dark-red S'sinn blood on the bridge deck.

Kitillikk's lance swung around, but the thing in Jim's hand flashed again, and half of her weapon vanished. Kitillikk flung the useless hilt aside and stood motionless, gaze fixed on Jim.

Kathryn stared at Jim in horror, horror brought on not only by the violence but by the thought that she had once shared her bed and her self with this man she no longer recognized. A mixture of shock and disturbing satisfaction swirled around her from the others on the bridge, but Jim remained perfectly blank.

He got slowly to his feet. "Very sensible," he said. "I don't want to kill you if I can avoid it; you're my best bet for making sure this war goes ahead as planned. Some of those Hunterships hanging around out there must still be loyal to you. Broadcast to them now. Order them to stage a mock attack on the *Unity*. By now the Earth ships know we've broken free. The captain here will send us on a course toward the Earth Fleet, as if we're trying to reach them. Your Hunterships will pursue. The Earth Fleet can't help but attack them, and then—"

"You've miscalculated," Kitillikk said, and Kathryn felt the coldness in her mind like a bath of liquid helium. "You think that I am like you. But I am not. You are human, and I am S'sinn, and you have slain my friend. The Hunter will devour you and spew you out—but I die with honor!" And with that she launched herself over the railing.

Jim's weapon flashed, severing Kitillikk's right arm and causing her wing to collapse, but momentum carried her into him. Her left arm gripped his neck and pulled him clear of the floor, feet twitching, surprise and terror on his face and finally, finally, flooding through the empathic blocks; and then her right foot came up and raked him from sternum to crotch, ripping through flesh and muscle, shattering ribs, spilling his viscera onto the floor of the bridge in a glistening, bloody heap. His legs jerked once more as his mind faded from Kathryn's horrified perception; then Kitillikk dropped him, planted her bloody foot on his ruined chest, and screamed, a sound of pure defiance and rage that rose to the limit of Kathryn's hearing and beyond.

The sound ended. Kitillikk staggered and fell to her knees, propping herself up with her good wing. The blood that had pumped from the stump of her arm now only trickled. She fixed glazing eyes on Jarrikk. "A true S'sinn," she gasped out in S'sinn, barely audibly, "dies with honor."

And then she collapsed across Jim's shattered body.

A stench like that of a slaughterhouse spread across the bridge, silent except for the quiet retching of the young ensign at the sensor panel. Captain Hall, face white, rose from his chair and walked on legs not-quite-steady to Kathryn and Jarrikk. "Course, Translators?" he said.

Kathryn looked up at him through the tears streaming down her face. "The Guildhall, Captain. Home."

"The *Unity* is on final landing approach," a voice said in Karak's ear.

"About time," Karak grumbled. He'd been waiting in his wetsuit for half a day; the *Unity* had somehow miscalculated her ETA. Probably it had taken them longer to deliver the bodies of Kitillikk and Ukkarr to the *Bloodfeud* than anticipated. There would have been questions to answer about that rendezvous before the Earth Fleet would have let them go, too . . .

His feeding tentacles wriggled thoughtfully. There were a lot of questions *he* needed answered, as well. Translator Ornawka's part in all this seemed clear, but what damage that would do to the Guild's reputation remained to be seen. Fortunately they had a lot of good will to bank on in the Commonwealth right now, thanks to Kitillikk's abortive attack on the Guildhall.

He felt badly about Ornawka, all the same. With

Earth authorities finally cooperating with the Commonwealth in tracking down the Humanity First ringleaders, they'd uncovered the truth about Ornawka's background. Like Kathryn, his entire family had been wiped out by the S'sinn—not during the war, but at its very start. He'd been on Kikks'sarr, in fact, part of the colony destroyed by Kitillikk in the initial confrontation. He and a handful of other children had escaped on board the colony shuttle, but when the ship stopped at the nearest human planet he had disappeared, only to be found by that passing Translator years later, living on the street. Those impenetrable shields must have been his idiosyncratic reaction to bondcut, and none of his Guild tutors had recognized the signs because humans were so new to the mix of races.

They'd been luckier with Kathryn, Karak thought. And with Jarrikk. Had he not put the two of them together, they might have gone the way of Ornawka. Certainly they'd both had reason for it . . .

Not now, though. Now, they were something quite special. A matched team of Translators who did not need programming. Of course, they could only Translate between humans and S'sinn, but there would be a lot of that to be done in the next while. They would prove invaluable in the process of building a lasting peace—and, of course, in strengthening the reputation of the Guild.

But he had to free them up for a research project, too. The Guild had to know just what they were capable of. Telepathy between themselves, obviously, but there had been hints . . . how had they escaped from the flagship, for instance? They said they'd convinced a guard to help them, but Karak wasn't sure they were telling everything.

A Translator cannot lie! he thought, and expelled a sigh-bubble. That was one myth they would have to work very hard indeed to rebuild in the Commonwealth.

Thunder overhead, then the *Unity* settled neatly to the blackened surface of the spaceport. Karak climbed into the waiting groundcar, and sighed again as it rolled toward the Guildship and he saw the scars on its hull and the twisted wreckage of the *Bloodfeud*'s docking tunnel still clinging to its side like a cancerous growth. Just the external damage alone would cost a fortune to repair. The Great Swimmer only knew what the S'sinn had destroyed inside the *Unity* during their occupation of it.

The hatch had opened by the time he reached the ship. There were Jarrikk and Kathryn, hand-in-hand. He got out of the groundcar and raised his manipulators in salute . . .

There's Karak, Kathryn telepathed. *Are you sure about this?*

I'm sure, Jarrikk sent. **Aren't you?**

He's not going to like it.

He's not going to have any choice.

Our Oaths . . .

We've been through *that* already. This is no different.

I suppose not.

Karak waited for them at the bottom of the ramp. Kathryn remembered how he had held her hand in his gloved manipulators when she first arrived on Commonwealth Central, a quiet, indrawn little girl, desperate for a family, for something to fill the horrible emptiness of bondcut.

But she wasn't a little girl anymore. And that hole— she squeezed Jarrikk's hand—was filled.

She and Jarrikk had decided, on the journey back to Commonwealth Central, that they could not allow the Guild to know about the power they had within themselves. They could not hide the low-level telepathy—they'd demonstrated it too often—but the other, the projective telepathy, and most especially the horrible possibilities of using their powers as a weapon, they would reveal to no one.

The Guild meant well, Kathryn supposed. It had made the Commonwealth possible, and so far it had kept the peace. But there were always strains, and nothing lasted forever. Someday there would be a new Guildmaster. The power they had found—the power to make anybody believe anything you wanted them to, and worse, the power to drive sentients mad—they must keep to themselves, or someday someone like Kitillikk or Jim would find a war it could serve.

As Jarrikk had said, they were still upholding their Oath to serve and preserve the Commonwealth. As they had broken the letter of the Oath once before to preserve its spirit, so they must do so again, but this time, it must be permanent.

They would leave the Guild. They would take Jarrikk to Earth, for regeneration therapy, and then . . .

Well, then, they had the whole galaxy to explore, and at least for the moment, at least in their small corner of it, it was at peace.

Here was Karak.

"Translators," he greeted them.

Kathryn cleared her throat. "Actually," she said, "that's what we want to talk to you about . . ."

About the Author

Edward Willett is the author of more than thirty books, including four young adult fantasy and science fiction novels, plus numerous nonfiction children's books on topics ranging from the Iran–Iraq War to Ebola virus, to biographies of J.R.R. Tolkien and Orson Scott Card. His young adult novel, *Spirit Singer,* won the Regina Book Award for best book by a Regina author at the 2002 Saskatchewan Book Awards. His short fiction has appeared in *Trans Versions, On Spec,* and *Artemis,* among other magazines. Ed is Web master and administrative assistant for SF Canada, www.sfcanada.ca. He writes a weekly science column for the *Regina Leader Post* and CBC Radio One in Saskatchewan, and is a professional actor and singer. He's married to Margaret Anne Hodges, a telecommunications engineer, and has a daughter, Alice. His Web site is at www.edwardwillett.com, and he writes a blog, Hassenpfeffer, at edwardwillett.blogspot.com.